I0608056

Charmer Boy, Gypsy Girl

Victor Harrington

Dedication

This book is dedicated to my daughter, Olivia, who once remarked to her father when she was a little girl. "Fate is imagination." I have remembered her words for their wisdom and simplicity of truth.

Daughters are to be cherished.

Acknowledgments

I owe heartfelt thanks to several people who over time continued to inspire me to complete this novel. I am deeply indebted to Carla Pamela Rodman, the first person with whom I shared my excitement and fear when the idea germinated inside me to write *Charmer Boy, Gypsy Girl*. Her continual kindness, quick wit, and unprecedented intelligence were an Elysian spring from which this author generously drank. She remains a talisman for myself and to everyone who has been lucky enough to have had her enter their lives.

Author Selden Rodman who with his gracious and old-fashioned New England reserve told me, after having read the first draft to the novel, "You have something here." I never forgot his words to me on that sunny afternoon in his kitchen surrounded by the hills of Ramapo Valley. Thank you, Selden.

To my sister, Denise Harrington Rideout, I shall always be grateful for her support. She never let this writer forget that there is no value for me to curse the darkness, but every reason to keep the candle lit within me.

I would like to thank Cory Morrison, a true flower child. Had it not been for her kindness and love for me, my journey as a writer would never have begun. Cory, you will always possess a special place in my heart, always.

Special thanks to Selma (Tommye) Rice; you always knew how much I loved you.

I must also thank Erica Beth Tarnoff, who kept me afloat and from drowning in more ways than I could describe in this brief space. Thank you, Erica.

No acknowledgment on my part would be complete without thanking my daughter, Olivia, who continues to inspire and confirm to her father that the best about life remains: Love.

Finally, I have the good fortune to be able to call upon a dear friend and remarkable educator, Ms. Karen Lust, for her keen insight and prescience about life. For this, I am truly grateful; it is a gift given to me by her. Thank you, Karen.

To all of them, my gratitude and thanks and to the many others that this one page would not allow me to list. You know who you are and how thankful I am to you all.

I owe a writer's debt to my editors, who provided me with their insight and wisdom.

Victor Harrington

In Sarajevo, there is peace within despair, love in the midst of hate.
From the once blood-soaked sidewalks and ancient walls,
it is said you can still hear the whisper of these two lovers:

Was there a time, my love, when we were not together?
Never... never a time we shall not be together.

'Nothing comes close to my city. It is the pearl on the earth, Saraj of springs and gardens, unique in the world.... High mountains around it, old and noble, snow peaks covered with mist are kissing the sky.... It is impossible, no doubt, to name all the beauties of this place...."

MUHAMED NERKES

Daedalus said: "Those suffer who have eyes...
Power is blind. What men want now is power,
Knowledge to spend and craftsmanship to arm.
In place of painted urn, the fire-glazed flower,
From every corner of this island rising,
Fiery beacons and hoarse alarm
Make beasts of men..."

Icarus said: "While we, being civilized, Father,
Shuttle in sleep from dream of cure to crisis
And back to dream again! What good is wisdom?"

THE AIRMEN
SELDEN RODMAN

PART ONE

Chapter One

December 31, 1983

Bosko stared into the mirror, uncertain of the image he saw. Who was that looking back at him? He glanced at his hands and thought they lacked strength. A knock on the door startled him back to the present.

"Come in," Bosko said.

The door swung open and his father, a tall, imposing man, stepped into the room. When their eyes met in the mirror, Bosko knew. He had become what some sons hope they will someday become: a reflection of his father. He possessed the same self-confidence as his dad—almost. Dragan entered Bosko's bedroom, reached into his pocket, and pulled out a roll of *dinars*. Grabbing Bosko's right arm, he placed the money in his hand and held it tightly. "The world will be coming to us in just two months. This will be a good year." Dragan kissed his son's forehead. Sarajevo had won the bid to host the Winter Olympics in February. On this night, however, only one thing mattered to Bosko and to the entire city: it was New Year's Eve, a few hours away from 1984.

"Thanks, Dad."

Dragan squeezed Bosko's shoulder. As he walked toward the door, he caught another glimpse of his son as their eyes met again in the mirror. He left, closing the door gently behind him, certain that the New Year's festivities were the only things on Bosko's mind. He plopped himself down onto his favorite recliner next to Rita, his wife. Picking up a newspaper, he said, "Well, he's ready for tonight. Any idea where he's off to?"

"Miro got them invited to some party. Don't ask me where." Rita had begun knitting a sweater for Bosko. She held the partially

1

finished sweater in front of her and began to count the stitches up and down. This would tell her how many rows she had completed and what row she needed to work on next.

Hearing a knock, Dragan said, "Someone's here." Rita looked at him briefly and went back to what she was doing, leaving it up to him to get up and answer the door.

"Mladjo," Dragan could be heard saying. "What a surprise. Come on in, it's cold out here in the hallway."

The moment she heard Mladjo's name, Rita rested the yarn on her lap and, smiling to herself, turned her head toward the hallway. She could hear, too, the two men embracing, then the sound of heavy steps growing louder as they approached the living room.

Mladjo was a tall, strapping young man in his late twenties. With a slight swagger that had returned to his walk, he strolled into the room.

"How are you, Rita?" Mladjo asked, softening his tone as he approached her and giving her a kiss on the cheek. "I brought you a couple of bottles of Refosk to celebrate the New Year."

Dragan, who was standing behind him, grinned with approval. "I'll be back in a minute. I'll go get Bosko."

"How are things?" Rita asked.

"I am well."

"Have you been able to get back on your feet?"

"Yes." His tone was confident.

Grabbing onto his wrist and looking up at him, she said, "You know, you can always come back. You know that, don't you?"

"Yes, Rita, I do. I am well. Thank you."

She shook his hand as if to acknowledge what he'd said to her and then replied, "Good." She left it at that.

Mladjo leaned forward to kiss Rita on the cheek once more, showing his affection and appreciation for what she and Dragan had done for him. A year ago, Mladjo had been released from prison; he'd been incarcerated for a near-fatal beating of a police officer. He was also a ruthless enforcer for a local gangster in Sarajevo. He'd spent four years in prison for his crime. And in that time his ruthlessness grew even more in scope, as he struggled to survive his term at Goli Otok, one of the harshest prisons in all Yugoslavia. When his sentence was completed, he'd been released onto the streets and had to spend month after month living and sleeping in the alleyways of small towns and villages. Eventually, he found his way back to Sarajevo from the island prison off the coast of Croatia.

The former gang to whom he'd kept his allegiance—never once giving up their names while being beaten by the police—had abandoned him. He was a liability. His childhood friend, Serge, Bosko's elder brother, had left Sarajevo to start a new life in Italy, and now Dragan and his remaining family were all he had left. In a moment of desperation, Mladjo had called Serge's father's home. Dragan said nothing except to offer the best friend of his elder son a warm bed. For the next six months, he had lived in Dragan's home as one of the family.

Mladjo was a wolf; as far as he knew, the world was filled by those who were wolves and those who were not. But he would not let his ways infect Bosko. He had stayed for as long as he needed, until he could find his own pack and become their leader. He would never forget Dragan's kindness when at his most vulnerable, when he was left to the streets and rivals who would want him killed. Dragan and Rita took him into their home. Mladjo's nature was like that of every Slav of the Balkans. To him, no good or bad deed committed is ever forgotten or not repaid in kind.

"Mladjo!" Bosko entered the room and they embraced.

"Good to see you. I brought your parents some wine to celebrate the New Year."

"I'm glad because they're going to spend it together. No partying for them tonight. What about you?"

"I have plans."

"I bet you do," replied Bosko.

"Open the bottle," Rita said. "You know where the kitchen is. Get some glasses."

Mladjo headed to the kitchen, feeling for the briefest moment that this home was also his own again. Bosko kept looking at his dad, who he knew had never passed judgment on Mladjo for the life he had chosen to live. Bosko found it curious that he hadn't done so.

"Bosko, hold this up against you. I want to see how it looks." Bosko held his mother's incomplete sweater against his chest.

"I like it. Looks good. Give it back."

"Here we go," Mladjo said, returning from the kitchen, more at ease than a few moments ago. He held four wine glasses upside down, the stems between his large Slavic fingers. Turning his palm up, he offered everyone a glass, then poured the wine.

Mladjo lifted his glass and made a toast. "To a great future for us all."

"To a great future," replied Dragan.

"To the future," said Mladjo, cracking a grin.

"Come and sit."

"I must be going, Rita, my friends are waiting."

"So soon?" Asked Rita.

"Yes, it was good to see all of you." Mladjo placed his glass on the table. He reached down and kissed Rita on her cheek and shook Bosko's hand. Then he and Dragan walked to the door.

When Dragan returned, he said merely, "A short visit."

"Seems like Mladjo is back on his feet," Bosko said.

"Looks like it, son." Dragan joined Rita and picked up the newspaper. Nothing more was said about Mladjo. Bosko realized he still had to get dressed. As he returned to his bedroom, he

4

checked his jacket pocket with the money his father had given him.

Slipping on the layers of clothing he'd have to wear to brave the cold outside, Bosko thought of how Mladjo had taken nothing from his parents when he'd stayed with them. His brother's bedroom was all Mladjo needed. His stay was hardly noticed, as he disappeared early in the mornings and came back late in the evenings. It was clear he was being the wolf, seeking out a new pack to follow him.

The few occasions that Mladjo let himself be seen with him, Bosko had noticed the reaction of strangers who recognized his friend and who would, with deference, acknowledge Mladjo. Everyone knew who he was, and what he was capable of. Bosko knew him only as a family friend who was always ready with a smile, but he couldn't deny that there was something menacing, impersonal, even alien about Mladjo.

He sensed something more lay hidden in Mladjo's personality, but Bosko was too young and inexperienced to know what it might be. Perhaps it was Mladjo's fierce loyalty, a loyalty to other people who'd done right by him, yes, but that seemed outweighed by his loyalty to abstract ideas, and by his need to acquire a greater share of power in his world in order to survive it.

"Bosko," said Rita as he entered the living room.

"Oh, you're not going to say it again are you?"

"Yes, just one more time," his mother said, without lifting her eyes from her knitting. "Be careful. Tonight is not like any other. Things can happen. Come and give me a kiss. I know you're itching to leave."

Without saying a word, Bosko bent down and kissed his mother. He walked over to Dragan, who was already standing.

"I'll be thinking of you both."

"I doubt that," replied his mother. "Remember what I said. Things happen."

Bosko and his father rolled their eyes as they patted each other on the back. "He'll be fine. He's a man, woman!" his father said.

"It was good to see Mladjo. How did he seem to you?" asked Bosko.

"Like he is determined to survive. He misses not having Serge around."

"I know. So do I."

"We all have to grow up, son, and find our way in this world. Serge has, so will you." said Dragan as he hugged Bosko tightly. "Enjoy this night—it comes only once a year."

"I intend to." Bosko glanced at his mother, who was looking at him intently.

In seconds, he was gone.

Dragan remained standing, lost in his thoughts. His two sons had left, one of them to be with his friends, the other to build a new life. They had grown up so fast.

Dragan reached for his wife's hand. Rita took his and together they walked toward their bedroom.

*

"Are you ready?" Zena asked as her daughter strolled into the family room. "Were you able to get the grease off?"

Admira lifted her clean hands to show her mom. "The car Dad's working on is missing a part I can't find anywhere in the city. I need Hugo's help. He always seems to know the right people."

She turned to her mother at the sound of a car approaching on the gravel road behind the house. Zena, feeling distracted, didn't get up from her chair. She was concerned about the chaotic celebrations that were already taking place tonight, and worried about her daughter being in the middle of all that dangerous excitement. Zena, however, kept her thoughts to herself. Admira also remained silent. They heard the car door slam shut.

"What's wrong?" Zena knew her daughter well enough to realize Admira had something on her mind.

Admira shook her head and smiled. Lena, one of her best friends from school, barged in, out of breath and tracking in snow onto the living room floor. "Come on, we've got to go," she said urgently. Taking a moment and drawing a much-needed breath, she walked over to Zena and kissed her on the cheek before turning to Admira once more. "Let's go, Admira. Hugo is waiting in the car."

Hugo was three years older than the girls and always had access to a car. Admira knew what her mother was thinking—an older boy with a car was the first step toward a girl getting into trouble—but her mother said nothing. It wouldn't have mattered if she had.

Zao, Admira's dad, had gone to a shop in the city to buy a small bag of coal. When midnight struck on New Year's Eve, he would enter their home carrying a basket of coal and a loaf of Zena's homemade bread. He would approach his wife and place the bread in one hand and the basket in the other. All of their lives, up until today, Admira and her sister would stand next to their mother, waiting for their father to place a single piece of coal into their delicate, outstretched hands. During this ritual, he would kiss his wife on each cheek and utter a silent prayer that their home would always have warmth and that his family would never go hungry.

On this New Year's Eve, Zao didn't insist that his daughters stay home. They were on the verge of becoming young women; the world awaited them, and they'd have to choose what traditions to keep. It was their time, now.

Admira and her mother embraced and softly whispered "Happy New Year" to each other before the girls ran out the door, laughing.

Outside, Admira reached for the passenger door of Hugo's car, glancing back at her mother who stood on the porch, wrapped in a woolen coat, waving.

Her mother mouthed the words "be careful," as she stood under the porch light.

Admira nodded and blew Zena a kiss. Then she and Lena jumped into the car, and in seconds it barreled down the snow-covered gravel road into the night.

*

Cold night air spiraled down from Mount Igman and hit Bosko as if it were the breath blown from a snow giant. While he stood on the walkway beside the Miljacka River waiting for friends, he recalled his father's words. "Saraj-Ovasi. The Field of Palaces. Never forget, Bosko, the soul of Sarajevo is its people."

The Academy of Fine Arts and the National Theatre were lit up, and a cold, wintry world sparkled around him as he sat on a large stone flowerpot, peering out toward the river.

"Bosko!" Miroslav shouted. "Are you ready?"

Startled from his thoughts but acknowledging his friend, Bosko nodded at his approaching friends.

"Look at him, just look at him," Matko said. "Look at that Elvis smile of his. I think he's ready."

"Well, Charmer Boy," Miroslav said, his deep voice resonating all around them, "think your Elvis smile and charm are going to get you anywhere tonight?" He lunged at Bosko. They embraced each other like two Cossacks, with a strong hug and a kiss on the lips.

"How you doing, Bosh?" asked Matko as he embraced Bosko.

"It's New Year's Eve, Mats. How do you think I'm doing?"

8

Matko reached into the breast pocket of his coat and removed his father's silver flask.

"Plum brandy made by Herzegovinian Croats who live in the Dinaric Alps. Fierce men, my people."

"Give it here." Miroslav grabbed the flask out of Matko's hand and poured a generous amount into his mouth before passing it to Bosko, who did the same, before handing it back to Matko. They tilted their heads back and, in unison, forced the brandy through their teeth, spraying it high into the air above their heads, baptizing their friendship. Sharing the bottle once more, they drank until their gullets were on fire and their eyes watered.

"Oh my God. Now that's a drink," Miroslav said. "Good job, Mats. I am king!" Miroslav yelled, running off with the bottle and slip-sliding away on the thin veil of freshly fallen snow.

"To Prince Lazar!" Bosko yelled.

Miroslav stopped and yelled back, "To the Maiden of Kosovo, the only wife a Serb should ever have!"

Bosko and Mats began to walk, following Miroslav.

"He's such a moron." Matko stopped.

Bosko looked at his friend. "Come on, Mats. Let's go!"

"How come your family doesn't have that painting hanging somewhere in your home?"

"Oh for Christ's sakes, how am I supposed to know? Come on, let's go. That asshole's going to drink all of our brandy if we don't catch up."

Matko didn't move. He stared at Bosko. "It's not just a painting. It's the Maiden of Kosovo by Uroš Predić and it hangs in every Serbian home I've ever been in, except yours."

"Thank you, Mr. History Major. Mats, I don't give a shit about a painting of some woman giving water to a wounded Serbian soldier."

"You know the painting."

"Yes, I know the painting. Dad prefers books. Now let's go,

you stupid Croat."

Matko didn't move.

"I swear to God, why do you get into these moods? I'm going to kick your ass if you don't move."

"It's just that you and your dad, your whole family, just don't give a shit about being Serbian. God, my father is always talking about having a Croatia for Croatians, a Serbia for Serbs. You know he's talking about moving us back to Croatia."

Bosko looked at his friend and said, "There's no Croatia, only Yugoslavia."

"Yeah, well, tell that to my dad and the rest of his Croat family. They could draw you the boundaries of Croatia from Zagreb all the way down to Macedonia. He keeps saying now with Tito dead, it's just a matter of time before—"

"Before what? Never mind, just let's go."

"He's convinced you know—"

"Mats, come on, please!"

Matko ambled over to the edge of the walkway and stared out at the Miljacka River.

"What is it?" Bosko asked, joining his friend.

"He keeps looking for any piece of news in the papers or on TV. Anything that will convince him about what he believes is going to happen."

"What are you talking about? What's going to happen?"

"I don't know, Bosh, but Dad is convinced he knows. He has so many newspaper clippings, articles with all kinds of stuff of shit that's happening. He keeps pointing to these articles and telling my mom that it's all going to change. It's changing already."

"Mats, nothing is going to change." Bosko turned to look in the direction Miro had gone. "Look at that, I can't even see Miro anymore. I want more brandy. Come on, Mats, don't start acting stupid. Where's this party, anyway?"

"It's just... I don't know what to do. I don't want to leave

Sarajevo. My father and his brothers never stop talking about going back to some imaginary homeland. He keeps going on and on about how things are changing, how it's all going to change."

Bosko heard the desperation in Matko's voice. He put his hand on Mats's shoulder. "You won't leave. This is our home." Bosko waved his hand, pointing in all directions of their city. "How could we leave any of this? She is the pearl of this earth."

"That's your dad talking."

"No, it's me talking! Just let your father rant. That's all he ever does. He'll never leave. And what's going to change? Nothing. Now can we catch up with Miro? Where's this party anyway?"

"I don't know."

"What do you mean, you don't know?"

"It wasn't me who got us invited. Prince Lazar up there knows someone who invited us."

"We're trusting him to get us into a cool party? He doesn't even like people."

Matko kicked Bosko's feet out from under him. Bosko landed hard on the walkway. Matko started to laugh. "You know what your problem is? You actually listen to my shit. You're so right. Dad can do whatever he wants, but I'm never leaving Sarajevo."

"You asshole!" Bosko struggled to get up.

The sound of Mats's laughter carried far on the now deserted walkway. Miroslav had heard it and, not wanting to be left out, headed back, running and sliding on the thin cushion of fresh snow. Mats extended his hand to Bosko just as Miro, appearing out of the darkness, careened into his friends like some dive bomber. They all lay on the snow-covered walkway, laughing and groaning and staring up at the night sky. Miroslav opened his mouth to let the snowflakes fall onto his tongue.

"Where's the brandy?" Bosko asked.

"Here you go." Miro handed the flask to his friend, leaned forward, and kissed him on the forehead. "Let's go, fellas."

Bosko tucked the bottle with the last of the plum brandy into his pocket. The three helped each other up, punching each other playfully and dusting off the snow. Matko strolled to the edge of the walkway, his two friends followed. They were the only souls around.

"It's snowing harder," Bosko said as they began to breathe in unison, three young men for whom each breath entered and left their bodies in a simple rhythm. They looked out across the river as they stood with their arms around each other's waists, the falling snowflakes blanketing them in a cocoon of white.

"She is beautiful," Mats said as he stared out into the city.

"Like no other place in the world," Miro replied.

They turned and began to skate away on the snow, arms around each other, singing, as the site of their collision disappeared under a veil of white.

*

The music was loud. Miroslav pounded on the door. When it opened, a huge plume of smoke drifted out to greet them. Matko and Bosko scoped out what they could see of the party, turning and smiling at each other. Young girls packed the house.

"Biljana," Miroslav shouted to the girl who fell from behind the door, practically landing in his arms. He grabbed her by the waist and lifted her off the ground with ease, reminding Bosko of something his father had often told him about a wife. *If she's not portable, she's not compatible.* Miroslav lowered her slowly, rubbing their bodies together.

"Do I have something for you," he exclaimed, staring into her eyes.

"We'll see who the gift giver is tonight. Well, come on in," she said, opening the door wider.

"This is Matko." Miroslav smacked the back of his friend's

12

head as he introduced him.

When Matko crossed the threshold, he brought his heel down on Miroslav's toes, causing him to let out a piercing cry. People stared in their direction.

"I'm Bosko," He said, shaking her outstretched hand, squeezing it gently.

"My friends call me Biljes," she said as she followed them inside and shut the door. "You can throw your coat on top of that table, with everyone else's."

She headed toward the bar, which was made from a long table draped with a white tablecloth and covered with plastic cups and bottles of soda, beer, and wine. "Bosko," Matko yelled, "be right back." He pointed to the girl he was about to follow into another room. Bosko gave him a thumbs up.

"Here you go," Biljana said as she returned and handed Bosko a beer.

"Thanks. Is this your home?"

"No, it's Ruza's. She and Miro are my friends. I'm the one who got you invited."

"Pretty cool of her parents to let her have this party with beer and wine."

"Oh, they're just down the road celebrating with neighbors. They figured that letting Ruza have her own party was the best way to keep an eye on us tonight."

"Who's Ruza?"

"That's her over there."

Bosko turned while he sipped his beer and noticed two girls standing together and laughing across the room. One of them brought a glass to her lips and turned toward Bosko. She looked straight at him.

"*Who is that?*"

Spotting the object of Bosko's focus, Biljana said, "Oh, that's just Admira."

Bosko couldn't take his eyes off the girl with thick, wavy black hair, high cheekbones, and almond-shaped eyes. She was a knockout but glanced away when she noticed his stare. Not wanting to seem too interested, he did the same.

"I see you already have a beer," Miro said, walking toward Bosko and Biljana.

"Yeah," he replied. After they clanked their bottles together, he casually turned his head in Admira's direction. She'd vanished; he didn't see her anywhere. Bosko gulped his beer, and without saying a word to Miro or Biljana, he walked away, pushing through a crowd of people in search of her. Bosko nodded at his friends while he moved through the room. Like a cat stalking a mouse.

A cloud of bluish-white smoke hung from the ceiling above those puffing away, and Bosko thought it was fitting that she had disappeared into the haze. For that brief instant, she'd had the appearance of not being real. He shook his head and began to think her disappearing act was her way of telling him she wasn't interested.

Seemingly out of nowhere, Admira stepped softly behind him. She was certain he was looking for her and it made her feel quite good. Not that it was unusual; young men found her very attractive. But she had a reputation for being a handful, for being strong-willed and independent, not easily controllable. She raced motorcycles and knew more about fixing cars than most boys.

She began to mimic Bosko as he strained his head trying to locate her in the crowd. Admira caught Ruza's attention; she shook her head and tried not to laugh.

Bosko was determined to find this girl who was playing hard to get. Who the hell did she think she was? He answered his own question: beautiful.

A soft voice behind him said, "Perhaps she's in the other room."

14

He started to turn around, thinking it was Biljana. "No, I don't think—"

"I had the strangest feeling you were looking for me." Admira's eyes met his. She stood very close to Bosko.

"Ah... yes, I was."

"Why is that?"

Bosko was exhilarated at being so close to her. He cleared his throat. "I thought you would like a drink."

"I have one," she said, raising her glass.

Don't smile. She'll think you're an idiot. "I'm Bosko. I live on Kosovo Hill." *Why did I say that? Who cares where I live?*

"It's a pleasure to meet you, Bosko from Kosovo Hill." His eyes were an unbelievable color. In an instant she remembered a wine her father had once brought home that was the same amber color of Bosko's eyes. She remembered how much she'd enjoyed drinking that wine, the little her father had let her have.

"You can leave out the Kosovo Hill part." He spoke softly, as if he wanted her to listen very carefully to everything he was about to say.

"Bosko of Mysterious Origin. How about that?"

"It'll do," he answered with the hint of a smile. "And you are Admira of..."

"You know my name? How?"

"I have this ability."

"You have a disability?" she said, struggling to keep a serious face.

"No, I said I have this *ability*..." It took Bosko a few seconds to realize she was having some fun at his expense.

"Really? To do what?"

"I can guess a person's first name. It's an ability I have. So, now you are Admira of..."

"Far and Wide, but I'm told I have limitations."

"Not too many, I hope."

15

"We'll see, won't we?" She didn't miss a beat in her response. He liked that—a lot. Without understanding why, Admira felt herself being drawn toward Bosko. Bosko was experiencing something less polite and very male.

"So, is it spelled B-o-s-h-k-o or B-o-s-k-o? I've seen both."

"Which would you prefer?"

"Boshhhhko. Do you like how it rolls off my tongue?"

"I do." He stared at her lips. "Say it exactly like that, once more."

"Boshhhhko," she said slowly. "Do you know Ruza?"

He hesitated a second or two before answering. Damn, no one had ever said his name like that.

"No. Matko and I just followed Miro. He has a friend here."

Admira smiled because that meant Bosko had come with friends and not a date.

Tonight, unbeknownst to her family and closest friends, Admira had set a plan in motion—one that she had been thinking about for quite some time. This would be the night she would become a woman. She would wait no longer, and what better night than this? Admira had waited because she knew what she wanted to feel when it happened. To her, making love for the first time was a rite of passage, she hadn't given into peer pressure like so many of her friends. It was not something to 'get it over with'. She couldn't deny the very real and palpitating attraction she felt toward Bosko. It had happened without any warning. Could he be the one?

"It's a beautiful night and the city is sparkling. Would you like to see it with me?" Admira blurted out.

"Yeah, I guess."

She grabbed Bosko's hand and led him through the packed house of hormonal teenagers. When they arrived at a door on the second floor, Admira knocked. When no one answered, she opened it and pulled him into the dark room. "Just wait."

He heard the lock click. Did she always take a man she barely knew into a room and lock the door?

"Close your eyes, Boshhhhko." There was a nervousness in her voice. Admira hesitated for a moment before walking toward the sliding glass doors. Would he feel swept away the moment he stepped out onto the balcony. Would he marvel at the scenery, at the sight of their fabled city, as if he were looking at it through her eyes?

Bosko stood still, his eyes closed. A single ray of moonlight shone into the otherwise dark room. He heard the sound of her footsteps approach. "Just a few more seconds," she said as she took his hand and led him toward the balcony. *Why do I have to show him what lies beyond the balcony? He's just some random boy I've met at the party—isn't he?*

Admira slid open the frost-covered glass doors. The cold air burst into the room, leaving Bosko's face tingling with a million pin-pricks. Holding his hand, Admira leaned forward and whispered, "Open your eyes, slowly."

Bosko did as she asked and looked out onto his city. Her lights sparkled like thousands of blazing gems.

"There's more. Come." She nodded toward the small wooden balcony. It was big enough for just two people.

Admira let Bosko take an extra step in front of her, and he stepped out onto the wooden slats and pressed himself against the metal railing. He remained completely still except to grab the wooden top of the rail with both hands.

She stood near him, their bodies barely touching. Turning her head slowly toward him, she gazed into his eyes. What was he thinking and feeling as he looked out at their mythical city on this New Year's Eve? She started to blow on her chilled fingers. Bosko wrapped his hand around hers and pressed it against his thigh to keep it warm. A frozen mist escaped their mouths. The cold night swirled about their faces while the warm air from the room blew against their backs. It mirrored Admira's emotions as she stood next to him. She felt the heat of attraction toward Bosko with a coolness that guarded her emotions.

She watched his eyes move up and down and side to side, imprinting the view of their city onto his thoughts.

Bosko slid his arm around her waist. She let him.

"What do you see, Bosko?"

He didn't know how to answer her. Not even from the balcony on his apartment was there such a view.

Every street and alleyway, even the banks of Sarajevo's river, glowed like molten lava. And the soft lavender haze that blanketed the rooftops were covered by a soft, powdery snow.

"Fire, I see fire—as if the earth were opening up. Look at the Miljacka. Look how brightly it's shining, as if it were a river of gold. Do you see it, Admira?"

She nodded her head. "Yes, Bosko, I see it." She squeezed his hand.

They should have both been freezing as they stood side-by-side on the creaking wooden balcony on this harsh winter's night, but they weren't. The heat of the moment, of being together, had cocooned them from feeling the cold. Bosko remained silent. He pressed himself against Admira; their hands entwined. They watched the kaleidoscope of their city in silence. It seemed as if the surface of Sarajevo itself was cracking apart and was about to release the lava stored beneath it.

The cracks they were staring at were in fact the streets and alley-ways, narrow and wide that separated the neighborhoods of Sarajevo. Along these countless ribbons of alleyways were street lamps, trees of light radiating a shimmering orange and gold brightness that spread throughout Sarajevo; these ribbons of light separated the city into its parts. Everywhere Bosko looked, Sarajevo spewed out a deep and glowing light, not from what at first had seemed to be the bowels of the earth, but from the city itself. A necklace of streets and alleyways lit up by those trees of light graced the city's body as if she were a beautiful woman. Its beauty almost had a sound, as if Sarajevo sang its own torch song. Their golden city of palaces had never seemed as gentle or as beautiful as it did at that moment with its countenance blanketed by a gentle snowfall.

Bosko looked toward Baščaršija, the ancient Turkish bazaar, then turned in the direction of the Gazi Husrev-beg Mosque. She followed his gaze, and they stared at the towering minaret, so brightly lit that from this distance it appeared as a giant ivory obelisk. From deep within its Byzantine arches glowed a soft and inviting yellow light. It was a mosque that had no equal in this part of the world, exquisitely built of stone and marble and a variety of inlaid woods.

As far as the eye could see, light from thousands of homes filled the valley and mountains surrounding Sarajevo. The wooden planks creaked under Bosko's weight as he leaned over the edge of the iron railing. He turned to Admira. "Why did you bring me here?"

"I thought you'd like to see this." Her heart sank, thinking none of this had made an impression on him. It was stupid of her to think it would.

"It's beautiful." He glanced at her for just a second before he turned his gaze back to his city. She wanted to leap into his arms. Those were the two most important words she'd heard from Bosko tonight, and it made her decision an easy one. "Look at all those lights. It's as if ..." The excitement in Bosko's voice was like that of a little boy. "As if the stars have fallen out of the sky and come to rest in every home."

"Yes, that's exactly it," Admira said. "You see it, too."

What was happening to them? They had abandoned their friends on New Year's Eve and spirited themselves away into a dark room because of some immediate and unexplainable

19

attraction for each other. And in the darkness, they had been greeted by an unearthly sight. Everything about this moment—their city, the balcony where they stood pressed against each other, the lavender haze, the ivory tower—had all become a Sarajevan tapestry woven together in a singular moment for only Bosko and Admira to witness.

"When Ruza and I were little and I slept over, we'd stay up really late at night and stare out at those homes and make up all kinds of stories about princesses who lived in them, needing to be rescued."

Bosko impulsively brushed Admira's cheek.

"It's a misty, moonlit night," said Admira, looking up at the sky.

"And Sarajevo burns like a flickering firelight." Replied Bosko.

They began to breathe in unison, each breath entering and leaving their bodies in a simple rhythm. Admira turned her charcoal-black eyes toward Bosko. She glanced at him for only a moment, realizing something had in fact happened to her, something that hadn't ever happened to her before with any other young man. It was an infinite and finite moment in the making, a decisive moment that occurs in the lives of two teenagers who meet for the first time. Chemistry was produced between her and Bosko. It was the scent of seduction. It lasted for only a few moments, but it had already altered their sense of each other, their sense of themselves.

He turned to Admira and said, "You locked the door. How did you know I wouldn't—"

"I didn't." Admira's tone was gentle, her eyes confident. She was certain of this moment, and of all the things that were about to happen—more so than Bosko.

The wooden balcony creaked and the snow fell between the wooden planks to the street below. Impulsively, Bosko placed his hand under her chin. Admira didn't resist or turn away. A snowflake landed on her lip. An energy had passed between them and it propelled Admira and Bosko from where they were in this life into the next moment of their existence.

They couldn't deny the inexorable pull of attraction they had for one another. Her entire being seemed to rise as her lips moved closer to his; Admira grappled with this sense of exalted fear, a fear toward all of the possibilities that might exist between her and him. Their warmth illuminated the night. Silhouetted against the night sky, he kissed her in a way he'd never kissed a girl.

"Wait here," she said, and she spun around on the snow-covered balcony, leaving him alone in a daze.

Her scent filtered by him, lasting for only a few seconds, long enough for him to breathe in the mixture of tangerine and jasmine.

"Here, take this."

She gripped the edges of two large cushions in one hand and dragged behind her a very large, thick fur with the other.

Bosko took the cushions and dropped them onto the snow-covered planks, then threw open the fur amid a flurry of snowflakes and wrapped it around his shoulders, making him resemble a grizzly bear. Admira slipped back into the room, leaving the sliding doors open. Bosko stood on the balcony, bound from head to toe in the large gray and white fur, staring out into the night.

Admira's palms were clammy and her heart pounded. She picked up a champagne glass but immediately put it back down, unable to breathe. Maybe she was having a panic attack. *What would he think of her later if she went through with this tonight? Would they see each other after the deed? Was it possible he would even want to see her again? Or would she have been just a*—Admira abruptly stopped thinking. She put every thought out of her mind except for one—

there *was* something special between them. She felt it. He wasn't like any other young man. "These feelings only happen," she said to herself, "when you meet someone very special, someone like Bosko." Admira was positive his inner vibration was attuned to hers.

Being near him made her—well, there was no other way of putting it—made her extremely horny. Those undeniable feelings convinced Admira that this was the moment to lose her virginity. A phrase she hated because she knew nothing was actually lost and everything would be gained if it was with the right person. "It is. He is," she said out loud to no one. She picked up the champagne glass and an opened bottle of champagne with the cork stuck back inside, and returned to the balcony. Bosko was still wrapped in the fur.

"Earlier, I put a bottle in a bucket of ice to toast the New Year while I looked out at Sarajevo. I don't know what made me do it."

Bosko took the bottle and the glass from her hand.

"I'm glad that you did because tonight we do have something to celebrate."

She nodded, but said nothing. Her heart was beating faster.

Bosko thought it had been a lot colder when he'd met his friends on the walkway. But as he and Admira sat huddled together, sitting on two very large and comfortable cushions, tucked snugly under the soft, thick fur, the world around them had warmed up considerably.

Admira moved the bottle and the champagne glass out from under the fur and placed both against the wall. She entwined her arm with his.

The white flakes continued to fall, turning them into snow sculptures. They spoke openly and at times whispered to each other about many things. It was a conversation that took on great meaning because they were so keen on listening to one another, wanting to know what the other was thinking. And what about their differences, how had they made them into who they were? That subject was too complex to be answered in one night.

Was there a God? Who had the best version? They laughed about trying to find an answer to that question. Did Bosko have any siblings? How did Admira enjoy living on the outskirts of the city? Was it almost like living on a farm? She explained that she did enjoy it because there'd been so much room to play with her sister when they were younger. The most difficult question, which neither of them could fully answer to their own satisfaction, was what their parents were *really* like. Bosko and Admira were spending the night thinking and talking as if they weren't sixteen. On this special night, they were mature beyond their years.

At some point, they began to feel as if they'd known each other forever. That realization was both exhilarating and frightening. When Admira mentioned it, confusion and joy showed in her eyes—and his. She reached out from under the fur and lifted up the bottle of champagne; the soft white powder encasing it floated away.

The Christian church bells began to ring.

"Happy New Year, Bosko," she said, offering him the bottle. He drank carefully so as not to spill the cold champagne and then he held the bottle in front of him.

"Happy New Year, Admira," he said, wiping the sides of his mouth with his hand. She took gentle gulps from the bottle. Finishing, she wiped the sides of her mouth with her hand.

Shouts from revelers echoed all around them. Bosko and Admira stood, snuggled together under the fur, and leaned forward against the balcony, watching as people ran into the streets carrying lit candles, wine-filled glasses, and champagne bottles.

"Happy New Year!" Bosko yelled to the people below. Admira joined him. People raised their heads and yelled back.

Once again, Bosko began to feel something less polite and very male as he turned Admira toward him.

She saw it in his eyes and felt it as his arm encircled her waist and they kissed the way that lovers do when they are leading each other to the most intimate act of all.

The New Year had begun.

"Charmer Boy, you son of a bitch, I know you're in there. I've checked every other room. Bosko, open up. I've got champagne. It's the New Year. What the hell are you doing in there? Mats and I are going to another party. Are you coming or not?"

Miroslav's interruption was like a brass band suddenly playing in the middle of High Mass. Admira and Bosko remained silent.

"It's a long way back, Bosh. Tvrtko came in a car with friends, and we can leave with them to another party. Open up." He banged his fist on the door again.

"Ah, let him be," they heard Matko say. "He's further ahead than we'll ever get tonight, lucky son of a bitch."

"We're leaving! Do you hear me?" Miroslav jiggled the locked doorknob.

"Let's go, Miro."

Bosko and Admira listened to their footsteps fade as they sat on the balcony in the dead of Sarajevo's winter. Wrapped tightly under the fur, their bodies emanated a very special heat and the bitter cold of what was now a New Year felt like nothing more than a cool breeze.

"Admira! It's me, open up. It's Lena!" her friend yelled as she pounded on the door.

Bosko looked at Admira. "Perhaps you should."

Admira handed Bosko the bottle of champagne, stepping out from under the fur and into the room.

"What is it?" she yelled.

"What do you mean, what is it? Let me in! It's the New Year! Why aren't you celebrating with us downstairs?"

24

Admira hesitated for a few seconds and then walked to the door and unlocked it.

"What are you doing here, in the dark?" Lena looked toward the balcony. From the look she gave her, Admira knew she had seen Bosko.

"So this is where you've been? I've been looking all over for you. I even got dressed and went outside in that friggin' cold! Why did you just disappear?" Lena started to walk into the room.

Admira held out her arm, blocking her friend's path through the door. She had no intention of introducing Bosko.

"Oh, it's going to be like that?"

"Yes."

"Do I know who he is?"

"I don't know."

"What's his name?"

"That's not important, Lena."

"Well, I hope he's worth it for you not to be celebrating with your friends." Lena leaned forward, quite drunk, clutching a champagne bottle in her hand. The moment Bosko heard what Lena had said, his first thought was that Admira wanted to be with him. Being *with him* in his mind could mean only one thing. After all, this was New Year's Eve; what else could it mean? In that same instant, he had another realization. He realized he had no idea what to do or how to do it. He felt a terrible nervousness; Bosko was clueless as to how to get things done. "Things?" he murmured to himself. "That's not how you're supposed to think of it."

Lena leaned closer into Admira. "Oh, I almost forgot. Hugo is going to some other party, if you're interested. I am. If you're not, he said he'd give you a ride home. He's trying to impress you. Going out of his way to drop you home," she said, falling forward. Admira grabbed her.

Admira turned to look at Bosko. Every fiber of her being

25

wanted to be with him. *Sleep with Bosko. Have you lost your mind?* Admira had planned a very special night. It was what she had wanted so desperately to happen, but as the seconds ticked away, she knew none of it was going to take place on this magical night. She knew she had to step back from the brink. Her first time had to be in a place more meaningful than in her friend's bedroom. And at a very special time—even more special than at this moment on New Year's Day. "Tell Hugo I'll be down in five minutes," she whispered to Lena. Bosko didn't hear her.

Lena took one last look at the balcony before Admira hurried her out of the room.

"Don't push, I'm going already. Happy New Year!" Lena drank from the bottle.

"Go then, already." Admira gently but firmly pushed her friend out of the room and shut the door. She turned and looked at Bosko leaning over the railing, shouting to the crowds and waving. "Bosko, the snow!"

He looked down at his feet.

She ran toward him. "The snow will make your feet slip out from under you if you lean over too far."

"Nothing bad can happen to me tonight."

She crawled in under the fur and pressed up against Bosko. Suddenly, she turned to him with an expression of urgency on her face and in her voice. "I need to go. My sister and I do something special with our father every New Year's Eve."

"You're leaving?"

"Yes, it might be the last time we do it with Dad. I don't want to disappoint him. Doesn't matter what time we get home, he'll be waiting up for us, but he'll be disappointed if I don't come home to share it with him." The first thing she'd done on this New Year's morning was to lie to Bosko, but she did it to save herself.

The first important thing on her journey to becoming a

woman hadn't happened. She was desperate that it should. It had to. But only with a man she could trust. Her emotions would overcome her if she stayed. Admira could see it happening tonight, on New Year's Eve, here in this room. *Stop it. Now is not the time. And this is not the place.*

"Meet me in front of the National Theatre at ten tomorrow morning, okay?" Without hesitating, she kissed his lips. "Now you have something of mine and I have something of yours." Stopping in the doorway, she looked back at him, standing by the glass doors; she'd always remember the color of his eyes. She very quickly pulled the door shut, lest she change her mind.

With the fur wrapped around him from head to toe and a flurry of snowflakes falling all around, Bosko picked up the champagne bottle and drank from it, staring out into the night, into their city of lights.

Chapter Two

Admira ran to the kitchen and threw open the curtains. "Calm down. You must be calm," she kept repeating. How absolutely wonderful it was to be sixteen. To be young and to believe the world had been made just for her. Every breath she took was reassurance that there were no flaws, no wrongs. Everything in her world was as it should be. She wanted to shout it out for everyone in the house to hear.

She had gotten up early and tried to be as quiet as possible as she showered and got ready for the day. The last thing she wanted was for her mother to wake up, come into the kitchen, and start asking questions.

Before Admira left the kitchen, she glanced at the frost on the window where she had written their names. Admira and Boshhhhko were barely visible; the sunlight had melted the letters into each other.

Admira packed the breakfast she had made for them into her backpack. Food calms the senses. She wanted to see the steam rising from the coffee cup he would be holding. What would his mouth look like as he bit into a sweet roll? Would he like the Polish jam? And what about the homemade sausages? Was she going overboard with her mother's homemade sausages?

She'd buttered three rolls and spread a thin layer of raspberry jam on each and wrapped each loosely in waxed paper, so they wouldn't lose their shape. A sweet roll is not a sweet roll if it becomes flat. She poured coffee into a large thermos, and took out two of her favorite *fildzans* from which to drink it. She hoped Bosko drank his coffee black. Her backpack sealed with its precious cargo, Admira was ready.

She wrote a note and slid it under a magnet on the refrigerator.

I met a boy last night. His name is Bosko. He's from Kosovo Hill. We are going to meet at the National Theatre at 10 a.m. Tell Dad. I know you'll read this first.

Love you both,
Admira

Because the family home was on the outskirts of the city, she'd have barely enough time to reach the National Theatre by ten. She grabbed her scarlet cashmere cap from the dresser, slung the backpack over her shoulders, and slipped into her sister's bedroom. "Happy New Year, Tonya," she whispered as she kissed her on the cheek. She tiptoed out of the house and walked down the path to the main road.

Spotting the tram, Admira ran after it, following rails that cut through the center of the city like a steel spine. She laughed as she chased after it, determined to catch up. As a gift to the most hardened New Year's Eve partygoers, the driver slowed down and opened the tram doors for anyone he saw meandering or stumbling along their way on the street or sidewalk. All they had to do was run up to one of the cars and jump in, which was exactly what Admira did. She found a spot next to the window in the empty, silent car.

She and the driver were the only ones on this particular tram, and she was alone with her thoughts. *What if he wasn't there?* A queasiness bubbled up into Admira's stomach. How foolish she would feel standing alone in front of the huge, stone National Arts Theatre, surrounded by only a blanket of white snow. "He will be there," she said aloud, squeezing the straps of the backpack resting on her lap.

The tram lurched, halted, lurched once more, and then stopped. Admira got up and approached the driver, who'd begun to curse.

"What's wrong?"

"This one, she's very temperamental. We'll have to wait a few moments."

Admira returned to her seat, forcing a smile now and again when the driver turned to look at her.

"It'll be okay. We'll be going soon," he said, mustering his own smile.

The minutes ticked away, and Admira's heart beat faster. Her palms were sweating. She ran each hand over her sweater more than once.

"Ah," the driver said.

"Great," she responded.

"No, not yet. Soon, very soon."

The minutes and seconds passed, excruciatingly slowly, as the tram remained still. Admira and the driver passed the time in silence.

*

Bosko saw the reflection of the clock on his nightstand. It was almost nine. A jolt flung him out of bed.

Ten o'clock. I have to meet Admira at ten o'clock!

For the next excruciating half hour, Bosko ran from his bedroom to the bathroom and back again, trying not to wake his parents as he dressed in a panic, overwhelmed with the fear of being late.

Outside, Bosko ran and kept running. The freshly fallen snow was kicked up from under his feet. His hair blew in the wind and his chest heaved in and out with his determination to meet Admira at the appointed hour. His long legs galloped across the streets of Sarajevo. He smiled; at who and what he didn't know, but it didn't matter. He simply couldn't help himself. *Run, Bosko, run.*

When the tram finally arrived, after stalling on the tracks for twenty minutes, Admira flew out of the car. *Calm down.* She hadn't stopped repeating those words to herself. You *gave yourself plenty of time.* She'd been sweating from the wait. *Oh no, do I smell?* Lowering her face in an attempt to get a whiff of her body, she said out loud, "Please, God, don't let me smell." If her watch was correct, she had ten minutes. With her backpack pulled firmly over her shoulders, she began to walk quickly, then slowly, and on more than one occasion almost came to a complete stop when certain thoughts began to overwhelm her as she got closer to the National Theatre.

An exaggerated stillness blanketed Sarajevo. It seemed to Bosko that he was the only person alive in the entire city. He'd sprinted and jogged all the way from his home to the National Theatre. Out of breath but exhilarated, Bosko bent over, his hands pressed against each knee as he gasped for air. Staring at the snow, he looked back at his footprints; they were the only ones for as far as he could see.

The Miljacka River was calm, its steady and slow current flowing effortlessly under the sheets of broken ice. Bosko was trying to be the same way. Be calm, he kept saying as he ran through the deserted, snow-laden streets of Sarajevo. A gentle breeze came up behind him, as if to nudge him on. From the moment he ran out of his apartment and down the stairs and slammed the entrance door open, his heart hadn't stopped beating furiously—it was going to burst at any moment. He felt euphoric.

Admira took off her cashmere cap and tucked it into her jacket pocket. "I would have slept with him the first night and now I feel like this—why?" Mumbling to herself probably wasn't a good thing. "Why does he make me feel this way?" She was happy, nervous, and hopeful. She'd never had these emotions all

32

at once.

As she walked, she picked up her pace. In a few moments they were both running, kicking up the otherwise undisturbed snow, approaching from opposite directions. Admira, jogging with her backpack slung over her shoulders, slowed down her steps. Her vision of their meeting suddenly became clouded by one thought. Was Bosko really going to be there? She tried not to think of her disappointment if, after she'd turned the corner of the Arts building, it would be only her standing alone in a silent field of snow. She looked up at the teacup-blue sky and envisioned, with every ounce of faith she could muster, that Bosko would be standing in the snow, waiting for her. Admira picked up her pace and in moments she was running. So consumed was she by that one thought that she flew past Bosko, just as he had turned the corner and was running toward her from the opposite direction.

"Wait!" he yelled as he caught sight of her.

They tried to stop from sliding and falling onto the snow, and as they struggled for their balance they burst out laughing. Their efforts almost catapulted them into each other's arms. Finally, they stood still, exuberant over the fact they were both here and standing only a few short feet from each other, only a few short hours after they'd stood on a balcony overlooking their bejeweled city at night. A white mist was being forced out from between their lips. *Is this real?* They began to laugh once more, it was a nervous disbelieving laugh. She was first to close the short distance between them until they were barely a foot apart. Bosko couldn't believe it. She remembered. Without hesitation, he kissed her, and she responded wholeheartedly. They were two lone figures standing on a blanket of powdery white snow, without another soul in sight.

"I wasn't sure you would remember, but you did," Admira said, moving a strand of hair away from his eyes.

33

"You look beautiful." It was all he could say.

"Thank you."

He was seeing her for the first time in the daylight and she appeared even more alluring than she had on the balcony last night. She took his breath away. The frozen mist that escaped their mouths took with it all of their earlier fears—fears that this meeting would not take place, fears that were now crushed into oblivion. The seconds passed and the rhythm of their breathing became one with a quiet joy.

Neither Bosko nor Admira knew where they were going; an internal compass seemed to be guiding them as they walked, holding each other's hand.

"Let's sit here." She pointed to some stairs facing the river. "Are you hungry?"

"Famished."

"So let's eat," she said, taking the backpack off her shoulders.

He watched her open the backpack and remove some fluffy rolls and the two *fildzans*, which she began to fill with black coffee from the thermos. Admira held the *fildzan* in both hands to warm the tips of her fingers. *Those eyes of his.*

They sat on the cold, concrete stairs watching the morning mist rising from a river squeezed between two banks in a city that was itself squeezed by the surrounding mountains. Each hoped not to ruin the moment by saying or doing something stupid.

Admira finally broke the silence while they enjoyed breakfast. "My mom once told me how her grandfather said, that as a young boy, his favorite memory of Sarajevo was in the summer when the Lombardy poplars would sway in the wind as if they were cooling the city. He said to her that if they were set on fire, those poplars would burn like giant torches and engulf the city in flames."

Bosko sipped his black coffee. It warmed him from the inside out. He squeezed Admira's hand affectionately and said, as he blew into his fildzan filled with hot black coffee, "It sounds as though they possessed competing inclinations those poplars—a dual spirit. Like Sarajevo."

Oh! She liked it very much that he could think the way he did, and answer the way he had. Her sense of him, that he contemplated his thoughts carefully, had started the moment they'd huddled under the fur. Some window or door to a part of who they were had been opened. What emerged had been a way of thinking, a way of saying things to each other that hardly ever happened when they were with their teenage friends. Admira couldn't understand why it had happened, only that it had. She felt more grown up, less of a girl, more of a woman when she was with Bosko.

Bosko kept his thoughts to himself as he sipped the strong, black coffee. He was feeling quite grown up. He noticed that she hadn't brought any milk. "The coffee is good, thank you."

"You're welcome, Bosko." Admira waited for a second before admitting to something from her youth. "I just had a thought."

"What is it?"

"When I was young, my dad would give me hot milk with a little Torani syrup sprinkled in. It was my favorite,"

"And now you drink your coffee black."

"I am older; I can handle stronger things."

What was it about being with Bosko that brought out her inner self-confidence? She removed a glove, wanting to feel his skin against hers. Taking his hand, she squeezed it. He didn't look at her, but he smiled, and so did she.

They drank coffee, and while they ate, the minutes passed. Her hand rested on his knee a long time, and all the while he squeezed her slender fingers.

"Come on. Let's go," he said. "There's something I want to show you."

She stuffed the untouched food back into her backpack and gulped down the coffee. "Okay, where to?"

"There." He pointed. He wanted to take her to a café, a *kafana*, nestled at the bottom of Mount Trebević. Bosko wanted Admira to himself, away from people and the city's awakening distractions. His wish was for them to be in a place where they could be alone, where he had her full attention and she had his. Off they went on a journey of hitching rides, catching trams, and walking—a lot of walking. Admira easily kept pace with him. Her stamina didn't go unnoticed by Bosko.

The sun shone like a piece of polished gold and nowhere were there any shadows in their city, on this luminous morning. Bosko ran ahead pointing to a one-story rustic brick and wood building; a cabin in the woods nestled below a teacup blue sky.

The snowball Admira had been holding behind her back rolled out of her hand the moment Bosko hugged her. They entered the *kafana* with their arms around each other's waists.

"Look." He pointed to the rainbows on the walls, ceiling, chairs, and tables. "It's the prisms from the windows that cause those rainbows. Cool, huh?" Bosko ran his fingers through Admira's hair, and then held out his hand in front of her and slowly opened his fist. Resting in his palm was a rainbow.

"What am I to do when I'm offered rainbows on New Year's Day in a *kafana* on a snow-laden mountain?" Admira asked.

"Enjoy," Bosko replied.

"I can do that."

Chapter Three

Tonya had been waiting for her sister to come home. The moment she heard Admira's voice downstairs talking to her parents, she ran into her sister's bedroom, flopped onto her bed, and waited.

"Happy New Year." Admira walked into the bedroom without looking at her sister.

"Where did you disappear to? Mom and Dad have been going nuts wondering where you'd gone."

"I left them a note."

"Yeah, I know, I read it. Who is this guy? Bosko! You didn't even come in and wish me a happy New Year this morning."

"I came in and gave you a kiss before I left."

"You did?"

"I did. Must have had a few last night—huh?"

"Never mind all that. Where have you been all day? Where were you?"

"Nowhere." Admira was barely able to contain her excitement. "How was your night?"

Tonya sat up on the bed. "Good. I got to drink beer. A group of us were down the road with the neighbors. Mom would freak if she knew. It's given me so much gas."

Admira couldn't contain her excitement any longer. She was about to explode. She knelt by the bed.

"What?" her sister asked, feeling Admira's excitement.

"I met someone."

"We all know. What else? Come on, give me details. Is he hot?" she asked, a sly grin on her face.

"Oh my God, you wouldn't believe what happened to me last night with Bosko," Admira blurted out to her sister.

Tonya grabbed Admira's hand. "You mean—him and you? What! What happened?"

Admira smiled. "I saved myself, but I almost didn't."

"What do you mean?" Her sister asked with her eyes widening.

"We were together, so close, and it felt so warm, so wonderful to feel him—"

"You *mean*—wait. You saved yourself, but you also—what?"

"From me, I had to save myself from me," said Admira, grabbing her blouse and twisting it.

"What do you mean, from yourself? You're not making sense."

"I almost—"

Admira stared at her sister. She had to stop or she'd admit that she would've let Bosko take her, ravish her, do anything to her.

Getting up from the floor, Admira walked to her vanity, sat in the chair, and looked at her reflection in the mirror. Last night she would have slept with Bosko, a boy she had never met before. She wasn't sure who that person was who was staring back at her.

"Go help Mom, Tonya. I'll be down in a minute," she said, after clearing her throat.

"Are you out of your mind? Go help Mom? No, no, no! First you tell me what happened. Come on, out with it. Come on, Sis, I won't say a word, really, swear to God—did something really happen? Did he, did you—you know. Did you?"

"You can hear all the gory details at dinner."

"Ah, crap. If you're going to talk to them about it, then there are no gory details. Nothing happened?" Tonya looked at her sister, unsure of what to really think. "Nothing, right?"

Admira kept silent. Her thoughts were still back at the *kafana*.

"Oh, I hate you." Tonya slid off of Admira's bed and started to leave.

Admira jumped up from her vanity, grabbed her sister, and embraced her. "Happy New Year, Sis."

38

*

Zena spooned the lamb stew into a large serving bowl and placed it on the center of the table beside a loaf of somun bread and fresh butter. Tonya was seated at the table and couldn't wait for the dinner conversation to start.

Admira hummed as she entered the kitchen. "The stew smells wonderful, Mom." She gave her mother a hug and smiled at her father. "Isn't it a great year?"

"The year hasn't even begun, and what are you so happy about?"

"Oh, I just know it will be, Pops."

"Know what?" He stared at his daughter, who was definitely acting out of character, and was filled with a gleam in her eyes.

"It's going to be a great year, that's all." Admira seated herself at the table.

Tonya glanced at her sister.

They all held hands and closed their eyes for a moment. Zao gave a simple thanks. "Peace be among us and may we always be blessed with food on our table." Admira broke a slice of somun bread into four pieces. Each piece represented a corner of the earth. She'd learned this from her father, as he had from his father.

"So, what's everyone been up to today?"

All eyes were on Admira. The real question was what had she been doing and with whom.

Admira served herself the stew, taking her time and dipping a piece of bread into it, then she smiled at her dad across the table.

"His name is Bosko. He lives on Kosovo Hill." She bit into the bread, savoring something far more pleasurable than the taste of her mother's stew—the sound of his name.

Zao filled Zena's glass with wine. They were Bosnian

Muslims, but alcohol was welcome in their home. She took a sip and glanced back at Admira.

"What is he like, this Bosko fellow?" asked Zao.

"Handsome. He's Serbian. Dad, please pass me the salt," Admira said all in one breath. With a respectful defiance in her eyes, she turned her attention to her father. Daughters save this expression to deal with their fathers. An expression that develops while in the womb, and it is reserved for when they become teenagers. It is only ever directed at their fathers and is never to be trifled with, and Zao knew all about it. He chewed his food very slowly while staring at Admira. Her mother dipped her bread into her stew but said nothing.

Admira's eyes darted back and forth between her parents. Bosko was a Serb and they were Muslim. But they were all wretched Slavs, as far as her father was concerned. He had said it so often.

"How old is he?" Zao asked.

"Sixteen."

"What else?"

"He speaks from his heart. His eyes are the color of a wine you once let me taste, Papa. And he isn't afraid to say what's on his mind."

"Do you love him?" Tonya blurted out.

"Tonya. That's a stupid question. She just met him." Her mother was not amused.

"Yes, I love him," Admira said softly, eyes focused on her lap.

"Oh God," her mother said, rolling her eyes to the ceiling.

Zao remained silent.

"But does *he* love *you*?" asked Tonya, pushing the envelope and hoping to get more fireworks out of the situation.

Admira raised her head. The seconds passed and she remained quiet. Everyone at the table kept staring at each other. Zena gave Tonya an unpleasant look. It was a stupid question to ask her sister. A thousand thoughts ran through Admira's mind. So much had happened to her since last night. A door to her private world had been opened, behind which lay her deepest thoughts and desires. Bosko had taken her to a *kafana* filled with rainbows. He'd sworn he'd done it with no other girl.

"Yes," Admira whispered. "He loves me." Her father and mother glanced at each other and watched their daughter, who had become very quiet and still. They waited for further revelations from Admira. She remained silent and kept looking into her bowl of stew.

"Well, then," Zao said. Admira cringed as she waited for her father to finish what she believed would be a sarcastic remark at best. "A toast to Bosko." Admira raised her head and a wonderful smile lit up her face as she stared at her father from across the dinner table.

"Wait a minute, just a minute. I don't understand."

"What don't you understand, Tonya?" Zao asked.

"My sister just told you out of the blue she's in love with a Serb, and you're just sitting there eating your stew. And now you're going to make a toast to him? You don't even know him."

"It's very good stew, that's why I am eating it. And as for me not knowing him, apparently your sister *knows* him."

Tonya shook her head with an aggrieved look on her face. "So, it's that simple?"

"What is it now, Tonya?" Zao asked, looking at his problem child.

"You're saying it's okay that Bosko's a Serb, and that he's got eyes for Admira, big ones. It doesn't bother you or Mom that she *loves* him? My God, wake up, both of you!"

"Tonya." Admira's tone was sharp. Her sister ignored her.

"What kind of a house is this, when Admira can come home one night and calmly announce that she's in love with a Serb? And you and Mom continue eating supper as if nothing's wrong and then you want to make a toast?"

Looking at his wife he asked, "Does it bother you, Zena?" Her mom shook her head. Of course it bothered her, not so much the Serb part, but that she knew nothing about him.

"So there you have your answer. Is there anything else, Tonya?"

"This is just not right. He's not one of us. You get that, don't you?"

"Stop it, right now," Admira said, rising from her chair.

"Why? You had to save yourself from this Bosko guy last night—"

The expression on Admira's face should have caused her sister to quit while she was ahead, but it didn't. "Oh my God, just stop."

"That's right. She had to save herself, Dad. You still *okay* with it now?"

"I'm more concerned for this boy. He has no idea what he's gotten himself into."

Turning to her father, Admira said, "What does that mean?"

"It means exactly what I've said. Now I want to eat my meal in peace. Why couldn't I have had sons? Both of you be quiet."

"Why are you giving up so easily, Dad?" Tonya persisted. "Come on, I know you've got it in you. Let's have some fireworks; it's been a while. What do you say? Be a pal."

Admira began to laugh.

"God, you can be such a disappointment at times, Dad. Ah." Tonya kept shaking her head.

Zao lifted his wine glass just barely; only Admira saw it. It was a private toast to her and Bosko, and only she had seen it. She'd met that first important boy in her life. Her gaze softened as she watched her Dad stick his fork back into his bowl of stew and continue to eat.

"Unbelievable," her sister grunted.

A frigid breeze blew through her slightly open window. Admira fantasized that Bosko would emerge from some shadow in her room and take her as his lover. The stars were gleaming, as if polished by the razor-like gusts that swept down the mountains. She pushed the window all the way open and took a deep breath, knowing he'd breathed in the same frigid air that was now blowing over her body.

On any other night it would've been easy for her to slip into her nightgown and go to bed, but tonight was different. She wanted him. Her young, innocent body needed him. The wind howled and Admira clenched her fists and listened to the same sound within her. She stood naked at her bedroom window with the freezing Sarajevo wind whirling around her, cooling her passion for a young man she'd just met. She slammed the window shut. She was angry and happy and alone with only one thought that overwhelmed her. *Bosko.*

Admira slipped her nightgown over her head and flopped onto her belly onto her bed, an arm reaching under the bed as she searched for something.

"Got it." She rolled onto her back. Her father always placed a piece of coal under his daughters' beds on New Year's Eve. The meaning was simple: *May this home always provide the warmth and security of family.* Admira turned back onto her stomach. Her arm dangled over the side of her bed. Bosko was her last conscious thought. Her fingers relaxed and the piece of coal rolled out of her hand and onto the floor.

Admira and her sister had gone to bed. The cold winter wind that swept around their home howled into the night. Zao, seated at the kitchen table, picked up a piece of somun and generously buttered its surface. He loved the fresh butter that he ate in large quantities, much to the consternation of his wife, which was produced on nearby farms. Zena had reheated a small portion of her stew and was about to serve it to him.

"Come sit."

"I'll be there in a minute," she replied. He got up, walked to the window, and looked out into the night.

"Another new year begins."

"She likes him, that's for sure."

"Likes him? She said she loved him. God almighty!" Zao turned and stared at his wife. "What is that?"

"Her backpack," replied Zena, who had emptied the breakfast that Admira had packed for her and Bosko. "She took sweet rolls, coffee, even my homemade sausages. My God!"

"Smart girl."

"She's never done that for anyone else."

"No, she hasn't. She feeds him because she likes him and after that, she's certain she loves him." Zao shook his head.

"Come on, sit, I've served you." Zena placed a plate on the table. "What is it?" He shook his head without saying a word but was thinking he was a blessed man. The love of his wife and family had remained the only constant in his life, even as he knew that the only permanence about life was its impermanence. Sitting back down, he bent his head forward in thanks and then immediately dove into the stew with his buttered slice of somun. Zena had made herself another cup of herbal tea, which she drank to help with her digestion.

"Well," she said after a few moments of silence. He looked up at her. "This is really okay with you?" Zao dipped his bread into the stew and swirled it around the plate, scooping up as much gravy onto the slice as possible. Just before he lifted the slice to his mouth, he said with a smirk on his face, "It's not like in Grandfather's time. Children now do what they want. They don't ask for permission from their parents. Besides, you gave birth to a

44

willful, stubborn child—and there's nothing you or I can do about what she has decided to do." Zao chewed down on the slice of somun. "Ahhh ... it's better this way. How much longer can she spend under the car with me covered in grease? She met a boy good for her."

"We don't know anything about him."

"I know. He could be a half-wit. What will we do with an idiot in our home, whom we'll have to look at and feed, for God knows how long? It doesn't matter anyway. She knows how cars work. How much more complicated could he be? She'll know exactly what makes him run. He has no idea who he's dealing with." Zao held his wife's hand and they both laughed softly, not wanting to wake the girls.

"Did you see the look in her eyes when she said his name?"

"Yes, like she was tasting the sweetest Paganini cake."

"Nine hours in a *kafana*. I wonder what they talked about."

"What youth talks about: everything and nothing." Zena held onto her husband's hand. He had been the good guy tonight. She knew that Admira was most likely expecting her parents' disapproval at the very least and possibly a fight. Yet it didn't happen. It didn't happen for many reasons. She sipped her tea, he ate his stew. The night wind howled.

"It will be okay," Zena said, rising and picking up Zao's plate and placing it in the sink before returning to the table with a cup of coffee for him. Zao had opened the day's newspaper to a specific article that should have been on the front page but wasn't. He wondered if that was a deliberate decision by the newspaper. To have had it on the front page instead of on page five would have placed the story in the spotlight. A story all too familiar to his generation.

"Things have changed in Yugoslavia. It's been happening for a while, but no one knows what it all means," said Zao, looking at the article that described how sides were being taken by different

45

groups throughout the country. Where once there had been no acrimony among neighbors who were Albanian, Serbian, Muslim, and Croatian, the next morning they would awake with a sense of alarm toward one another, brought on by rumors and innuendo about what the other side was planning to do. Neither of Admira's parents knew what it meant or what it was leading to. Neither spoke of these events happening all over Yugoslavia to Admira and Tonya. How could it be explained to anyone? "It says here the Albanians keep pushing to have more autonomy in Kosova. They won't get it, the Serbs won't give it to them. They will tear each other apart for the same scrap of meat. Then what will that mean?

"It says Serbian farmers in Kosova had their crops burned in the night. No one knows who did it. Cows and goats were killed. People have also been killed, and yet it says none of our leaders do a thing to settle these problems." Zao shook his head. It felt like a terrible dream had commenced and he and everyone else would be a part of it.

Zena's keen observation of things, she always shared with her husband. "They do nothing because to do anything would be to admit there is a problem much larger than anyone, even you and I, want to believe is true. After all, have we not lived in peace all these years? To think otherwise is to admit that this has all been an illusion."

Zao had a disgusted look on his face as he squeezed his wife's hand and said, "And now with Izetbegović going to prison, it gives the Serbs, his enemies, even more ammunition."

Zao was referring to the group of Bosnian Muslim nationalists convicted several months earlier in Sarajevo, who were sentenced to thirteen years in prison under the Socialist Federal Republic of Yugoslavia law that prohibited spreading international hatred. Izetbegović was one of them. It was a dubious charge for which he and the others had been sentenced.

46

"He was quoting saying, 'There can be no peace or coexistence between the Islamic faith and non-Islamic societies and political institutions.' The Serbs are saying he's intent on creating an Islamic republic in Bosnia."

"Enough, Zao. It's New Year's. No more talk of this nonsense."

He sipped his coffee, and Zena sipped her tea.

Chapter Four

May 1984

Zao sat bare-chested on a lawn chair in his back yard near a stockpile of chopped wood. He'd just finished his first two cups of coffee when he heard the back door open.

Admira carried a plate of *alva*, a delicious dessert that Admira's mother made out of flour, sugar, butter, saffron, and rosewater. She pulled a patio chair close to her father.

"So, Dad, are you ready for tonight?" She was unable to hide her excitement. It would have been impossible for her father to miss the nervousness in her tone.

It was so important to Admira that Zao like Bosko, whom he'd met, and his family, who would be visiting for the first time. *How can I choose between my love for my father and my love for Bosko? I can't.*

Admira set the plate on his lap.

"What are you and Mom going to do and say tonight when Bosko's parents get here?"

Zao popped a piece of alva into his mouth.

"You've made a choice to be with a Serbian boy. And my feelings about it are mine. Why should it concern you?"

"I love him. I know you and Mom think it's crazy, but I do."

"If we told you not to see Bosko ever again, would you?"

Admira looked away. Zao reached out and held his daughter's hand.

"Look at me. Would you stop seeing Bosko if we forbid it?"

Admira shook her head. She wouldn't stop being with Bosko no matter what her parents said or did.

"I just don't understand why you haven't ___"

"What, Admira?"

"I was certain you would fight me, just like Tonya thought you would. Why haven't you? Mom's been real quiet about it. The truth, Dad. Were you and Mom just waiting to meet his parents and then unload? You've been so stoic about us being together. What gives? What are you really thinking?"

"Do you know that I've been inside a Christian church and sung in its choir?" Zao's tone was filled with pride as he looked at his daughter with a calm stare. "How many Muslims do you know who've done that?" He tugged at her hand playfully. Wanting to know more about what her dad has just revealed to her but more concerned about what he and her mom felt about Bosko and her being together, she said, "Are you going to answer my question?"

Zao bit into his dessert.

"Everyone in the town I grew up in knew that a Muslim boy was singing in a Christian church. It was me. Imagine that."

"Is that really true?"

"Cross my heart and hope to—"

"Stop, don't say those words."

He settled into his chair and pushed the dessert plate away, so Admira knew he was about to tell a long story.

"I even learned Christian blessings from the priest and used to bless myself, a Muslim, with Christian prayers. After my father passed away, my best friend, who was Serbian, adopted me and treated me as if I were his brother. When Karl and his family went to church, I would go along. The priest liked my singing voice so much that he asked me to sing in his choir. Me, a Muslim. In my youth, I sang praises to a Christian god. Maybe the Muslim side of God appreciated the humor more than the Christian side? What do you think, huh?"

"God doesn't have a Muslim or Christian side. What happened to Karl, Dad?"

Zao took a breath within a breath. He squeezed Admira's hand. "In those years the pro-Hitler fascists in Croatia began rounding up Serbs. One night many of them came. All of them were armed and they went into each Serbian home and pulled

50

people from their beds. They had a list of every Serb family in our village and were searching for certain people. When they found them, they separated husbands from wives, children from parents. Karl's family disappeared and I never saw any of them again. The Muslim families were spared that night because those Croatian bastards were only interested in Serbs.

"My aunts and uncles knew they would be back and come for us, so we ran like so many other refugees did, going from one town to the next village to the next, hoping to meet long-lost relatives who had also managed to stay alive. Everyone tried to stay alive any way they could while the slaughter continued on all sides."

Admira briefly noticed anger in her father's eyes, and then it was gone. He tried to smile away his palpable resentment.

"I pray to *no* god anymore. And I stopped singing songs of praise to God the day they took Karl and his family away from me. God has forgotten about us Slavs—as he should—because we don't know how to live."

"Don't say that, Papa."

"You and Bosko and all your friends are our future." Zao still held her hand. "It's the old ways that must vanish, but this is not the time to talk of such things."

"I'm sorry for what happened to Karl."

Zao said nothing but stared out into the distance at the mountains that surrounded his city. Admira saw in her father's eyes a longing, a yearning, to have his best friend with him once more. He squeezed her hand and said, "Go meet Bosko. Tell him I'm looking forward to meeting his family tonight."

"Really?"

"Yes, Admira, really."

She embraced him. "I love you so much."

Zao returned her hug. "Hey, now let me eat the rest of my alva in peace."

51

Admira left her father to be by himself. Walking up the concrete steps, she took one last look at her Dad, just before she pulled open the kitchen door.

Zao bit down on the delicious alva, savoring its unique taste. There was another taste in his mouth that hadn't gone away and had been there for quite a while. The nation he'd help to rebuild as a young man after the war was showing ominous signs of fracturing apart. He was well aware that since Tito's death in 1980, three fundamental problems continued to plague Yugoslavia, to which none of their leaders could provide an answer. He was a Muslim and he had Croatian and Serbian lifelong friends. But he had seen it: divergent ethnic interests kept getting stronger. Yugoslavs faced an economy that was inefficient at best and corrupt at worst. And Zao knew, as many others had always believed, that the little that existed of Yugoslavia's institutional structure was totally incapable of doing the most important thing of all: retaining Yugoslav unity.

He kept his thoughts to himself. He knew no one could predict what the future might be. There was no need to raise the alarm. What good would it do, anyway?

Zena entered the kitchen and Admira ran to her, grabbing her and dancing with her around the kitchen. They all laughed.

"What's gotten into you?"

Admira squeezed her mother's cheeks and kissed her. "The old ways are gone forever."

"What are you talking about, child?"

"It's just such a wonderful life, isn't it, Mom? I finally know what Dad thinks of Bosko." Admira turned and dashed out of the kitchen.

*

Dragan had been sitting in the living room since the early morning hours, looking out the large bay window as he relaxed into the sofa. He'd squeezed a wedge of lemon and some honey into his tea and stirred.

"Dad?"

"What are you doing up?"

"What are *you* doing up?" replied Bosko.

"I couldn't sleep so I decided to have some tea. Don't wake your mother. She won't give me any peace if she gets up. It's early. Go back to bed, Bosko."

"I know it's early, but I'm up, I'll join you." Bosko didn't give his father a chance to reply, but headed to the kitchen. He placed two tea bags in a cup and poured the water from the kettle into it, then a teaspoon of honey and the juice of half a lemon.

"It's going to be a gray day today," said Dragan when his son rejoined him.

"Looks like it." Bosko sipped his tea. His dad seemed a bit off to Bosko.

"So, tell me, how is Admira these days?"

"Fine."

"I like her."

"I'm glad."

"Not that it would matter one way or another to you whether we liked her or not."

"It would matter." Dragan glanced at his son.

"For you to see that I love someone that is like me, my kind, my ilk."

Dragan smiled at the irony of Bosko's words. Both men became silent as they watched the sudden emergence of the sun between the overcast clouds. Its glistening rays appeared for a brief moment but then disappeared behind large waves of silver gray clouds moving slowly over the skies of Sarajevo. Bosko observed his father, who, as far as Bosko could tell, was somewhere else in his thoughts. Lately, he'd heard Dragan get up, go to the living room in the early morning, and sit by himself. His mother had not said anything about his dad constantly getting up so early. Her silence had put Bosko's mind at ease.

"So what have you and the boys planned for later today?"

53

"Not sure." Bosko became silent. He wanted to ask his dad a question but wasn't sure how to go about it. So he tried a different tack.

"Matko's dad hasn't given up on going back to 'Croatia.' He's always making Mats feel that Sarajevo was never good enough for all of them. I've never liked him. He's never seemed to be a happy person."

"Go on."

"He's always kept telling Mats that our generation is clueless about what's important in life."

"My grandfather used to say those exact same words to my father, and he in turn to me," Dragan said.

"He did?"

"Yes. My grandfather was quite something, according to my father."

"Do you miss your father?"

"Yes, wouldn't you?"

"Like you wouldn't believe," said Bosko.

Both men smiled.

"So what is this all about, Bosh?" Dragan turned to his son as he sipped his tea. "What's bothering you?"

"Nothing's bothering me. It's just ..."

"What is it?"

"You know I've never cared about being a Serb and all of that. I don't even know what that means. It just hasn't mattered to me." Bosko waited for his father's reply.

"I know that, son. Not your fault. Your mother and I have not been the best examples of card-carrying Serbs."

"Why? Why aren't you like Mats's dad? He's so into being Croatian."

"I suppose because your mom and I have seen this country change so much in our lifetime. Things that neither one of your grandfathers dreamed of; you and Admira take for granted. It's good, it will make you and Admira and all your friends demand better things. Your standards will be higher."

Bosko glanced at his father.

"Grandfather wouldn't have approved of Admira."

"It would have been more than just disapproval on his part."

Bosko felt his face tighten. "Times have changed for the better," Bosko said.

Dragan reached out and placed his hand on Bosko's cheek.

"Yes, they have changed for the better. Even though these days a lot of people keep snarling at each other."

"It doesn't make sense to me. All of this bravado and posturing—what's it all for?"

"Bosko," Dragan turned to his son. "Whatever may happen to you and Admira, let it be because you both want it."

"We'll never let anything come between us. Besides, what can happen?" Bosko asked, his eyes glistening.

"She reminds me of your mom. Very headstrong; the best ones usually are."

"She can be quite scary at times."

"So can your mom." They tried to muffle the sound of their laughter.

"Mats keeps telling me and Miro that his dad wants to leave Sarajevo. His dad has been saying the same thing ever since we were kids. He keeps telling Mats that things are changing. I mean, we all know that, we see it happening. So let it change. Who cares, what does it matter? His dad just wants to go back to Croatia, he keeps calling it home."

Dragan held onto Bosko's arm and said, "This is *our* home."

"I know. Poor Mats. He's had to suffer listening to his dad about going back to Croatia for so long. All I know is Sarajevo. When I think of myself, it's never as being a Serb. I'm Sarajevan, it's the only thing I know."

"Someday it will matter, that you are a Serb."

55

"Why?"

Dragan turned to his son. A sharpness had suddenly entered into his eyes, but they softened when he looked at Bosko. "It will matter because that is what you are and everything you do in your life must reflect on the fact that you are. So always be proud you are Serbian. Never deny or shame your heritage—understand that, son." Bosko nodded.

"Son, we live in Sarajevo surrounded by all kinds of people. We make it our first priority to get along with each other. In this city we've always done as we please and married whom we wanted. Fact is it makes us better people in the long run, less conventional, less inbred." Dragan laughed. "We are like mirrors for each other. Our light as a person is reflected by the light of others. That is why you can find a synagogue, a mosque, and a church all within a few yards."

"What happens outside of Sarajevo is always so different than what happens here."

"It wasn't always that way, Bosh," replied Dragan.

"But it's that way even now." Bosko tone was damning as he spoke. "And when I think of all these shit-stirring politicians who keep telling everyone about how things should change and cause people like Matko's dad to think the worst of something is heading our way, they should vacation in Sarajevo. They'll get to see how people should live and do live."

"You're right. Admira and all of your friends are the future. So whoever will lead you will be your decision. In grandfather's time, they didn't choose so wisely. Don't you and your friends make that same mistake."

"I won't," Bosko said, almost seething as he spoke.

Bosko's expectations from life and a future had no connection to being a Serb. None of their parents ever wanted to talk about those dark times from their past. It was always meant to be avoided and thoroughly forgotten.

"Have these thoughts anything to do with the dinner we'll be having with Admira's parents tonight?" Dragan turned his head slowly toward his son.

"Well it's—it's just that her parents haven't said much about, you know, me being a Serb and all. Her dad looks at me sometimes as if he's seeing something or someone—I don't know really what Zao is thinking when he looks at me the way he does. So I was just wondering how you and Mom really feel about the fact that—"

"Bosh, the only thing that matters to you is Admira and nothing else. I was just like you when I met your mom. I wouldn't have noticed if heaven opened up and the angels came calling. If you are happy, then so are your mother and I."

"You've made my day." Bosko reached over the arm of the sofa chair and playfully punched his dad on his shoulder.

"Good to know. So tell me more about Admira. She's headstrong, huh?"

"Yes, and she races motorcycles."

"Looks like you got a handful with her."

"It does look that way, Dad, it definitely does."

Chapter Five

May 1984

Zena's preparations over a three-day period were going to produce a feast. Zao couldn't remember when she had prepared such a meal and with such attention to detail.

"What time will they be here?" Zao asked.

"Six o'clock," Zena answered.

"Well, I hope that's soon," Tonya said as she entered the kitchen. "I'm famished. Mom had me running all over the city so Admira could have a perfect night, while Admira did next to nothing except hang out with her lover boy." Without giving her parents a chance to respond, she turned and ran out of the kitchen.

"That is a very strange child," her father said.

"No more than the other," Zena answered.

Tonya walked into Admira's room. "You're not even dressed."

"I can't decide."

Admira dumped an armload of dresses onto her bed while Tonya sifted through her sister's wardrobe with the speed of a corn harvester, picking out three.

"Well, the white one looks good," Admira said, staring at the dress on the hanger.

"How do you feel?" Tonya asked. Her sister sat down on the bed and became silent. "What is it, Admira?"

"That's the thing. I know how I feel... and I don't. It's so confusing but also so crystal-clear."

Tonya draped the white dress over her arm and sat next to Admira. "Listen, just go with it. Whatever you're feeling, don't try to explain it to yourself. If it scares you, let it. If it makes you happy, let that happen too. Go with everything your gut tells you to do. I know I will when it happens to me."

Admira hugged her sister. "What would I do without you?"

The sound of a car approaching the house on the gravel road put an end to Tonya's serious, sisterly advice.

"It's going to be fine, just relax and be yourself. You look beautiful, Sis. I'll see you downstairs."

*

Tonya took the stairs two at a time as she raced down from the second floor. "They're here," she yelled as she ran into the kitchen.

"We know. Calm down. Come, let's go greet them," her father said.

"I'm calm. I'm cool."

"Where's Admira?"

"She'll be down in a minute, Dad."

Zao held out his hand to his wife and they all went outside on the front steps of the back porch to meet their guests.

Bosko was taking flowers out of the trunk.

"Welcome," Zao said, waving.

Bosko moved to meet Admira's family, placing both bouquets in one arm and extending the other to greet Zao and his wife. Dragan was standing next to his wife, watching his son looking so at ease in the presence of Bosko's parents. Rita had her arm linked with her husband's, her steel blue eyes revealing nothing about how she felt about this moment. Dragan stood still, his thick, shiny black hair combed back across his head. His doe-shaped eyes softened his chiseled face with its straight-edged nose and strong, triangular jaw. Bosko looked like his father. Moving his hand behind his back, he gently pressed the driver's side door shut. Turning to Rita, Dragan kissed her on the forehead.

"It seems we've lost a son," he whispered, realizing how, in just the short period of time that Bosko had known Admira, he had fallen completely under her spell.

"So it seems," Rita replied, wondering whether that was such a bad thing.

Bosko had his hand against Zao's shoulder and was leading him and Zena toward his parents. The late-afternoon light reflected off Rita's blonde hair and her fair skin glowed. They were both happy for their son.

"This is my mother, Rita, and my father, Dragan."

Zao shook Rita's hand and then Dragan's. He introduced his wife and daughter.

Bosko presented Zena with one of the bouquets.

While the families were making small talk and walking toward the house, Admira stepped out onto the concrete stairs, standing there for a moment in silence. All eyes turned toward her.

Bosko broke away, his pace almost turning into a run as he approached her. He didn't care how it looked to her parents or his. He had no plans for his life, nor did he know where his life would take him; none of these things mattered as he embraced Admira. He was sixteen and in love. He handed Admira the other bouquet of flowers, wishing they could leave right away and be alone.

She smiled and buried her nose in the bouquet as their parents approached.

"Hello, Admira," Dragan kissed her cheek.

"I'm so glad you could make it."

Bosko's mother squeezed Admira's hand affectionately.

"Let's all go inside," Zao said as he gently reached out to usher everyone into the house. He glanced at Bosko's father, then his mother. They all returned glances, acknowledging that their children had forgotten that any of the adults existed.

"I should put these in water," Admira said nervously.

Once inside, Tonya followed Admira into the kitchen.

"His father is handsome," she said. Opening the cupboard and reaching for a vase, she handed it to her sister. "Are you nervous?"

"Yes." Admira picked up a knife.

"You shouldn't be. It's not like you and Bosko have given them a choice—right? I'm going back to check on things. I'll give you a report if it starts to look bad."

"Thanks for the encouragement." Admira stuck her tongue out at her younger sibling.

Tonya was headed to the door but turned around and asked, "Have you?"

"Have I what?"

"Have you and Bosko given them a choice? You're the passionate one, remember?"

Admira placed the bouquet of geraniums and carnations in the sink. They were Bosko's gift to her mother. After filling the vase with water, she dropped a handful of colored marbles into it. They sparkled like gems as they reflected the light.

The dozen roses in her own bouquet were the darkest red she'd ever seen; from some angles they seemed almost black. Staring out the window, her mind drifting as she cut the stems, she didn't notice that a thorn had pricked her until she felt the warm stickiness of her blood between her fingers. Looking down, she saw a tiny stream of blood flow into the center of her palm. *Is it the right or the left hand that predicts a person's fortune? Where's my life line?*

It was her right hand, and she was sure it had her life line, as well as her heart line. Admira rubbed her fingers against her palm, fascinated that a tiny thorn could cause so much blood. She held her palm outstretched, hypnotized by the streaks of red, and thought it was his rose and her blood. Together it sealed their fate.

"Admira."

Startled, she refocused her eyes and saw Bosko standing in the doorway.

"What's on your hands?"

"A thorn from a rose pricked me." Admira held out her bloodied hand for him to see.

"One thorn did all that?"

"They're your roses."

He approached her at the counter, reaching for the roses, ready to toss them into the sink. "Ah. They got me too. I'm going to throw these out."

"Don't you dare! Come here, my impetuous Serb."

A tiny drop of blood had gathered on Bosko's finger. She touched her finger to his. "Now we are joined by blood. We will never be separated."

"You've made me forget everything and care for nothing but you."

"Oh, I am so glad." Admira could not have sounded more alluring or provocative.

Bosko pressed his mouth against hers. They were mad for each other and needed to consummate this passion or else they would become two mindless blithering fools.

"Stop..." she could barely say, and then she let her head fall against his chest. Admira wanted to drag Bosko up to her bedroom, even as their parents remained downstairs. Raising her head she said softly, "It's time for us to leave. Let them sort it out."

They each carried a vase of flowers into the living room.

"If it's alright with everyone, Bosko and I would like to take a walk. We won't be long."

"On your way back, light the torches, Admira."

Admira acknowledged her father's request and glanced at her

63

sister. "Would you like to join us?"

"May I?" she asked her parents.

"Go on," Zao said.

The evening air was cool as it drifted down from the mountains. Admira and Bosko walked with their hands clasped along the gravel road toward an open field. Tonya remained silent as she walked by her sister's side, wanting to say something but the occasional quick and stern glances from her sister, prevented her from any outburst or off color quip for which she was known. God, she thought to herself, there were so many outrageous things she wanted to say to her sister and Bosko, at the moment.

"Look!" she said, turning to Admira and pointing.

Nestled in Bosko's curls were the fanning orange wings of a monarch butterfly.

"Maybe it brings luck," Bosko said as it fluttered its wings and landed on Admira's shoulder.

Tonya inched her finger close to it, but it rose up and flew away.

"It landed on both of us. I wonder what that means," Bosko said.

Oh this was great, a perfect in to whatever she wanted to say. "Well, my grandmother, who was a gypsy—"

"Grandma was not a gypsy. Those were just stories Dad told us," Admira said.

"Believe what you want, but we have gypsy blood. It was your gypsy blood that let you fall in love with Bosko the first moment you saw him. Fact is you would have—"

"Stop it right now." Admira grabbed Tonya but she broke free.

"Would have what?" Asked Bosko.

"Best if she's the one who tells you," replied Tonya, staring at her sister defiantly.

"Sounds like there's a story here, guess I'll have to ask."

"It's true from the first moment she saw you."

"That's enough." Admira tried not to blush at her sister's comment but couldn't help it. Her reaction hadn't gone unnoticed by Bosko, who leaned closer to her.

"But I want to know more. Keep going, Tonya," he said, egging her on.

"Enough. Understood?" Admira knew full well how her sister was capable of blurting out anything.

She playfully pushed her sister away and said, "Don't encourage her. Tonya, stop this."

"What? Like I can't see what's happened?" Tonya rolled her eyes, and then in a more sensitive tone said, "I guess I'm saying all of this because I kinda wish it was also happening to me. I don't see you a lot anymore, Sis. At least if I met someone like Bosko, not that Mom or Dad would even let me start dating, I wouldn't feel—" Tonya rolled her eyes once more as her thoughts trailed off. "Well, I wouldn't feel so lonely and jealous if it did happen."

Admira reached out and hugged her sister.

Bosko watched the sisters embrace. In a loving voice, Admira said, "I'm sorry. I've been so childish."

"Tonya, I too have been very selfish," Bosko said, taking a few steps toward them. "We haven't been acting very mature."

Admira hugged her sister even tighter.

"I will do my best to share from now on."

"Good luck with that. I'm not holding my breath," Tonya replied, staring at him.

Admira began to laugh. "Oh, you. You make me laugh. Do you know that?" She shook her sister gently and hugged her again.

"We always could make each other laugh," Tonya admitted.

"Tonya?" Bosko asked. "What else does your gypsy blood tell

you?" Tonya and Bosko were locked in a stare. "I would still like to know..."

"Well, go on, tell him what your gypsy blood believes."

Tonya stepped back but remained between her sister and Bosko. She looked at Admira for a second, and then turned her gaze to Bosko.

"Three of us are standing here, and yet the butterfly chose to land on only you and Admira. Don't you see?"

"What?" Admira said softly, taking a step toward her sister.

"Just as the butterfly was once a caterpillar, you and Bosko were something different before you met. The two of you were always meant to become something grander."

Tonya glowered at her sister, who remained silent. Suddenly, she spun on her heel and turned her back to them. "I'll see you guys back in the house. Three's a crowd. I'll light the torches." Over her shoulder, she shouted, "Nice to know you Bosh— alright if I call you Bosh?"

"Works for me." Tonya nodded her head as she kept walking.

*

Three hours had passed since they'd finished their meal. Rita and Zena were sitting in wicker chairs in the backyard. Zao and Dragan had gone into the house to play backgammon and drink *Vinjak*. Bosko and Admira had wandered off on their own again.

"It's incredibly peaceful here compared to Kosovo Hill," Rita said, resting back against the back of her chair.

Zena picked up her cup of steaming black tea and said, "I wasn't very happy when we first moved here; I seemed cut off from everything that was happening in the city. It took a little getting used to." She rested back in her chair much the way Rita had, feeling very much at ease in being able to talk to another woman her age about their children, who were now lost to them.

66

Placing the teacup back onto the table, she continued, "I was always afraid when the girls would go out to play that they would wander off and get lost. I asked Zao to put that bell in the yard. When they went too far away into those fields and I couldn't see them, I would ring the bell and they would come back. Admira was always the last to return."

Bosko looked toward Sarajevo in the distance. The lights from the city's large buildings and small homes, the marketplace, and the walkway on the Miljacka, those secret places and the not- so-secret places of their city, transformed Sarajevo into a bright and burning, dazzling star. The night was glimmering, and he thought he could hear all the people who were happy and their laughter.

A cool breeze blew past, bringing him back to reality. In truth, Bosko had only one thought: he wanted to run off with Admira to some soft, grassy knoll under the stars and make love to her, ravish her. He was desperate and it was unbearable that he had to restrain himself. Knowing he'd have to wait was a horribly stultifying feeling. All of his teenage male desires would go unfulfilled. He was so close to her, touching her, feeling her soft skin brush against his. Her lips were swollen from his kisses. She never stopped him. But he may as well have been the Man on the Moon because his desires were so far from being satisfied. Wanting to distract himself from those thoughts, he said, "Oh, I didn't tell you. Mats is dating Valencia. He met her at the New Year's Eve party; he really likes her."

"So was it a good thing that you all came to the party?"

"Speaking for only myself, absolutely." They continued to walk, with Bosko falling into a palpable silence.

"Something on your mind, Bosh?"

"You might say that."

"Anything I can help you with?"

"You might say that."

In a tone that sounded humid and languishing and expressed her own sexual desire for him, she said, "Tell me."

"You task me—you have no idea how you task me." He grabbed Admira and pressed her to his chest. The uncontrollable urge to make love to her was more than he could bear. His heated breath had a sweet pungent scent to it.

"Shh..." She pressed her lips to his. "I want you with every aching beat of my heart," she whispered into Bosko's ear as they trembled in each other's embrace, feeling the unbearable yearning to make love, to savage each other. To unite. Admira could wait no longer. She had to have Bosko, have him as she had wanted him on that New Year's night.

"I will come to you, soon."

"I'm going mad not having you."

"You will have all of me, every part of me. I will be yours." She ran her fingers through his black curls. "Oh, you are my wonderful, impetuous Serb." Admira kissed him with such abandon. And as they continued to walk, both imagining that moment when they would be each other's mate, they listened to a symphony of nocturnal sounds. Hearing the soft lyrical sounds of the night Bosko remembered a Bosnian folk song, written by Bosnian Serb poet Aleksa Šantića, about a young Serbian boy who fell in love with a Muslim girl named Emina. So he began to whistle the tune and then, turning to her, sang the first words to the song.

And lo, in the garden, in the shade of a jasmine,
There with a pitcher in her hand stood . . . Admira.

He was seducing her, doing to her what she was longing for him to do. "Tell me more, my troubadour."

Admira squeezed Bosko's hand and a tear formed in her eye. Of the countless things her father had told her, it was that one particular belief that she could never put out of her thoughts: *God has abandoned us, Serbs, Muslims, and Croatians, because we do not know how to live.* Her own answer contradicted her father's belief. *I will never lose you; God has not abandoned us.*

Chapter Six

While Bosko's parents were visiting his brother in Italy, he invited Admira to the family's apartment on Kosovo Hill for a picnic. On a blanket spread out over the carpet, he'd placed a bowl of bread, all kinds of cheese, a variety of grape leaves, including ones stuffed with lamb and olives, and a bottle of white *Traminer*.

She was wearing a simple, pale yellow, cotton dress; the cut and material were meant to reveal as much as they were meant to hide. The fabric clung to all of her curves. Admira was young, un- tested, and still a virgin. She had waited—deliberately—and during that time she'd understood how she wanted to look and what she wanted the man of her choosing to feel. She was sixteen and wasn't about to lose anything. On the contrary, she knew Bosko loved her, and this moment was meant to give that love its meaning through flesh and blood.

Think, Bosko. Say something, anything. Nothing came to him, and he couldn't believe how dumbstruck he felt. *Oh my God*, he kept repeating to himself.

Admira undid some of the large herringbone buttons on her dress. She'd gathered her hair to one side and let it hang over her shoulder in a lush black twist. She stopped fumbling with her hands and took a deep breath, trying to relax.

Bosko's heart was beating so hard he thought it would explode. *She's finally here, alone with me—be a man. No, no. Take it easy, don't be a brute. She's a work of art. But just don't act weak or indecisive. Don't be a punk.*

They stared into each other's eyes once more, afraid to look elsewhere. He forced a smile.

Say something, anything. You're going to lose the moment.

Sitting on the blanket, Bosko held onto the neck of the wine bottle. "There's a story..." he blurted out.

"Tell me," she said, sounding relieved. Her fingers wrapped around his free hand as she edged closer.

"A long time ago, a Mughal emperor and his army of thousands entered the fabled land of Kashmir in conquest. As the days and weeks passed and he ventured farther into this fabled land, he was overcome by what he saw."

Both Admira and Bosko were overcome by the sight of each other. The emotional layers that had kept them apart were being stripped away, and though they hadn't moved while on the blanket, it seemed as if they had, in fact, gotten much closer than they were. So close that everything inside of them said they were locked in a passionate embrace.

"You were saying, Bosko?" whispered Admira, breaking the silence. "What did this emperor see?" The feeling of an unstoppable force, the kind that can breach the walls of a dam, was overtaking their sense of time and reality; the walls seemed to wobble and the floor seemed to rise and sink at the same time. In Admira's thoughts she had revealed to Bosko the most intimate parts of her body.

"Something unexplainable happened to him," Bosko said.

"What?" She was filled with expectation.

"His soldiers realized he'd begun to weep as he sat on this magnificent black stallion with its mane sweeping back and forth across its neck."

"Weep? Why?"

"While he firmly held the reins of his stallion, sitting atop this marvelous animal, he watched the wrenching blue sky above. It was the kind of sky so clear that every thought you have is the truth. The emperor gazed at the orchards surrounding him and his army. As far as his eyes could see, he and his army of thousands saw untouched forest valleys and crystal-clear streams. The scent of jasmine and hyacinth filled the air. There were trees everywhere—almond, peach, and apple. Golden saffron collected in mounds like hives of gold dust, and he was mesmerized by the tallest mountains in all the world surrounding him. The emperor climbed down from his stallion and began to walk beside a stream that was filled with melted snow from the highest peaks. And as he listened to the bird song that echoed around him, he realized—"

"What?" she asked, inching closer.

"It was he who had been conquered and made prisoner by all that was beautiful before him."

"Go on."

"Through the tears his soldiers heard him say..." Bosko's voice was barely above a whisper.

"What, Bosko, what did they hear him say?"

He leaned forward and whispered into Admira's ear.

"If there is a paradise on this earth

It is here

It is here

It is this."

A shiver passed through her as he brushed his mouth against hers. They tasted each other and the fruits of paradise. "It is this."

Bosko popped the cork and Admira jumped. Before he could pour them each a glass of wine, she reached for the bottle and placed it against the wall. They knelt on the blanket, afraid and exhilarated by the moment. Admira began to undo a button on her dress. He placed his hand on hers. "Let me."

Each button came undone with ease and after enough were opened, she pushed the dress down past her thighs till it gathered at her feet. Her cotton camisole and panties were the only things separating them. Bosko removed his shirt, and she admired the taut muscles of his shoulders, arms, and chest.

"Stand," she instructed. Admira removed his belt and then his pants, flinging them near her dress. They lay down on the blanket facing each other.

She held his shaking hands and placed them against her hips, guiding him to peel away her panties.

"From the moment I saw you, I haven't been or felt the same. I swore to myself—"

"Shh, I know. Kiss me, my impetuous Serb." He did and couldn't stop. Bosko didn't think about what he was doing. They guided each other, relying on sheer instinct, breathing in the other's breath. Moving to kneel between her thighs, he began to kiss her, starting at her neck and inching slowly downward.

Admira did not try to stop him. Her young body was as fragile as a leaf caught in a storm, and yet she held nothing back. She was in love, and all things were possible. Her back arched and her hips began a slow, rhythmic dance of sex. She pushed her body closer to his mouth each time it was near. Her eyes closed and her head swayed from side to side in a rhythm only she could hear.

Bosko was overcome with a need to be daring—both with himself and with Admira. The wait was over. A voice within told him to *take her*. He meant to please her. He coveted her. He loved her. Time passed. Seconds ticked away. Minutes came and went. The hour unfolded. And with each passing moment, she let go of the uncountable inhibitions possessed by every girl that hold her back from releasing her essence to her lover for the very first time. She gripped Bosko's hands and he held on tight. Her body began to shake and a sound she'd never made before stirred within her and then in one violent, sensual moment escaped her lips. He'd brought her to her first climax. He rested his cheek on her thigh.

He was sixteen, but beyond the thinking of an ordinary sixteen-year-old boy. Lifting his face, Bosko gazed into Admira's eyes. As he slowly raised himself onto his knees, he left a trail of kisses in a line all the way to her mouth. Without hesitation, she reached between his thighs and caressed his manhood with her supple fingers. Pulling him toward her and kissing him, she wrapped her legs around his waist, not wanting him to move.

Bosko pressed his chest to hers and she felt the beating of their hearts. The sound of Bosko's was unlike anything Admira had ever heard. If a heart can have a gender, then his male heart was beating with a rhythm that was bestial, vulgar, and impolite. But it was also a heart that was possessed by a love for Admira that could only be described as elevated, passionate, and sublime. He entered her and she let out a gasp and dug her nails into his back.

He stopped and stared into her eyes with wonder.

"Don't stop."

Bosko would never fully appreciate or understand the pain she felt, but to Admira it did not compare to the pleasure of knowing that Bosko was her first.

He drove deeper into her, and the growing heat inside of her surrounded her every thought. He couldn't stop. This was love and lust; it was male and female. It was everything. Time had no meaning. It languished, seeming to come to a standstill. She dug her nails into his back once more and each breath he drew burned in his nostrils. It was a moment in time not to be hurried. And they waited, together, for that moment of climax, enjoying every moment leading up to it. She pressed both hands firmly against his spine, forcing his body deeper into hers. This was the moment they had both been waiting for, and everything surrounding it.

The pain, the joy, and the union of their bodies added a "foreverness" to this moment. He was a comet hurtling toward earth on a pre-destined course of self-obliteration. He cast every part of his being, every fragment of his emotions, deep inside of her to be embedded forever. The impact incinerated the Bosko of the past and changed Admira's world forever. She was euphoric because they had each experienced making love for the first time.

It was with each other and it was glorious.

Admira lay on top of Bosko, her naked breasts pressing against him, her breathing laborious and so wonderful to feel. She pressed her ear to his chest, listening to a sound that was elevated, passionate, and sublime. And then it came to her: it was what she thought had happened to the first man and woman of creation in that first garden when they had first made love. It was the sudden and beautiful awareness that their lives were filled with every possibility. She raised her head and stared into Bosko's wine-colored eyes.

*

When they woke, it was late afternoon. Admira put on her dress, went into the bathroom, and washed the small blood stains away that painted the insides of her thighs. She tried to gather all of her thoughts and feelings—every emotion that flew in and pierced her conscious and unconscious self—and lock them away in some special place of her being. But most of all, Admira tried to hold on to this feeling that swept over her like a tidal wave and in which she felt she was drowning.

It was a feeling of dying and being reborn, a feeling of complete and utter euphoria. She'd been yearning to feel this way ever since that night when she'd stood naked at her bedroom window with the bitter Sarajevo wind blowing over her. That night, her young and innocent body had needed and wanted Bosko while she'd listened to the night wind howl. The sound was the very same within her now. It had happened as she'd imagined it would, and she wanted to cry out of sheer joy. They'd made love to each other for the first time and it had felt good. More than good. It was confirmation that they were meant to be. Just Bosko and her. There could never be anyone else.

Admira stepped from behind the bathroom door and

watched Bosko get dressed. He was happy and it showed.

"You must be hungry," he said. "I'll make us each a plate."

"Let's eat out on the balcony," she said as she watched a cluster of low-hanging clouds pass by. They appeared so close she might reach out and touch them. "Maybe we'll grab one of those clouds." She liked the idea of catching a cloud and smiled at the thought.

"It's a cumulus cloud," said Bosko.

"The soft, puffy kind? When I see them, I'll always think of you."

They filled their plates and went outside to eat and dream. "You look like you've stolen all the gold from Fort Knox," she said.

"I feel like I have," he said, biting into a stuffed grape leaf. Bosko was famished, as was Admira, but he offered her the larger piece first. His gesture didn't go unnoticed. She gazed at him, and her lust for him showed in her eyes. But for the moment, they leaned back in their balcony chairs, trying to comprehend the moment and the fact that they had made love.

"Bosh, how did you know about that story?"

Pouring them more wine, he said, "About a year ago I was passing a small bookstore in the old marketplace and for some reason I stopped to take a look inside. But just as I was about to walk in, I noticed this book about the Mughals displayed in the window. I remember it was opened wide and the sunlight was shining off the golden edges of the pages. And there was a beautiful painting of the Taj Mahal and a short paragraph about this Mughal emperor and his journey of conquest. The quote was at the end of the story."

"Say it to me once more."

"If there is a paradise on this earth it is here. It is here. It is this."

Admira stared at him in utter silence.

"It's strange how I've remembered the words that were also written in Persian."

Hearing that, Admira became even more aroused.

"I don't know why, but when I stared at the words, it seemed to me it would be wrong not to remember them. It was just one line."

Peering through the wine in her glass, she stared at the studious expression on his face and said softly, "Please recite those words to your gypsy girl."

Bosko pulled her hand gently across the tile table toward him. The look in his amber eyes softening, Bosko said, "*Agar firdaus bar roo-e zameen ast, Hameen ast-o hameen ast-o hameen ast.*"

"You should not do this to me; seduce me like this. I have no way to fight back."

"Good. I mean to take away any chance that you ever could, Gypsy Girl."

"Tell me another story, Charmer Boy," she said as she gently massaged the sole of her foot against his calf.

"If I am to be your storyteller, how am I to be paid?"

"Ah, I see. What would satisfy you?"

"I'll leave that to your imagination."

Sliding the wine and plate of food to one side and holding her hand, Bosko said, "A village in northern Slovenia was once called Jerusalem."

"Really?"

"Yes. Really. In the book about the Mughals, there was also one other short story."

"Tell me, my storyteller."

"Well, the heart of the story is this. The town was called Jerusalem in Slovenia. It wasn't the city of King David, Christ, or Mohammad. The story said that a very long time ago, warrior knights took a special oath upon their swords that they would make the journey to Jerusalem—the greatest quest for

78

the knight crusaders. Some succeeded in their journey to the Promised Land, but many others were killed, or grew too weary or sick to continue, and found themselves in this village in Slovenia called—"

"Jerusalem."

"Exactly, and those knights who couldn't continue on their quest ended their journey in that village, trying to convince their hearts that they had kept their oath and had reached their true destination."

"But they hadn't," Admira said.

"No, they hadn't."

"But it was wrong for them to believe their own lies."

"It was."

"If you swear an oath, it must be kept, no matter what."

"Yes, Gypsy Girl. No matter what."

"So is that it? That's the end of your story?"

"Pretty much."

Looking a little disappointed, Admira said, "Well, I was expecting something more spectacular."

"There is," Bosko said. "I said I was going to tell you the heart of the story. The last part is this..."

His gaze had a possessiveness, the kind that's seen in the eyes of a man who is obsessed with the woman who feeds his life force.

"When I stood on that balcony alone on that New Year's morning, still thinking of you, smelling your scent after you'd left me, I listened to the sound of every bell ringing from every church. And I took an oath."

"What kind of oath?" Her eyes softened as his hardened.

"I swore that we would never be apart. And no one else would have you, and I would have no other girl, no other Jerusalem. I promised myself that I would kill, strangle the life out of, anyone who tried to touch you or ever tried to take you away from me."

Admira lowered her head. "You are my terrifying Serb, aren't you? In a *kafana* filled with rainbows, Bosh, I once said to you that one day you would tell me how you felt being with me. Do you remember?"

"Yes."

"And now you have. And I told you, one day I would do the same."

"Yes, you did." Bosko held her hand.

A sense of peace welled up inside of Admira. Staring into his eyes, she said, "I knew from the moment we met that it would be you and only you."

"What?" he replied, a devilish smile on his face.

"Only you, crusader, will make love to me till the end of my days."

PART TWO

Chapter Seven

July 1989

Zena observed her daughter quietly staring out the kitchen window, watching her father chop wood. Her firstborn was all grown up. Gone was the grease from under her finger nails. She no longer helped Zao change the truck's oil, or spent an afternoon helping him hoist an engine out of a car.

Admira was a woman now. Her raven black hair curled upward as it rested on her shoulders; her face appeared to be a flawless gem. She carried herself like a buoyant and self-assured woman. Going to her mother at the kitchen table, she fell into the same thought she'd been having all day and couldn't shake. Admira couldn't believe five years had passed since she and Bosko had met. How could that have happened so quickly? "I was thinking," Admira said, "of how quickly time has passed. It seems as if it was just last night we were sitting at this same table and I was telling you all about this guy I'd met. Tonya was making me angry and making me laugh at the same time."

"And that was five years ago," replied her mother.

Admira nodded. "Does it always happen this way when things are good? Your life rushes past you?"

"Yes."

"It doesn't seem fair."

"It isn't. You're telling a mother who still sees herself running out into the backyard to ring that bell so that you and Tonya come back home from playing out in those fields. It feels like it was only yesterday when I was doing it."

Admira had blossomed from being an attractive teenager into a beautiful, even sultry-looking young woman. She slid her arm across the dinner table and held her mother's hand.

81

"What is it, Mum?"

"I keep seeing that young girl I used to know barge in after coming from her father's garage, covered from head to toe in grease, wearing grease-covered overalls, trudging through the kitchen on her way to her bedroom."

"It's been a while since I was under a car changing the oil or helping Dad hoist up an engine. I miss it."

"Your dad misses it even more."

"I think I'll surprise him in the garage next week wearing my old overalls and help with whatever he's working on."

"He'd love that. So what's all this?" Zena was looking at what Admira had arranged on the table.

"All of Bosko's letters that he wrote to me when he was in the army for those very long twelve months." Admira had every letter he'd written to her tied together in various bundles and stacked side by side on the table. "It's a year out of both of our lives. I always like to reread them and I didn't know which one I wanted to read today, so I brought them all out. I still can't decide."

"I used to do what you're doing. Carve out chunks of my life that were only a part of me and your dad before you and Tonya came along. And after the two of you were born and were growing up, I started to put away little things belonging to you and Tonya; remembrances of our lives. The trunk in our bedroom is full of things from when your dad and I first met and then from the two of you."

"I don't think Bosko will ever let me put this dress I'm wearing away in some trunk or closet. He never wants me to get rid of it, he's forbidden me to do it."

"Why is it so special to Bosko?"

"I was wearing it when he told me a story of a crusader and the oath he had taken."

"How does that matter to the dress?" Admira glanced at her mother briefly and then pulled out a letter from one of the

82

bundles. "It's one of those things, Mum."

"And what is this?"

"This is the piece of coal Dad placed under my bed that New Year's night after I came back from the party. I keep it wrapped in one of Bosko's handkerchiefs. I think of it as representing another year of my life. So far I have three years of my life since I met Bosh displayed on this table. The letters, the coal, and this dress I'm wearing. I'm missing two years.

"No, you're not. They're all in there." Zina tapped Admira's temple. She stared at her daughter, whom she knew cared nothing about life, only about the man she loved. "Sometimes I think you and Bosko have everything to look forward to, and then sometimes I get so afraid because I start to wonder if it will all change."

"If what will change?"

"Life. His feelings for you. I'm not saying Bosko will. I know how he is about you. It's just a mother's worry—you're right, it's silly."

Admira's stare slowly turned into a glare. She reached out with both hands and held onto her mother's wrists.

"Mum. Who can he love but me!" Such an unshakable belief by Admira made the hair on her mother's arms stand up. "There will be nothing, nothing that will ever keep us apart."

"I don't think that poor boy knows what he's gotten himself into."

"Oh, I know he doesn't."

Zao stopped swinging his wood splitters' maul, turned his head toward the open kitchen window, and listened to his wife and daughter laughing. He wished there was more laughter to go around these days. Zao, like many other Yugoslavs, had watched an ill wind of radical nationalism rise up these last few years, stoked by what many in Yugoslavia saw as a fictitious prosperity that was leading to an economic crisis. There was a $21 billion foreign debt, fifteen percent unemployment and estimates of annual inflation of 250 percent. Yet none of their leaders had a realistic plan to deal with this economic cancer. The anger and frustration it was causing infected everyone, every wretched Slav. He swung his maul hard against the stump of oak and it split in two. Looking at the two halves lying at his feet, Zao began to think of those who were swinging the ax that was slowly splitting their nation apart piece by piece. One name amongst a few others kept cropping up: Slobodan Milošević was now president of Serbia. He was taking center stage in the decisions that would ultimately determine all of Yugoslavia's future. Zao had seen before what was happening now: Milošević stimulating and exploiting age-old Serbian nationalism to gain political support and greater power.

Zao placed another stump of wood onto the chopping block. He held onto the wooden handle with both hands; the cold metal wedge that would split the wood into two or more pieces lay in wait to complete its job. Zao rested the maul against the chopping block and sat down. He picked up the solid piece of wood, running his palm and fingers up and down against the log. It was firm and strong; it would provide his family with much needed warmth in the coming winter months. They would sit around the fireplace and Zao, would regale all of them with stories from his youth, the good times that he could remember. They were all like this one piece of oak whose strength lay in its ability to provide warmth and unity for their collective survival. But Zao had watched in silence, as had his wife, the splintering of their country taking place. He and Zena along with every Yugoslav watched as the ancient monster, that was so rooted in their psyche, reared up its head once more.

In the five years that had passed since the Olympics had come and gone, every Yugoslav had become witness to the rising expression of a collective racial nationalism that fostered a growing animosity toward other ethnic groups. Zao knew that in their history as a people, there had never been a catharsis that could expiate the monster of racial nationalism that continued to dwell within their collective soul.

He stood up placed the oak log onto the chopping block. He had kept his thoughts to himself; doing so had made Zao want to speak of things, of anything, with much less frequency. With one swing of his maul, he split the oak in two.

"Did I tell you? Bosko is thinking of starting a business. He's very good with electronics and wants to open a store that sells and repairs anything electronic. I think it can work out."

Admira was convinced Bosko could make a go of it, even as every part of the country was constantly faced with workers striking for higher wages and demanding that prices be lowered on milk bread, meat, and produce. Trying very hard not to become glum about the situation, she said, striking a happy tone, "I still have to figure out my university courses."

"Good, that's what you should be thinking about."

"Mum..."

"Yes."

"I wonder if I'll be enough for him. I mean, in twenty years will he still feel the way he feels about me now?"

"In twenty years, you'll have your answer."

"I suppose I will." Zena's straightforward answer to her daughter's question was typical of her. She never gilded her answers to any of her daughters. Admira shuffled the letters around on the table, her thoughts split between which letter she wanted to read and the future with Bosko.

"What are you thinking about, child?"

"After Dragan died so suddenly, something changed in Bosko. I can see it. It's as if a hole had opened up inside of him that will never be filled."

Zena squeezed her daughter's hand and remained silent.

85

"It was all so ordinary, everything that followed after his father passed away. Bosko and his mom made the arrangements for the funeral and service. It was all so matter of fact. A person lived and then died and the only thing he or she left behind was the memory of their existence, carried on by family."

"That's the way life is."

"On the day of his father's funeral, Bosko couldn't even remember what the date or even the day was. His mind went completely blank. And when all the others had left the grave site —you and Dad, all of his friends, Serge and Rita—Bosko stayed. He couldn't leave his father. I was there watching, standing next to a tree, feeling so helpless."

"What did Bosko do?"

"He needed to talk to him. He knelt down on his knees, curled his hands into fists, and pressed them into the grass. Years later he told me what he'd said to his father."

Admira stopped moving the letters around on the table. She began to recollect Bosko's words.

"He told Dragan, 'I always thought we'd have more time. There are so many things I didn't tell you.' Mom, I don't know if I can fill this hole he has inside of him. I don't know if I ever will."

"Listen to me, and don't you ever forget this. When you get married, that hole will get smaller and will keep getting smaller. Having children and doing for them, sacrificing for them, having them love you will fill that hole of longing that Bosko still has for his father."

"How can you be so sure?"

"There was a time, my child, when we all had to fill a monstrous hole that was left in all of our lives. We did it by marrying and having our children. After what we had—" Zena stopped.

"After what, Mum?"

"After those dark days."

"You and papa have hardly ever talked about those days. Why?"

"It's the past, and it's best forgotten." Banishing thoughts of a dark time in their past, Zena put on a smile for her daughter and said, "So now, what are you and Bosko going to do today?"

"Oh, we're meeting everyone for drinks. Mats said something to Bosh about wanting to go to some rally tomorrow or the next day, I'm not sure."

"What kind of rally?"

"Who knows, with Mats. I wish it was just Bosh and me having drinks. You know, I'm so selfish, Mum."

"I know."

"I've always hated sharing Bosko. I know it's wrong but I can't help myself. I wish he was going to be with me tomorrow and not with Miro and Mats. Is there something wrong with me to feel this way? I can't help myself."

"There's nothing wrong with you. You are selfish and willful. That is all."

Admira and her mom began to laugh.

"It's a good thing you haven't gotten tired of his company."

"Tired of being with Bosh!" She looked at her mother as if she were mad. "I love it when he takes my hand and presses me gently into a café seat and we chat forever as the world spins on its axis and the day becomes the night."

"He's a lucky man, your Bosko."

"He is, he really is." They laughed. Admira walked over to the window and stared out at Zao splitting those thick oak stumps. "I know what letter I want to read." Walking back to the kitchen table, she gently shuffled apart the folded pages till she found the letter she wanted. Kissing her mom on the cheek, she headed for the screen door.

She sat on the stairs and took Bosko's letter out of her pocket. Her jeans were sculpted to her long legs, and her white blouse loosely fell over her broad shoulders. She was barefoot.

The sun's rays were blocked by a large cloud. "Cumulus," she said as she looked up at the sky. It was the same kind of cloud that had hovered outside the window after they'd made love for the first time.

She glanced at her father, who was still chopping wood. Her dad had become more silent in these last months. He was speaking less than at any other time in their lives that she could remember. He seemed preoccupied by something. Admira thought that maybe it was because she and Bosko had created their own lives together and her dad, the first, most important man in her life who had taught her much about being strong and caring, was no longer that most important man. Admira kept looking at him as he dutifully kept splitting the logs. Her mother was staring out the window at Zao.

It was time to get reacquainted with her father. It was long overdue.

She slid Bosko's letter back into her pocket and walked over to the well and filled the empty pitcher. She smiled as she pressed the metal pitcher against her side, remembering Bosko's song to her those many years ago.

And lo, in the garden, in the shade of a jasmine,
There with a pitcher in her hand stood... Admira.

She picked up an empty glass that was lying next to Zao on the grass and began to fill it. Holding the out the glass, she said, "Dad, have some water. So now, tell me: have you become the silent type, pouting away because you think your eldest has abandoned you?"

Taking the glass out of her hand, Zao said, "How did you know?" He drank and kept drinking. When he had finished, father and daughter continued to stand there, looking at each other, saying nothing.

88

Chapter Eight

June 1989

Miro let his head fall back as he settled into his chair. He closed his eyes and enjoyed the cool, early morning breeze sweeping down from the mountains whose forests were now a dense and lush green. Last night they had all gotten together and spent the entire night drinking and dancing. His head ached from a hangover.

"Thank god this old geezer opens up his place as early as he does," Miro said as he kept his eyes closed. They were seated at one of their favorite cafés in Baščaršija, the old market place in Sarajevo.

"Agreed," replied Bosko while he poured from each dzezva resting on their table into each of their *fildzans*, which had a single cube of sugar, and a small amount of a dark rich coffee. Bosko had a sweet tooth and was already eyeing the *rahat lokum* treat that had been placed by the old geezer on the table. "Dad used to say the best coffee in the world should be as hot as Lucifer's feet, as sweet as a virgin's thighs, as black as your lover's heart."

"You know," Miro said, opening his eyes and leaning forward in his chair, "your father was a wise man." They sipped their coffee and enjoyed the tranquil morning as the gray cobblestones that lined the street began to glisten from the first rays of sunlight and the scent from a lime tree next to their table permeated the air around them.

"The lime trees are blooming along Vilsonovo Avenue."

Bosko nodded at Miro's words, which also brought a smile to his face. He couldn't wait to take Admira to the place of lime trees. He, like Miro and every other Sarajevan, looked forward to June and their blooming. It was June 28: the trees were in bloom and the effect of their scent on every Sarajevan who came to visit them was noticeable. Bosko would see it happen to himself and to

Admira when they strolled along the avenue watching their fellow Sarajevans. Life at that very moment just seemed to become more agreeable; they had no cares or worries. When the scent of the lime tree fragranced the air, it was also a time for the bonds of friendships to be rekindled and forged anew. In their city of palaces where the scent of the lime trees suffused the air and the beauty of Sarajevo was the backdrop to all of their lives, the effect on Admira and Bosko and all who were of their ilk was always the same: it made their love-making indefatigable.

Yet even on this beautiful June morning, as he and Miro sat at the café enjoying their coffee, Bosko, along with every Sarajevan and Yugoslav, could not avoid thinking about it: the reality of what had become a quarrelsome time among all Yugoslavs, bringing with it an unknown future into all of their lives.

"So, how you holding up?" Bosko asked.

"You're asking me this question so early in the morning, after you forced me to join you and Mats for—whatever this is that Mats wants us to do? How do you think I'm doing? I'm struggling like everyone else. And you?"

"As best I can, Miro."

"Bosh, do you realize we were in the army three years ago? Remember how, when we all got back home, that first night when we all got together with the girls and we celebrated a brand new life and we all cheered to the future? Remember?"

"Yeah, I remember."

"Things have not gotten any better. Fact is, everything has gotten worse. You know there are times I wish I was back in the army, seriously. I haven't been able to land any worthwhile job since I've been back. It's just crap out there. I think we should protest!"

"Protest over what, Miro?"

"Bosko, there are no real jobs. No really good, paying ones. But somebody must have those jobs. It's just not us. Something has got to be done. I'm not a farmer, and I'm sure as shit not going to my granddad's sheep farm—that's just not happening. Anyway, enough of this depressing shit. How are things with Admira and her university?"

"She's happy."

"Are you?"

"We're managing as best we can. Miro, if it wasn't for her I don't know what I'd do."

Bosko and Miro, like every other citizen in Yugoslavia, was grappling with an economy whose foreign debt had increased to an unmanageable figure.

"I read in the papers that the price for electricity, for food and clothing, just the basics, is rising sixty percent every six months."

"Yeah, I read that too," replied Miro. "Things can't stay this way. Something has to happen, something has to change."

"You know, the only people making money are those Russian cocksuckers and their mafia. They're making billions of dollars while the French and Germans, who get six weeks' paid vacation, do hardly any work. What they get paid for those six weeks is about the same as we make in a year. It's just not right. Things just aren't taking off in Sarajevo, but those goddamn Europeans are doing great while we bust our nuts to make a quarter of what they do. The Italians hardly ever work, and the Greeks never pay taxes. I'd like to take a Howitzer to all of them. We can't go on living this way and have a life with a family."

"I never thought I'd live to hear the day you would say that word."

"Yeah, it frightens me every time I say it."

"Smartest thing you ever did, letting Biljana know how you felt about her. God, it took you long enough to figure it out." Bosko sipped his coffee and peered out at the green forests of Mount Trebic and Igman. "We'll make it, Miro. Haven't we always?" Bosko patted his friend on his back.

"Yeah, yeah, always surviving but never thriving, that's our motto, you know."

"Whose?"

"We Yugoslavs, that's who."

"Things will get better, Miro."

"You think? Maybe in our lifetime? But all that aside, this is the stupidest idea Mats has come up with. I can't believe you agreed to it."

"It's important to him that we go to this rally, and it's only one afternoon out of our lives. Humor him. We've dragged him to so many—"

"This is different, Bosh. We don't belong there. Something like this has nothing to do with us, or Mats."

"We'll only be gone for a few hours, and then we'll come back and get drunk."

"Alright, alright, the more I think about it, the more it pisses me off."

"There he is, pulling up in his dad's car."

"Let's get this over with," said Miro, gulping down the last of his coffee.

Matko had pulled up to the curb across from the café on the only paved street that allowed for vehicular traffic. Bosko and Miro jumped into the backseat of the car.

"This has to be the stupidest idea you've come up with, Mats," Miro said as he shut the car door. "Don't say anything. Just shut up. I'm going to sleep. Wake me when we get there."

"Mats," Bosko said, leaning forward in his car seat. "Don't ever ask us to do something like this again."

"Alright, alright."

Bosko looked at Miro, who leaned back and closed his eyes. Then Bosko did the same, wondering to himself whether going to this rally really was a good idea.

In a few short minutes, he and Miro had dozed off.

*

"Holy shit, look at this. Wake up you guys. We're finally here."
Bosko and Miroslav slowly opened their eyes and sat up.

"There. Must. Be. Thousands. Here," Mats said as if to
understand there was something ominous about this moment.
The car to a stop.

Bosko leaned forward in his seat. "Well, come on. What are we
waiting for? You brought us here. Park the car—this is a good
spot—and let's go see what all the hype is about."

"Absolutely. Let's get going." Mats flung open the car door
and jumped out. Bosko and Miro climbed out of the back seat.
They were crowded on every side by men of all ages, who stepped
on their feet as they pushed, squeezed, and rushed past them. Bosh
and Miro glanced at one another, not knowing what to think about
where they were and what was happening, before turning and
following their friend into the crowd.

Bosko, Miro, and Mats, after having been squeezed on every
side by throngs of men, all of whom were slowly edging forward,
found themselves entering into an open area—a very large,
mountain-rimmed meadow, an ancient battlefield. They'd never
seen anything like it. A wall of humanity surrounded them. The
moment they stepped into the meadow, an incessant hum filled the
air, like the drone from thousands of bees. Only it wasn't bees but
the voices of thousands of Serbs, young and old, who'd gathered
on this ancient, hallowed ground, a symbol of patriotism to
countless Serbs, all of whom were waiting for something
momentous to happen.

"Bosko, what is this place?" Miroslav yelled above the noise.

Bosko's face turned ashen as it dawned on him where Matko
had brought them. Miro leaned closer.

"What's wrong?"

"It's the Field of the Blackbirds. We shouldn't have come

93

here."

"What the hell do you think I've been saying all day?" Miro yelled. "This is a bullshit political rally. I told you we didn't belong here."

Bosko grabbed Miro. "It's not the rally that matters, it's that we are *here*. A place where nothing good will be said."

Miro looked at Bosko. "I have no idea what you're talking about."

"I read about this place in one of my father's books."

"Yeah, so?"

"It's a battlefield and cemetery, a place where—"

"A place where what? Bosko, start making sense!"

"Nothing good will come from what is spoken here today."

"You've already said that," Miro replied staring at Bosko.

"Mats only said it was going to be on some field. What was he thinking of, coming here? Let's get him and get out of here. Now."

"You know between the two of you, I've fucking had it."

"We have to find Mats."

"Alright. Fuck! You go that way and stay in my line of sight. If you see that asshole, wave. I hope for his sake you find him first, because if I do I'm going to grab him by his Croat neck and drag his ass out of here."

Bosko fought his way through the crowd, looking for Matko. Having to jockey for space just to be able to breathe as he pushed his way through the throngs of men added to his sense of claustrophobia. He was hemmed in on all sides by men young and old. He tried to jump up to look above everyone's head, but it was impossible for him to rise up even a few inches. They were crammed together tightly. The hum from the crowd of thousands kept getting louder. At times Bosko thought he was imagining its sound. "Mats!" he yelled out, but the sound of his voice was drowned out by the hum.

94

Bosko became more aggressive and began to push himself forcefully through the crowd.

"Mats!" he yelled out once more. With every passing second came a sense that he had been lowered into a pit filled with a pack of ravenous dogs. But these were his fellow Serbs, so why should he think that? Bosko knew what this place was from reading the history books his father owned. "The Field of Blackbirds." The "heroic" last stand of prince Lazar and his Serbian army against the Ottoman Turks. They had been defeated. What words could be spoken in this place, a graveyard, except to remind the thousands present to remember that day and what its meaning is for all Serbs. A meaning that was open to interpretation in these times.

"Bosko, over here!" Miro shouted.

Bosko pushed his way toward Mats.

"Let's go, Mats. We don't belong here," Bosko said.

"What are you talking about? We just got here," Matko protested.

"We're leaving. This place is a graveyard and has only one meaning: to dredge up a past that has no place in our lives," Bosko shouted, giving his friend a push. Some other men crowded around them, turned, and stared at Bosko and Mats.

"No, Bosko. Don't you see it? Look around you. We're standing at a moment in history. I couldn't let it pass without being a part of it. I wanted both of you to share it too."

Bosko tried to grab Mats's arm, but he wrestled it free. "Just listen for a second," Matko yelled over the din. "Imagine if we could go back to a pivotal point in history, like the battle of Borodino, and watch the seeds of Russian victory planted even as they lost battle after battle to Napoleon on their own soil. Or imagine being in the crowd when Lincoln delivered the Gettysburg address. Hitler at the Reichstag in 1941 or in the 1930s in Munich. History, Bosko. This is a moment in history.

95

"I brought us here to witness the future before it begins and wanted the three of us to experience it together. That's what makes this moment so incredible. We're together. To witness it. The six-hundred-year anniversary of the battle of Kosovo when prince Lazar was defeated by the Turks. No Serb has ever forgotten this date. How can you not want to know what Milošević is going to say—today of all days?"

"This place is cursed, Mats. It's not Gettysburg and the man who will speak is not *Lincoln*."

The roar of the crowd grew louder. And to Bosko, the entire meadow had become its own ecosystem. The air that they were all breathing, the sunlight that was beating down on them, the breeze as well as the stillness, existed only in this meadow and nowhere else. It had become a heated cauldron of Serbian passion for their mythic and heroic past. Even the ground seemed to shake beneath the feet of the thousands of men who were standing upon it. Bosko looked down at the grass, at the ground beneath his feet, thinking it was about to give way and fall into some dark hole from which would emerge—what?

Standing next to him was a young man who began to tap his chest with an open hand. Soon another man began to do the same, others began to follow. All around Bosko, young as well as old men began to pound their chests in unison, in a rhythm that for them was the beating of their collective Serbian heart, the beating of a drum. A call that implied they were a band of brothers, just like their ancestors who died to the last man on this "Field of Blackbirds."

Miroslav tried to grab him, but Matko curled his hand into a fist and gave him a look that stopped Miro dead in this tracks. "I will not be denied this moment. I want to say I saw it. Our future begins here. Can't you sense it? Can't you hear it? Look at them Bosko, how they pound their chests. It's happening right at this moment, the future."

"You have no idea what you're talking about, Mats."

"Fucking retarded history major," said Miro.

Matko lowered his fist. "This is a call to destiny, that's what I'm talking about. The ground beneath us has the blood and bones of your ancestors. Prince Lazar and thousands of Serbs died here trying to win their freedom from the Turks. Look around you at all these Serbs. They do give a shit about their history, and they do have thoughts about their future." Matko turned and pushed his way through the throng of men. Another roar shook the ground and reverberated all around them. "Come on," he shouted in the direction of his friends.

"He's not going to leave. Do you want to try and drag him out?" Miro asked.

"No," Bosko replied vehemently. "That would be too ironic —starting a fight here on this day. Let's just try to get out of here as soon as possible."

Bosko and Miroslav inched their way through the throngs of men until they reached Matko. They shrugged their shoulders and nodded to each other, wondering what the hell was happening.

The roar finally gave way to a strange silence as a helicopter appeared and began to descend onto the stage. All eyes were on the platform. Slobodan Milošević exited the helicopter and strode confidently across the stage toward the podium. He looked out at the throng of thousands, silent and waiting. Moments passed and still he didn't speak. The crowd had become eerily silent finally, his speech began.

"Comrades, comrades. One of the greatest battles of all time took place here in the heart of Serbia in the Field of Kosovo, six centuries ago. By the force of social circumstances, this great, six-hundredth anniversary of the Battle of Kosovo is taking place in a year in which Serbia, after many years, after many decades, has regained its state, national, and spiritual integrity.

"The lack of unity and betrayal in Kosovo will continue to

follow the Serbian people. The concessions that many Serbian leaders made at the expense of their people could not be accepted historically and ethically by any nation in the world, especially by the Serbs who have never conquered and exploited others."

Bosko watched the faces of people in the crowd; each seemed mesmerized by the words.

"Disunity among Serbian politicians caused us to lag behind, and the inferiority of those politicians humiliated Serbia. The Kosovo battle contains another great symbol. This is the symbol of heroism. Poems, dances, literature, and history are devoted to it. Kosovo heroism has been inspiring our creativity for six centuries and does not allow us to forget that at one time we were brave and one of the few that entered the battle undefeated.

"Six hundred years later, we are engaged in battles and quarrels. They are not armed battles, although such things cannot be excluded yet. Regardless of what kind of battles they are, they cannot be won without resolve, bravery, and sacrifice, without the noble qualities that were present here on the Field of Kosovo in days past."

Bosko and his friends remained still as they listened to Slobodan Milošević's speech, which was getting the crowd riled up, about how their past leaders acted as weaklings in the area of politics instead of showing the Serbian people the glory of their past, their courage on the battlefield, and their sense of honor amongst nations. Their leaders up until now had been cowered by neighboring countries and their ethnic groups. Bosko turned his face to the man standing to his right and then to the man on his left. They were both mesmerized as if they'd been put into a trance by Milošević's words.

Bosko sensed that within each of them stirred a calling to a great cause that had been long overdue, fanned by Milošević's words. Yet Bosko did not have such feelings. The expulsion from the land of Kosovar, which had been their homeland in ancient times, by the Turks with the help of their Albanian henchmen at the battle of Kosovo, needed to be revisited and dealt with in a most serious way. Bosko could hear in his words, as could they all, the belief that now was the time to reclaim what had once been the ancestral land of the Serbs. For the Serbs to do such a thing would lead to only one consequence too frightening to contemplate.

Was he the only one who cared about the consequences of such an attempt? The men, for as far as Bosko could see, hadn't stopped cheering Milošević's words. They clapped and they roared. But Bosko remained silent, he wanted to hear no more words, no more chanting. He had to leave. They should not have come here.

Pushing his way toward his friends, Bosko grabbed Matko's arm and whispered into his ear. "Let's go. We don't belong here. Now! Come on." Mats didn't move. "Mats, we have to leave; this is not where we belong." Matko remained still, his eyes focused on the podium and Milošević, who was still speaking. "Mats, we don't belong here." Bosko grabbed his other arm firmly. "These people are not our family—let's go." Matko turned his head and stared into Bosko's eyes.

"No, they're not *my* family."

Then, without saying another word, Mats turned around and began to push his way past the crowds of men, with Bosko and Miro walking behind him.

The three of them walked back to the car in silence, weaving in and out of the crowd, which had spilled out beyond the field. As they approached the vehicle, Miro turned to Mats and said, "So what did you think of all of that history? Was it worth it? Dragging us out here to hear it?"

"There's nothing for me to say. Except that history is never mute. It will speak for itself, far beyond Milošević's words," Matko replied.

"What the fuck does that mean?" Miroslav asked.

"You shouldn't ask so many questions about things you don't understand. Sometimes it's best to remain stupid."

"I'm the one who's stupid? You fuck—"

Bosko grabbed Miroslav by the shoulders. "Enough. I'm sick of always being your goddamned referee. Let's get the hell out of here."

Miro pushed Bosko aside. "We just spent I don't know how long standing in the hot sun—for what I don't even know. Let me tell you something, Matko. I don't know what this circus was all about and I don't care. But I will tell you, you Croat, insulting a Serb, friend or no friend, is never a good idea. That's a history lesson you should always remember." Miro shoved Mats out of the way and walked to the car, leaving Bosko alone with Mats.

Bosko said, grabbing his arm, "What doesn't make any sense to me is why a Croat gives a rat's ass about what a Serb has to say. Miro and I are Serbs and we don't give a shit what Mr. S&M had to say, dredging up all of our fucked-up past. What made you think we would want to hear any of that?"

Bosko left Matko standing there alone, got into the back seat, and was overcome with frightening thoughts he couldn't quite understand. He kept thinking of Milošević's words.

"Six hundred years later, we are engaged in battles and quarrels. They are not armed battles, although such things cannot be excluded yet."

*

Is it a coincidence, Bosko, in life and history, that Serbia and you will regain the dignity that was lost to us but never forgotten? We shall celebrate the history of our past together, our ancient past and our glorious future. Did you not say, Bosko, those many years ago in a toast with all of your friends gathered, that the

100

future is filled with possibilities?

Bosko was dreaming. He had never left that mountain meadow; the crowds of men surrounding him had parted, leaving Bosko standing in the middle by himself staring at the man who was standing on the podium and was staring into Bosko's eyes.

On this day, you have come before me, along with these men, young and old, and those who give our men their strength—our wives and mothers.

Bosko thought he saw his mother and grandmother standing on the stage.

All of you have come to this hallowed ground, on which it has not rained for longer than anyone can remember. But Bosko, there is no need for rain to fall here. Look down and see how this field has been nourished by the souls of our Serbian dead, the dead whose blood lies interred beneath the earth on which you stand.

On this day, every Serb on this field understands that once the thunder of horses, the clash of war, and the cries of the fallen whose hopes for their people were never vanquished, could be heard here.

A thunderous and deafening roar passed through them all like a shock wave, and Bosko felt it in the marrow of his being.

Bosko. The blood of our ancestors has clung like tears on every blade of grass beneath your feet, bidding us, the living, to remember those monsters who are not like us but live amongst us. Every Serb who stands before me on this, the Field of Blackbirds, must now embrace our destiny to make Serbia a greater reality. We must face our enemies. By the sword, if necessary.

In his dream Bosko stared down at the ground. It began to shake. The spirits of his ancestral dead had been awakened and were struggling to free themselves from this graveyard to embrace the living. The past could become one with the present. It was an embrace felt all over the Field of Blackbirds as he heard the roar of a half million Serbs screaming as if from every connecting tissue that made up their heart and soul. It was a volcanic sound of acceptance from every Serb present that finally it must be this way.

*

Bosko awoke with a start, covered in sweat. He stumbled out of bed, pressing himself against the wall and knocking over a lamp. He didn't know where he was as he faltered around. His eyes were wide open.

"Bosko, it's okay. It's alright," Admira said. "You were having a nightmare. It's okay, I'm here." She slipped out of bed to join him. "I'm here. It was just a bad dream." She picked up the fallen lamp and placed it back on the dresser. Bosko stood in front of her, staring at her as if she were something monstrous—because she was not a Serb like him.

"Come." Admira reached out with her hand. "Come back to bed. It was only a nightmare." Her tone was gentle and calming. "Come here," she commanded. "Give me your hand."

He grabbed her hand and pulled her into an embrace.

"It was so real... it was so real," Bosko kept saying.

"Bosh, it wasn't real."

He looked at her. "No, it was real."

"It was a bad dream. It's over. Come to bed." Bosko couldn't climb into the bed with Admira, not yet. Instead, he tucked Admira under the covers and sat on the bed beside her in the darkness and waited for her to fall asleep. An hour later after she had fallen asleep, he was still staring at her. How could he have ever thought that she could be something monstrous?

*

The morning mist crept along the grassy banks and above the clear, ice-cold streams that cut through the mountains of Sarajevo, a ghostly messenger that moved over wildflowers, lush green hills, and river valleys, descending past the open fields and into neighborhoods that bordered the city. Soon it enveloped Sarajevo in a shroud of white.

Bosko stood on Admira's veranda and watched the mist inch forward as it rolled down from the Trebević and Igman mountains. He clenched his fists as Milošević's words from the dream echoed in his head.

Every Serb who stands before me on this, the Field of the Blackbirds, must now embrace our destiny to make Serbia a greater reality. We must face our enemies. By the sword, if necessary.

"That's not me," he said aloud.

Admira was in the kitchen brewing a pot of her mother's strongest tea. Reaching for two mugs out of the cupboard, Admira set them on a tray along with a teapot and a couple of sweet rolls. She pushed open the screen door and joined Bosko on the veranda.

"Where did this mist come from?" she said. Only the very top of the stone minaret of Gazi Husrev-Beg was visible; the rest of Sarajevo had disappeared.

"Out of nowhere. It's hiding Sarajevo."

"Hiding Sarajevo from what?" She looked at him quizzically.

"Just a thought," he replied, watching her and trying to smile.

She handed him a mug of black tea. Admira sat in the chair opposite him. Grabbing Bosko's hand and shaking it playfully, she asked, "What happened yesterday?"

"I don't know. I wish I did but I don't."

An eerie quiet overtook their world on this particular morning. Even the sparrows had stopped chirping.

"I'm a good listener." She leaned back against her chair and waited for Bosko to find the words.

"The blood of my ancestors is theirs, not mine. I don't care, do you hear me? I don't give a shit."

"What are you talking about?"

"It's what he said, what he told me."

"Who spoke to you, Bosko?"

"Mr. S&M."

"Who?"

"Milošević."

"Slobodan Milošević?"

Bosko nodded. "We were standing on a battlefield. A graveyard. That's where Mats took us. The Field of Blackbirds near Prestina. Because Mr. History Major was convinced it would be a moment in history that we will never forget. He wanted all of us to experience it. For what ungodly reason, I don't know. I would have never gone if I'd known where he was taking us." Bosko sipped his tea, glanced at Admira, and looked away.

"What is it?" she asked him.

"We are coming apart, it's true and it's been happening for a while—slowly, but it's been happening." Bosko was talking of how Yugoslavia was fracturing into different pieces. What were he and Admira to do? What were all of their friends supposed to do?

She thought of her father's words. *You and Bosko and all your friends are the future. It's the old ways that must perish.*

He was right. The old ways would perish. It was up to them and their friends to make sure it happened. The old ways had come back to haunt Bosko in his dream.

Bosko was leaning against the railing. Admira got up and stood beside him.

"The best thing about the last twenty-four hours is that I could come to you here while your parents are away visiting friends." Admira squeezed his arm.

"Something wrong is happening to all of us. I feel it. I know you do; we all do. It's like we're becoming infected with something that's making us think and feel things we never have." Bosko stopped himself. Admira caressed his cheek. "No, that's not true. We have always had these feelings haven't we?" He was staring into her charcoal-black eyes. "We had them once before in grandfather's time. It's happening all over again."

"Bosh, nothing is for certain. Nothing."

Bosko embraced Admira and she squeezed him tight. Her hair had the scent of citrus. Pressing against her while they stood on the veranda in the backyard, Bosko looked up and saw how the mist had enveloped almost all of Sarajevo. Looking at his city blanketed in a shroud of white, he said, holding on to Admira, "That night," he placed his hand on her cheek, "when I met Mats and Miro on the walkway and we were heading to a New Year's Eve Party, Mats kept going on about how his dad wanted to leave Sarajevo. About how his dad kept telling him everything was changing and not for the best. I kept telling him that nothing was going to change and his father was never going to leave Sarajevo. That was over five years ago. What his dad had been saying all along was true. He knew it then. These feelings infecting everyone have been a dark shadow that has remained over our heads, weaving itself into the story of our lives for the longest time."

She tried to press her fingers against his lips, but he gripped her hand and said, "We will never be able to live together."

"Stop it! That's not you talking. We've ignored it, Bosh, because it was a shadow, it didn't seem real. It isn't real."

"It's as real as you and me. It's flesh and blood, and its words are spoken from the mouths of so many who have convinced everyone else that we're not meant to live together."

"It's not the future. It's not our future. Bosh, it was only a dream."

"But where we were was real, Admira!" He stepped away and,

leaning on the railing said, "If I could dream that he spoke to me, asking me to accept a history that must be made by the sword." Bosko leaned closer and looked at her, his brow wrinkled. "What if those thousands of men who stood by me and Mats and Miro believed in what Milošević said? Did they go home and, when they were asleep, did each of them dream of him speaking to them, and did they hear the same things he told me? And if they listened to his words, as I did in my dream, what did they hear? What did they start to think and then want to do?

"What do people do with all that anger that's been held inside for so many years? Where does it go? What happens to it?"

Admira thought of her father speaking of his best friend, Karl. Somewhere, deep down in a place no one was allowed to go to except for him, there had to be anger and rage toward those who had killed his friend. There had to be.

She held Bosko close. Over his shoulder she saw that the minaret had finally succumbed to the mist and had disappeared, like all of Sarajevo. Admira closed her eyes, remembering her father's belief, one she could never put out of her thoughts. *God has abandoned us, Serbs, Muslims, and Croatians, because we do not know how to live.*

She hugged Bosko even tighter, and whispered, "I will never lose you, and God has not abandoned us. Bosh," she said as she pressed her hand against his cheek, "who among us would want that time to come back? The time that our parents and grandparents never want to talk about or when they do, their eyes always fill with tears and a silent rage? If that past is the future being offered to you in your dreams by Milošević and whoever else, in reality, who would want it? I know our friends wouldn't want it. Can you think of anyone who would?"

"But don't you understand, Admira? Don't you see it? What is to become of all of us, if I should have dreams like this? And if others who were there, had them as well?"

106

"Shh." She pressed her fingers to his mouth. "What is stronger and more lasting, the fading meaning of a dream or us?" They held on to each other in the absolute quiet that surrounded them. To Bosko and Admira it seemed only the two of them were alive. Only the two of them existed.

Chapter Nine

November 19, 1989

The storm had subsided for the moment and a soft powdery snow fell on Sarajevo, bringing with it a numbing warmth that blanketed the city. Bosko stopped running and looked around at the familiar sight. Those first hours of a snowfall always brought out the young and the old to play, lovers to reaffirm their love, and those who walked in silence still searching for love. Miro ran up to him.

For the next couple of minutes, they horsed around and slid on the walkway by the Miljacka River.

"Look. There he is," said Miro, pointing to Mats in the distance.

"I'll race you." Like little boys they ran, slipping and sliding on top of the freshly fallen snow. As they laughed and hit each other, pedestrians moved out of their way.

Mats stuck out his tongue to taste the falling snowflakes. "Mats!" Miroslav called out but Matko didn't respond. "He's daydreaming as usual. A grown man who still daydreams."

"He didn't sound right on the phone," Bosko said.

"Who knows, with him? Maybe he broke up with Vails or they had a huge fight."

"He didn't break up with Vails. She would have called Admira or Biljes right away. He better have called us out here for a good reason." They reached each other. "Mats, what's going on? Why did you make us come all the way out here so late and in this weather?" Bosko said.

Without saying a word, Matko embraced both his friends.

"What's going on? What's the big secret that couldn't wait till the weekend? You and Valencia getting married?"

"No, it's nothing like that, Bosh."

"What is it, Mats?"

"I'm going away for a while."

Now Miro was pissed. "You made us come all the way out here to tell us that? Why didn't you just call us?"

Mats had a very subtle but pained look on his face. Miro seemed too pissed to notice, but Bosko picked up on it right away.

"My uncle has a house in Konavoski Dvori. He got my dad a job working with him in one of the big hotels there." Mats turned away from his friends and stared out at the Miljacka as if he were in a trance.

"When was this decided?"

"It's been in the works for a while. We leave for Dubrovnik tomorrow." Mats reached into his pocket.

"Tomorrow? Mats..." Bosko grabbed his friend's arm.

"I suppose you've been reading the papers, huh? Uncle Tudjman is bringing all your clan back into the fold of mother Croatia."

"Shut up, Miro. Mats, what about Valencia? Does she know you're leaving?" Bosko asked, flabbergasted.

"Yes, I was with her all afternoon. She was quiet and cried a lot. I don't want to leave her, with all my heart I don't want to leave her. This is the hardest thing I've ever done, but I know I have to do it. I have to. I love her as much as you love Admira."

"You just told her now, that you're leaving tomorrow? Mats, don't you understand what that's done to her?"

"I know. I'm sorry."

"Sorry." Bosko grabbed Mats by his coat and shoved him back. "Sorry. That's what you say to Vails? I'm sorry. She's the woman you love, the woman who loves you. And you're just going to leave her? Have you lost your mind?"

Bosko grabbed Mats by his coat lapels and pulled him closer until they were only inches apart.

"I always figured that with all the stupid things you've come up with to do, somewhere in that head of yours," Bosko jabbed Mats on the side of his head, "there was a twisted reason to do it that made sense." He shoved Mats away. "This time, there is no reason."

"I don't expect either of you to understand."

Miro stepped closer to this friend. "I'm telling you, you will regret to the last moment of your life doing this. Do not do it, Mats."

"I don't have a choice. This time my dad is right. It's all going to change. It already has, and this is just the beginning. We're not going to be able to control it."

"Control what? What are you talking about?" Miro asked.

"I'm talking about our home, you stupid, ignorant Serb. Our lives are going to change," Mats said, glaring at Miro.

"Good luck to you and your dad. Send us a postcard." Miro turned to walk away.

"Miro stop, relax," Bosko turned to his friend. "Mats, why is your father leaving Sarajevo?" he asked.

Mats faced his friend. "You asked me that day when we left the Field of Blackbirds and stood together. Why am I, a Croat, interested in what an asshole Serb had to say? Now I'll tell you why. For as long as I can remember, my family has always believed in one thing. A country of Croatians for only Croatians. They believed it was the best thing for everyone."

Bosko was unable to hide his rising anger as he glared at his friend.

Matko continued, "I thought it was a stupid idea and belonged to another time and way of thinking. We've been living together, Muslim, Croatian, and Serbian for years in Yugoslavia. We marry each other and celebrate each other's holidays together. And we do it better here in Sarajevo than in any other place in Yugoslavia. But my father understood something that I now realize was always true. Yugoslavia was never going to last,

111

because we are not meant to live as brothers, together."

"But, Mats—" Miro tried to interrupt.

"So before its final demise occurs, I think dad hoped that somehow, and in some way, we would just separate and live where we were all meant to live; Serb, Muslim, and Croat, each in our own little country. The way things are going, do you think it's going to be that easy?"

Miro rolled his eyes at his friend.

"Bosh, you know what I'm saying is true. The Slovenian parliament abolished twenty-seven Yugoslav laws on Slovenian territory—what does that say to you?"

"Mats, I don't know anything anymore. I can't make sense of what's happening to all of us, no one seems to be able to."

"That's right!" Miro chimed in.

"Mats, all I and Admira and Miro and Biljana can do is to take it one day at a time. That's what we're all doing in Sarajevo and everywhere else. It's all we can do."

Matko placed his hands on Bosko's shoulders. "No, that's not all we can do." He turned and walked to the edge of the walkway and stared out at the falling snow settling on the river.

"Mats, what is it?" said Bosko, standing next to his friend.

Turning to Bosko he said, "History never repeats itself in the same way—when it does."

"What the hell does that mean?" Miro replied.

"Miro, there is a chess game going on between our vaunted leaders who will break up this country. It's not that different from what took place during grandfather's time."

"So it breaks up. Who cares? Maybe it's for the best."

"Miro, think before you talk. It will not be for the best. Croatia's Mr. Tudjman has a political strategy. His ultimate goal is to have a separate nation carved out of what was once Yugoslavia, a Croatia for Croatians. Partitioning of a nation never occurs without a terrible cost.

"The flag of Yugoslavia no longer flies in Croatia. Now it is the red and white checkerboard shield, a historic symbol to Croatians—but most definitely not to any Serb."

Matko looked at his friends, both of whom were Serbian. Walking up to Miro, Matko said in a soft voice, "Even you, Miro, know what that means, that red and white checkerboard shield."

Miro felt a flush in his face at the image of the checkerboard shield.

"Let us not forget for a moment that the Ustashi regime of the Croats during the Second World War flew that same flag... and murdered countless thousands of Serbians under that banner. Were I a Serb living in Croatia, I would be very angry to see a symbol that once meant the death of thousands of Serbians, now flying above my head." Matko looked at Bosko and at Miro, waiting for an answer. Finally, Bosko said, holding onto Matko's arm, "Mats, you have to have some faith that the worst will not happen once more. A new century, a new millennium, is just around the corner, and it comes with a different way of thinking. We are not who our grandparents were, we're not!"

"Such an optimist and romantic." Matko hugged his friend.

"It's better than being a fatalist." Said Miro.

"I agree, Miro, you're right. But even as we speak, what has happened? Belgrade, and Zagreb, have eliminated each other's TV programs from appearing on their local channels—you know this. For the longest time, it was one of the best ways for all of us to observe, laugh, and cry about who we all were, wasn't it? But even that simple thing we can't do anymore. We're being cut off from each other piece by piece—by walls that are real and invisible, separating us. It's been happening for a while.

"What's going to follow? Economic and then political fragmentation? It's already happened. You and Miro have heard the news about how the new Croatian Army has been purchasing weapons from Poland, Germany, and Czechoslovakia, even

Uganda. They are preparing for a war. If war does come, I have to be there to protect my family. My dad wants to be home when it happens, when the fighting begins. Because there *is* going to be a country called Croatia and whoever tries to prevent it will be made to pay an unbearable price for trying to stop it from happening.

Do you watch the news anymore? I don't, because it's all propaganda; one side accusing the other of something true or not true. Yet not enough people care to know what the truth is. It's because people really enjoy living with their fear and a sense of being persecuted. I went to hear what Milošević had to say to confirm what I believe is already true."

"Stop, you're ranting. I'm sick of hearing it," Miro said.

Bosko started pacing nervously in circles while running his hand through his hair.

"Miro is right. Just stay with us, and we'll face whatever the future is, together. It's what friends do."

"I know that, and I would." Mats grabbed Bosko's arms. "But I can't because there is something I must do."

"What could be more important than being with Vails and us?" Bosko asked.

"My father may want to make Croatia for Croatians. I couldn't care less. All I want is for my family to be safe—for him, and my mother, and my whole family to be safe wherever they are. And wherever they are, that's where I have to be. I have to watch over my mom and dad—I have to. It's what I must do. Besides, it won't matter for much longer where we are. The madness will be everywhere."

"The historian speaks yet again," Miroslav said in a derisive tone.

While Bosko listened to Mats, in his heart of hearts he knew his friend wasn't completely wrong.

"This time it's not about that, Miro. Your family has lived

here for how many generations, four or five? They've been surrounded by every kind of Slav there is. But has anyone in your family married anyone who is not Serbian? We live together, but we've always lived separate lives. If that weren't true, would any of this be happening? It's not history I'm speaking of, only a simple fact. Our peoples are not meant to live together."

Bosko kept listening to his friend, knowing that Mats had delved deep into his psyche and into all of his fears when he spoke. But Bosko still couldn't accept that the history of their grandparents would repeat itself the way Matko was certain it was about to.

"That's the reason things are happening and will continue to happen," Bosko said, holding his friend gently by his shoulders. "If we let ourselves continue to believe in what you've said, Mats."

"If I'm wrong, then the only thing that will have mattered was that I was wrong. I have no choice but to take care of them, Bosh. They are my parents. Could you leave your mother or Admira if you knew they were in danger? Miro, would you be able to leave Biljes or abandon your parents and not protect them?"

"No, Mats, I could never leave Admira or my mother."

"You would protect them with your life—wouldn't you?" Bosko nodded. "You too, Miro, you would do everything to protect Biljana. It's what I must do with my family."

Bosko didn't know what more to say to his childhood friend, whom he knew had no other choice. Mats gave them a smile that turned into a smirk and said, "Don't fret. Maybe nothing will happen, and Mom and Dad will be very happy living near the coast. Then I'll come back."

He reached out and held Bosko by his arms and said, looking into his best friend's eyes,

"When there's no choice given, then an act of courage is called for. This is mine because there's no other choice for me."

Mats pressed his forehead to Bosko's. "You will always remain the idealist and the romantic. It's why I love you and why Admira is in love with you. Forever seeing things as you wish them to be, not as they are. But no wishful thinking can change what's happening. You and Miro have been brothers to me, the only people I could ever count on and who have always protected me. Now it's my turn. I have a chance to be protector to my family, to show them they can count on me."

Matko reached into his breast pocket and removed a bottle of brandy. "Toast with me to the day we meet again on this spot," Mats said, raising the bottle. "To our friendship." He drank from the bottle, then held it out, daring one of them to take it. Bosko looked at his friend, then grabbed the flask out of his hand. Mats smiled.

Bosko drank and then held out the bottle to Miroslav, who took it and did the same. Then he handed the bottle back to Matko.

"To our resident romantic and to our local cynic." Matko held the brandy bottle in his hand as he motioned to Bosko and Miro in order. "To Admira, Biljana, and Valencia, to friends and friendship, the greatest protection one can have in this cruel world." He swallowed the last of the brandy.

The crowd on the walkway had thinned. No one had passed them in a while. A silence enveloped them as did the falling snowflakes. Never could Bosko have imagined a moment such as this. A stinging pain passed through his heart.

Matko threw the empty bottle of brandy high into the air. It sailed toward the freezing waters of the Miljacka, its silver shine cutting through the curtain of falling snowflakes, before disappearing out of sight. Mats embraced Bosko. Nothing was said. Everything was felt. Bosko released his friend.

"Take care of your Croat hide. It's much too pretty to have something happen to it," Miroslav said, grabbing Mats and kissing him on the lips.

"Take care of yourself, you big stupid Serb."

"Ignorant, not stupid. How many times do I have to tell you?"

"Watch over Bosko, Miro. He's always taken care of you and me. Make sure to take care of Biljes. And Bosh—tell Vails, tell her..." Matko was trying to hide his tears. He didn't finish.

"We'll tell her, Mats, and she'll be with us, waiting for you. Understand?"

"Understood." Mats turned around to leave. Bosko and Miro stood together. Neither could speak as they watched Matko disappear into the night behind a curtain of snowflakes.

"There goes a student of history. Good luck to him," Miro said in a solemn whisper.

"Is it so easy for you to let go?" Bosh asked.

"You're the romantic. On that point he wasn't wrong. He's doing what he has to. In the end, we all will—whatever that might be."

Bosko looked at his friend. "Sometimes I don't think I know you, Miro."

"There are times Bosh, when even I don't know who I am."

The wind picked up and started to blow the snow around in swirls.

"Looks like we're in for another storm."

"Yeah, looks like it," said Bosko. They spun around and the two of them headed into the tempest.

⁂

Bosko had said his goodbyes to Mats just a few short hours ago. The snow storm outside had gotten more intense. He ate his entire meal staring at the tablecloth, without saying a word. Rita had made his favorite soup, a kind of bouillabaisse or fish soup

Alaska corbar. Admira and Rita glanced at each other, neither wanting, nor even knowing how, to start a conversation with him.

"Rita, your *punjene tikvice* was amazing."

"Thank you, Admira."

"Bosko, I still have *duveč* I made yesterday. I can heat some up if you don't like—"

"No. It's fine." He looked at Rita, and in a softer tone said, "It's fine, Mom. Everything is good."

"Then I'll leave you two. Let me clear the table so I can wash up—"

"Sit down, Mom, please."

"I need to clean up these dishes."

"Sit down. Please. Admira, did Vails call you?"

"She called me and Biljes. We went over to her house to be with her. She's so upset, Bosko. She understands why Mats had to do it, but she's so afraid for him. Bosko leaned back against his chair, and pushed his plate aside. After wiping his mouth with a napkin, he said.

"Mom, I want to know something, and I want the truth."

"What is it?"

"I want you to tell me about that time when they took your father away. Everything you remember."

"That was a long time ago. I don't remember much. I was so young," Rita said.

"Now, I know that isn't true. You and Dad, and even Admira's parents, have always avoided talking about what happened during that time. The only thing I know is that all the adults have always called it 'the time of madness.' But they always avoid speaking about those times. So now I want to know about that time. People talk about war and its calamity, how it affected them, and the horrors that came with it; it's normal and natural. The Europeans have glorified it, built memorials to it. Why is it that our people do not talk about *our* war? The Nazis, the

118

Chetniks, the Ustashi—why has that history been swept away and not dealt with?"

"I will not talk about it." Rita abruptly stood.

Bosko slammed his fist onto the table. "Mom, do your son a favor and tell him the truth. What is there to hide? All I want to know is what you remember."

"Son, this is not the time to speak of—"

"Not the time." Bosko jumped up. "Don't you see what's happening everywhere? This is exactly the time."

"What I can tell you is it was a time of madness in all of our lives."

Rita lowered her head. Pulling his chair closer to his mother, he sat down and held on to her hands.

"Mother, I am your son."

Rita grabbed Bosko and embraced him. "Yes, you are, and I love you so much."

"Then tell me what you remember. I need to know."

"I don't know how it all started," she whispered.

"How can you not know?" He looked at her in disbelief.

"It just happened, Bosko. Wars just happen."

"No, they don't. Wars do not just happen, and we can never accept that as a truth."

"What is it you want me to say?"

"Only the truth, because none of it is being said these days. What can you remember from that time of madness?"

Rita glanced at her son. In her eyes he could see she had vivid memories of those days so many years ago. Her voice cracked as she began to speak, still staring down into her lap.

"The war in Europe suddenly came to us, to our doorstep, to every town and village."

Bosko wrapped an arm around his mother's shoulder. "What happened to you, to your friends, to your homes, to the people you loved?"

"What happened is what happens to everyone in a time of war. We lose the ones we love. We've never had 'wars' as Slavs. It's always a barbaric freak show for us and for the rest of the world to shake their heads in disbelief.

"And with us, it was so easy for the Nazis to exploit age-old hatreds. But it wasn't the Nazis who were to blame." Caressing Bosko's face, Rita said, "No one else is to blame for the things we do."

"So we are to blame? We all agree, and so would the Nazis. But that doesn't explain why."

"I do not know why, son. No one knows why. But we gave them quite a show. It even embarrassed them to see how we could tear each other apart. How does anyone embarrass a Nazi? But we did. All they wanted was to secure this part of the world before they invaded Russia. They found allies who were more than willing to help them if they got what they wanted: a country to call their own, a greater Serbia for Serbs, a Croatia for Croatians. It's what has always brought out the monster in all of us, which leads us to tear each other apart. Nothing seems to have changed. Now almost fifty years after the war, we're at it again."

"Why did you and Dad not talk to me about the things that happened to the family? No matter how painful it was to speak of, you and father owed me that."

"Yes, you're right, we should have told you, but it was too painful to talk about." Rita lowered her head.

"Everything that's happening now is as if it's all happened before. How is this possible?"

"I don't know son," replied, Rita her head still lowered.

"Mother, look at me." Rita stared into her son's eyes. "Tell me of that time. I need to know."

"No one, not Serb, Croatian, or Muslim was without blood on their hands in those days."

"I know this, Admira knows this, we all know this——."

"No, Bosh you and Admira don't. The Mufti of Jerusalem met with Hitler in Germany to discuss matters of his homeland and the Jews. No one, Bosko, was without the mark of Cain."

"Don't quote the bible! Everyone does who thinks they have a direct pipeline to the intentions of God."

Rita held onto her son's hand.

"Mother—"

"Listen," said Rita, looking up at Bosko. "You want to know, so I am telling you. The Mufti helped to recruit more than 20,000 Muslims into the SS who helped kill Jews in Croatia and Hungary. So much happened to all of us during that time of madness."

"I don't want a history lesson!" Bosko sat back in his chair. "I can find all that history in the library. Tell me what you remember what happened to your friends and family." Bosko leaned forward in his chair. "Mum, you were a young girl when the war began. What do you remember of what happened to your family?" Bosko was holding onto his mother's hand as he leaned forward, his amber-colored eyes glistening. "What do you remember? Is there something that you and Father never wanted me to know?"

The howling wind blowing against the windows and the balcony doors under a dreary gray sky created an eerie atmosphere in the room. It whipped the cascading snow into a white squall, drenching their city and its mountains in a monsoon of drifting snowflakes.

Bosko looked out of one of the living room windows; the snow storm had swept into the valley, pummeling Sarajevo. Large, shimmering snowflakes flew against the glass and clung to the surface, leaving a pattern resembling Christmas decorations. Admira reached across the white tablecloth and held Bosko's hand.

Rita's tears rolled down her cheeks. "It's what I can never forget that you are asking of me."

Admira got up and, pulling a chair away from the table, sat at

Rita's side. Without any emotion in her voice Rita said, "I will tell you. The village I was born and grew up in before the war entered into all of our lives had many Croatians, who had been living there for generations. When the war started, sides were taken. No town, no village, was safe from soldiers. The Ustashi, the Chetniks, and the Partisans fought each other and cared nothing for the people in the villages and towns they killed. A father or mother, a young boy or girl they suspected was a traitor to them, were killed and entire villages destroyed.

"But that didn't stop my father from hiding a Croatian friend's son in our cellar from the Chetniks who were killing any Muslim or Croatian they found. Afterward, the young boy was found by a group of Chetniks who went house to house looking for Croatians in our village. All the mothers and daughters of the village were herded into the counsel house and made to wait. Later in the day the leader of the Chetniks came into the room.

"He walked into the middle of all of the mothers and daughters sitting on the floor, and then he said, 'It is a strange thing, why a neighbor would want to help his neighbor and become a traitor in these times.' He was talking about my father. Mother held onto me as tightly as she could while he talked. 'It must be because of the goodness that we all possess in our hearts that we want to help a neighbor.' I remember how he turned his head and, staring at my mother said, 'I am not a good man. I am not a bad man.'

"He turned toward the door and it opened and two men dragged my father into the room. He had been beaten so badly because of what he had done, because he'd hidden our neighbor's son. They threw my father onto the dirt floor and my mother immediately went to him, but they grabbed her by the hair and kept kicking her with their boots as they dragged her back."

Rita stopped. Her tears kept rolling down her cheek and landing onto the white lace table cloth.

122

"I've tried so hard to forget his words and what happened to my mother and father. But I just can't—I can't. It's branded into my soul. The leader walked over to my father, whose face was so swollen and bloody from being beaten. He motioned to one of the men, who walked to the door. Then he grabbed my father's hair and, twisting his head toward the door, said, 'Look, it's your neighbor!'

Admira pressed Rita's hand into her chest. Bosko remained silent.

"A naked man, the young boy's father, was tied to a wooden door and carried into the room and placed next to my father. That Chetnik turned to my father and said, 'You saw fit to hide this man's son in your cellar. You must redeem yourself in our eyes, traitor. Your act of redemption shall be to bite off his testicles.' My father refused. I can still see his face battered and bloodied. He stared at my mother, knowing he would be killed, and I remember the look he had in his eyes. It was telling my mother how much he loved her. He was a Serb, they were also Serbs. But it didn't matter. To them he was a traitor. He was killed, as was our neighbor and his son, and thrown into a pit with hundreds of others. We had to be taught a lesson. It was war. The Croatians were the enemy. We were Serbs and we were to never forget it.

"There was one more lesson to learn, and they were going to teach it to the women. So instead of killing us, he dragged my mother away. Ripped her out of my arms as I screamed and tried to claw my way back to her. The other women held onto me as I watched my mother being dragged away. They brutalized her. Raped her over and over, and then when they had finished, they dragged her back so that all the women would see what had happened to her. She was made into an example. If any of us in our village ever helped a Croatian or Muslim, this is what would happen to them.

"When they brought her back, I barely recognized her. She had been so badly beaten; she was bloodied and she had been raped repeatedly. But I didn't know it at the time. Years later she told me how those men had violated her. I remember the terror I felt inside of me at seeing what they'd done to her. Seeing how my mother had been hurt that way. The other women helped her to walk and they brought her to me. The only thing that mattered to her at that moment was to comfort me and to know that those men could have done the same thing to me. Her little girl was safe in her arms.

"Before the Chetniks left, their leader came to us while we were still huddled in that room. He was the kind of man who felt his invincibility when he could hurt a woman. He spat on my mother. Then he told her that my father's body was thrown into a pit with all the other Croatian men they had killed. She looked up at him. He was hoping to see a broken woman. Her face bruised and bloodied. Her body violated. But she was not broken. Mother spoke in a whisper through her badly bruised and swollen lips. In that whispering voice she said to that Chetnik: 'You have won nothing by killing my husband. You have not dishonored me. My husband's love touched my being in ways you will never understand. His love makes what you've done to me meaningless. Every woman you think you've broken and destroyed will survive. What will you tell your children you did during this time?'"

Rita brought Admira's and Bosko's hands together on the table.

"My father and mother loved each other so much, and it is the only thing I want to remember about those times. Their love. Only that and nothing else."

Admira held onto Rita. She knew how women will always be left to bear the worst and most bestial side of a war waged by men. Bosko asked for the truth from his mother. She'd given it to him. He wished at this moment that he had never asked.

"Mother, I'm sorry for asking you. I didn't know."

"Son." Rita lifted Bosko's face until it was turned and they were looking into each other's eyes. "Don't be sorry. It was having our children that helped all of us to heal from the wounds we'd savaged upon each other. So why should you, our children, know of these things? Why should our children be told of such a time when they had brought back the reason to want to live and fall in love again? The ugliness and brutality of our past needed to be done away with—forgotten forever. Otherwise, this cycle of madness will never end." Rita held her son's hand and then, kissing it, said, "Your father and I never talked about what happened to his family and mine, to so many, many families, for that reason."

The wind outside howled louder as if in agreement with Rita's words.

"It's what your parents wanted, too, Admira, to end this memory of hatred. So when the war finally ended, it was the young and old together who rebuilt everything that had been destroyed. And it worked. We built a country. We married and had children. This time we were not just Serbs or Croatian or Muslim. We were Yugoslavs, and we mixed and mingled. And we tried to put the past behind us." Rita attempted a smile. Bosko kept shaking his head.

"Mats was right. Everyone who has kept saying it for years was right. It's all been just one big illusion. We were never one people. Maybe... maybe if we'd been taught about that time, truthfully, talked about it honestly, discussed it in school and university, in *kafanas*, on street corners, and every church and mosque there is— if we had done it, we *would* have learned something about our past and the mistakes made and how not to repeat them. It should have been taught over and over again instead of trying to bury it and forget what had been done."

"Bosko, no one can teach us how to live together."

"Why not?"

"Because, my son, so far no one has come along who has been wise enough to show us how to do it. To learn from our mistakes."

Hearing his mother's words, Bosko stared at Rita, feeling a sense of foreboding overwhelm him.

"Listen to me." Admira reached across the table and grabbed Bosko's hand. "No matter what happens, we will always have each other, our family, and our friends to help and to protect us, and that's all that matters. Understand? It's the only thing that matters." Bosko remained silent.

"Bosko, for your dad and I the only thing that mattered was for us to get on with our lives and enjoy being alive. What would it have mattered to tell you about the past? The future is what mattered. Always the future."

Without saying another word, Rita stood up. She had remembered in one night what she had tried in a lifetime to forget. Reaching her bedroom, she quietly shut the door behind her. Admira wrapped her arms around Bosko. It took him a few moments to try and comprehend what his mother had said to him and Admira. It made sense. The future is what mattered, but even as he believed in that idea, Bosko understood something else.

He held Admira at arm's length and said, "Mats' left us. He abandoned Valencia, the city he loves, and everything he knows to be with his family. He said to protect them. I understand why he did it. I would do the same. But if all of us begin to truly believe the end is near, and that only the worst is about to happen, if everybody starts to think this way, history will repeat itself—and in the end, we'll begin to see only the monster in each other..." Bosko didn't finish his thought. He kept staring at Admira for the longest time before he whispered, "In the end we won't have a war. We'll have a barbaric freak show that'll tear us apart." The winter wind howled as if in agreement with Bosko's words.

PART THREE

Chapter Ten

Summer 1990

Dragging her feet along the cobblestones as she walked, Admira held onto Bosko's arm and at times tried to playfully pull him along as they strolled on the walkway next to the river. Sarajevo was quiet except for the singsong of the wood larks that kept flying above their heads.

"Will you see Vails later today?"

"Yes, Biljes and I are going to visit. We've been visiting her a couple of times every week. Buck up her spirits while Mats is away. He keeps writing to her. It's a good sign, it has to be."

"Why is that?" asked Bosko.

"Because the worst hasn't happened—whatever that was supposed to be... and maybe it's not going to."

"Wouldn't it be something if that fool Mats suddenly shows up one day? God, I'm going to get so drunk with him and Miro when it happens."

"Me and the girls will join you."

"How is Vails?"

"She holding up, she's going to be fine. His letters to her take weeks to get delivered but they come so that's a good sign. She lives for his letters." Bosko nodded but remained silent. Mats had left seven months ago. He'd stayed in touch by writing to Vails constantly. Life continued at its slow, monotonous pace and Bosko was so glad of it. "Are you going to be the big, silent type for the rest of the day?"

"No," he said, picking her up by her waist and spinning her around. "I think we should go dancing. Let off some steam."

"I'd love that."

"I know."

"Tonight."

"Tonight and tomorrow night. Every night till our feet ache and we can't dance anymore."

"I knew you were the guy for me. You know me so well."

"I do. Let's go see our lime trees and pick up some things on our way to munch on."

"Now you're talking."

"And when we get there, I'll make you a garland out of lime leaves for your hair." He released Admira and she slid down his body. They were taking these long walks to nowhere in particular every other day and enjoying the simple connection that occurs when two people block out the "noise" of everyday life and just focus on each other.

It had become very apparent to her and Bosko, to everyone in Sarajevo, that their lives would no longer remain as before. Their country was indeed undergoing an upheaval. Where this would lead them no one knew. And that was the precise reason everyone got on with living their lives. Simply waiting for some unknown and possibly dire end to occur was not something that anyone could sustain and keep their sanity. So they and everyone else went about living their lives as best they could, while they listened and watched everything occurring around them.

"The Greens of Slovenia was created? Did you see that in the news? It's the first environmentalist party in Yugoslavia."

"I heard," he replied as they continued to walk.

"We can be quite modern; we're not as medieval as the world thinks of us as being," said Admira as she squeezed his arm. Bosko had also read in the papers of how the Croatian parliament elected Franjo Tudjman as president and how a protest of 50,000 Serbs from Croatia and Serbia took place in Petrova Gora against him, whom they condemned as being as genocidal as the Ustashi.

The list of antagonistic goings-on throughout "Yugoslavia" continued unabated, it seemed, every hour of every day. And yet no major conflict had erupted. Was it possible, thought Bosko, that the momentum that had seemed unstoppable due to some horrible circumstances had now deflated? Mats was safe. Their world was changing but it hadn't imploded—and maybe, just maybe, it wouldn't.

The wood larks continued their singsong as they circled above. They, like Admira and Bosko, were not aware that the Serbian leadership and President Slobodan Milošević had met to determine the future of Yugoslavia. It was agreed. Only one outcome was possible. War in Croatia and Bosnia and Herzegovina was inevitable. When and how was the only part that remained an unknown— fate and circumstance would make that decision.

*

"Can you reach it?"

"Yes, Dad, pass me the wrench." Admira was decked out in her grease-covered overalls, lying under her dad's truck about to change the oil. Her hair was tied into two pigtails and her face was covered with streaks of grease and oil. Her dad bent down and handed her the wrench. It was a cool fall afternoon and she could hear the leaves being blown about on the grass outside of the garage as she lay under the truck helping her dad change the oil in his truck.

He had already opened the oil cap under the hood. Admira had crawled under the truck, taking the oil pan with her, which she had put under the engine near the front of the truck. Placing the head of the wrench around the bolt, she gripped the handle of the wrench tightly then with three quick bursts against the bolt, the way Zao had shown her to do it, since she was a little girl, she was able to loosen the bolt and remove it. She let the oil drain completely out of the engine, then she tightened the bolt back up.

129

She rolled herself out on the dolly and sat up. "Piece of cake." Zao sat next to his daughter and handed her a clean cloth to wipe her hands. In the old days, he'd make her wash her hands thoroughly before they would sit down and have a bite to eat. But that little requirement didn't mean much to him these days. He wanted to spend as much time with her as possible. Admira and he had been fixing one problem after another that plagued his beat-up truck. This was her way to reconnect with her dad. It was the one thing only the two of them shared with each other. He offered her half of a very large sandwich that his wife had made for the both of them.

"Here, it should be good. Mom's Princip sandwich." His remark made Admira smile.

"Dad, you have a strange sense of humor."

"You think?" Admira had seen how her dad had gotten to be quieter. He wasn't morose or depressed, just more silent. His remark was more in keeping with the dad she had always known. He possessed a wry black humor.

"You've never believed it was true," she said before taking a bite of her sandwich. Zao did the same.

"Who knows if it's true," he replied. A Princip sandwich, as her father had labeled it, had become something of a tradition in Sarajevo, and could be bought in some cafes, though its symbolism was not wholly appreciated by everyone. It had its roots in a long-held belief by some people about what had happened on that fateful day in 1914 in Sarajevo, though many others said it was absolute rubbish. Admira continued to enjoy her sandwich, as did her dad. He handed her a flask filled with lemonade. They continued to eat, saying little to each other.

Admira rested back against the truck, her thoughts wandering back in time to the morning of June 28, 1914, the day a Serbian nationalist, Nedjelko Cabrinovic, had thrown a bomb at a car carrying Archduke Franz Ferdinand and his wife, Sophie. Fate and circumstance at that moment caused the bomb to roll off the backside of the vehicle. It exploded and wounded an officer and some bystanders, leaving the archduke uninjured. Later that day, Franz Ferdinand decided to visit the injured officer. The archduke's procession happened to take a wrong turn at the meeting of Appel Quay and Franzjosefstrasse. One of Cabrinovic's accomplices, nineteen-year-old Gavrilo Princip, happened to be loitering at a deli, where legend says he was eating a sandwich when the archduke's car happened to stop directly in front of him. Allowing fate and circumstance to finish what had not been accomplished earlier in the day, Princip fired point blank into the car, killing both Sophie and the archduke. That singular event triggered the bloodiest conflict the world had ever known: the First World War.

"Well, whether he was eating a sandwich or not, it was that wrong turn taken by the car that sealed his fate. It sealed all of our fates." Zao's last words were spoken with a creeping moroseness. It was the first time in a long time that she had heard that tone in her father's voice. "We've been taking a lot of wrong turns for quite a while now."

Like everyone in Yugoslavia and around the world, Admira and her family watched Slovenia march off to independence. The first piece of what had been Yugoslavia had broken off like a piece of rock from an escarpment, and this rock had now become the kingdom of the Slovenes. What was also occurring in Croatia was that the Croatian government had begun to fire Serbs from their jobs in the police, the government, and state-owned firms. What made this situation even more volatile and intolerable to Zao, his wife, and countless older Yugoslavians, regardless of their ethnicity, who had memories of the last war, was the bringing back of historic Croatian symbols, especially the dreaded red and white checkerboard shield that had been used by the Ustashi during the Second World War.

Hundreds of thousands of Serbs had been murdered by the Ustashi soldiers, who had flown that banner and worn it on their uniforms. Franjo Tudjman, the leader of the Croatian Democratic Union whose political party was in power, refused to condemn the atrocities committed by the Ustashi regime. To Zao and to countless older Yugoslavians with vivid memories of the past, these actions by Tudjman and the Croatian government could only lead to something catastrophic: a bloody and barbaric response by every Serb in Croatia. Their growing fear was of Tudjman wanting to restore the Ustashi regime, which seemed inevitable in their eyes.

"Dad... Dad, what are you thinking?" Zao had been staring out at the backyard while eating his sandwich, having said hardly a word to his daughter.

"Nothing, I'm just so happy we can do this again. It's been a long time."

She could see her dad was thinking of the events happening all around them and how powerless he felt as a man to change any of it, how afraid he was as a father for his family. Admira placed her sandwich on the dolly and, reaching up, wrapped her arms around his neck. "It will all be okay, Dad, you'll see." Zao kept hugging her for the longest time.

"Yes, you're right, let's eat our sandwich and finish fixing this truck."

"Okay."

*

Winter 1990

"Well, it's been quite a while," Valencia's mother, Slavenka, said as she strolled into the living room of their apartment, "since I've heard the three of you laughing so loud."

"We were remembering that time when Mats convinced us all

to rent bikes. Mom, come join us." Valencia patted the sofa cushion next to her. Slavenka sat beside her daughter.

"Alright, but only for a minute. With your father having to stay at work so late these days, it's given me more time to meet friends and catch up on gossip and the news. There's so much of both these days.

"It was quite a sight, the six of us as we cycled in a long line around the Sebilj fountain and to Baščaršija and across Princip Bridge." Admira sounded wistful at recalling those past days. "We went everywhere we could. It was so much fun, wasn't it?" Admira looked at Biljana and Vails. "You know what?" Her eyes lit up. "That's the first thing we'll do when Mats gets back." They nodded their heads enthusiastically. Admira continued to usher her friends back to their past, to a happy time in their lives. "It turned out to be such a beautiful day, and what a view we had when we sat on our picnic blanket. You know, I think it was at that picnic when Miro finally got it... how much he loved you, needed you, Biljes. That dumbhead finally realized how you felt about him."

"It took him long enough to figure it out," Biljana admitted.

"But at least he did," Admira replied. "And coming down, Bosh and Mats' decided to race and somehow their bikes got tangled up and they fell off and rolled down into this ravine."

"And you," Valencia said, looking at Admira, "chased after them, riding down the side of the hill on your bike. Sometimes, girl, you have no sense. Their pants were torn, their arms all scraped up. Mats had a gash on his temple. Bosko's knees were bloody. And their two bikes were completely destroyed, so they had to carry them all the way back into the city."

"Bosh and Miro and Mats got into a fight with the old man, the owner of the bike shop, because he was demanding twice the amount of money the bikes were actually worth," Admira chimed in.

"Yeah, but do you remember what happened after?" Vails asked. "Remember that guy? He was a friend of Bosko's, though he was older. What was his name? There was something about him that made me feel—I don't know—I guess scared. He was with friends passing the bike shop when he noticed Bosh and the guys arguing with the owner."

"Yeah, I remember," Biljes said. "There was something very brutish, no, not brutish, dangerous about him. God, he was big and sexy, too. He had a girl on each arm. So did his friends. After the owner saw him and realized he was a friend of Bosko's, his attitude completely changed. Like all of a sudden he was very afraid of Bosko's friend. God, what was his name? He actually ended up paying for the damaged bikes—wouldn't let Bosh pay for anything. Mladjo, that's it. Mladjo was his name. Why would I remember that?"

"Probably because you found him sexy," Admira teased, smiling at Biljes.

"You know, it didn't make sense that Bosh would know someone like him. They acted as if they were best friends even though he was older than Bosh." Biljes sipped her tea.

"There really was something frightening about that guy. Bosh never told us who he was. Did you ever see him again, Admira?" Vails asked.

"No. That was the only time. Bosh has never talked about him either. But you guys are right, something about him made you want to take a step back."

"Looks like you three have everything under control," Slavenka said, kissing Valencia tenderly on her cheek and standing up. "Before you know it, all three of them will be back together again."

"Thanks, Mum. Go and enjoy your gossip with your friends."

*

134

Valencia leaned back against her sofa chair and stared into her half-empty tea cup. Admira glanced over at Biljana. They both knew what the other was thinking and were ashamed of it. They were so glad that it wasn't Bosko or Miro who had left. They still had their men.

Vails scooped up a small triangle of baklava from a tray, which she had placed on the center table in the living room. They all began to pull off small pieces with their forks.

"I received a letter from Mats almost two months ago; I'm amazed it actually got here. I'm so grateful it did because I don't know when I'll be hearing from him again. He said everyone is fine and coping. He doesn't like Dubrovnik. Nothing particularly wrong with the city, he says, but it's not Sarajevo. I know he's going to wait till things get better—whenever that is—and he's sure everyone is safe before he tries to come back here. I can't understand why the Yugoslav Army is besieging Dubrovnik—it's Dubrovnik, pearl of the Adriatic."

Admira almost threw the piece of baklava back onto the tray. Eating and enjoying the taste of baklava while a city that was special to all of them was being bombarded seemed to her crass and perverse.

"It's just as if it were being done to Paris or New York. That would be unthinkable, and yet it's happening. Everything Mats said would happen has come true."

Her friends said nothing.

"And can you believe, just like that, a truce was negotiated between Slovenia and Yugoslavia a few months ago? Now all Slovenes will have their dream, an independent country." Admira looked at her friends who stared back at her. What could they say?

On TV and in the newspapers, they also learned of how Dubrovnik, an ancient city in Croatia, but special to all Yugoslavs, was now being bombed. It was a completely irrational act to Admira and her friends and to everyone in Yugoslavia. The bombing and destruction of a beautiful city didn't make sense. No one knew how or when it would end.

135

"Mats told Bosko just before he left that 'perhaps we will slit each other's wrists, but not each other's throats. Perhaps the consequences of what could really happen will bring everyone to their senses.' Maybe he was also right about that. The war with Slovenia lasted only ten days and only eighteen people were killed; at least that's what I read in the papers.

"Or was it eight people? I feel so dirty even saying only eight or eighteen people were killed. What if we knew some of those people? They wouldn't just be numbers. But, if they could have what they had, with hardly any horrible things happening... it's possible, isn't it... that the same could happen all over?"

"Anything is possible, Admira," said Biljes.

"You really think that could happen, Admira?" Said Vails.

"The Serbs can't keep bombing Dubrovnik. It's the worst thing they could have done. The whole world is watching, and they're being seen as nothing more than barbaric monsters."

Admira couldn't stand any more of the depressing political talk about war. "How about a toast? There has to be something we can toast to," she said. "To us, women of the Balkans, we don't break easily, if ever." Admira felt a tug in her gut as she said those words. She knew it would be the women—Muslim, Croatian, and Serbian—who would pay an unspeakable price because of so many enraged men. "And to you especially, Vails. I know Mats loves you more than anything. And to the women of Sarajevo." They brought their cups together in a soft clink and enjoyed the silence as they sipped their tea.

Chapter Eleven

December 1991

"Mats, hurry," his father yelled. Mats ran back into the house. Turning to his wife, Matko's father said in desperation, "You must leave now with the girls. We'll catch up. No questions! We don't have time; every second counts. You have to leave now!"

"Andro, I won't leave you—I *won't!*"

"This one time you will not argue with me. We'll be right behind you." His breath had the stench of fear.

She tried to grab his arm as he pulled it away from her. "I won't, I won't!"

"Go now. Stick with all the others leaving. You will have more protection in numbers. We will be right behind you. Go now!"

"Andro—"

"I love you. Go!" Mobs of people were running from their homes with only the clothes on their backs. Houses and barns were being set ablaze and the sound of gunfire and exploding mortar shells grew closer.

"Run!"

Matko's father watched his wife and two hysterical nieces disappear into the crowds of screaming people, who were all running for their lives. The sound of artillery fire kept getting louder; it was almost on their doorstep. Plumes of smoke billowed into the sky. Countless homes were engulfed in flames.

"We're all here. Let's go, Andro, there's no more time. Where are the girls?"

"They're with the others, running. Where's Mats?"

Matko's uncle and two cousins were standing with his father in the front yard.

Matko flew out of the front door, wearing a jacket. "I've got it," he yelled as he ran toward his father.

The first shot hit his youngest cousin between the shoulder blades. A rooftop sniper had seen the men and made a choice. It was not immediately lethal. Matko's cousin fell into his own father's arms. Before they had a chance to respond, another shot rang out, instantly killing the wounded man's brother. His uncle fell to his knees as he held a wounded son in one arm, a dead son in the other.

Matko picked up the bolt action hunting rifle that fell out of his uncle's hand, raised it in the general direction from where the last shot had been fired, and squeezed the trigger. The chamber was empty. There were no bullets in the gun. Another shot rang out and suddenly rounds were being fired from all directions. Matko's uncle, still holding his sons in his arms, yelled, "Mats, get back in the house."

His dad grabbed him by the waist, and his uncle dragged his wounded son in his arms as they struggled the few yards to the house. They dove in through the front door and crawled away from the entrance. Matko lay on the floor in the living room, his heart ready to burst. He couldn't breathe. His whole body was shaking. He heard his uncle, Josip, groan from the last shot taken by the sniper, whose intent was to shatter his uncle's pelvis, which he'd accomplished.

"Mats?" his father yelled from where he sprawled across the living room floor. "Mats, answer me."

"I'm okay, Dad," he replied, lifting his head with glazed eyes, staring at his father.

Sweat poured down his father's face and his whole body shook uncontrollably. They were trapped. "Josip!" he shouted.

Andro's brother couldn't answer him. He was fading in and out of consciousness.

"Josip!" Andro's voice had lost all its calm.

Matko turned toward his uncle and cousin, who were lying together in the passageway.

"He's hurt badly, Dad. What do I do? Tell me."

Andro wiped his mouth and face. The sweat of fear oozed out of every pore. They were surrounded and trapped in the house, as the sniper had planned. "Dad, what do I do?" Matko shouted in desperation.

"Stay where you are. I'll come there." Realizing they couldn't escape, Andro ignored the barrage of bullets tearing up the walls and windows of his home. He crawled over to Josip and Mats. Andro and Uncle Josip reached out and pulled each other close. Andro tried to turn his brother onto his side, but Josip screamed in pain.

"Get the boys out, Andro," Josip implored his brother.

"I can't. They're everywhere."

Matko looked to his father, who was on the verge of tears.

Josip's breathing was labored while he lay on the floor in agony. One arm was wrapped around his critically injured son, who was now barely conscious. His other precious boy lay dead in the front yard. "Go," Josip said, "watch the front. I'll try to reach the back." Matko's father embraced his brother as their tears flowed. They kissed each other and Matko's uncle looked at him and said, "Help me."

Matko threw down the hunting rifle. He grabbed his uncle and cousin by their jacket collars. Josip cried out in pain, but Mats dragged them to the safest location down the hallway to the back of the house.

"Mats, hurry," his uncle begged him.

"What do I do, Uncle Josip?"

"Be strong and stay with your father. No matter what, stay with your father. I'll watch the back. Go. Andro needs you." He was barely able to squeeze Matko's hand. He struggled to wrap one arm over his youngest son, who was now dead.

Matko was in a daze. How had all this happened? They were leaving only a few moments ago. He crawled on his belly toward his father. The shooting had stopped. It was replaced by the sound of laughter coming from outside. They were trapped and surrounded by Serbian and Montenegrin irregulars who were going to have a little fun tormenting everyone in the house.

"Mats, help me with the sofa."

Matko and his father turned the sofa onto its side to act as a barrier, to shield them against the barrage of bullets. The glass from the large living room window had been shot away and a cool breeze blew inside the home and dried the sweat on their faces. It caused them to shiver. They were both in shock. As best they could, they kicked and threw furniture, clothing, and lamps toward the doorway—everything and anything within reach that might slow down an intruder from entering the house. But what good would it do? They were trapped and unarmed.

"Josip. Josip." Matko's dad called out to his brother, but there was no answer. He crawled away from the sofa, leaving his son hidden by it and braced himself against a heavy upholstered chair. He was the only one with a loaded gun. Matko's father kept watching the hallway that led to the entrance door. Everything had become eerily quiet. Andro watched his son and tears welled up in his eyes. He hated himself for bringing his son to this place. Matko had never wanted to leave their home in Sarajevo.

"I'm sorry... I'm so sorry my son. I'm sorry."

"No, Dad, don't be. We're together." Matko tried to sound brave. He even smiled at his father. "I would have it no other way, Dad." A sudden barrage of bullets coming from all directions tore into the living room. Chunks of plaster were ripped out of the walls and fell to the floor. Every glass window had been shattered and the sound of the gunfire grew louder and kept getting closer. Matko lay flat on the floor, covering his head as he listened to the sound of every bullet streak past his head and body. The assault continued for another minute and then suddenly stopped. Mats waited for a few seconds before raising his head slowly.

"Dad?" He yelled out. "Dad are you okay?

His father stared at him. Then a stream of blood gushed from his mouth. A jagged piece of wood from the sofa chair had been shattered by the gunfire and its pointed end pierced his father's chest. Matko was about to run to his father.

"No, stay!" Andro gasped as pools of blood escaped from his mouth. He was still trying to protect his son with his last conscious thought and breath. His eyes remained open for just a few seconds longer while the image of his son staring back at him with tear-filled eyes faded away. A steady stream of blood oozed from his mouth, his head fell forward, and his body lay still against the sofa chair.

Matko couldn't take his eyes away from his father. *Miro, Bosko, where are you?* He wanted to be with them, wanted them here with him. They would know what to do. It seemed as if he had called out their names a thousand times.

"What should I do, Dad? What should I do? Please tell me." Matko banged the side of his head with his fists. "What should I do?"

Caring nothing for himself he got up and ran toward his dad. Reaching out to grab his father's hand, he felt the bullet pierce his back between his shoulder blades and he stumbled to the floor, unable to reach and grab onto his father's hand to pull him to his side.

*

Mats opened his eyes, thinking he heard a footstep. He was fading in and out of consciousness. How long had he been like this? When had he been shot? Mats had no memory of the moment it happened. Nothing about the moment or what led up to it made any sense. Where was Vails? He kept hearing her voice.

141

His eyes were open, and he was certain he'd heard the sound of footsteps... and laughter. Men were outside in the front yard relaxing and resting. It was time for a coffee break. Because the living room window had been blown away, he could hear his family's killers only a few feet away.

Then he heard one of the men say, "They found those three this morning hiding in a barn. Those fucking reservists found them and fucked the shit out of those cunts. Three openings to fill. Lucky bastards. When the two of us got there, they told us we were numbers forty-nine and fifty. Is that Croatian pig still alive inside?"

Mats had remained alive, unwilling to die because he had to get back to Vails. She was waiting for him. Each desperate breath of air he took barely filled his lungs and as it did, the pulverized dust from the destroyed plaster walls and ceiling seeped in. He heard footsteps once more, sounding heavy and vengeful. Boots on a wood floor stepping on broken pieces of glass and plaster.

He concentrated on listening to each step as the stranger walked down the hallway toward the rear of the house, toward the bodies of his uncle and cousin. Then everything stopped; the house was quiet. Mats tried to listen for any sound or hint about what the stranger might be doing, but there was only silence.

Ivan knelt down beside Josip and his dead son, reached into his pocket, and pulled out two square pieces of cloth. He placed one on top of each body. The cloths were replicas of the new Croatian flag.

Ivan remembered that day, as did every Serb in Croatia. To Croatians the checkerboard was seen as an emblem of ancient historical importance. To most Serbs, this was the same emblem on the flag that was flown by the Ustashi government during World War II. That same government had murdered three quarters of a million Serbs. How could any Croatian not understand what it would mean for a Serb to see such a flag resurrected?

By placing the flag on top of the bodies, Ivan and his fellow Serbs were sending a message that this was the future for Croatia and its new flag. After a long silence, Mats heard the stranger's boots crunch down on the hardwood floor and debris once more. It sounded like the dried bones of the dead being ground into dust beneath his heel.

Mats tried to make a sound to call out to this stranger as he heard his footsteps pass the opening to the living room. But there was barely enough strength left in Mats to take even the shortest breath. Realizing he couldn't make a sound, he began to scratch the wooden floor with his fingernails.

The stranger stopped and glanced briefly into the living room. He was about to exit through the front door when he thought he heard a faint sound. He stopped and remained absolutely still. Did he imagine it? There it was again. No, it was real. His finger squeezed delicately against the trigger of his Kalashnikov. He saw nothing but the dead body of a Croat pig lying next to an overturned sofa chair, a jagged piece of wood stuck in his chest. There it was again, a strange sound coming from somewhere near the sofa. Ivan saw the fingertips of a hand protruding out from one end of the over-turned couch.

"Come on. Jump up. I'll give you a chance," he said.

The hand stopped moving.

Ivan inched closer until he was able to raise his boot and smash it down hard onto the hand. Bones broke. He heard them. But the hand didn't move.

Ivan's trigger finger was itching. He grabbed one end of the sofa and in one swift motion rolled it away. Mats was still alive, staring up at him with soft green eyes. The two men stared at each other for long moments, before Ivan unslung the Kalashnikov from his shoulder and placed it by his side as he knelt beside Mats. A dark red, almost black, pool of blood had encircled his body from wounds inflicted by Ivan's fellow gunmen. The dried blood had hardened like a glue. Ivan picked up the bolt action hunting rifle lying next to Mats, pulled back the bolt on the rifle and looked into the chamber. It hadn't been fired in a long time. He placed the rifle back by Matko's side. Mats continued to stare at Ivan as he whispered, "Vails."

Neither one of them could imagine what the other was thinking. Ivan lowered his head. Matko's lips were only inches away. He was trying desperately to say her name: "Vails." Blood had hardened around his mouth and in his throat, making it difficult to utter her name. Somehow he had to let this stranger know that there was someone alive whom he loved with all his heart. Someone who was waiting for him to return. Someone who loved him. He had to convey that one thought to this man who knelt next to him. With only his eyes Mats tried to reveal to this stranger what was in his heart.

"Tell... Vails... I... love her," His eyes said. "Always... love her."

Leaning forward, Ivan whispered, "Suffer in these last moments of your life and while you do, remember all of whom you have loved."

Ivan tucked the flag back into his pocket. Matko listened as the sound of the stranger's retreating boots crushing the plaster laying on the floor faded away.

Chapter Twelve

January 1, 1992

Bosko had spent most of the day preparing for Admira, Miro, and Biljes. Everyone was getting together to celebrate the New Year a second time at Bosko's apartment. Vails had been depressed from not having heard from Mats in quite a while. She was in no mood for any kind of celebration, but insisted that they have a drink to her and Mats. Rita had cooked a feast before she left the house to visit friends. For Rita and most Sarajevans, it appeared that their world was spinning out of control. She had told Bosko that visiting friends and neighbors, now more than ever before, gave both her and them an increased sense of security.

Sarajevans provided each other with moral support while they tried their best to ignore, even as they tried to understand, what in the hell was happening to their world.

*

The doorbell rang. Bosko wasn't expecting anyone until eight o'clock.

"Are you Bosko Brkić?" the stranger asked twice, giving Bosko no time to answer the moment he opened the door.

"Yes," he answered.

An elderly man in crumpled, dirty clothes stood at the front door observing him.

The man stuck his hand into the leather satchel hanging at his side and said, "I have a letter for you." The man held out an envelope. Bosko tried to take it, but the man held onto it firmly. The elderly man looked at the number on the door as if to make sure he had the right place. He glanced up at Bosko once more and then released the large brown envelope into Bosko's hand.

As the messenger turned to leave, Bosko grabbed his arm. "Wait. Who are you? What is this?"

The pale gentleman stood still with his eyes cast down at the floor, but said nothing.

"Please, come inside just for a moment."

Bosko stepped aside and motioned the stranger toward the living room.

"Would you like some coffee? Are you hungry?"

"Coffee would be nice. No sugar, just black."

Bosko nodded. "I'll be right back." Before he entered the kitchen, he glanced at the envelope that he'd left on a side table. He hurried to pour the coffee. Instinct told him that this man would only stay for a brief time. Rushing out of the kitchen, he said, "Here you go."

"Thank you," the man said quietly.

"You know my name. May I know yours?"

"I am Vlado."

Bosko shook his hand. Bosko was puzzled at this unexpected visitor showing up at his door. "Where are you from?" Bosko asked.

"I do not know anymore."

"You are not from Sarajevo?"

"No."

Bosko noticed how the man's hands shook while trying to hold his coffee mug.

"Can you tell me, Vlado, where it is you're from? What is happening out there? We hear and see so much on television and in the newspapers, but we don't know what is real and what is a lie. No one can seem to tell us." Bosko leaned forward and steadied Vlado's hand as it continued to tremble.

Vlado lowered his head and stared into the blackness of his coffee. "It is madness everywhere."

Bosko's chest tightened. "Madness?"

146

"Yes, everywhere." Vlado sipped his coffee. Every time he raised the cup to his lips he seemed to grow calmer. Bosko waited. He didn't want to press him because the man seemed so fragile. Vlado kept closing his eyes, as if every mouthful of coffee tasted like nectar. He clearly hadn't tasted it in a very long time. "I am from the town of Glina. Do you know it?"

"No, actually," Bosko replied, trying to sound as gentle as possible. Then he asked again, "What happened, Vlado? We see and hear so much of what is happening everywhere, but no one in Sarajevo knows other than what the politicians and foreign press want us to know. We live in a bubble that has yet to burst."

Vlado nodded. He saw the fear in Bosko's eyes. "My family and I have lived in Glina for many generations. Not anymore; the Croatians have made that clear to every Serb. We are now a national minority and need to be herded off to some dark place and left there to be forgotten. Or be forced to live somewhere else. But I know of no other place in which to live, and although I am Serb, I care nothing for a greater Serbia or greater Croatia. I don't even know what that means. I just want to go back to my home in Croatia, to my family's home of so many generations."

"What happened in Glina?"

"Every day I saw one Serb after another become more paranoid and bitter. The elders in our town still remembered what had happened to their families and friends at the hands of the Ustashi. How eight hundred Serbians were locked up in our church and then the church was set on fire. Memories of such a day can never be forgotten, even though it happened forty-five years ago. Then one day, out of nowhere, men I have never seen before started coming into Glina. They were Serbs like me, and we all thought they were there to help calm the situation. We soon found out that was not their purpose. Instead of helping us, they made it worse for every Serb in town."

Vlado set the empty coffee cup down. "They began to spread

147

lies that were mixed with the truth. It came to one point when no one knew what was true and what a lie was. They kept telling us of situations happening to Serbs in towns all over Croatia. About how Serbs found themselves suddenly losing their jobs for no reason. How they'd been fired from the police force, released from every level of education. Even employment in hospitals and medical institutions wasn't secure anymore. The tourist industry and private firms no longer wished to hire a Serb. But this was just the beginning, they kept telling groups of people who came to listen to them.

"They kept repeating the warnings coming from Milošević and others that every Serb in Yugoslavia faced annihilation. It was a replay of events at the hands of the Ustashi during World War II, who murdered almost a million Serbs. These men brought weapons with them and started selling them to the Serbs, telling them if they didn't carry weapons they would have no way to protect themselves from their coming annihilation at the hands of the Croats. Those of us who had always lived in Glina supported the political party of the town. These men were our Croatian friends and neighbors we'd known all our lives. Then one day those Serb pigs who had come to Glina attacked the police station without provocation."

"Who were they?"

"Garbage. There is no other word for it. No Serb from town took part in it. We didn't even know it was going to happen. The men who did this were Serbs from the town of Knin. They were the Marticevci extremists who only wanted bloodshed, and as much of it as possible—why, I don't know. It made no sense."

Bosko had heard about these Serb extremists. Their leader was Milan Martić and the men who had flocked to him had begun to terrorize non-Serb populations in the region of Krajina Croatia.

"They killed every Serb who refused to join their group; they thought nothing of killing their own kind. Or they threatened to wipe out the families of Serbian men who refused to put on their uniform. They gave us no choice, and many Serb men wore their uniforms because their families would be killed if they didn't. Many just tried to run away, refusing to do it."

Bosko sat in silence, hanging on every word.

"I managed to hide and escape because I will never put on a uniform and kill anyone. My family had left a few months earlier with little more than what they could carry on their backs. We had seen the writing on the wall and I sent them away. If it wasn't the Croatians who were going to kill us one day, then it would be our fellow Serbs because we refused to fight our Croatian friends and neighbors. What kind of madness is this that we have all succumbed to? I stayed to protect my family's home from being robbed and torn apart, not that I could have stopped the looting. A bullet would have seen to that. But Glina was my home, home to generations of my family. I just couldn't leave it. It is all I have ever known. Now I am here. I came to give you what is in this envelope."

Bosko reached out and took Vlado's hand.

"What's in this envelope, Vlado?"

"It is best that you read it when I am gone."

"Who gave it to you?"

Vlado had a gentle but frightened look in his eyes. He didn't answer the question.

"Where did you run away to?" Bosko pressed. "Where have you been living all this time?"

"In my memories," Vlado answered as he stood to leave.

"Don't leave now."

"I have to go."

"But—"

"Take care of yourself and those you love. I don't know where this monster in all of us has come from, but it will be a long time before we can get rid of it. A long time." Vlado walked toward the front door. Bosko reached for the doorknob and opened it for him. "Thank you for your coffee."

Vlado patted Bosko on the shoulder affectionately, turned and stepped across the threshold and into the apartment hallway. He turned one last time to stare at Bosko. It lasted only seconds, then he hurried away and down the stairs.

Bosko closed the door and walked back into the living room. He didn't know what to think about Vlado. Another thread of insanity was weaving itself into what remained of the shredded fabric of their world. *Why have so many of my friends simply disappeared? Where have they gone?* Bosko rested his head in the palm of his hands. Peering at the envelope on the table, he picked it up, stared at his name written in black ink, then turned it over. He didn't recognize the handwriting, but before he had a chance to open it, Admira stepped into the apartment. He hadn't heard the key in the door.

He greeted her with a passionate kiss and held her hand, leading her to sit with him in the living room for a while. Admira sensed something was troubling Bosko, but she remained silent and just happy to be with him. The minutes ticked away and nothing was said by either of them. He let his head fall backward on the sofa and shut his eyes. Admira climbed onto Bosko's lap and pressed her face into the crook of his neck. He could feel her warm breath blowing against his skin. A knot formed in the pit of his stomach from his anxiety and fear. What was their collective future going to be?

Bosko reached out again to grab the letter from the side table when the doorbell rang. "That's Miro and Biljes," he said, giving her another kiss. He held on to Admira for a second longer, staring into her onyx eyes before letting her slide off his lap to answer the door.

Admira reached for the knob and flung open the door.

"Here we are, early as always, with champagne in one hand

and *strudla* in the other," Biljana said.

"Come in, Biljes." Admira grabbed her in a tight embrace. Bosko also strode up to Biljana and hugged her.

"It feels good for us to be together," Miroslav said as he embraced Bosko.

"Yes, it does," Biljana agreed, looking at him.

"I'll be right back." Miroslav headed for the kitchen.

"So what have you and Miro been up to?"

"The same, not much. And you?" Biljana asked.

"The same," Admira replied. "There's precious little we can do these days."

"Hey." Bosko put his arm around Biljana. "I hope everyone's hungry."

"What do you think, Bosh? I'm starving," Miro yelled back from the kitchen. They heard him uncork the champagne.

"What's that?" Biljana asked, pointing to the envelope. She walked toward a plate of hors d'oeuvres and helped herself. Admira did the same.

"Ah, the mystery envelope. I don't know."

"Are you going to open it?"

Bosko went to the table and picked up the envelope, tearing open the flap and pulling out some sheets of paper. He began to read the letter silently to himself.

"Well, here we are. Five glasses of the best champagne in the entire city. One for each of us and one for our absent friend," Miroslav said, appearing from the kitchen and placing the tray on the table.

Bosko stared at his friend, eyes glazed.

"Bosh, what is it?"

"Mats is dead."

"What?" Miro ran to Bosko and grabbed the letter out of his hand. "It says he was killed in December. That's a month ago!" Miro's whole body reeled backward as if he'd been gut punched.

151

"How?" Admira asked, trembling.

Biljana fell into a chair, her face pale, tears filling her eyes.

"It says his father, his uncle, two of his cousins, and Mats were all killed at his uncle's farmhouse in Konavoski Dvori." Miro's voice was barely above a whisper as he read. "But I thought they were all in Dubrovnik. That's what he said in his last letter to Vails."

Suddenly, Bosko picked up a chair and smashed it against the floor and the wall.

"Bosko!" Miro yelled. He ran to his friend. "Stop it." Bosko pushed him aside and walked away. Biljana got up and motioned Miro to her side. Admira wanted to go to Bosko, but she saw how his emotions were on edge. He was building up a rage that in a moment of utter despair he would lash out at anyone. Biljes held Miro back; she saw the same thing as Admira and knew it was best to wait.

"I told him not to go. I told him to stay here where it's safe. But he had to do it. He had to prove to his father that he wasn't afraid." Bosko screamed. It was a primal cry of rage. He grabbed another chair and smashed it, against the wall. It split apart. A shaft of wood pierced his temple and then fell to the floor. He began to bleed. Admira jumped up and ran to Bosko and pressed her diminutive body against his.

"Stop, dearest, stop." Bosko could only see a white light and not Admira. "Stop this. It won't help." She pressed both hands against his chest. "Look at me. We're together. Here with Miro and Biljes."

"I told him not to go. I saw the fear in his eyes that day. So did you, Miro" Bosko said. Tears slipped down his cheeks. "I should have stopped him. I should have—"

"We both should have," Miro yelled. Then, lowering his voice and walking to his friend, he embraced Bosko. "Nothing could have stopped Mats from leaving—nothing. You know this is true." The two friends leaned their foreheads together and closed their eyes.

Bosko's blood began to trickle down his face; a few drops fell onto Miro's hand.

"Now look, I have your blood on my hands. That's not something I want."

"Neither one of you is to blame," Admira said, returning with a napkin and dabbing it gently against his temple. Biljana stood beside Miro and wiped Bosko's blood off his hand.

"Leave it!" Bosko yelled at Admira. "Do you think this is anything? Mats is dead!" He grabbed the napkin out of her hand and threw it to the floor. Biljana pulled Admira back and held her. "We're eight years from a new century, a new millennium. This should not be happening. Not now. None of it!"

"Bosh, nothing can change what will be."

"Miro, what inevitability do you want us to accept?"

"What do you think we can do?"

"Stop this," Bosko yelled.

"How?" Miro looked at Bosko incredulously. "Everybody thinks they have an idea of how to stop it. Do we even fucking know what *it* is? Yet it continues and keeps getting worse."

Bosko sank into a chair with his head in his hands. He needed someone to blame. "We are eating each other alive."

"Yes, Bosh, we are, and the whole world is watching, and they don't give a shit. Why should they when we don't?" Everyone in the apartment became still and a silent. Finally Miro said. "Bosko, read the letter out loud."

Admira and Biljana sat side by side, holding hands. Miroslav leaned against the wall, his hands shoved into his pockets. Bosko picked up the letter, his hands shaking, and read.

Bosko,

I'm writing this letter to you and to Miro. It is for you both. My Matko and my beloved husband are dead. My husband's brother and his two sons died with them in December. I do not know the actual day it happened. What I know was told to me by our neighbors who managed to escape and came here to Dubrovnik.

I am entrusting this letter to an old friend of my husband's family. It is such an irony that after all that has happened, the person I can trust the most with this letter is our Serbian friend, Vlado. Serbs killed my son and husband and it is a dear Serb friend who must bring you the news of their death. He too has lost everything from his hometown in Glina. He's bringing this news to you from me because he is searching for a sister who he believes escaped Vukovar after the siege ended and managed to get to Sarajevo. I hope to God she was able to make it.

Vlado got to Dubrovnik before the bombing began. My husband and I ran into him by chance one day on the street. Neither of us could believe what was happening and how we had been brought together. We stayed in touch with each other while in the city. Thank God we did. Bosko, if you can, please look in on him. Anything you can do for Vlado, I will forever appreciate.

Bosko stopped reading; he realized now why this stranger had refused to tell him where he had been staying. If he had mentioned Dubrovnik, Bosko would have known that this letter came from the only person he knew who was there, and that something terrible had happened. He continued reading:

We had gone to Matko's uncle's farmhouse to bring back family heirlooms. Mats's uncle and my husband said that many of the things we were bringing back were irreplaceable and thought it best to bring what we could back to the city. Most of it was of no value to anyone but us.

The bombing and shooting happened fast and without any warning. Andro made the girls and me leave first. We ran with all the others to escape. He promised they would be right behind us. Somehow they were separated from the others who were fleeing. They were spotted running into the house. That was the last anyone saw of them.

Bosko stopped. The next line on the letter was blurred by her tears.

"I..."

He hesitated, and then continued.

I needed to write this letter to you and Miro to take the numbness away. I want to die because I'm already dead inside. What I would give to have them all back. Sometimes I stand by the door thinking I hear their footsteps. I keep thinking it was all a mistake. That they're out there trying to make their way back to me. Nothing in Konavoski Dvori remains. It is a wasteland. The farm, the house, everything was destroyed and burned. I have no son. I have no husband. My nieces and I managed to get into Dubrovnik just as the Serbs had started shelling the city. May God forgive me for agreeing to leave Sarajevo. We should have stayed where it was safe.

I do not know when I shall write to you again, or when I shall see you and Miro. We will remain here with my husband's family and his other brother. What is this madness that has taken hold of us? How can any of this be happening?

Bosko, you were my son's best friend, you and Miro. Mats loved both of you so very much. Thank you for having been his friend. I'm sure he thought of both of you till the very end. And his precious Valencia. I know he spoke her name with his last breath. Take care of yourself, your family, and Admira. If Miro is with you when you read this letter, tell him that Matko talked of him often.

155

He missed their differences. God be with you both. Please tell Valencia. I do not have the strength or courage to write to her. Ask her to forgive me.

May god protect you and all those you love.
Sabina

Bosko stopped reading. He looked up and stared through the balcony doors at the lights of Sarajevo. The pages fell out of his hand, and without saying a word Bosko walked toward the balcony, slid the doors open, and stepped out into the freezing night.

Admira didn't know what to think, or what to believe. It seemed as if they were trapped in a crawl space and the air was gone and they were all gasping for every last breath. Biljes squeezed Admira's hand.

"Go on. He needs you," she said softly.

Admira got up. Bosko had left the doors open. The cold night air swirled into the apartment.

Miroslav turned to Biljana. She wanted to say something kind and gentle to him and was about to caress his face, but he pulled her hand away and held it, his own trembling. With a wild look in his eyes, he said, "It's going to happen to us here. Isn't it?"

*

Rita came home late after visiting her neighbors. Bosko told his mother about Matko's death. She hugged her son for a long time and sat with him and the only other best friend he had left in this world. Each time Rita thought she might have some words of comfort and was about to say something, she would catch herself. She realized there was nothing she could say that would make any difference. So she sat with her son and Admira and their closest friends. And they huddled together, like all of them were lost in a daze of conflicting emotions. Rita heard her thoughts keep repeating and getting louder. *Once more it is happening. The worst of our Slavic past has risen up, and it will consume us all.*

Rita made them coffee and they drank and watched the night sky begin to brighten.

Finally, Bosko broke the silence. "Mom, I'm taking Admira home, I'll see you later." Without saying a word, everyone at the table stood. Rita joined Bosko and walked with him, thinking of how, at this moment, she felt completely inadequate as his mother. She was unable to give her son and his friends any answers about why Mats had been killed. Rita hugged everyone at the door as they left the apartment.

"Come back soon," she said to Miro and Biljana.

"Don't I always?" Miro asked, hugging Rita once more.

Admira and Bosko waved to their friends as they drove away. It was a cold and bright dawn in Sarajevo.

It was only the second day of the New Year. On its first day they had been told of Mats's death. In the past every New Year had brought with it only the best memories of every year that had passed. Once long ago they had all met on New Year's Eve. Love and intimacy had been borne out of that first meeting; it took root that night when they had all met, and since then they had toasted to the hopes of a grand future that they believed would happen. Now none of those hopes seemed at all possible.

After hours of walking aimlessly through narrow streets, past unopened shops, watching the early morning sun bounce off the orange roof tiles, they decided to take the tram. No one standing or seated around them on the tram knew about Matko. A good man had died in a horrible way, like so many others. It was too much to even consider what kind of nightmare could suddenly and inexorably become their future.

When they finally reached Admira's house, on the outskirts of the city, she tugged at his arm. "Come inside. Have some tea or *vinjak.* I don't want you to be by yourself," Admira pleaded.

"I'm okay."

"No, you're not. Come inside. My dad will know what to do, what to say."

Bosko put his arms around Admira. "I need to be alone."

"Where will you go?" Admira asked.

"I don't know." Bosko released Admira, kissed her on the lips, and turned to begin his long walk down the gravel road toward the city. He was heading toward some place where he and Mats often met. Admira stood by the fence and wrapped her arms around herself. *Why, God, have you forgotten us?*

She climbed the stairs and opened the back door into the kitchen where her family was seated at the table. Her father said nothing. Zena began to get up from her chair but Zao pressed his hand to hers and Zena sat back down. Something terrible had taken place. Her mother had heard it in Admira's voice when she'd phoned the night before telling them that she was staying with Bosko. She'd given no reason, and quickly hung up.

Admira took her seat at the table. "Mats was killed a month ago in Konavoski Dvori. So was his father, his uncle, and two cousins. Bosko received a letter yesterday from Matko's mother letting him know." Zena reached across the table to hold her daughter's hand, but Admira pulled away. Tonya was quiet. Her father bit down on a wedge of orange without looking at his daughter.

"You knew this would happen, didn't you?" She studied the expressions on both her parents' faces.

Zao didn't answer. Zena shook her head. She had kept her fears to herself. She did not know. How could anyone know anything? Should she and Zao have talked to Admira and Tonya about how things had been changing for quite some time in Yugoslavia? And what it meant? She looked up at her husband, who knew what she was thinking. Yet what could have been said that would have made sense, that would have allowed any of them to look into the future and know what would be? For Zao it was clear: the more voices that were added to the conversation of what was going to happen to all of them, the worse it seemed to get. He like many others were waiting for the voice of reason to show itself. Only then, thought Zao and many others, could a real conversation take place about all of their futures. But Zao and every other Yugoslavian had yet to see the emergence of a calm voice on all sides. Instead, what he saw taking place was the exploitation of their differences and the horror of their history being dredged up. And that was something that most Yugoslavians were loath to discuss and want to remember. Yet that was exactly what was being exploited by the leaders of all sides—their individual barbarism toward one another and how it was about to repeat itself. How could any parent talk to their children about such matters? None of what was happening made any sense.

"Why won't you look at me, Dad?"

Zao turned his head to face his daughter.

"You knew it would happen," she said again.

"I did not."

"Why is it happening again? Why?" Admira yelled at her father.

Zao didn't answer.

"You have to know why," she pleaded.

Zao stared down at the kitchen table.

"If *you* don't know, Dad, if no one knows, how will it stop?"

Once more Zao did not answer.

By his silence, Zao had given Admira his answer. She stared at her father, angry at him for not knowing the answer to her question. She pushed the chair away from the table, got up, and left the room. Tonya followed, unusually silent.

Zao raised his hand to one side of his face to cover his tears, not because he was embarrassed, but because he couldn't bear for his wife, his woman, to see the shame and guilt he felt as a man. His shame was for each man who was leading this parade of death. He raised his head. Zena gripped his hand and kissed it. She could no longer hold back her own tears while she held onto her husband saying.

"Why, when they know better, do they incite this age-old hatred and fear, that has always taken hold of the lives of every Serbian, Muslim, and Croatian?"

Zao knew. The situation had become unstoppable. All of their leaders were stoking the flames of ethnic nationalism, which he knew would lead to "ethnic cleansing."

Chapter Thirteen

Without telling her that they were coming, Bosko, Admira, Biljes, and Miro showed up on Vail's doorstep. Two nights had passed since they'd first read the letter.

"Oh my God, you guys. What a surprise. What are you doing here? Come on in." They entered the house single file as she hugged them. "I'm so glad you came. I've been on pins and needles waiting for another letter from Mats. Come on in. Let's have some coffee. It's only Mom and me at home. Dad's off doing his thing, spending time at work even on the weekend." Vails disappeared into the kitchen. Bosko and the others sat quietly together in the living room. Vails yelled out from the kitchen, "He's being such a monster not writing to me. Maybe he plans to surprise me and that's why he hasn't. What do you guys think?"

Bosko lowered his head, unable to answer. The sound of the cabinets being open and shut stopped. Her friends turned their heads toward the kitchen entrance and saw Vails leaning against the wall staring at them. Admira and Biljana got up and approached Valencia, who started to tremble. The shaking got worse as they came closer. The moment Admira and Biljana hugged her she let out a primal cry.

"No... no... no... no!"

Bosko pressed his face into his palms. His tears flowed and wouldn't stop. Vails pushed her friends away so she could look at Admira and Biljana for a moment before she stared at Bosko.

"Tell me," she said.

"He's dead, Valencia."

Valencia's body stiffened.

After hearing what she was certain was her daughter weeping, her mother did what many mothers do. She instinctively went to her side to comfort her. She knew instantly as she sat next to

Valencia what had happened.

"No, it's not true. He wrote to me just a couple of months ago. Mats said he missed me and was going to do everything to come back. It's not true. I have the letter." Vails went to a bureau, pulled open a drawer, and took out a folded sheet of paper. "See? It's right here. He's alive. Don't you say he's not. Don't you dare! Mats is not dead," she screamed.

"Vails, with all my heart I wish it weren't true," Bosko said, his voice cracking.

"But I have his letter," she said, running up to Bosko and waving it in his face. "He's not dead. He's coming back to me. See, it's in here because he said so."

"I also have a letter." Bosko reached into his jacket pocket and handed it to her. "It was delivered to me two days ago."

Valencia held the two pages in her trembling hands.

She began to read, and then let out a wail from the pit of her soul. Bosko and her friends closed their eyes and lowered their heads, while they listened to Valencia weep uncontrollably.

"It can't be. He's in Dubrovnik," she said vehemently.

"Vails, I wish it wasn't," said Bosko.

"But—we were all so sure Mats was coming back. I could feel it. I knew he was coming back. This can't be true. I don't believe it. It's a cruel joke. I know it is."

"Vails." Bosko got up from his chair and knelt next to her. Taking her hand in his he said, "With all of my heart I wish it wasn't true. For two days, I've kept telling myself it's a dream. I'm going to wake up and feel like we all do after we've woken up from a bad dream. I'll say, 'Oh thank you God, it was only a dream.' But it isn't, and I don't know why it happened. No one I ask will ever be able to give you or me or any of us the reason why it happened."

"I'm sorry, so sorry for every bad thing I ever said about Mats. I never meant any of those things, Vails. You have to believe me. I didn't," Miro said, tears streaming down his cheeks.

"I know that, Miro, and so did Mats."

Miro turned his head away and Biljana comforted him as she listened to his muffled sobs.

"It wasn't supposed to happen this way," Valencia said. Her voice was frail. "We were supposed to go to that exact spot when you all met to come to that first party. Every New Year's Eve we were going to have a drink on that exact spot, until we grew old and couldn't do it anymore."

"What am I to do now?"

"Survive. It's what we all must do," Miroslav said quietly.

She looked up at Miro. His words were never truer than at that moment. She reached out to embrace her friends.

"I just don't understand why," Vails repeated. "He has to come back to me because he promised. He promised me."

No one was able to make any sense of the new reality of their world.

"I don't understand... Why? Why did it have to happen?"

Admira had once said to Bosko, "Who among us would want that time to come back? The time that our parents and grandparents never want to talk about, or when they do, their eyes always fill up with tears and a silent rage? If that past is the future being offered to you in your dreams by Milošević and the others, in reality who would want it? Would our friends want it? Can you think of anyone who would?"

In the quiet of her living room, Vails and her friends sat silent, unable to comprehend the meaning of their lives.

＊

Valencia sat on her bedroom floor holding Matko's last letter to her.

My dearest Valencia,

I am so tired of everything. Nothing is the same. I am out of place here. It all feels foreign, and I long to be back with you. That's all that can make me happy. Dubrovnik is beautiful, but I don't feel like I'm Croatian like my father. I miss my city. People are very tense and afraid here. They don't know what to do.

My father keeps telling my mother that everything will be all right. This is just a phase that we have to go through. He says that since we are all ethnically the same, we need to have our own country. He says it is good for our future, that there will be a Croatia, but such things can't happen without great cost.

I feel so afraid, Valencia. You are the only one I can tell and not feel ashamed. I think Bosko knew how afraid I was about leaving. If something should happen to me, please, please, don't ever think I didn't love you, that I abandoned you. It was the hardest thing I've ever done, walking away from your love. But if I hadn't gone with my family, I'd feel more ashamed now than I do for feeling afraid about the future. You must do everything to stay alive no matter what happens. Live!

Who knows, maybe these thoughts I have about the future are all wrong and we will laugh over this letter in years to come. Maybe Miro and Bosko are right and we shouldn't expect the devil to come when we haven't seen him yet. Tell those two that I miss them very much. But nothing matters to me more than you.

I ache at nights because I can't hold you. I will do everything in my power to come back and be in your arms. I've already started my next letter to you. It's in my thoughts just waiting to be written. I will love you... always and always.

Mats

"Valencia," her mother called as she pushed open the door to her room. "What are you doing? We're leaving. Get packed. My God girl, this is not the time for you to be reading your—" She looked at Valencia, who had her arms wrapped around her knees and was rocking back and forth. "Oh, my baby." She knelt beside her daughter. "We have to do this. It's our only chance."

Valencia nodded through her tears and looked up as her mother said, "So many of our friends have already left or simply disappeared from Sarajevo, and nobody knows where they've gone."

Sarajevo's citizens were emigrating. It was only the beginning. Soon there would be a desperate attempt by hordes of people to leave while they could. Anyone who was able, through whatever means possible, was making arrangements to abandon their homes. Lives were being severed and families torn apart in a desperate bid to stay alive before whatever happened, happened. But what was going to happen, no one knew. No matter where you were in the city people kept hearing of a calamity that was fast approaching, but no one knew what it was because it was without shape, breath, or being.

"We'll come back. You'll see. Everything will be like it was before. Our friends will still be here. You'll see, nothing will have changed."

Valencia remained silent. She didn't believe in anything anymore. It was all words with no meaning.

"Slavenka, what's going on?" Valencia's father asked as he burst into the room and saw them both sitting on the floor. She made a motion for him to leave while she comforted their daughter. He appeared worried. "We have very little time. We're not waiting for your friends to show up."

Valencia's mother held her daughter close as Vails clasped Matko's letter to her chest. It was her most precious possession.

"I have no one, Mother, no one. The only man I've loved is dead. And I'm abandoning the only thing left that keeps his memory alive, Sarajevo. We have nothing to believe in anymore, nothing to be proud of."

"We have each other and our lives. Isn't that worth something to you?"

"We're leaving because Dad is an official and he has used every channel available to get us out. All our friends whose fathers are officials have done the same. All that secretive business he wouldn't talk about, disappearing at night for meetings, was to get us out of here. He was making deals." Valencia wiped her wet cheeks with her sleeve.

"Would you rather stay? He has information that no one else has, and yes, he has channels open to him that most people do not. That is why we are able to go. It may seem wrong that he can leave while others can't, but Vails, I can live with that guilt for the rest of my life. I could never continue living if anything were to happen to you."

"So we must give no explanations to those who are staying. Even Ruza and her family have already disappeared without saying goodbye. Sentimentality is a luxury these days. I am a coward. We are all cowards," Vails cried.

"No, you are not. We are not," her mother said. "We must live. You must live. The train lines have already been blocked with so many desperate people trying to escape. Anyone who is able to leave is doing so any way they can. You are my only child and I will not allow anything to happen to you while I still breathe. Plus, we are all your father has in this world."

"Valencia," her father said entering her room, "Admira and Bosko are here."

Valencia placed Matko's letter on top of her open suitcase. Matko had told her to live. She'd do her best. *No matter what. Live.*

"I'm sorry, so sorry." Valencia began crying as soon as she saw her friends waiting for her in the living room.

"No, Valencia, you mustn't be sorry." Admira embraced her. Against her father's wishes, Valencia had broken her promise to him and called Admira to tell her that they were all leaving

166

Sarajevo. She couldn't run away without telling her best friends. She wouldn't do it.

Bosko shook hands with Valencia's parents and Franjo embraced him. "Take care of yourself." It wasn't lost on him that a Croatian father was telling him, a young Serbian, to be careful. Valencia's father caught a glimpse of Admira and his daughter. "Sarajevo has always had the most beautiful girls," he said. Franjo embraced Admira and whispered into her ear, "Stay safe."

"I'll never let anything separate Bosko and me," she answered.

He stared into her eyes and felt the certainty of her words. "No, I don't believe you ever will. Can I get you and Bosko something to drink before we go?" he said.

Admira smiled at Franjo's good manners, remembering to be a good host even at this time when they were about to abandon their city and leave all of their worldly possessions behind. She and Bosko shook their heads. There was nothing that they needed.

"Then please excuse us. We have some last minute details to attend to." The tone of his voice said there was not much time left to say their goodbyes. They would be gone soon. Franjo's eyes showed no shame for the strings he had pulled and the officials he had bribed. He was left with very little money to start a new life with his family, but they would be alive and safe. His family came first, above all else.

"Let's sit." Admira motioned Valencia to the couch. "Everything will be okay. Think of it as only a vacation."

Valencia stared at the floor and nodded. "I called Biljes, but no one answered so I called Miro, and no one picked up there either. I don't know where they are. Several times I called and left messages. Have you seen them?"

"No," replied Bosko. "I'm sure Miro's with Biljes; they're fine, not to worry."

"I can't believe I'm not going to see them before I leave."

"Where are you going?" Admira asked.

"All my dad keeps saying is *west*."

"Vails," Admira said, "we'll tell Miro and Biljes. They'll understand."

"No, they won't. We're just leaving, running away as if it doesn't matter that Sarajevo was our home. We're leaving everything. Everyone we love. We can take only one suitcase each. I haven't said goodbye to anyone, to any of our friends. Dad wouldn't let me. I dropped to my knees and begged him to let me call you and Biljes. I just couldn't leave without seeing you and saying goodbye."

Bosko knelt by the sofa and said, "Thank you."

"For what, Bosko?"

"For caring enough to call us."

Valencia hugged Bosko tightly and he embraced her.

"He's doing the right thing, Vails."

"I know you don't mean that, Bosko."

"Vails. He's your father, and it's his job to keep you and your mom safe. It's good that your father is taking you out of Sarajevo. At least we'll know that you're safe."

"We've been on a list," she said with a terrible sense of guilt. "My dad has been waiting to get the word. He got it today and just like that, we're running away. You have to believe me, Admira, he made me swear not to tell anyone what was happening. I gave him my word. I'm sorry." Valencia's crying turned into sobs.

Admira held her. "You must go and be with your family. Whatever happens, when it is over we will be back together. All of us. You'll be back and we'll be here."

Valencia smiled. "You don't hate me? Admira, please don't hate me."

"Vails, how could you ever think that?"

168

"What will you and Bosko do if..."

"We'll be together... whatever happens."

Bosko thought of his father, who had worked for the United Nations. *If he were still alive, would he have done the same as Valencia's father and gotten his family out of Sarajevo?* Bosko knew one thing: he would never have left without Admira.

"Please don't let anything happen to you and Admira. Promise me. Promise me. You are all I have left."

"We will always be together. I promise you," Bosko said, holding her hand.

"Valencia," her father said, "it's time. We cannot be late." Franjo rolled out his daughter's suitcase.

"I want to give you something." Valencia began a desperate search for something inside her suitcase.

Admira stroked Valencia's hair and then, holding on to both of her hands, said, "Vails, bring us back something from wherever you end up. We'll be waiting."

Valencia hugged them. This could not be happening. How could her family be leaving Sarajevo? What a tragedy for friendships to be severed, with no tomorrows to think of.

Bosko shook her father's hand once more, then he kissed Valencia's mother on the cheek. "Good luck."

"Good luck to you and Admira," Valencia's mother said with tears in her eyes.

"I love you, I love you, I love you," Valencia murmured, hugging Admira again.

"Shh," Admira said. "We'll be together someday soon, you'll see."

Valencia looked at Admira and asked, while wiping away her tears, "Does your dad still bring a piece of coal and a loaf of bread to your mom on New Year's Eve?"

"Yes, he always does."

"I hope he never stops."

169

"Valencia, please, we have no time left," said her father in desperation.

Bosko and Admira walked to the door.

"Take care of yourself, son. With all my heart I wish you and your family the best."

"Thank you, sir."

Admira slid her hand into Bosko's. They knew they'd already spent too long on goodbyes. It was time for them to run.

"Remember me," Valencia said.

Bosko stopped at the entrance of the door. He and Admira turned and waved.

"Love you." Admira's voice was soft.

Valencia nodded and wept as she watched her two best friends disappear from sight and out of her life. The door shut and she began to sob uncontrollably. She heard Admira and Bosko crying and hoped they could also hear her.

*

Her dad sat across the aisle from his wife and daughter with a sense of indescribable joy. He'd upheld the ultimate responsibility of a father and a husband—keeping his family safe. His wife reached across the narrow aisle of the bus and held onto his hand. He looked at Valencia sitting next to her mother with her head bowed, crying. All of his daughter's tears meant nothing to him because he knew when the monster and its gaping jaws finally showed its face, it would devour his city, but not them.

Some of the passengers sat in silence and shock; tears rolled down their cheeks. For others, the guilt and relief of being able to leave created nervous laughter and an inability to sit still. Relatives, exhausted from crying, standing outside on the pavement, blew kisses to their families. They called out to them and mouthed the words to phone, write, or to simply remember them. Some reached up and touched the bus windows and were in turn touched on the other side of the glass by the hands of loved ones.

Suddenly an elderly woman on the sidewalk, a stranger, placed her hand against the window next to Valencia.

Valencia did the same, meeting finger against finger, palm against palm. Valencia rested her forehead against the glass and began to weep. The elderly woman smiled and shook her head as if to tell her not to cry. Her facial expression told the story without words, begging Valencia and everyone on the bus not to forget those left behind.

The driver closed the door and started the engine, causing a pathetic wail from inside the bus and out.

Valencia's cry broke through the quiet sobs on the bus. "This cannot be happening!"

Hands that had been pressed against the glass lowered into laps as passengers turned to look away from the window. Peering through her own fingers still pressed against the glass, Valencia saw her world, the last images of Sarajevo, through a rose-tinted window.

Chapter Fourteen

Six weeks later

Zao couldn't take his eyes off a newspaper photograph taken by a journalist in the summer of 1991. The photo was of Slobodan Milošević, leader of Serbia, and Franjo Tuđjman, the Croatian leader. Both men were walking with Alija Izetbegović, once a political prisoner and now Bosnia's president, who stood between the two them as all three strolled along a deserted, sun- drenched beach somewhere in the Adriatic.

Zao turned to Zena. "This journalist is right in what he says. Look at how only the two of them are smiling, like barracuda. The more I look at it, the more it appears true. I'm sure Alija wasn't aware that as they walked he was really being led toward the water's edge, as if he were about to be drowned. It's what the journalist also saw and what he wrote."

Tuđjman and Milošević had completed their war with each other and had signed a peace agreement ending combat operations. The more Zao studied the photo, the clearer the image became. It could have been Hitler and Stalin in that photo, leading Chamberlain to the water's edge. Both Hitler and Stalin knew they were going to go to war, but they weren't ready. First, they had to sign a non-aggression pact because they were going to carve up Poland between the two of them. Milošević and Tuđjman had already had their war and now had peace. Only one other place was left to carve up in what remained of Yugoslavia.

"Alija has only two choices: seek independence for us in Bosnia or join with Milošević." Zao kept pounding his fist on the kitchen table. Zena finally grabbed his arm to stop him, and they sat there holding onto each other. Both realized that either choice would be fatal for all remaining, in the one place left for them to carve up: Bosnia Herzegovina.

Chapter Fifteen

March 1992

The evening was cool with a breeze blowing down the mountainside. The leaves from the poplar, birch, and ash trees rustled in the wind like chimes. Bosko had been talking to Admira on the phone throughout the day. They had argued and she kept insisting, but he was unyielding. Under no circumstance was she to attempt to come into the city.

The mood in many of the neighborhoods of the city itself teetered on a strange and undeclared truce between Serbs and Muslims. Sarajevo had been given a respite. A week prior, a Serbian wedding party had been held in a predominantly Muslim enclave of Sarajevo, on the first day of March. Throughout the day, wedding guests waved the Serbian flag in celebration. Out of nowhere a sniper had fired shots at the wedding guests, killing the father of the groom and wounding a guest.

Tempers flared and barricades went up blocking entry into Serb and also Muslim neighborhoods in Sarajevo. Within a few days, the barricades came down in the city. Residents knew they were sitting on a powder keg and the only thing missing was the spark to ignite it.

Bosko and Admira sat in silence, waiting for the other one to say something.

She spoke first. "I can't stand the silence, Bosh. I want to hear your voice."

"I don't know what more to say. No one knows anything more than what the radio or television tells us. The papers tell us to have hope and trust in modern society, not medieval ways. Most of them say it won't come to that. I think they're right, at least I hope they are. I wish my father were here. I'm not as strong as he was."

"You are your father's son. And you are just as strong."

175

"You think so?"

"I know so. I want us to do something," Admira said. Her tone wasn't happy but neither was it desperate. "I want us to talk about the future, about children. And about the everyday things we used to talk about when we got excited about having fun together. We've stopped doing that—why?"

"I don't know."

"Well, we're going to start doing it again. It's the future that counts. Nothing else."

"You're right."

"There is something else I want us to do."

"Whatever you want."

"I want to go to Vilsonovo Avenue the first moment the lime trees begin to bloom. It's only a few months from now. We always did that. I want you to stick the leaves in my hair like you always did before. Will you?"

"Of course."

"Their fragrance makes my soul feel calm. And makes me want to think of things as simple as children's laughter and homemade soup and cutting tomatoes and feeding you the slices. I can't help thinking of sentimental things or of a secret you once shared with me when I breathe in that fragrance. It makes me want to make love to you and never stop."

She gripped the phone even tighter. "It makes me think about everything that is still beautiful about Sarajevo."

"On that first day when the lime trees are in bloom, we will be there."

"You promise?"

"Absolutely."

Admira closed her eyes as she stood at her living room window. In the distance, the lights of Sarajevo flickered. In her mind's eye she saw Bosko standing on his balcony looking at her. She pressed her lips against the phone, wishing she were standing a hair's breadth away from him. "Good night, crusader, till the end of days."

176

Chapter Sixteen

April 5, 1992

"It's eight o'clock, Bosko. How come you're dressed up so early?"

"Good morning, Mom," he replied, and he took his place at the table with Rita. She placed a mug of tea in front of him and sitting across from him sipped her tea in silence, not taking her eyes off her son.

"Where are you going?" she asked, sounding a little apprehensive.

"There is a march—"

"Bosko."

"Hundreds, maybe thousands, will be there. It's a march for peace, and I'm going to be there in the thick of it."

"Don't do this. These things always turn out badly. Please."

"Mom, I walk past the Grand Hotel Europa almost every day and you know what I see not far from the entrance? Crowds of men selling sniper rifles, Kalashnikovs, bazookas, and handguns of every description to anyone with the cash. Every day for months they've been doing this and no one stops them. All it does is feed into the growing paranoia of every Muslim, Croat, and Serb in Sarajevo who fears for his survival. Everyone has begun to suspect the worst from his neighbor. So what should I do, Mom? Hide in this apartment? For how long? Till what happens?"

Rita frowned. She knew whatever she said would fall on deaf ears.

"This is how you want me to make my voice heard—by doing nothing?"

"The city is unstable. Crowds and marches will only make things worse."

"If we don't do this and show them that we are willing to

177

die—"

Rita jumped up from her chair and slammed her mug down on the table. "Don't you ever say that to me again," she screamed at Bosko. "Do you understand? Not ever. How dare you."

"Mom, I just—"

"What?" asked Rita, tears forming in her eyes.

"I just can't do nothing."

Rita walked over to Bosko and held his face between her hands. "Don't you ever say that word to me again. I brought you into this world to live. Do you understand? To live."

"I'm sorry. I just want you to know how important this is to me."

"Bosko, it's—"

"It's time I do something to make my voice heard. I have to."

What Bosko and his fellow Sarajevan citizens were unable to see at the moment were the 260 tanks, 120 mortars, anti-aircraft cannons, sniper rifles, and small arms too numerous to count, in the hills encircling the city. All in the hands of those comprising the newly formed Army of Republika Srpska, thousands of men who were once soldiers of the former Yugoslav People's Army. Their ranks were now also filled with Serb Orthodox officers and eager young recruits from various other areas of Bosnia and Herzegovina. And amongst this pack of wolves were many hundreds of foreign Orthodox Christian volunteers, many of whom had come from as far away as Russia. They were all being led by General Ratko Mladić.

No view of the city was hidden from someone behind a gun turret, or from someone with a finger on a trigger. Citizens of Sarajevo on the streets and in their homes, museums, churches and mosques, the marketplace, cemeteries, and hospitals were all in their sights.

Earlier in the year, Bosko and every Sarajevan had witnessed Radovan Karadžić, with help from Milošević, use his supporters and militias to set up barricades in neighborhoods throughout the city, in effect Balkanizing Sarajevo. His group had even taken control of a central police station. Yet he'd also seen firsthand, when he had approached the barricades manned by Muslims or Serbs, that there was an absolute reluctance within both groups to confront one another openly on the streets or when any Muslim or Serbian needed to pass through the barricades.

Mothers, wives, and daughters set up barbecue, cheese, and pie barricades. Anyone who wanted to walk through, regardless of nationality, had to take a bite before proceeding. There were even cigarette barricades created and credit provided by the vendors to their customers.

Bosko at times wanted to laugh because he saw people cover their heads with stockings so that their neighbors passing by wouldn't recognize them as guarding the barricades. When the barricades were taken down after just a few days, Bosko ventured out again to see what was happening in his city. As he passed many of the cafes, he would hear a song, "A Stocking on Your Face," constantly being sung by Sarajevans, both Muslim and Serbian, who were on opposite sides just a few days ago but were back again, drinking and hanging out as they always did at the cafes. This singing went on for weeks after the barricades came down. Like many other Sarajevans, Bosko and his mother remained convinced that peace would prevail and the worst events that had happened elsewhere would not happen in their city.

Bosko stepped out onto the sidewalk in front of his building. Once on the street, he watched groups of people walking together, some carrying banners heading to what he thought was a gathering point. One of the many signs being carried by demonstrators read: *No to extremists who think they can rule our lives.*

Jumping into the crowd, he was immediately overcome with the same exuberance he felt emanating from them. It was good to do *something.* The hour passed and more people joined the ranks of the marchers. Their numbers swelled into the thousands. They paraded toward the Holiday Inn that had become the Serbian Democratic Party headquarters. Its co-founder, Radovan Karadžić, was seen by many Sarajevans as an extremist of the worst kind. This peace march was one way to let *Karadžić* and other extremists know that in the end, they would not prevail. Civilians would take control of the former Yugoslav Army.

Bosko remembered one of Mats's favorite quotes: "The only thing necessary for the triumph of evil is for good men to do nothing."

"I'm here, Mats," whispered Bosko under his breath. "I hope you're proud of me."

The throng of thousands continued toward the Holiday Inn. Some were singing, others laughing. Many chanted, "Peace will prevail."

Bosko noticed how the white clouds sailed along effortlessly across a blue sky. The momentum of the crowd remained steady. Nothing could stop them now. A young man his age walking alongside him started to chant, "Peace will prevail." Bosko hadn't stopped. The sound of hundreds of men and women chanting the same words produced a conviction among them that yes, peace would prevail. Some in the crowd held hands, others locked their arms together, and others had their arms around each other's waists. They moved as one mass of people possessed of an unshakable belief that they were not going to allow their lives to descend into a barbaric hell.

Bosko locked his arms with the young man next to him. He was overcome with the same exuberance and conviction that had overcome the throngs of people that were now in the thousands. And Bosko felt another emotion—anger. It was brought on by the realization that he and his family and everything and everyone he loved could at any moment be taken away from him. In his thoughts he heard himself say, "that will not happen. I will not let it happen."

He turned to the young man at his side as they both chanted. They were smiling almost to the point of laughing out loud. Yes, they were unstoppable, they were indeed going to prevail over their leaders who were seeking to divide Serb, Muslim, and Croatian. The same leaders who were setting them upon each other's throats.

Out of nowhere, a roar was heard. It was coming from the throngs of men and women who were far ahead of him and the people around him. The movement of the crowd slowed. People in front of him started to look around and peered above each other's heads to see what had happened. Why had they slowed down? Then a second sound broke into the air. It was wasn't a sound made by people. Seconds later the same sound was heard. Everyone near Bosko looked around, thinking they were imagining it. It was real. Shots were being fired. Bosko looked at the young man who stood next to him, both of them feeling as if the world as they knew it, had ceased to exist. Bosko stood still; the air around him felt fresh and clear and so breathable. It was because the massive crowd had dispersed and they were no longer huddled together. Instead, they were all running in every direction, looking as if they were thousands of beads that had scattered after being dropped onto a floor. People ran in every possible direction, yelling and screaming to friends and strangers to do the same.

The young man who was next to him grabbed Bosko's arm and dragged him along. Soon they were both running as fast as they could to nowhere in particular. They could both hear the sound of gunfire. It seemed to be coming from every direction.

The seconds and minutes passed, and soon the entire city seemed to be in utter chaos and pandemonium as thousands of people scattered, not knowing if they were running toward or away from the Serb snipers, who were hidden in hotel rooms at the Holiday Inn.

Finally, at one point Bosko realized he was running by himself. The young man whom he'd met briefly and with whom he hadn't exchanged any words, only the experience of that brief moment of feeling, together, invincible in their cause, was no longer beside him. The yelling and screaming of thousands of people running in every direction saturated the air. To run home like he was some young boy who'd been beaten up in the school yard seemed cowardly to Bosko. He wanted to run toward those who were firing into the crowd and rip off their heads.

"Run, boy, run," an elderly man repeated desperately as he ran while trying to push Bosko along. "Run!" he said, staring into Bosko's eyes. Everything had happened so quickly. His body began to shake out of anger, out of fear, out of desperation. But as he ran, Bosko realized he wasn't afraid for himself—he was afraid for the future. He felt the panic of some inevitable fate that was about to engulf them all. His mind was overwhelmed with thoughts that he could not make any sense of, as the adrenaline pumped though his body. His heart was beating furiously. Bosko ran past familiar bakery shops, pharmacies, and office buildings, and as he did it seemed to him that he was running in slow motion. He noticed the smallest details of random things, like the letters on the signs of stores, the colors of doors, the clean plate- glass windows of shops, and even the cracks on the sidewalk as he kept running. Bosko saw a young woman who had been knocked to the ground by the running mob. He grabbed hold of her and lifted her off the pavement. They were both shaking.

"Thank you," she was barely able to say. She left Bosko standing by himself and began to run, disappearing into the crowd.

Bosko felt like a coward as he watched the countless, faceless people run, some of whom had been shot and may have ended up paying with their lives for their beliefs. He'd waited too long. He should have been marching a long time ago. Matko's words came back to haunt him.

The only thing necessary for the triumph of evil is for good men to do nothing.

Chapter Seventeen

Bosko made it home unharmed. Since that moment of seeing her son enter the apartment, Rita's whole body hadn't stopped shaking. She still trembled as she stood at the kitchen counter trying to serve them their dinner. Holding onto a large wooden spoon, she shook uncontrollably. Bosko stood silently at the doorway watching his mother, whose back was turned to him. Rita burst into tears again. He knew that her only thought was of what could have happened to him. The spoon fell out of her hand, and she pressed a hand to her mouth to muffle the sound of her sobs.

"Mom." Bosko walked into the kitchen and embraced her. She couldn't stop herself from crying. "It's okay." He held onto his mother. "I'm here with you."

She kept nodding. Bosko was safe beside her, was Rita's only thought.

They ate dinner without much conversation. Later, he helped clear and wash the dishes. Rita left him in the living room and went to her bedroom.

Admira had called, extremely worried by the news of the shooting and other instances of violence that had erupted. Six people had been shot and killed who had marched in the crowd and several others had been badly wounded. At first, Bosko was not going to tell her that he'd been in the crowd marching and chanting. He didn't want to worry her. What was there to be concerned about if he'd been safe and cozy, locked up in his apartment with his mother?

So many Muslims, Croatians, and Serbs were acting with courage, throughout what was once Yugoslavia trying to protect each other and paying for it with their lives. What Bosko had done wasn't brave at all, and nowhere near what could have been thought of as courageous. He finally admitted to Admira that he'd been part of the march.

A long silence followed while she listened to his account of the events. He told her everything, about what he'd done and why. She finally broke her silence by saying in a soft yet firm voice, "I will keep my promise and wait for that moment when I can see you again. But this you must promise me. Whatever you do from now on, you do it with me. Promise me. Say it."

"Together—I promise."

"Say it again."

"I promise."

*

Bosko sat on the sofa in the dark and became mesmerized by the flickering light emanating from the TV. A bright blue and white light illuminated the room while he stared at the blurred, flickering image of the anchorman informing all Sarajevans of the day's events. The city's residents had now become like Roman gladiators, who were inexorably bound to live and die in an arena. Tonight's broadcast provided the list of the first casualties.

Olga Sučić and Suada Dilberović had been shot and killed by Serbian snipers. Olga was a thirty-three-year-old Croatian woman, and Suada was a twenty-three-year-old Bosniak medical student at the University of Sarajevo. These two women were now dead, along with Nikola Gardović, a groom's father killed at a Serb wedding on March 1, 1992; they had become the first casualties of an insane play being acted out in front of Bosko and every Sarajevan. He kept listening to the sound of gunfire breaking up the quiet of a city that seemed to be slipping into some dark hole of despair. Where the shooting was coming from, he had no way of knowing.

Bosko turned off the TV and all of the lights in the apartment. His mother's bedroom door was shut. He began to pace about in the darkness of the living room. So many other thousands of Sarajevans were doing the same at this very moment, all of them not knowing the meaning of what had begun outside on the streets of their darkened city. Bosko stopped and stood in front of the window and peered out into the night. He imagined the thousands of eyes that were doing the same. A gun battle was taking place in his city between two or more sides, none of whom could be seen. Bosko watched the night being lit up by the use of tracer ammunition used for nighttime gun battles.

His heart began to pound. The sound of the gun battles taking place on the streets below his apartment made him want to be a part of it. It made him want to hunt down those who had fired into the crowd. He kept listening to the sound of gunfire when he thought he heard the sound of muffled voices yelling out. He ran to the balcony, slid open the glass doors carefully, just a few inches, and pressed his ear against the opening.

"Run back," he heard a voice yell out. It was coming from somewhere on the street below.

Another voice yelled, "No, this way."

Bosko easily recognized the sound of a Yugo M70 on auto mode being fired in an attempt to keep "the enemy" in one place, and behind cover. It was the beginning sound of a war. How could all of this be happening? How can a war just begin? And as he asked himself that, he heard his mother's words: "It just happened, Bosko. Wars just happen."

"Wars don't just happen," he had responded angrily to his mother, and yet here he was watching it occur outside of his window, listening to the unmistakable sound of it.

"Back, back there!" a number of voices yelled out as the sound of gunfire tore open the silence of a Sarajevan night. He looked out at the neighboring buildings and across the expanse of his city and Bosko saw the bright red and white light of multiple explosions taking place. Parts of Sarajevo were being bombed heavily, and like a swarm of locusts an onslaught of bullets of every caliber kept hitting and piercing or ricocheting off the thin walls of apartment buildings or the stone façades of office buildings. Glass was being shattered and death had descended upon Sarajevo. The shouts of its victims couldn't be heard, only the sound of their killers.

Explosions of shells from heavier guns were increasing, a prelude to a still unheard requiem. This night a darkness unlike any other had overwhelmed Sarajevo. In that darkness, Sarajevans heard the beating heart of their own fears.

Bosko stared out at the silent moon in a cloudless sky. He kept repeating her name—Admira. He stretched his arms out in front of him and pressed his hands against the glass, now terrified out of his mind for Admira, and for his mother. What future would they have had, what would have happened to either of them, if a bullet had struck him at the march? What would his mother have done if that had happened to him? He would have left them with the image of him lying in the street, his blood pouring out of him while people ran screaming, no one to help him, dying alone? What would it have been like for his mother to find him that way? Or Admira?

Bosko swore to himself that whatever future was in store for him, for Admira, for his mother, he would protect them with his life and he would face it with all of the courage he possessed.

A hand rested on his shoulder. He instinctively wrapped his arm around his mother and together they stared out into their city. Into oblivion.

"It's begun, hasn't it?" He turned and frowned at his mother. She nodded in silence.

The shouts of strangers coming from the streets below continued into the night.

PART FOUR

Chapter Eighteen

April 6, 1992

Admira and her family stood in the backyard looking toward Sarajevo. What they saw defied reality. In the distance, explosions went off one after the other. All through the night and early morning, they had listened to the faint sound of explosions coming from the city, four miles away, sounds that didn't make any sense. Sounds that were out of place in their city of palaces that was surrounded by tranquil forests and pristine mountains. Yet as they stood huddled together looking toward Sarajevo, they became numb by what they saw. White mushroom clouds emerged instantly after the explosion of a shell, popping up like pieces of popcorn every other second. The sound took a few seconds to reach the ears of everyone in their neighborhood, who were now standing in their backyards watching the destruction of their city.

Zena placed her arm around Tonya and pulled her tightly to her side. Watching the destruction of Sarajevo felt at that moment as if she were standing on a street corner and was watching helplessly as a stranger ripped her daughter out of her arms, dragging her away to suffer a horrible end.

Admira's first and only thought was for Bosko and his mother. She watched the rising and increasing amounts of black smoke reach up into the sky. She looked in the direction of the Theatre Arts Building where she and Bosko had met on that first New Year's morning, and saw large plumes of white smoke rising. Her heart sank. It was being destroyed at this very moment as she stood in her backyard, helpless to do anything. The scent caused by what had now become hundreds of explosions occurring throughout Sarajevo remained like a thin membrane that hung

189

over the city. It was a reminder to all Sarajevans of what their future had now become. They were all trapped in Sarajevo, with no chance of escape. The stench of death would now mingle with the smell of exploding shells. In Admira's thoughts, she saw the images of mothers and fathers clutching their children as they ran down familiar streets and alleyways, trying to escape the gunfire and the next exploding shell. In her heart Admira felt the slow accumulation of the death of the city's citizens taking place; they all did, as they stood in silence looking out into the distance at an unbelievable sight. But it was in fact real, it was happening.

"Bosko is okay," said Zao, turning to his eldest. He could see how her mind was racing and how at any moment she would have plunged herself headlong, running into Sarajevo. Zao held onto Admira's hand and, squeezing it, said, "He will be okay. He will protect Rita. She needs her son now more than ever."

"Dad?" Tonya's tone was somewhere between asking a question and stating an unbelievable fear. Tears filled Zena's eyes. A huge pit had opened up in Zao's heart.

"Admira, where are you going?" her father asked as she walked away.

She didn't answer; she was determined to get to Bosko.

Her father grabbed her. "Admira. Stop."

Zena and her sister joined them.

"He's fine. Bosko is safe," Zao said, determined to prevent his daughter from leaving their home. Tonya wrapped her arms around her sister and kept pulling her back. "Don't go, please don't go," she pleaded, holding onto Admira with all of her might, whose own embrace grew tighter around Tonya with every passing second. Many families from their neighborhood stood together, each in their own backyards, not fully realizing that they had been thrust into a reality without meaning, without hope.

Turning to his wife, who was already by his side still clutching on to her youngest, Zao felt the sharpest pain in his chest when he realized that on the 6th of April, 1945, Sarajevo was liberated from the fascist occupation during WWII. And now on the same day, forty-seven years later, on the 6th of April, 1992, Sarajevo had become engulfed in yet another war.

The siege of Sarajevo had begun.

*

Early the next morning, Sarajevo was filled with the silence of the dead. Admira was beside herself. She desperately wanted to leave and go into Sarajevo to make sure that Bosko and his mom were okay. But her father would stop her. Her whole family would prevent her by every means possible from leaving her home. So she had to wait; but for how long could she stay away from Sarajevo, not knowing if Bosko and his mother were safe? The phones had gone dead. No one knew when and if they would be able to speak to Bosko. Restless and unable to sleep, she had come down from her room and remained in the hallway leading to the kitchen, after hearing her parents speaking softly as they sat at the kitchen table.

"It feels like some conspiracy has always existed against our city. Fate toys with us, Zena, it always has—always," Zao said. "Like Troy, we seem doomed, not once, but over and over again to repeat over and over again what we cannot stop ourselves from doing. Gravilo Princip in grandfather's time initiated the Great War in Sarajevo. Now, here we are, not even a hundred years later, and another war has begun, again started by a Serb in the same city. What is the madness in these people? What is our collective Slavic fear that runs so deep that generations upon generations suffer for it?"

Zao rested his hand on his wife's shoulder. Neither of them had an answer, and even if they did, it would not matter nor would it affect whatever future lay in store for all of them. Yet like

191

Zao and his wife, so many Yugoslavs had let themselves believe, as they had rebuilt their nation after a brutal barbaric war, that maybe they had finally succumbed to a peace that would last. But all it had been, these forty-seven years since the last war, was a brief respite from their age-old hatreds for one another.

Admira crept closer toward the kitchen, pressing herself against the wall so as to listen to what her father was saying to her mother.

"Alija Izetbegović, our Bosnian president, do you know what he said not so long ago?"

Zena listened to her husband, who, like her, was terribly afraid for his family. She knew he was loath to have to pick up a gun and become part of the killing—but he would. She and Zao knew many would do it to protect their families in Sarajevo. They would do it at any and all costs.

"Alija said the choice to become an independent country or become part of a greater Serbia was like facing a choice between having leukemia or a brain tumor."

Zao knew whatever choice the president of Bosnia-Herzegovina was to make would be a catastrophe. He'd asked the European community for its recognition of an independent Bosnia barely four months ago, in December of 1991.

"There is one last irony to all of this."

Admira crept even closer toward the kitchen.

"Earlier today I heard on the TV that Alija Izetbegović's hopes have been realized. Twelve European community foreign ministers representing their respective governments recognized Bosnia-Herzegovina as a nation. Imagine that, Zena. Bosnia- Herzegovina is now a nation. Just like that, the Europeans say Bosnia is now a country. We are independent and free. What's that supposed to mean? That we can freely and independently get killed because the ones with the guns freely and independently shoot at us?"

Zao hadn't talked to anyone in the neighborhood since the bombardment of Sarajevo began. His neighbors had remained in their homes. No one mingled or exchanged words about what was happening. What could they say to one another, except repeat the same thoughts they were all having about the future?

The irony of her father's words made Admira feel sick to her stomach.

Zao slammed both his fists against the kitchen table. Zena moved closer toward her husband. She, like Zao, had realized what everyone would very soon come to realize: the lifting of that curtain of recognition for Bosnia and cities like Sarajevo lowered the blade on the pendulum that had now begun to slowly swing at the throat of every Bosnian and Sarajevan. An independent nation of Bosnia was an anathema to Serbian leaders Slobodan Milošević and Radovan Karadžić. It could never exist. It must never exist.

Today was April 6, which most times would be a beautiful spring day in Sarajevo. Today, Serbian General Ratko Mladić ordered the artillery to obliterate from memory this city surrounded by palaces. An independent Bosnia would be doomed.

Zao lowered his head onto his palms, which were resting on the kitchen table. Zena rested her head against his hunched-over back. And an absolute silence filled the room.

Admira quietly climbed the stairs back to her bedroom. She lay in bed staring at the ceiling. Tonya was still asleep beside her. She had left her own bedroom to be with her sister. Fear allowed her to sleep. It kept Admira awake. She hadn't seen or heard from Bosko for a couple of days. And it was too dangerous for either of them to leave their homes and travel the four miles each way. Lines of demarcation shifted and changed all the time. An area controlled by one group today, making it possible for people to move about, could change hands the next day, making safe passage no longer possible.

For now, she and her family were relatively safe because their home was not part of any area controlled by Serbs. It was located in a zone that had come under the control of one of Sarajevo's hastily put together militias, mainly comprised of Muslims and some Croatians. One of those militias was being led by a dangerous and vicious criminal named Mladjo. His ruthlessness as a gangster was unparalleled, and he used every ounce of it to fight back and kill whenever he and his gangster friends came upon Serbs who were taking part in the destruction of the city.

Districts within the city were now controlled by either Serbs or Muslims. The Yugoslav People's Army in Sarajevo was comprised of Serbs who had carried out attacks on the central tram depot and also on older districts of the city with mortars, artillery, and tank fire. They had also taken control of the airport. No place in Sarajevo was safe from bombardment or sniper fire.

Tonya slid her hand across the covers. Their fingers entwined. "Admira—are you awake?"

"Yes."

"Me too. What are you going to do?"

"I don't know."

*

Throughout the city, people had already begun to hoard and ration their food. Bosko made his second cup of tea using the same tea bag. He knew he could use it at least twice more. It was one small way of extracting as much from a food item as possible; other ways were soon to follow. During this time of uncertainty, all consumables were worth their weight in gold. It had only been a week since the shelling began, and all everyone could do was continue with their lives as best they could.

The amenities of life—electricity, running water, the telephone, all items taken for granted—would soon be practically nonexistent. The Serbian guns firing from the hills were dismantling Sarajevo's infrastructure. Nothing could be bought easily or cheaply anymore. Store shelves were empty. The first military rule of a siege was to have control of everything and everyone entering or leaving the city, to begin its slow strangulation leading to an agonizing death.

Rita entered the living room, and Bosko gave her his biggest Elvis smile. "I've made you tea with a fresh tea bag." Rita joined him at the dining room table. "We'll need to find some sleeping pills; there's too much of a racket going on." She sipped her tea in silence and studied her son across the table.

"You know I have to go," he said.

Rita said nothing.

"Mom, we've been holed up in the apartment for a couple of days. It has to end. I need to see what has happened and know what stores are still open. Where can we buy food and toilet paper? Is the bakery down the street open? Are there are any pharmacies left? I need to buy canned food if there's still any remaining on the store shelves. We have to know what kind of world is out there if we're to survive. All of our neighbors are out and about coping with whatever it is we are now facing. None of us has a choice. We have to survive.

"I'm the only one who can go; not you. Look at the clock on the wall. I'll be back at five o'clock—just seven hours from now."

"Bosko. You can't be out there for seven hours. I won't let you leave this apartment."

"Mom, I need to find out if there's anything I can barter for what we need. It will take time. I'll be careful." Rita kept shaking her head as if she weren't going to let it happen. "Do you have a better idea? Besides, I'm not the only one out there. Everyone is doing this. All of Sarajevo is out there. We're all fighting for our survival. Maybe those guns will stop firing at us tomorrow or next week or next month, but until they do, we have to survive. See?

195

I've got a bag."

He pulled out a leather bag from under the dining room table. "It's not heavy. It's got some of my clothes and some of Dad's old tools. I'm going to try and sell them or see if anyone will barter with me for something we need. I have some money and I will buy the things we need to stock up on like toothpaste and toilet paper. This is our world now, Mom. The more we fight it, the worse we'll make it for ourselves."

"Are you going to try and get to Admira?" his mother asked softly.

"Yes, if I can get through the checkpoints and militias."

"Bosko—"

"I know. I'm a Serb and those people who are shooting at us from the mountains are Serbs. And because of it, there are a lot of angry people out on the streets running for their lives. Being a Serb in Sarajevo is not such a good thing right now."

Rita covered her mouth with her hand but didn't say a word. Bosko reached for her hand and squeezed it. "I'll be okay. I promise. It's what Dad would want me to do. It's what I know I have to do. When they start shelling this area again, you go down to the basement. No being defiant and stubborn. All the others will be there. Take your recipes with you. You can trade recipes with the other women. Go to the basement. Don't think of waiting it out in the apartment. Mom—are you listening?"

"Yes. I promise."

"I'll be okay. I'll be back soon."

Rita knew she couldn't hold Bosko back. Even though her eyes were closed, she held on to his hand and kept kissing it. She had to stop herself from crying and stay strong for both of them.

"Go," she finally said as she stood and kissed him on his forehead. He grabbed his leather bag and they walked toward the door. She couldn't wave to him from the balcony and wouldn't go down the stairs with him. Rita couldn't take the chance that the last image of her son would be him running away from her. One minute he was standing in the doorway flashing his Elvis smile, and the next minute he was gone.

Bosko heard sounds of life coming from the other apartments as he raced down the stairs. He wasn't angry, desperate, or scared; he was impatient. In search of answers. What was becoming of his world? How bad was it really? He had to know firsthand. He was finally going to Admira and couldn't wait to get there.

Stopping inches from the apartment building entrance, he stood by the sheet of wood that had replaced the glass removed from the door. A week ago, he and some neighbors had cut circular holes about three inches in diameter into the wood to act as peepholes so residents could peer out at their world from behind the safety of the wooden door and see what it had to offer them that day. He pushed open the door and stepped outside. Within seconds, he was walking, taking quick steps, but he couldn't keep up with his fast-beating heart.

Bosko had pushed himself through a crowd of men and women who were in a grocery shop that had suffered severe damage from the shelling of the last few days. People were jostling with each other, grabbing the remaining food items off the shelves, and many times fighting with each other over the last remnants of canned food or any kind of foodstuff that remained on the shelves. He swept two of the last cans of red peppers into this bag. He and everyone else in the store were trying to grab whatever they could. The fear of what each of them thought the future held was kept in check by the immediate need to find and hoard as much food as possible.

Bosko was about to grab a whole flat bread that was at the very end of the top shelf that no one had seen. Then he saw an old woman with absolutely nothing in her bag who had been unable to get even the smallest item for herself. No one was talking to her and no one tried to help her. She was being pushed and shoved and had almost fallen to the floor several times. Yet she stayed, hoping that maybe she could come away with something—anything.

Bosko held onto the somun and, pushing himself through everyone, handed it to her. She placed it into her bag. "There is nothing left," he said, "you should go before someone takes this somun from you." She nodded. Bosko could see she was proud as much as she was frail. Perhaps she was all by herself, alone in Sarajevo. Yet she was determined to live and survive however long she would be able to. He looked around at his fellow Sarajevans in the store as they ransacked it and fought with each other. No one had come to her aid or even cared that she was alone and old. Bosko wondered if this were ultimately what they would all descend into, becoming nothing more than a pack of rabid dogs, bent on survival even at the cost of disemboweling their neighbors and friends if need be. He refused to believe it would happen to them. In the end, though, Slavs of his kind always turned their war into a barbaric freak show—weren't those the words of his mother?

Bosko held the old woman by her hand and they walked out of the store together. Her gray eyes thanked him. He smiled. Then he watched her walk away, caring nothing for the gunfire or explosions that were taking place. The yelling and shouting in the store had gotten louder. Bosko held onto the leather bag and walked away at a brisk pace, constantly ducking his head at the sound of each burst of gunfire.

He'd noticed, as he walked briskly and at times ran like hell, that on the streets were women and men emerging from their apartment buildings or basement shops wearing their slippers, pajamas, and housecoats. Many women were still in their dressing gowns after running for cover. They had remained hidden during another night of bombardment and gunfire. Bosko noticed that many of the streets and sidewalks were covered, blanketed by the spent gray-brown cartridges that in the light of day appeared as a dirty brown carpet. Who had fired those guns in the city? No one knew.

Traveling in Sarajevo for anyone was dangerous. Anything moving was prey for hidden predators. Those who dared to venture out hid in the shadows created by buildings still standing, behind tree trunks, or crouched down on all fours, crawling on the sidewalk or behind a concrete barrier next to a road or a bridge. They were always looking for the next doorway to hide in as they moved from one dangerous place to another. If you braved the streets, you ran.

Those who ventured outside did whatever possible to make themselves less of a target. Exactly how that was achieved was anyone's guess and left to the individual imagination. Men, women, and children, old and young, would make a mad dash, sometimes in a straight line, toward a doorway—always with the hope that the gunman had paused from looking down the barrel of his gun because he was hungry, thirsty, or needed to take a toilet break.

Bosko knew he had to get to Admira. If she tried to get to him, she might be killed. Streets no longer existed as they once had. Hundreds of buildings and whole neighborhoods were obliterated. Tall buildings were reduced to skeletons. Hundreds, and at times well over a thousand, shells exploded within the besieged city in just one day. Admira wouldn't know where to run or hide. But worst of all, she would be at the mercy of the snipers, who killed anyone in their crosshairs, even children.

He'd heard from his neighbors that the rumor going around the city was that every few hours a Serbian sniper collected 500 German marks—the bounty on any Sarajevan. It was a form of ethnic cleansing. Some of his neighbors told Bosko that they'd heard from family or friends that former classmates and drinking buddies were now those very same Serbian snipers who were trying to kill them. Friends of friends had disappeared from the

199

city only to reappear in the mountains as her destroyer. Or they had taken up positions in the city and from their lairs were shooting and killing their fellow citizens. What was this madness that had turned neighbor against neighbor no one knew.

*

Zena and Zao stood in the shed next to the garage, which was now used to store her jars of canned produce. The wild fruit and berries that grew all around them were perfect for making jams. Every fall she'd dutifully fill each pantry shelf with her bottled jellies, preserves, and pickles.

When it was possible to get TV reception, Admira and her family sat huddled around the television and watched a broadcast showing the continuing devastation of their city or images of someone's neighbor or friend lying dead in the street. The coverage included photos of buildings that had become raging infernos as they were systematically reduced to rubble. Fires continued to burn without enough men or water to fight them. Smoke and the smell from exploding shells filled the air.

On every street, cars had smashed into the sides of buildings, trees, or traffic poles. Passengers travelling at breakneck speed trying to get to their intended destinations, generally never made it because a shell exploded a few feet in front of the car, or the driver was shot by a sniper. Maybe someone else in the car had desperately tried to take control as the car careened all over the street and then smashed into a cement wall. If the crash hadn't killed them, and by some miracle one or two of them crawled out of the car, they were shot almost instantly.

*

Admira and Tonya bustled around the kitchen, trying to finish their cooking. "Admira, do you think they'll like it? It's the first time I've attempted to cook something for everyone. Dad didn't look too pleased that Mom let me cook lunch. He's given up on me ever becoming a good homemaker."

"Your vegetable stew is delicious. Dad's in for a surprise," Admira said, reassuring her sister. Meat, poultry, and even fish were no longer on the menu for Sarajevans.

Tonya went to the cabinet and removed four plates.

"Bosko's going to love your stew," Admira said as she walked to the cabinet and removed a fifth plate and placed it on the kitchen table as she laid out the knives and forks before walking back to the stove.

"How do you know Bosko's coming?" Tonya looked at Admira, confused. Admira stirred the pot of stew. "What makes you think—"

"I just know he is," Admira replied, turning around slowly and staring at her sister.

"And I suppose that's because of your gypsy blood?"

"I guess."

"You know, you're strange, Sis. You've always been just a little off. Mom, Dad, and I have always known."

Admira hugged her sister.

As they stocked the shelves with the preserves, Zena and Zao turned their heads toward the open kitchen window and listened to their two daughters laughing. Thank goodness there was still laughter in their lives. Only Admira and her sister could make it happen.

"You really think Bosko will come today?"

Admira nodded.

"But why today and not tomorrow or even yesterday? What's so special about today? The shelling and explosions haven't stopped. Sis, it's impossible for Bosh to get here. You'll drive yourself crazy thinking about it. How can he leave Rita? Admira, look at me." Admira knew her sister was trying to be helpful, but she was certain about Bosko. "He's safer if he's home."

"I know that, don't you think I do? But Bosko won't stay

home—he has to see me. I can sense it. I can, in here." She pointed to her chest.

"Sis, don't do this to yourself."

"It's not like I have a choice. Or even Bosko. I have to see him and he has to see me. Every day when I wake up, a force is pulling me toward him and him to me, no matter what's happening in the city. Our thoughts keep getting stronger about the same thing. We have to be together."

"God, I wish you'd stop being so strange sometimes. It's so spooky. Get a grip on reality. There's a war going on, people are being slaughtered, and all you can do is think of Bosko."

"I know how selfish it is to be this way, but I can't help myself. Bosko and I have always had a special connection. It can't be explained, no one can explain it. Not even us."

Realizing that there was nothing she could say that would make a difference about the insane idea of Bosko travelling four miles to their home while the city was being destroyed, Tonya decided on another tack. Nudging Admira, she said, "Well, come on. If Bosko is going to be here, we need to finish up." In her heart, Tonya wanted to believe that Bosko would make it the four miles from his home, but she didn't—not for single second. Admira kept staring at her. Tonya stepped next to Admira and took the wooden spoon out of her hand and turned her attention to the stew on the stove.

*

"That smells terrific," Zao said, as he and his wife stepped into the kitchen. He rubbed his hands together and approached the stove.

"Can I have a taste?"

"Sure." Admira raised the spoon for her father.

"My God, that's good. Good job, Tonya."

"Thanks, Dad."

"Zena, come, I'll wash your hands." Zao turned on the sink tap and affectionately washed his and his wife's hands together. Then he grabbed a hand towel off a wooden peg on the wall and wiped her hands dry. "Come, now. Let's all sit down and have a meal together."

"I'm waiting for Bosko."

"He called you? He got through?"

"No."

"I don't understand."

"He's coming today, Dad," Admira said as if it were a fact, like the next day's sunrise.

Zao glanced at his wife and turned toward Admira. "How do you know this?"

"Gypsy blood," Tonya murmured. That comment produced a sharp look from her mother.

"I can feel it. I'm going to wait for him."

"But what if he—" Zena began to say.

"I guess we could wait awhile," Zao interrupted his wife.

"I've been trying to beat your mother at backgammon anyway. Let's have a few games while we wait."

"Doesn't anybody care to ask me if I'm hungry?" Tonya said.

Looking at his daughter, Zao asked, "Can you wait?"

"Of course I can. After all, Dad, what are a few bombs here and there? He's a big, stupid Serb who doesn't know any better. He'll be here. Bombs won't hold him up."

Admira hugged her sister and they both started to laugh.

Zao sat down at the backgammon table. He looked at the board and began to calculate his moves while trying to figure out what to do if Bosko didn't come. "I hope to God he makes it today," Zao whispered to Zena. He was asking for something from a God he didn't believe listened to his kind anymore. But in his heart he hoped that maybe, just maybe, a God somewhere had realized he'd ignored their kind long enough and now at this moment some generosity filled his heart.

He was a father who loved his daughter, a Muslim who had sung praises in a Christian church. Didn't that mean something? To some God that was out there, it had to have meant something. Zao knew it was only a matter of another day before Admira would risk going into the city to see Bosko. No one was going to stop her. *Please, God, if you are real and listening,* Zao whispered in his thoughts, *give us one more day with her. Protect her always.* His prayer was to the same deity he had once believed had abandoned all Slavs because they didn't know how to live.

*

Bosko listened for sounds he couldn't hear, looked for things he couldn't see. The noise lodged in the throat of this city was the sound of people being murdered every second of every day.

He stepped behind a section of concrete wall and crouched down to catch his breath. The wall had been blasted apart and appeared ready to collapse at any moment. He peered around its jagged edges at the rubble of buildings around him. *Run, and don't look back. Just run.*

Bosko jumped up and ran and kept running toward shadows cast by buildings and the bombed-out doorways of any structure he could reach. He ran as fast as he could through crossroads, knowing to avoid streets that were perpendicular to the mountains; they were openly exposed to the snipers. So Bosko ran through alleyways and streets shielded by buildings on each side that blocked off the view of the mountains and therefore of him. He had begun to sweat but also felt a chill throughout his body. He made sure that when he ran, he jumped over pieces of concrete rubble lying on the street or sidewalks; if he tripped or twisted his ankle, he would fall helpless onto the street. A shell or sniper's bullet would surely hit him.

People barely looked at each other as they ran. Bosko hid behind the wall of a building, listening to bullets whizzing past. He wasn't in some arcade playing video games—this was real. The sound of his own breathing was labored after darting and dodging and staying out of death's grip. *Not today.* He wasn't going to die today. Carefully peeking around the corner of a bombed-out building, he watched his fellow Sarajevans running for their lives. Bosko turned in the direction of Logavina Street and couldn't help but smirk. He and Admira had spent hours at Cafe Elvis, located at the foot of the street.

Bosko counted down the seconds before making a mad dash to the next point of safety. He was positioned in a sprinter's stance, about to make his break, when he saw a man across the street at the intersection, kneeling next to another man. He was desperately trying to lift the wounded man but was unable to carry him. Bosko couldn't take his eyes off the two men caught in the open as one of them was trying desperately to lift the other and carry him to safety.

Also watching, but unable to help was a group of men and women hiding behind a white van. Each time the young man tried to lift the wounded man into his arms, he stumbled and they both fell onto the deserted street in full view of anyone watching. He kept trying over and over again to lift his wounded brother, who kept pleading with him to leave him.

The man simply wasn't strong enough. The group of people hiding behind the van kept screaming for him to leave his friend, but he was his brother and he couldn't, he wouldn't ever leave him.

Without thinking, Bosko dashed across the street to the wide intersection, toward the two men. Throwing his bag on the ground he yelled, "Give him to me. Grab my bag." Bosko yanked the wounded man out of the arms of his brother, lifted him

205

against his chest, and ran toward the people near the van. Bosko reached the sidewalk, tripped and fell over the curb, and the two of them rolled toward a wall where the others hid. The men ran to him, thinking Bosko had been injured.

"Are you okay?" they asked. Bosko nodded, trying to catch his breath; his heart was pounding, and he couldn't speak.

"That was a mad fool thing for you to do. You could have been killed," one of them said.

"No, not today," Bosko replied, still gasping for air as he knelt down on his hands and knees on the sidewalk. "Today, I have somewhere special to go." Stooping next to the stranger he'd carried, Bosko turned his head and they stared at each other without saying a word, fully realizing what had just happened. They had cheated death—together. With only one thing for them to do, they smiled at one another. It *was* something to smile about. The injured man's brother waited for Bosko to stand before he embraced him.

"Thank you." He kept repeating the words with tears in his eyes.

"Glad I was here," Bosko said, patting the man on the shoulder. Bosko watched as he knelt beside his brother and they embraced, thankful to be alive.

"What's your name?" the wounded man asked.

"I'm Bosko." They shook hands.

"Thank you for what you did for me, Bosko. I am Muris, and this is my younger brother, Vedran."

"You are welcome."

Vedran handed Bosko his leather bag.

"Well, I'll be running along. Someone's waiting for me and she can be very impatient." Bosko's wry comment brought smiles to everyone's face. He stood by the front of the van, carefully raising his head just enough so that his eyes allowed him to peer through the glass of the passenger side door. He squinted and scanned the area. Bosko waited till the moment was right, then turned and said, "We will all get back home today—understand?" In their faces he could see that their nerves were frayed. Their hands and legs were shaking, and some had tears in their eyes, but they all nodded in agreement. He looked around the front of the truck once more, then extended one hand behind him. Someone grabbed it and squeezed hard. The instant his hand was released, he ran. Their words followed him: "God's speed."

Bosko ran and never looked back.

*

The trams were still running, though they were targets for snipers who could be hiding as close as 200 yards away. There were signs hanging from lamp posts or painted on the sides of buildings in black, orange, or white, all saying the same thing— PAZI SNAJPER, "Watch out Sniper." Courage and pride kept the motormen and bus drivers at their jobs even if it made them stationary targets, along with the passengers who huddled inside.

Burned-out buildings and homes served as snipers' nests. Bosko ran with people a few feet in front of him or watched as strangers passed by in the other direction. If you were in range— and who wasn't—you were a target. Life or death on the streets of Sarajevo was a roll of the dice. He ran, he kept running.

Bosko hadn't seen any pharmacies that were still open, or bakeries, with their doors open their customers waiting in line to buy freshly baked loaves of bread. The continuing destruction of his city and its people being targeted for death is what he saw.

He hurried himself along, keeping his wits about him. He observed everything and everyone around him. Everyone was a pair of eyes for everyone else. Neither he nor his mother nor their neighbors could fathom the intent of those who were hidden in the mountains of Sarajevo and firing into their city. How long was this going to continue? Bosko thought surely some government would act to end this growing nightmare that had gripped Sarajevo.

Think only of Admira and your mother, he scolded himself, immediately bringing himself back to the reality of his surroundings. Bosko knew if he was lucky enough to get a tram, it could cut down his travel time immensely, but the tram was a large target. Risk had become relative. If catching a tram worked, he would be able to spend more time with Admira. Take the risk, he said to himself as the red and beige streetcar came toward him. *What a beautiful sight.* He tried to calculate where he'd have to be to jump onto the tram if it didn't stop. At the same time, he listened to the unending sound of automatic weapons being fired, each side, defenders and besiegers, taking aim at one another. Moving into the open and waving the motorman down was definitely not a good idea. Too many people were being shot at bus and tram stops.

The sight of other people waiting for the tram boosted Bosko's spirits. Sarajevans were still trying to retain a semblance of order in their lives. Food was still delivered into the city, when possible, by the United Nations. But convoys and their trucks were constantly fired upon by Serb gunners or held up for hours or even days; some were not allowed to enter the city at all. If any of the trucks reached the relief centers, most of the food ended up on the black market where it was sold to profiteers by corrupt, unscrupulous peacekeepers in the U.N. protection force. People in Sarajevo went to their jobs, if they still existed—and many didn't return home. Occasionally, Bosko's eyes locked with someone else's in an unspoken conversation that said many things: *God's speed. We must be nuts. What are we doing out here?* Sometimes it was a smile, even a smirk, conveying what they were each thinking: *Hey, we've cheated those bastards of their quota of killing today. We're still alive.* But most times Sarajevans greeted each other with, "Take care."

Bosko walked up to a small crowd of men and women, who were nervously milling about, their eyes darting back and forth looking for any potential threat to their lives. He smiled; those that looked at him barely smiled back. He made sure to keep a certain distance from whoever was next to him. If they suddenly all had to turn and run, scatter in different directions, the last thing he would want to happen would be to run into someone as they, like him, were trying to make their getaway.

Most everyone who had gathered to wait for the tram kept looking about in every direction. Their hearing as well had become highly attuned to any sound close or nearby. Distance was part of every Sarajevans calculation of to how to react to an explosion or to the crackle of gunfire.

Bosko tried to remain calm and alert. He heard a sound of relief coming from the others as they saw the first car of the tram approach them in the distance, its steel wheels grinding down hard on the steel rails it followed. The motorman standing in his cab behind the glass was a perfect target.

The two cars rolled up next to the group. Both sets of doors on each of the cars were already open. Scrawled in white paint across the side of one of the cars were the words: *Why are you shooting and wasting your bullets, can't you see I'm immortal?* Sarajevans hadn't lost their sense of humor, only their lives. The women jumped in first, followed by the men. It made Bosko smile that even in these, the worst of times, the men of Sarajevo hadn't forgotten their manners. No one chose to sit on any of the red or gray triangular plastic seats next to the windows. Everyone was crunched together, standing in the aisle. The tram jerked, its wheels grinding hard against the rails as it lurched forward, picking up speed. Bosko and the other passengers saw the many bullet holes that had pierced the metal of the cars. Some of the windows had been shattered but most remained intact for now.

209

There were single bullet holes that had punctured the glass windows but did not break the glass. Bosko and the others looked down onto the floor exactly below those holes in the glass, and they all were overcome with a silence. The floor was stained with what must have been blood—a lot of blood. Sarajevans had been killed in that spot as they stood or sat on a seat.

"Hvala—thank you," they began repeating once they'd turned their heads in the direction of the driver standing in his compartment. He nodded without saying a word, remaining focused and defiant toward his would-be killers, who must have seen him. He had courage, a lot of it, and his passengers knew it. He was completely exposed as he stood in the front section of the tram behind a large sheet of glass. A perfect victim for a sniper.

Bosko watched Sarajevo pass by as they sped down the tracks. In just a few days it had already begun to resemble a very different city. With every explosion that had taken place, a little more of the colors that made of Sarajevo a bright and vivid Renaissance painting, was being removed. The many homes and buildings that were painted in beige and cedar brown, in yellows, light blues, and greens, were being replaced by a gray-black resin and residue that had been pasted onto every building and house, every façade and rooftop, that was bombarded and then obliterated. The rich hues of the walls and façades of Sarajevo's buildings and Mediterranean-style stone homes, the countless thousands of red clay, fishscale tiles that were also maroon and orange in color and that covered the roofs of homes large and small in a city that was a living tapestry of color and beauty—it was all being destroyed, peeled and stripped away by her besiegers.

Left in their place was a black-looking tar that now caked itself on every wooden structure and onto the white stucco walls that were left to burn, while crumbling beams of steel were falling into an ever-widening pit of crushed stone, ash, and burning embers. Their city. A city that had begun to fill with the stench of dried blood and rotting corpses. Bosko, like everyone next to him, remained silent as they watched their homes, their city, being turned into a living graveyard. There was so much anger, so much hate, so much sadness that consumed his and everyone else's heart, in having to bear witness to such a calamity.

The wheels of the tram ground hard against the tracks as it lurched and struggled to get to all the official and unofficial stops where people waited in relative safety. The tram stopped and some more people dashed in through the shot-up, mangled, open doors.

Those who didn't enter from the front and side doors of the tram, climbed through the blown-out back window. Barely audible words of gratitude and praise greeted the motorman once again. No one sat near the windows. Everyone was tightly pressed against one another. The heat of the ordnance exploding around them baked everything it touched; their city had become an oven of death.

Bosko wanted to say something to some stranger—anything! But the people in the tram didn't look at each other or exchange words, not yet. Everyone needed more time to calm down before they chattered and even laughed to keep from crying. Bosko thought about how they shared a common destiny that each, would face differently. Perhaps those who thought of themselves as weak silently tried to read the thoughts of those they believed were strong. Maybe they could absorb that stranger's strength. Even if it only lasted for a day or even just an hour, they would be better for it.

A woman in her thirties took out a small thermos and cup from her bag. She started to pour coffee into her cup, but her hands began to shake. Unrelenting, she paused and tried again. Each time she tried and failed. Out of shame or fear, she began to cry for every reason a human being would when faced with the

211

humiliation and terror that they all faced while huddled together in a tram car.

Without a word, an elderly woman rose from her seat. She had had to sit down. She didn't care if she had let herself become a moving target; she was old and she was tired. But now she approached the young woman. She reached out, steadied the young woman's hand, and together they poured the coffee into the cup. When it was full, they raised the cup together to the young woman's mouth and everyone on the tram applauded the simple victory. The elderly woman caressed the stranger's face as if she were her granddaughter.

"You must not cry, child," the old woman said. "Think of those you love, and that you will see them again." Bosko and the others watched the young woman nod while her hand shook even as the old woman held onto her. Crouching low as he walked to the front of the tram car, Bosko turned to the driver and said, "Don't stop. I'll jump. Just keep going."

"Land on your feet and run. Understand? Do not hesitate," the driver replied. Bosko nodded. Another fifty feet and he would jump. He leaned forward, placed his hands on his knees, and turned to the driver who gave him a thumbs up.

"Good luck," Bosko said.

"You as well, son."

Bosko jumped off the tram, landing hard on his feet, but keeping his balance, and made a mad dash for cover, turning the corner onto a side street.

He breathed hard, covered in sweat, as he ran to a bombed-out bakery, not knowing who or what might be waiting there. Once inside, his footsteps kicked up a plume of plaster dust, which flew up into his face. He coughed and gasped and fell to his knees, pounding his fists on the ground. The situation was so bizarre. Serbian men in the hills killed fellow Slavs in the city they'd all called home. Neighbors and school friends were shot and killed as if they were vermin. Beautiful Sarajevo was being destroyed brick by brick, street by street, home by home, set ablaze in a cauldron of death. The unseen fingers behind the crosshairs of a telescopic sight or an exploding shell were painting the city in the bold, bright color of red and every other color the human body gave up when flesh and bone exploded into countless fragments.

Dead bodies had become the new expressionist art being created in Sarajevo.

Decapitated bodies and severed limbs littered the streets and alleyways close to children lying lifeless next to a curb. A grotesque gallery of decaying bodies littered the roads, or lay still in door-ways, or were sprawled out in the middle of the street.

Anger and loathing had replaced happiness and pride in his people—these Serbs, his own kind. He wished that in one fell swoop he could kill them all. But he couldn't. What he could do —what every remaining Serb in Sarajevo could still do—was to never join those murderers. Bosko and Sarajevo were as inseparable as heart and soul. Bosko the Sarajevan had now forever abandoned Bosko the Serb. The two would never meet again.

*

Tonya turned off the tap at the sink and brought the bowl of garden tomatoes to the kitchen table. "Here, help me dry these," she said, handing Admira a clean dish towel. They began to dry the handful of vegetables one at the time. "Dad must be starving," Tonya said. "I'll take him a tomato and some salt. That will keep him quiet awhile longer." Admira's focus was directed out the kitchen window. *Am I wrong about Bosko coming today?*

She felt her heart sink and was ashamed of being so selfish. Truly, she was a wretch who could never control her feelings

213

about Bosko. People were dying, being murdered in the city every minute of every day, and the only thing she could think about was seeing her boyfriend. But deep down in the pit of her soul she didn't care about how selfish and self-centered she was, because the truth was seared into her heart. The only way she and Bosko were going to survive this madness was by not forgetting for one moment what they meant to each other.

"Come on, let's go eat the last of the *alva*. Then I'll give Dad his tomato." Tonya picked up the bowl of tomatoes and placed them in the sink. "God," she said, glancing out the window. "Look at this cloud, Admira. Come quick and take a look before it passes. You can almost reach up and grab it." It took Tonya a few moments to realize that as she stared up at the cloud, Admira had quietly pushed her chair away from the table and walked out of the kitchen.

Admira jumped off the back porch steps, her mind blank except for a memory. She ran toward the fence. After they had made love for the first time and were about to walk onto the balcony to feast on another kind of banquet, she saw a cluster of low-hanging clouds pass close by. At the time she had said, "Maybe we'll grab one of those clouds."

"It's a cumulus cloud," Admira remembered Bosko saying.

She'd replied, "The soft puffy kind. When I see them, I'll always think of you."

Admira leaned over the fence, shading her eyes with her hand, gazing down the gravel road. A figure waved in the distance. She laughed as tears welled up in her eyes. She looked up at the cloud.

"Cumulus," she whispered, and then leapt over the fence and ran headlong down the gravel road.

Tonya ran into the yard. "Admira," she yelled. "Wait. Where are you going? Come back. Mom. Dad." She turned and yelled back at the house, "Admira's heading for Sarajevo. We have to stop her!" Tonya ran to the gate and desperately called out to her sister, who was running down the gravel road. Her eyes were drawn away from Admira for a split second when she saw Bosko in the distance running toward Admira.

"My God! Mom, Dad. It's Bosko," she yelled. "It's Bosko! He's here. He's really here." Tonya turned and ran back to the house. She jumped onto the top stair and nearly ripped the screen door off its hinges. "Mom, Dad."

Zena and Zao came running.

"It's Bosko. He's coming. He's on the road. Admira knew it."

The gravel kicked up from beneath their feet as Admira and Bosko ran to meet each other. He dropped his leather bag; she leapt into his open arms, her legs wrapped around his waist.

"I love you... I love you... I love you," she kept saying as she squeezed him close.

Bosko forgot every ugly image he had seen on his journey. The only reality in his life was feeling Admira's body pressed against his chest and the scent of her as his face nestled into her neck. They couldn't stop kissing each other. He was alive and they were together.

Her parents and Tonya rushed out into the yard to greet him. Zao ran ahead of Tonya to the fence. His heart was in his mouth as he flung open the gate. His prayer had been answered. That's when he saw the two of them, walking quite casually, their bodies pressed together, arms wrapped around each other's waist. They were laughing. The shock of seeing Bosko next to his daughter made him laugh as well and in a moment, Zena was standing next to him doing the same. Admira's sister cried and laughed. They all walked down the gravel road to meet Bosko.

Zao embraced him. "It's good to see you. What took you so long?"

"Traffic was unbelievable," he deadpanned. Zao kept hugging Bosko, unwilling to let him go. They were relieved to see each other but for very different reasons.

An enormous weight had been lifted from Zao's heart.

"How is your mother, Bosko?" Zao asked, breaking the silence.

Bosko didn't know how to respond. *How was anybody in Sarajevo?*

"I told her that, when the shelling starts, she should take her recipe book and go to the basement with all the others. Exchanging recipes will break the monotony of waiting it out."

"I'm glad to hear she's okay."

"She is strong."

"She is, Bosko," replied Admira's dad, who turned to look at his wife. She was as relieved as Zao to see Bosko, and she was still in shock. She said the first thing that's often in a mother's thoughts. "Are you hungry?"

"Famished," he said, embracing her.

Bosko held out his palm to Tonya. She slapped it hard.

"I told them."

"What?" he asked.

"What's a few bombs here and there? You're a big, stupid Serb. They won't hold you back." Before Bosko could answer, she jumped up and hugged him. Looking at her sister, she said, "Well, now that he's here, we don't matter much anymore, do we?"

Bosko grabbed Admira by her waist and lifted her up into the air. She rested her hands on top of his shoulders. He asked, "Did you know?"

"What?"

"When an immovable object meets an irresistible force—"

"They surrender," Admira answered immediately, still a bit out of breath as she slowly slid down his body, planting her feet next to his. "Spooky, isn't it?"

Chapter Nineteen

They all went inside and sat at the kitchen table. Zena looked at the clock. It was exactly one o'clock.

For the next hour, glances were exchanged, hands were held, and smiles were given—all in silence. They had food, when so many others did not. They had shelter, when so many others hid in dark ruins. They were alive, when so many others had died. The ritual of having a meal together had never had a greater significance to all of them than at that moment.

Bosko got up and walked over to the kitchen sink. "So many of my friends have gone to the mountains or have just disappeared. Some of them are probably shooting at us right now. How can they do this? I don't understand it, Zao." Through the kitchen window, Bosko watched the plumes of smoke rising from the city in the distance.

"Come and sit down. Staring out that window will not give you answers," Zao said. "In the end, people will always do what they believe they must."

Bosko turned and stared piercingly at Zao.

"What is it?" Zao asked,

"Miro once said that to me."

Zao stood and motioned for Bosko to join him outside. "Bosko and I are going to take a walk. Some coffee would be good."

"I'll make some," Zena told him.

"Don't worry," her father said, looking at Admira. "I won't keep him long."

"Make sure you don't," her mother answered.

Bosko rested both hands on the same spot of the fence he'd seen Admira jump over.

"I don't know what to do, Zao." For Bosko and his mother, being Serbs in Sarajevo was beginning to matter more and more

217

with each passing day. "I haven't seen Miro in weeks. The last time I talked to him, he said he was planning something big and he couldn't wait to tell me about it. And that was before this madness started. I don't know what's happened to him or Biljes. I wanted to go to his apartment, but I haven't left Mom's side, except for now. I can't lose another friend."

Zao studied Bosko's face; he sensed there was an unsettling thought that Bosko was unable to voice. "You and your mother are welcome to stay here with us anytime for however long you wish. You don't have to stay in Sarajevo."

"What will your neighbors say, taking in two Serbs? I can't let you do that. But thank you for the offer."

"Now you listen to me. I will deal with my neighbors. My daughter is in that house and we both know what she's planning to do. If you were here, she would not have to go into the city to see you."

"The militia will come for us when they find out two Serbs are living out here. They'll think the worst. Besides, Serbs make better hostages if they are in the city. There may be another way to keep my mother safe, but she will not agree."

"Agree to what, Bosko?"

Again Zao noticed an unsettling thought surface in Bosko's face as he turned to look at Zao. Bosko said, "Leaving me. Mother has to go away, get out of Sarajevo. She has to."

Admira pushed open the kitchen door and walked out onto the porch.

"If there is a way, then do it," Zao said, squeezing Bosko's shoulder. "Do it." Zao turned his attention toward Admira, who was standing on the stairs. She gave Zao that "it's time to go, Dad" look.

"Ah, that's my cue. I've been taking up too much of your time. He's all yours, Admira." Both men stared at each other intensely for a moment. That look said everything.

218

Zao patted Bosko on the back and went into the house. "I brought us some coffee," Admira said, holding a precious mug of black coffee in each hand.

"Fresh coffee—what a luxury." He took the cup out of Admira's hand and they both sat down on the steps next to each other. He sipped his coffee, and he felt so ashamed at this moment for being a Serb.

"Tonya, stop that; zip up Bosko's bag." Zena snatched the leather bag out of her daughter's hands. "What's the matter with you?"

"I'm just curious. All he's got in there are some old tools and shirts and stuff and two cans of peppers. Why is he carrying these things with him?" she asked. Her father motioned her to sit next to him at the kitchen table. "What did I do now?"

Zao took her hand in his and said, "They're items to sell on the street. So that he can get things for his mother and himself. I guess he plans to do it on his way back."

"Zao, he's got to go back with food, even a little of whatever we can give."

"Let's get started," her Dad replied.

"Sit with me," Admira said, motioning to the back porch stairs while they sipped their coffee. Faint sounds of explosions could be heard in the distance. "Close your eyes." Their entwined hands rested on her lap. Bosko closed his eyes. "Don't move," she said, whispering in his ear. "We're all alone."

Without another word they snuggled as close as possible, shoulders and arms pressed against one another. A slight breeze blew against their faces. As one passing second became another, the silence they'd summoned enveloped them. It kept them separated from feeling the despair of their world spinning toward some unexplainable end. Time had stopped and they floated into neutral space, without the reality of yesterday, today, or tomorrow. They were two lovers existing together in a silent world, and there was nothing else and no one else with them. And they sat in the stillness of their surroundings, pressed against each other, for a long time.

The minutes continued to tick away. That strange current they both felt was made of the molecules and atoms of his life force passing through him and into Admira and the atoms of her essence entering Bosko. In this primordial space they shared, they were not flesh and blood, nothing about them was corporeal. What Admira felt as much as Bosko as they sat pressed against each other was the existence of a pure energy flowing between them.

"When do you have to leave?" she asked, hating every word.

"Soon; there's a curfew. At the last checkpoint, one of the militiamen said to me that they won't let anyone pass after curfew, and anyone seen trying will be dealt with severely."

"I'll bring you a surprise tomorrow when I come and visit," she said in a matter of fact way.

"Admira—I want you to listen to me. You must not come into the city. It's best if I come to see you. I know the streets that are more passable than others, and the buildings that have been destroyed, where to hide, and the neighborhoods to avoid. I know which streets are full of rubble that has made them impassable. Sarajevo is no longer a city you would recognize. Whole neighborhoods are obliterated and barricades and blockades are everywhere; they go up and come down every day. If you wait for me, I promise I will come as often as I can to visit."

Admira didn't respond. She continued to hold onto his hand. She gripped it tighter to get his attention. When he turned toward her, she finally said, "Bosh, do you really think we're so special?" Her tone was a mix of gentle anger and of disbelief as she stared at Bosko. "Do you? I don't think so. We're like every other couple who refuses to give up what they have—each other—even though those pigs hiding like frightened sheep in the mountains

220

or in their rat holes will try to kill us. But it doesn't matter. This!" She raised their clenched hands. "This is the only thing that matters. Only this!"

"Admira—"

"You made me a promise that whatever you do from now on, you do it with me. We will do with our lives what we must, together. Do you remember that promise you made to me?"

"This is different. You don't understand what's happening. There are—"

"Do. You. Remember?"

"Yes, sure I do. But you can't come into the city. It's madness. You must listen to me."

"Whether I travel to your home and back or whether you step just a few feet away from your doorstep, we can't know which is more dangerous."

"Yes, we can."

"No, we can't. You know that." Admira grabbed Bosko around the waist and shifted to face him. "No one can know what is more dangerous—to walk miles or only a few yards. Listen. I know how afraid you are about me coming to see you. But do you think I could sit here day after day, week after week, month after month waiting for you? I'll die. I will go mad.

"Then one day when I can't stand it any longer, I'll come hurtling into the city because I am so desperate to see you because I listened to what you said to me today. If I do, it's not me being strong. It was me being weak by listening to you. That weakness will make me careless. And those eyes that see everything in the city will see my desperation and carelessness for a split second. Is that what you want?

"Bosko—we're no different than every other man and woman in love. It's the only thing that will protect us from the savagery we know is out there. Shh..." She pressed two fingers to his mouth. "Let me finish. Remember when you told me how

221

when you, Mats, and Miro were on the Field of Blackbirds that you heard a deafening hum coming from all those people?"

Bosko nodded.

"Now it's our turn to let those savages in the mountains hear what's in the heart of every Sarajevan. It's our will and *it* will not be broken. We'll endure no matter what they try to do to us. And lovers will die someday, but they will never separate us. All of us, every single one of us who remain in love. That's the song we all will sing, and they'll hear it through our tears. People will all hear it long after this siege is over and they will never forget the song we sang here in Sarajevo."

*

"Mom, do you think that's enough? Maybe another bottle of your apricot jam?" Tonya asked as she and Rita began to fill Bosko's leather bag with food items. They had taken out the shirts and tools and replaced everything with food and supplies.

Zao was standing between them, checking the items they loaded in the bag. "It mustn't be too heavy. Make sure the loaf of bread is not being crushed," he said. He lifted it off the kitchen table. "That's not too bad. It shouldn't slow him down."

"He's a Serb," Tonya said. "Nothing slows him down. Look how far he'd gotten with your daughter after only a few short months."

"Child, what did we ever do to deserve you?" Her mother asked trying very hard to not laugh.

"I don't know, Mom." Tonya said. Both Zao and Zena saw the fear in Tonya's eyes. They wrapped their arms around her and hugged her tightly. They all knew that Admira would be going into the city to be with Bosko. Nothing would be able to stop her.

Bosko remained silent after hearing every word spoken by his gypsy girl. Shaking him playfully out of his silence, and possessed by an unyielding resolution that nothing was going to stop her from coming to Sarajevo, she said, "So tell me. Paint a picture of what I must know. Tell me how I can stay alive."

She meant to say it that way. Bosko had to know they were in it together. No matter what happened, it was going to be the two of them—together.

His tone was soft, but stern-sounding. "Stay away from the streets that are perpendicular to the mountains. Those streets are in full view of the snipers. You will see signs hanging from a street lamp or on a tree, saying, 'Sniper, Beware.' Just run, don't look back. Always know where you are going and what street you are going to take. If a street you chose is inaccessible because of barricades, make sure you have a second and third choice." Bosko had seen how Sarajevo was becoming less recognizable with each passing day. The options of where to run and where to hide for a minute or an hour changed constantly. To have any plan for Admira to follow, when there were so many unknowns she would be facing, perhaps did not make sense. But a plan, any plan, however real or worthless it might become to her the moment she found herself running for her life, would keep her alert and focused on the task ahead of her—to survive.

"Don't guess about your choices; always know them ahead of time. Don't rush; it takes however long it takes you to get to us. Do not worry, don't rush, *and do not be careless.*

"Wait, and watch the others who are running. Everyone out there is a pair of eyes for everyone else. Watch for the rubble on the street; don't trip over it, or slip and fall on shards of broken glass. It's everywhere. You will see people being shot. Someone might be killed a few feet from you. You will see blood everywhere. There's nothing you can do for them. Just run. Do you understand, Gypsy Girl? Think of nothing but staying alive." Bosko gripped Admira's arms, shaking her. "Can you do this?"

"I promise. I'll do everything as you have said. Tomorrow.

223

Shall we say one o'clock?" They embraced one another unlike at any other time. The scent of Admira and the feel of her body against his, the soft rise of her chest against his own, overwhelmed Bosko's senses. He absorbed her, taking in the tiniest detail to reconstruct later.

Chapter Twenty

The following morning

Admira sipped her tea as she sat near her open bedroom window. The morning breeze fluttered the sheer curtains and she breathed it in; it filled her with all the anticipation and anxiety of the race of her life ahead. It would be her first, and hopefully not her last, she kept telling herself as she moved to sit in front of the vanity, staring at her reflection.

"Admira." Zena's voice was soft.

"Mom, come in." Admira jumped up and met her mother at the door. They hugged each other, neither one wanting to be the first to let go. "You didn't sleep, did you?" Zena shook her head side-to-side. "Dad too?"

"We were both awake all night."

"Come sit with me." They sat on the edge of her bed, neither of them knowing what to say to one another. Finally, Admira took Zena's hand. "I'm sorry, Mom. I hope you and Dad can understand."

"Don't say a word. The only thing that matters now is you thinking of nothing else but what you must do to get to Bosko's. Your dad and I know..." Zena's voice faded and she lowered her head, about to cry. "You are going to travel four miles each way to reach Bosko in a city under siege—" She couldn't stop her tears.

"Mom, I'll be okay. I know I will." Admira grabbed her mother and held onto her tightly. Zena nodded. She released Admira.

Staring into the eyes of her firstborn, Zena said, "I know you will. Don't think of anything—of me, your father, your sister, of Bosko. Have only one thought while you travel: staying alive."

"I promise," Admira said, hugging her mother once more.

"I have something for you." Zena reached into the pocket of

225

her housecoat and pulled out a small plastic bag. She placed it in Admira's hand.

"This is your makeup. I have my own."

"I know—" Zena choked back tears.

"What is it?"

"On the radio I heard them saying that the women in Sarajevo never leave their home without wearing makeup. They think that wearing it will make them look prettier, so if a sniper sees a pretty girl he will think twice before pulling the trigger. I don't know if it's true, but I brought these few things for you, so you'll have more choices of what colors to use."

"What colors do you want me to wear? What do you think looks good on me?" Zena didn't answer. "Tell you what, give me a few minutes and I will surprise you and Dad with my new look."

Zena nodded and started to get up from the bed. Admira pulled her gently back down, her volcanic eyes serious. "I'll be okay. Bosko is waiting and I'm not going to disappoint him. Mom —thanks for everything. For understanding."

Zena kissed her daughter. Tonya walked into the room. "I heard you and Mom talking."

"Come sit with us," said Admira.

"No. You need to be focused and thinking of being safe." She turned around and left Admira with her mom.

"Tonya's right. You need to get prepared. I'll see you when you're done."

Zena left her eldest and went to comfort Tonya who was alone in her bedroom.

Admira sat in front of her vanity mirror, staring into the eyes that were staring back at her. She placed her mother's cosmetic bag in front of her, opened one of the drawers, and took out some blush, lipstick, and eyeliner. Think of nothing else—not your love, your fear, your impatience to get to him. Think of nothing except staying alive. She repeated it to herself. Looking into the mirror, she wondered if every woman spent a long time meticulously painting her face to look as beautiful as possible. Would it make a difference to her potential killer? When they were done, did every woman see the mask of eternity, the one she would wear from that moment on if a bullet ended her life?

She held her right hand with her left as it began to shake.

"Breathe," she said, staring at herself in the mirror. After a few moments, she reached out and picked up her eye shadow. A soft lavender color. She brushed it on, careful not to apply too much. Then she applied eyeliner to accent her almond-shaped eyes. She'd been told they were one of her best features. Whoever was going to look at her today through their telescopic lens would see determination in her eyes. Picking up a mascara brush, she brushed a smooth layer of black onto her long lashes. She batted them as she stared at herself in the mirror.

Holding another brush in one hand, she picked up a small circular container and stroked the surface of the powder. Then, holding the brush close to her lips, she blew away any excess blush on the end of the soft bristles. The powder scattered in all directions, forming a mist in the sunlight that had tumbled into her room, its rays focused on her chest as she sat in front of her vanity. With gentle strokes, Admira covered each cheek with a faint pink tint. After a few moments, she stopped and marveled at her face in the mirror. Only one last task was left.

She picked up a tube of deep, blood-red lipstick, parted her lips, and stroked the color over her top lip, then the bottom one. She brought both lips together, rubbing them to distribute the color evenly. Slowly and very sensually, she parted them as if she were about to blow a kiss to her would-be killer. She was satisfied that her mask of eternity wasn't garish, but arresting enough to make a sniper pause for a moment. A moment might be all she'd need to disappear from his sight, like a ghost, gone in an instant.

The reflection Admira saw in the mirror was the image of a warrior. She was ready.

Her dad was sitting at the kitchen table, waiting for her.

"Morning, Dad," she said. She reached down, giving him a tight hug and kiss on the cheek. She purposely left an imprint from her lipstick on her father's cheek. "Where's Mom and Tonya?"

"They're in your sister's room. She's upset, so your mom's trying to comfort her."

Admira pulled up a chair and sat next to him. "I know Tonya's upset. I wish I could say something to her. Tell her—"

Zao quickly changed the subject. "Your sister will have us to be with, that's all that matters right now." Looking at his daughter he said, "You look beautiful."

"Thanks, Dad. You don't think it's too much?"

"No."

Admira placed her hand on top of her father's. "I'll be back soon."

"I know."

Admira wasn't taking any food; she needed to travel light. "I'll try to be back by five this evening. It's not even ten now, so I'm getting a good head start."

Zao nodded and tried to smile.

"Look, I even put my hair up. It makes me streamlined, more aerodynamic, less resistant to the wind when I run. Dad, look at me."

He did. She sipped a cup of black coffee her father had put on the table for her. "I'm faster than anything they can shoot at me. No bullet can catch me." Zao tried with every fiber of his being to seem calm, to not be upset and therefore upset Admira. He knew she had to have a clear head and her thoughts and instincts to remain sharp.

"Okay, okay, I know you must go." He hated himself for

saying those words as he squeezed her hand. "I don't want to hold you up."

Admira picked up the two empty coffee cups from the table and put them in the sink. "I'll wash them when I get back."

"Alright," her father said. Admira could see how Zao was having the hardest time hiding his sadness.

"No one will touch these two coffee cups except you because you've promised you'll be back to wash them."

Tonya and her mother entered the kitchen.

"I've been waiting for you guys," Admira said.

"I couldn't stay in my room. I had to see you." Her sister ran to her and held her close.

"It's going to be okay, Sis. I'll be back. I promise."

"I'll be waiting," Tonya said. "Just come back."

"You have my word. And when I'm there, I'll give Bosko tons of kisses from all of you."

"I don't want to see you walk down that road," Tonya said. "I don't want to see that."

"Okay, you don't have to watch me go. Promise to keep Mom and Dad company while I'm gone. Mom, ring the bell at five and look down the road. You'll see me coming."

"We'll be waiting," Tonya said.

"Don't let Dad cheat at backgammon either," Admira said.

"It wouldn't help. He's too reckless when he plays. Don't you be."

"I won't."

Admira pushed open the screen door, walked out onto the porch, and jumped off onto the yard. Without stopping, she reached out and tapped her mother's bell. It made that all too familiar sound she and her sister had heard throughout their youth. Closing the gate, she took a deep breath and began her long, four-mile odyssey that would lead her into the heart of Sarajevo.

Zao stepped out of the kitchen and hurried toward the fence to watch his eldest daughter walking toward their city under siege. In his thoughts, its complete destruction seemed inevitable.

Admira stopped. All she had to do was give him enough time. She turned and saw her father in the distance standing at the fence. She raised her hand, waved, and blew him a kiss. He had come out of the house. She'd known he would. Zao kept waving to his daughter until she was out of sight.

*

Run, just keep running. She tried as hard as she could not to focus for even a second on any ghastly sight she came upon. Bosko had prepared her and nothing she saw or heard would cripple her or make her forget the most important thing—getting to Bosko. Admira ran along a street and sidewalk lined with rubble. A carpet of fallen concrete and glass lay at her feet. Those hiding in the hills were attacking the UNIS towers from every direction with every kind of explosive device. Glass from their windows was being blown out, causing shards of lethal debris to fall onto the street below. Admira could hear her heart beating wildly. She'd passed the many checkpoints as she kept making her way to Bosko and Kosovo Hill. She remembered his words and hadn't stopped repeating them under her breath.

"You will see signs hanging from a street lamp or on a tree, saying, 'Sniper, Beware.'" She had seen them. Large black or yellow letters written on the exposed metal beams and on the sides of buildings, hand-painted signs warning Pazi Snajper, sniper, beware. Admira repeating his words to herself: "Just run, don't look back." She had ducked down onto her hands and knees behind a concrete barrier. The sound of gunfire had kept getting louder and closer to where she was hiding. Peering above the top of the concrete, she saw a white truck with the letters

RADA attached to its grill jump the curb across the street near a supermarket and crash into the tree. It was being fired upon. A man jumped out of the passenger side and was immediately shot dead.

The blue tarp that covered the back of the truck was being shot at, and then suddenly two other men jumped out from the back of the truck. One was shot in the back and collapsed onto the street, the second man was shot in the leg and was trying to make his getaway by crawling on his hands and knees along the sidewalk to a bus shelter.

Armed men appeared from nowhere and were yelling at him. She didn't understand what they were saying to him. Her mind had shut down. She didn't know who they were. Two men ran up behind the barrier next to her, and for a split second she thought they were the same people who had shot the men in the truck and now they meant to kill her. Lowering his Kalashnikov, one of the men turned to her; she could feel his breath on her face.

"Stay down, and don't move," he ordered her. His companion was yelling orders to other men who were now firing back at someone, but at whom, Admira couldn't tell. Then it came to her they must have been part of a militia unit. She had heard of them on the radio. Hastily put together to defend the city, they were also now trying to root out Serbian snipers who were killing Sarajevans. The two men jumped over the concrete barrier and along with the others kept firing and moving away from Admira. He had said not to move, but Admira knew that to stay would only make her a waiting target. Either choice, to stay or to run—there was no way of knowing what the outcome would be. She waited. Peering over the concrete barrier once more, she saw a fierce gun battle was taking place and she was caught in the middle of it. Bullets flew over her head or ricocheted off the streets and sidewalk. The sound of men yelling to each other to find these Serbian killers, to Admira's ears, was the sound of human savagery unleashed.

"Always know where you are going and what street you are going to take. If a street you chose is inaccessible because of barricades or gunfire, make sure you have a second and third choice," she heard Bosko's voice say to her.

She could see both the UNIS towers burning. They were being bombarded by mortars and tank shells. Hundreds of plate- glass windows were obliterated and shards of glass were blown out in all directions as the orange and red flames of a ghastly fire consumed several floors of both buildings. "Run," a voice in her head instructed. "Run, girl, run."

Her breath was erratic and her heart was beating uncontrollably. She had to figure out where she was when at the moment nothing that was happening around her seemed to be real—and yet it was. Then in one blinding flash, she realized she'd finally seen it. The thing she had never really given much thought about till now. It had become clear to Admira as she sat behind the barrier trembling—the fragility of life. And how the fabric of what binds us together can be so easily torn to shreds, and we become the monsters that human beings are so capable of becoming.

She had to get to Bosko; she was determined to get to him. Looking around, she recognized her location and some familiar signs, *kafana* and TRIGLAV side by side, placed high on the outside wall of the café that she and Bosko had often visited.

She scrunched down behind the barrier, shutting her eyes for just brief moments at a time as she kept hearing the sound of men hunting for their prey. Her face was covered in sweat and the pulverized dust that filled the air was coming from buildings that were collapsing all around her. Admira figured she had to run in a straight line as fast as she could. Whoever fired at the truck was being hunted. Perhaps he and other snipers wouldn't see her, now that their hiding place was being sought by many militiamen who had fanned out and were on the hunt for them.

Not glancing back but keeping her eyes on what was in front of her, she jumped up from behind the concrete barrier and ran in a straight line as fast as her legs would take her, jumping over rubble and debris and around destroyed cars and truck. "Run, Admira, run," a voice kept saying.

A young man on a bicycle sped past her, riding for his life. A young father was carrying his young daughter in his arms and was sprinting down the sidewalk. More people began to appear and were running and not stopping to help anyone who had slipped and fallen.

"Don't fall—just run and don't fall," she commanded herself. Finally, Admira slowed down for only a moment, out of breath. She passed a woman about her mother's age, who was kissing a loaf of bread she held in both hands. Ignore everything else. Run, the tiny voice inside instructed her. Run. She hurried from doorway to doorway as she maneuvered around the many trams that had been shot up and destroyed and fallen lamp posts. She saw out of the corner of her eye a red metal sign the size of a chalkboard nailed to the side of a building. In white letters were written "Run or R.I.P." Admira did as the sign said, and she ran hoping that no mortars would be fired in her direction. They were deadly accurate. She knew that running out in the open made her the most vulnerable.

Passing a bombed out building, she noticed the deep shadow its walls cast on the sidewalk and a car that had crashed into it. If she could make it to the car, she could hide in the shadows. She needed to catch her breath. Her legs were tired. Just for a minute, she said to herself.

She sprinted out of a doorway and ran as fast as she could toward the wall and the car that had crashed into it. The closer she got, the more she felt her powers of survival would prevail on this day. The pop, pop, pop of bullets echoed as they flew above her head. People screamed, but she didn't look back. Bosko had told her, "Never look back, never." She slammed into the side of what had once been a red car, now covered with a thick layer of ash and dirt. Admira scurried behind it and into the shadows.

Dropping onto her hands and knees, she tried to catch her breath. It seemed as if her heart might explode inside her chest, but she concentrated on slowing down her breathing. Just for a minute, she reminded herself once more. As her breathing began to slow, she noticed the overwhelming stench in the air. When her eyes became accustomed to the dim light, she noticed that barely five feet in front of her lay a young woman's corpse.

The car had been shot at and she had lost control and slammed into the wall. She had crawled out of the driver's side and in seconds had been shot by a sniper. Her skull had been blown away but most of her facial features remained intact, making her face have the appearance of a flattened, unworn, rubber mask. Blood had splattered from her skull and covered the woman's face in red droplets. Her mouth was open and she still had her teeth. The eyes had been sucked out of her skull, and her head was turned to the side as if she faced her killer. The corpse rotted, fouling the air. Admira covered her mouth and nose with her hand.

The reality of the siege grabbed her by the throat for the first time. It was no longer simply a blur of dead bodies she'd run past. Like the young man she saw bent over a bicycle rack, his body hanging lifelessly still, a gaping hole in the side of his chest through which a basketball would fit. A woman her mother's age lay sprawled out on the sidewalk, her simple dress having flown up past her knees and thighs, the indignity of the most private parts of her body being displayed to all the world. And here, five feet away from her, was a young woman—about her age—dead, murdered. She was lying just a few feet from Admira. She had black hair and a simple and cherubic face. It felt to Admira as if

234

she were staring at her reflection.

Admira glanced in the direction the young woman's face was turned, suddenly overwhelmed by fear. Had this woman also run to the shadows between the car and the wall and not driven it? Had it been her fatal mistake? Was someone watching and waiting for her to emerge from the shadows too? Admira dropped to her belly on the cold, hard concrete amid the rubble, the filth, and the dried blood that now pressed against her face. Was someone out there waiting and watching? Could she run faster than the bullet? Maybe the sniper could already see the look of terror on her face. Was he playing with her? His finger was probably on the trigger, waiting.

"Make a run for it," she whispered to herself. "You can't stay here. Do it. Get up, and run and never look back." The seconds began to tick away and Admira breathed heavily, inhaling the dust and filth of the street. She spread her fingers across the sidewalk and lifted her body inches off the ground as if doing a push-up. Waiting a few more seconds, inching higher, still in the shadows, she brought her legs forward and raised her head. Hands on the ground, knees bent, ready to sprint, Admira turned to the dead woman and said, "I'm sorry." And with that, she flew out of the shadows, running as fast as her legs would take her.

Following another simple piece of advice, she remembered more of Bosko's words: "If you can see the mountains, they can see you." Distances between the city streets and certain points in the hills, once considered substantial, weren't anymore. No matter where Admira was in the city, she was never far enough away to avoid a sniper's bullet or an exploding shell.

She could barely see in front of her. Where was she going? She didn't know and couldn't remember. Her heart raced. Screams filled her ears, but an inner voice kept telling her to run and hide, run and hide.

She caught glimpses of the shallow graves dug in front of and

235

between apartment buildings. People buried the dead anywhere the soil was deep enough to cover a body. More dead bodies were piling up in the city than graves being dug. She scanned the area to see if she recognized the street. Most of the surrounding buildings and known landmarks had been destroyed.

Where is God? Where? She damned God for being invisible. Then she said his name—Bosko. She said it again and again. Each time she did, her resolve grew stronger. Admira inched her head up above a pile of concrete rubble and steel beams that had fallen onto the street from a bombed-out office building. Suddenly she knew where she was: maybe a half hour from Kosovo Hill, if all went well.

With renewed hope, she set her sights on a building about two short blocks away. Should she run from the start or emerge cautiously? An eerie silence enveloped her. She jumped up and ran, but her feet seemed to have gained fifty pounds of dead weight. Just run, her inner voice shouted. Run.

*

"Here you go, Mom." Bosko handed Rita a cup of black tea. There was no milk and they were conserving whatever sugar they had left. When the water in their apartment had mysteriously come on, Bosko, his mom, and all of their neighbors scrambled to fill every container they could. Every bathtub was filled with water. With the electricity still on, they were able to boil as much water as possible on the stove. Clean drinkable water was vital; without it, survival was impossible. Running water was becoming an extremely rare commodity in Sarajevo. It appeared intermittently throughout the city, and how long it would last in any neighborhood or in any building was always a mystery. Sarajevo's infrastructure was being destroyed by the Serbian guns.

Rita sat knitting another of her famous sweaters. One for

Bosko and one for Admira. She still had to figure out what stitches and weave to use to conserve as much of the wool as possible. Like everything else in town, it was in limited supply.

"There's no tennis on TV?"

"No," he said. It was a bizarre comment for Rita to make. But when the electricity came on, people turned on their televisions. They watched the news and different sports as buildings collapsed around them and people were gunned down in the streets. Sometimes even a tennis match was broadcast. Bosko wanted to laugh. Life in Sarajevo had become both full-blown comedy and tragedy.

He jumped up out of his chair. There was nothing to laugh at or about—was he losing his mind, his sense of reality? Laugh at what, he yelled at himself. Bosko began to pace the living room like a caged animal; the wait for Admira was agonizing. He and Rita kept saying their prayers to a god that didn't seem to exist or care what happened to all of them. Yet they prayed to this god to keep her safe and to reach them soon. Once again Bosko heard a familiar and damning thought. Why were they not being smart and staying in their homes, remaining apart, waiting for that day when this madness would end? It would have been the sane thing to do. He'd said this to himself a thousand times. And the answer he got was always the same.

Have you ever been in love, the kind of love that cares for nothing and no one, only for what is selfishly loved?

These words echoed within Bosko just as they did in every man and woman in Sarajevo who dared to remain in love and could not bear to be apart.

A knock sounded, shaking him from his thoughts. Bosko ran to the door and flung it open.

"How are you doing, Charmer Boy?"

Miro and Bosko lunged at each other, holding each other tight.

237

"My God. What's happened to you? Where's Biljana? Are you okay?"

"One question at a time, my brother. Invite me in?"

"Get in here, you fool," Bosko said, pulling Miroslav into the apartment.

Miro immediately went to Rita. He kissed her on both cheeks.

"Miro, where have you been?" she asked, her voice almost failing her.

"Enjoying the party," he said with a grin.

"Where have you been all these months? Where's Biljes? Where's your mom and dad?"

"I have no idea where I've been, Bosh. It's as if I've been sleepwalking in a nightmare," Miroslav said as he plopped down on the sofa. "This is all a bad dream. Any moment now I'm going to wake up. I'm still waiting for the alarm to go off. Sorry for not getting to you sooner. I had to take care of some matters. I haven't been in the best of spirits lately." Miro's last words were tinged with his sardonic sense of humor.

"How about a drink?" Bosko asked, smiling at his friend's last comment.

"Whatever you've got."

"Miro, it's so good to see you. You bastard, why didn't you come sooner? Where's Biljes? Tell us."

"When is the right time to do anything? I had things to deal with."

"What things?"

"How about that drink, then I'll answer your questions."

Bosko walked to his father's cabinet and took out the Refosk, their last bottle of red wine. He couldn't believe his only friend left in Sarajevo was here with him, alive and safe.

Bosko brought the bottle of wine and glasses from the cabinet and sat down opposite his friend. He poured the wine and offered a glass to his mother and then handed the other to Miro.

238

"To us—huh. What a lovely life it's become."

"To all of us." They gulped their wine. Rita kept silent.

"What happened to you? How is everything? How's Biljana? For God's sake, out with it," Bosko fired questions at his friend.

Miro looked around the room and said, "You've covered up all the windows and your glass doors. We all have to; if we can see the mountains, they can see us."

"Miro, what's wrong?"

"Biljana and I were married." He blurted out the words and then filled his glass and downed more wine. "I'm a married man. Can you believe it? Me—married? It was the big surprise I was waiting to tell you. The big thing I'd planned. We got married the day before those guns started blasting holes in our lives."

Bosko jumped up and extended his hand. Miro shook it.

"Smartest thing you've ever done. Congratulations! Well, go on, tell me everything. When did it happen?"

"She's gone."

Bosko grabbed him. "You don't mean—"

"No, no, she's fine. She's just not here." Miro looked at Bosko. "Her parents pulled a lot of strings and were able to get some big shot in the French government to get them all on a U.N. flight out of the city." Miro wiped away his tears. "I love her, more than anything in this world. I love her."

"I know you do, Miro."

"If I could have, I would have gone with her. I wouldn't have said good-bye. Not to you or to anyone. I would have gone. I hate this city and what it's become."

"I feel the same way. We all do. And I want to kill every single man who is doing this to us. I want to kill those Serbs. I do. But we'll prevail. They won't bring this city to an end."

"Always the romantic. Good to know certain things remain the same."

"Where is Biljes?"

"She's in Paris. Can you imagine? It took every connection her family had to get them on one of the last planes out of the city. A lot of money was exchanged in just a few hours between her parents and the U.N. officers. I told her she had to go, and no matter what happens, one day we would be together. I knew if she stayed, it would come to no good. I keep telling myself that I did the right thing. Didn't I?"

"Yes. Sure you did," Bosko said.

Miro wiped his tears. "You know, her parents used to spend a lot of time vacationing in Paris. I guess it finally paid off. It's always who you know in this world that makes the difference. At least in this hell it does. Don't be angry with her. There wasn't time to say good-bye even though she wanted to. I guess it's why I hadn't come to see you earlier. I'm not in the best of spirits without her. I don't know what to do with myself anymore. Don't be angry, I just couldn't bring myself to go visiting after she left."

"How could I be angry? She's safe, that's all that matters."

"I keep telling myself that every day. But I miss her so much, more than you can imagine. Everyone I know is gone, Bosh. I don't see any of our friends anymore. Even neighbors I would see almost every day, they've disappeared. Some have already been killed, others I don't know."

"Many are in the mountains or hiding in buildings and are shooting back at us."

"Mats was right." Miro dropped his head into the palms of his hand. "He was right all along when he told us this would come to a no-good end."

"Miro." Bosko walked up to his friend. "Mats was right, but we have to survive, we can't let those bastards win."

Miro nodded his head but remained silent.

"My parents were making plans to leave Sarajevo when they saw the writing on the wall last year. When they left for Trieste, they took as much money as they could with them. Thank God for that. The last thing I told them when they were in Trieste, and that was over the phone, was not to come back. I couldn't leave Biljes in Sarajevo. All of this happened some months before that maniac with his tanks appeared in the hills. Thank God they're safe. Now there's just you, Admira, and me. How is she?"

"She's good, I'm waiting for her. Why don't you wait with me? I know she'll be so happy to see you."

"Bosh." Miroslav looked at Bosko incredulously. "That's—"

"I know. It's a long way from her home to mine."

"Are you both mad? Rita, how can you allow that? How can her parents allow that?"

"We can't stop them."

"You've been out to see her?"

"Yes."

"I'll never understand you, and..." Miroslav paused.

"And Mats?"

"Both of you. You and he always refused to see things as they are. He knew what was going to happen to him but he refused to accept it."

"He had no choice, Miro."

"Yes, I know," Miro said sounding so terribly sad for his friend's death. "And you and Admira doing this, it's lunacy."

"Miro, I don't have a choice either. We're not going to live our lives like cowards hiding away, waiting for this to end. All of us have to stand up to those bastards, by showing them our faces. They cannot kill us all."

The sound of exploding shells kept pounding away at their city. But they spoke quietly to one another. The apartment building shook from the concussion released by the exploding shells.

"It's not going to end in a good way for us Serbs in the city, Bosh. Like you said, those are Serbs in the mountains shooting at people in the streets and it doesn't matter who."

"I know, Miro." Bosko was more afraid for his mother than he was for himself.

Looking up at his friend, Miro said softly, "And you both walk four miles in each direction. You must not do this. Admira must not do this. We're not going to survive by gambling with our lives. Maybe this will end in a month or so. Wait it out. Both of you."

"And if it doesn't end, do we stay hidden and become cowards behind our doors?"

"What about your mom? You owe it to her to stay alive."

"Mom knows how I feel." Rita remained silent. "As determined as those animals are in the mountains to destroy and obliterate our city, Admira and I are just as determined not to ever be separated, not even by a day." Bosko put his hand on Miro's shoulder. Their eyes met. "We're going to outlast them, that's what we're going to do. They just don't know it yet."

Miroslav nodded his head. "Survive any which way we can. It's what we have to do—right?"

"Yes, it's what we all have to do—Serb, Muslim, and Croatian. Survive for another day and every day after that."

Rita got up and sat beside Miro. Holding his hand she spoke to him as a mother. "We will survive this together." He nodded, but Miro really didn't believe Rita's words.

"How, Rita? Do you know how? Dead bodies litter the streets. No one dares to pick them up; they're too afraid of being killed themselves. So they're just left there to rot in the sun and rain. The city is crumbling all around us, and soon there will not even be any rubble for anyone to live in. The Sarajevo that used to be our mythological city—it's gone and forgotten by everyone as if it had never existed."

Bosko rested his hand on Miro's shoulder.

"Don't, Bosh," said his friend. "I don't want to hear it." Miro became silent. Bosko could see that his friend wanted no tender or grandiose explanation from him as to how they were all going to survive. He didn't believe it. They were doomed.

"What is it, Miro?"

"I—I hadn't thought of Mats till this moment. I had forgotten about him. Put him out of my thoughts. I don't know why or how I could do such a thing, but I had. It's as if we will have to forget everything about our past lives and think of only how to survive. Nothing else matters anymore but that."

He stood up, looking around at the apartment. "We're shrouded in the darkness of our fears, of where we run to and hide. There's no light in our lives. Those bastards see everything and we can't hide from their guns. Look at my hands, look how they're still shaking. My legs can't run as fast as I want them to, and I always have the taste of vomit in my mouth. I still go to Biljana's apartment and sleep in our bed and try to pretend she's next to me. I keep rolling around in the sheets and blankets we both slept in on the last day she was here. That way I can still smell her. I'll never wash those sheets. This is not a way for anyone to live."

"You'll find a way, Miro. You must," Rita said, gripping his hand tighter as she stood next to him. "You are not alone. You have us." She put her arms around Miro and he hugged her back. "You'll find a way to survive," she said. He nodded, raised Rita's hand, and kissed it.

"Biljes would have said goodbye, but there wasn't time. You have to believe me. There just wasn't time." Miro was desperate for Bosko to understand.

"Biljes is safe. That's the only thing that matters, the only thing." Bosko hugged his friend.

"She said to tell you and Admira that she'll be back. You have her word."

"I know she will. Now, let's talk of other things."

"How are your neighbors treating you? Have they said

anything?"

"We try to get along."

Miro tried to smile but failed at it. He and Bosko were Serbs in a city under siege by Serbs who were slaughtering its citizens, the implication of which was very clear to him and Bosko. He became silent for a brief moment and then, looking at Bosko, said, "Think of only how to survive, Bosh, you, and Admira. Think of nothing else. I will do the same." He turned to Rita and said, "I know Bosh will take good care of you—he always has."

"Miro," Rita stood up. "We will take care of each other." He hugged Rita and then turning to Bosko said, "I should go."

"You just got here. Stay, you fool. Don't leave now. Admira will be here soon and she'll be so disappointed if she doesn't see you."

"There are some things I must keep doing. I've been checking Biljana's apartment building every day. It's been shelled a few times, but so far her unit is untouched. People are moving into abandoned apartments and buildings. It can't be stopped. But while I can, I'll stop people from moving into her place or stealing her things. It's the only connection I have to her. I'll be back in a couple of days. We'll talk then. Tell Admira I can't wait to see her."

"Miro, stay. Let's talk. We have a lot to catch up on. Don't go."

Grabbing Bosko, Miroslav said, "She's coming to see you, not me, and I'm not going to take a moment away from you both by hanging around. That's some lady you've got. You know that?"

"I do."

"God, what would we be without our women?" He looked at Rita. "All of the women we love. Be well, my friend. I will see you soon. Give my love to Admira."

Miroslav embraced Rita. "I'll see you both very soon." At the door he turned. "Watch out for the neighbors. We Serbs are not the most popular people these days."

"I will. You do the same."

Bosko opened the door and Miroslav left. He shut the door and kept his hand pressed against it while he listened to the fading sound of Miro's footsteps. His best friend was still alive, after Bosko had believed the worst might have happened to him and Biljana. If he hadn't shown up today like he did, Bosh had intended to look for Miro and Biljes by going to her apartment.

Rita sat beside her son.

"She'll be okay. Don't let yourself believe anything else. Understood?" Rita held onto Bosko's arms and shook him. "She'll be here." His mother repeated once more, "Be patient."

"I'm going mad, Mom. I should have never agreed to it— never."

"That girl has a mind of her own. Nothing could stop her from coming to you. Wait for her. She'll be here. I have some more knitting to do for the two of you. I think I'll go lie down," Rita said. "I'm feeling a little tired. If I fall asleep, wake me when Admira arrives. It was so good to see Miro. Thank God he's safe, and Biljana was able to get out. Be patient. When you open that door, make sure you hug her for the longest time. Understand? She'll be here. I know she will."

Bosko tried to appear reassured by his mother's words, but the look on his face said otherwise.

Rita kissed him and grabbed her yarn as she headed to her bedroom. "I will try to finish both of your sweaters soon."

With every step she took, she prayed to an unseen god to protect all whom she loved.

*

Bosko sat hunched over a chair in the living room. It was only the three of them now. Biljes and Vails were safe. Mats would be

245

happy. And now Miro was married. Bosko's concern for Admira grew. He needed her and wanted to be with her every day. When did she leave? Was she hiding somewhere in the city because it had become impossible to be in the open for even a few seconds? Or... Bosko grabbed his head. "No," he heard himself say, "she will be here." He smacked his fist against the palm of his hand. At that moment another shell struck close to his apartment building on Kosovo Hill. He sat still, unflinching as the sound of the explosions continued.

Where was Admira? He sat in his chair and watched several photos in their frames fall off the wall and listened to the wine glasses in his mother's china cabinet rattle, as did the windows from the continuing explosions occurring outside of his apartment building. He looked up at the ceiling where there were more hairline cracks that had become visible. The lights hanging from the ceiling were swaying. Even the large sliding doors to the balcony vibrated from the blasts that had become much more frequent and closer. The hallway and the stairwell had many cracks on the walls and on the stairs. The windows had been completely boarded up with wood and with two-inch holes drilled into them to allow for sunlight.

Bosko smacked his fist into his other hand once more. Where was Admira? Her first journey into the city. Why did I agree to it? He should have never listened to her. If only he'd forbidden her to come. He jumped up and once again paced around the living room.

When the shelling began and the snipers had started their slaughter of the innocents, he'd wasted no time in covering up the all of the windows and the sliding glass doors to the balcony. He'd ripped out every closet door, including all of the wooden shelves, and cut them to the size of each window in the apartment before he nailed them together to form one sheet of wood. Then he drilled several at an angle, two-inch holes into each sheet of wood, so the sunlight would stream through in a downward angle. He screwed the hinges from the closet doors onto those large square pieces of wood and fixed them to the window frame. He'd attached a hook to the wood that could be clasped onto a thick screw in the frame. This prevented the wood from swinging forward. For very short periods of time, Bosko would unlatch the large pieces of wood and swing them open just slightly on their hinges, to let his mother and himself see what the outside world looked like on that day. Bosko then took the thickest darkest curtains his mother still had, fastened them to curtain rods, and then he nailed each end of the rod above every window, over the wood, blocking out any view of the interior of their home to the world outside. He did the same thing to the sliding doors that led to the balcony.

When the curtains were drawn open, daylight shone through the holes in long tubes of light, falling onto the floor and walls, illuminating the living room. The scene was reminiscent, Bosko thought, of the wide shafts of sunlight that flooded through the highest part of the glass windows of the train station onto the floor of the reception hall.

Leaning back against a wall, he slid down to the floor and then raised his arm, moving it back and forth through the beams of sunlight cascading into the living room. The shafts of light warmed his body and distracted him as he waited for Admira.

The concussion of exploding shells close by reverberated throughout the apartment building, and the constant barrage of gunfire from automatic weapons rattled his nerves.

Bosko could see it in vivid detail with his eyes closed: thousands of explosions and then the tons of stone, cement, jagged shards of glass, and burnt wood fall onto the streets of Sarajevo.

The beams of sunlight continued to warm his face and neck as he sat pressed up against the wall, listening to the bombardment of his city. Think of only her, Bosko kept telling himself, only Admira. I'm with her and I'm bringing her to me.

Suddenly, Bosko leapt to his feet. He waited a brief second as he turned his head toward the door. Had he imagined it? A faint knock. Running to the door, he heard it again. He flung open the door. The knob smashed against the wall.

Admira held back her tears. Her face began to quiver just slightly, but in those black, charcoal eyes could be seen the resolve that had brought her to Bosko's doorstep. She leapt into his open arms and Bosko held onto her. She was here with him. Her scent was intoxicating amidst the dirt and grime that covered her. She placed his face between both her hands.

"Traffic was unbelievable," Admira said as she tried to smile.

PART FIVE

Chapter Twenty-One

They fell into each other's embrace. Bosko lifted Admira into his arms, turned, kicked the door shut, and carried her to the sofa. She clung to him tightly. Bosko could scarcely believe it, but it only made the reality of him holding onto her all the more scary. The frightening part was that she was here, and they were in each other's arms. *What if one day I wait for her, but she never comes?* That thought kept his heart beating as if it were about to burst.

Rita got out of bed. The blue ball of yarn fell off the pillow and rolled toward the door. She picked it up and listened for the sound of voices. But Bosko and Admira remained silent. Rita walked back to her bed. Her place was here; they needed to be alone.

Holding onto Admira while she sat in his lap, Bosko rocked her back and forth, brushing away the dirt that covered her face and her hair. Beneath the layer of Sarajevo dust and dirt, her lips were still blood red. They were sitting amongst the myriad shafts of sunlight that entered into the living room. It felt serene and comforting to have their warmth beating down against their necks and shoulders, their faces and lips. They kissed each other, their lips meeting in a beam of sunlight. Bosko stood, with Admira still wrapped in his arms.

"Pick up the candles for me," he said to her, pointing to a couple of red candles. "And the matches." She grabbed the candles and a precious box of matches.

When they reached the bathroom, Bosko took the candles from her hand and placed them next to each other on a shelf by the bathroom mirror. Then he struck a match and lit both candles. The pitch-black room was filled with a soft glow, and on the ceiling and walls appeared the flickering movements of their shadows. In the dim light, she saw the shimmering surface of the water he had saved in the large, white, enamel tub.

"No, Bosko, you need to save every drop—"

"Shh," he said as he began to undress her, stripping away each layer of clothing from her beautiful, young body and dropping them onto the floor. He pressed his face against her belly and the scent of her was overwhelming. Standing, he scooped her up and gently lowered her into the fresh, clean water.

Her spirit came alive as he kissed her. Bosko unfurled her black curls that had been swept back into a tight twist. Her hair fell around her face, and her beautiful eyes that had once stared at him from across a room, stared back at him now, surrounded by the soft hint of lavender eye shadow. Admira submerged herself beneath the water and then broke the surface, her hair and face drenched.

Neither spoke as Bosko slowly lathered her body with soap, lifting her arms one at time. He pressed his hand against her breasts and watched the bubbles form over her skin. Admira rested against one end of the tub and let her leg dangle over the side, exposing her voluptuous thigh. His focus shifted to washing her feet, her ankles, her calves, followed by her thighs, sliding his hand upward toward her waist. Still silent. His hands moved over every part of her, caressing, washing, rinsing. And they felt cocooned by time. They made every minute spent together seem like it was an hour that had passed. And the only sound in the dimly lit room was the sound of their soft breathing.

*

"Bosko..." Admira's tone could not have sounded guiltier. "All this water, you've wasted on me."

"I would have bathed you in it forever if I could." The dirt and memory of the day circled down the drain with the water. He lifted her out of the tub and placed her feet on a clean towel on the floor. Kneeling in front of her, he gently pat her dry. She played with the curls of his hair as she watched him dry her body, kissing her everywhere and arousing her, creating a very different world, one that was void of the harsh and brutal reality that surrounded them.

Admira urged Bosko up, pulling him close to her, pressing their bodies together. Kissing him passionately, she undressed him. She'd prepared for this moment before she left home, diaphragm in place, because she'd intended to make love to Bosko as soon as she arrived. They would concede no part of their existence to those who were so desperately trying to end it.

The shadow of their bodies entwined as they made love in silence. They were together and heard only the song of an unbounded love. Were they imagining it, or had the shelling and gunfire abated? The only reality was that they were making love to one another, surrounded by the light of the two burning candles, and every passing second felt a world away from the one that was being destroyed.

The only way to remain defiant against the will of their killers was to show them that lovers would never stop moving into each other's arms to make passionate and gentle love, while being subject to a reign of terror. It was the glue that kept their city from being completely ripped apart. In the heart of every Sarajevan man and woman was one thought: never stop sharing with each other moments of an unbounded love.

And it felt to these two young lovers as if they had spent untold hours together.

*

Holding each other's hands, they finally strolled out of the bathroom; he led her toward the kitchen. He'd dressed her in one of his clean shirts and a pair of pants fitted with his belt.

"I have some biscuits to eat with our tea. Oh, and I have some great news. Miro came to visit us before you arrived."

Admira grabbed Bosko. "What? He's alive? Oh, thank God. How's Biljes? Was she also here?"

"Biljes and Miro are married, but they aren't together. Biljes managed to get out of Sarajevo some months back. Her family has connections. She's safe in Paris."

"Thank God."

Admira embraced him. He felt her trembling in his arms. He held on to her tightly.

"Miro felt so guilty that she didn't say goodbye. He kept asking me to forgive him."

"There's nothing to forgive. She's safe. That's all that matters. Both she and Vails are safe. It's a good sign. It has to be."

Bosko lifted the whistling kettle of boiling water off the stove and filled their cups.

"Why didn't he wait? I wish I could have seen him."

"Why do you think? He knew this was our time and didn't want to intrude. He has Biljana's apartment to go to and take care of. He misses her so much. But he has us now. There's only the three of us, so we'll have to make it together. I think we'll be seeing a lot more of Miro. He'll be back."

"And so will I," she said.

"Come on. Let's have our tea and biscuits in the living room. I think my mom has been waiting for the right moment to say hello. We've kept her cooped up in her bedroom long enough. It's time to let her know it's safe to come out."

"Well—you've been a very naughty boy."

"Mom." Bosko knocked on her bedroom door and then stepped away from the door and waited. The door opened. "Want to say hello to a crazy girl?" Bosko asked.

"Admira—"

Admira didn't give Rita time to say another word but rushed to her and they embraced. "Oh, I'm so glad you are here, so extremely happy."

"Me too, Rita—me too."

"Come sit down. I won't take your time away from Bosh. How are your parents, Admira?" It was so good to feel a soft sofa beneath her as she sat down.

"Dad and Mom are hanging in there. I suppose for them, and you, this is nothing new. It's why they haven't lost hope that this will end. They've seen it all before. You want to know something, Rita?" Admira put her cup on the table and took Rita's hand.

"What, dear?"

"Knowing how you and Mom and Dad survived helps me to be strong. To never think of giving up. You made it, and so will Bosko and I."

"I know you will," Rita said, squeezing Admira's hand. "I've taken on a project that I should get back to. The constant noise from all these explosions breaks my concentration so I'm not as fast as I used to be. It's going to take a little while to complete. But, when it's done, I think you both will like it." Rita kissed Admira, stood, and turned toward the hall to her bedroom.

"Mom, stay a little longer."

"I've stayed long enough. Admira came to see you, not me."

Rita kissed Admira and as she began to walk back to her bedroom, she thanked this unseen god for keeping Admira safe.

*

Admira rested against Bosko's chest with one of his arms draped across her breasts; the other held a book. They were lying together, snuggled against one another on the sofa. The rays from the late afternoon sunlight bounced off the book.

"I'm ready. You can start anytime."

253

The best and only way to enjoy whatever time remained for them to be together, was to lie in each other's arms and feel each other's breath, hear the beating of one another's heart. To devour every moment of time, as it was experienced by them. Bosko had a treat waiting for Admira. As they lay together on the sofa, he was about to read the story of a young woman and her lover, who had written a remembrance of their lives together, and what it meant to him after many years had passed. The preamble to his story began with a poem. Bosko kissed Admira's neck, sending a shiver down her spine. The sound of violence and impending death from the outside world grew faint the moment Bosko began to read aloud.

There came a wayward moon
So brilliant were its rays
That brick and stone would gleam
As heaven I thought would seem
But nearer to heaven was I
And deeper in its bosom
Then all the winged creatures
For certain I heard them sigh
Oh what heady days those were
When I recall them now, when music
Filled these walls within and mischief we allowed
Colored were our evenings like the setting sun
From flames of waxen candles and wine we had begun
Ah... but now those days are lost
Though sweeter for the passing
And though all days must end
Tomorrow shall descend
Wait for me in the morn
And watch for me at noon
See the coming dusk
And my shadow upon it soon
You asked if I would remember
I said to you I would
In ten years I will remember
For a thousand years I could.

Chapter Twenty-Two

July 1992

What couldn't be bought was traded for household items. People scavenged among destroyed or abandoned cars and buildings, looking for anything salvageable. Batteries and headlights, still intact, that could provide light for a living space were incredible treasures. Wooden benches began to disappear. They'd be used for fuel in the coming winter.

Everywhere the streets were more deserted than ever. Each passing day depicted the slow, excruciating disemboweling of their city. Death followed in the steps of every Sarajevan. Black and gray were the colors left by exploding shells that covered one building after another, whether it was left standing or left in a pile of rubble, and there was always the smell that hung in the air caused from the hundreds of exploding shells. The familiar sounds of a city were no longer heard. There was no singsong of birds or the rustling of leaves in the wind. There were fewer and fewer trees to be seen. Their only purpose now was to act as fuel. The sound of children laughing or screaming with joy was no longer heard. In the briefest time, a city of a half million souls had become silent but for the sound of its continuing destruction. The silence in between the explosions played havoc with their nerves, yet Sarajevans had become defiant toward their killers. They continued to find ways to fight back.

A gray sky hung over Sarajevo. There were more days occurring like the one today. The vibrantly colorful palette of what had always been Sarajevo was now a city lit by a dim and sickly sunlight that fell onto its streets, revealing the shadows of people running. Faceless people.

Bosko and Rita had gone to collect water. He walked behind her as they passed the newly and repeatedly bombed *Oslobodenje* newspaper building. But not even bombs could stop the papers from rolling out. The word *Oslobodenje* meant freedom. Hunched over, they hurried past a wall behind a line of people, none of whom bothered to look at the graffiti scrawled there—a large skull and cross bones drawn in black. Written next to it was *Welcome to Hell*. Only ten minutes before, they'd passed a wall on which was written *Welcome to Sarajevo. Have a nice day*.

"Look, there it is." Bosko and Rita hurried along with the others, all moving toward a makeshift water station. From his shoulders, Bosko lifted the four plastic water jugs he'd strung together. Whether he'd be allowed to fill all four today was yet to be seen. Rita walked up to the person in front of her and stopped; her son stood closely behind her. He remained silent, as did Rita. Better to gauge the mood of the crowd than to speak to one another. People were dressed in their normal day-to-day clothes, just like he and his mother; the same clothes in which they could be killed at any moment. It was a surreal experience for Bosko. Sarajevans not dressed in tatters, not looking like their city. They were wearing their jackets and light woolen coats; some women were wearing red or burgundy or white jackets. Their dresses and slacks were still clean.

After the few brief minutes that he and his mother had been standing in line, Bosko looked behind him. Another hundred or so people had been added and were now awaiting their turn. Some of the women were chatting, but not loudly. Others who were mothers or wives remained silent. Some of the men who were not talking had turned and noticed Bosko and his mother standing in line, and a growing displeasure could be seen in their eyes.

They knew he was a Serb. The line moved along, and with it, Bosko and his mum. Rita stared back at anyone who looked at her. She knew they could push her and Bosko out of line or do much worse, but she remained calm and so did Bosko.

People in line were anxious to get their share before the water was shut off. Being a target for a hidden gunner was making every one very edgy. Finally, it was Bosko's turn. They stood in front of a long pipe connected to and fed by a hose. Jutting out from the pipe were several nozzles from which the water gushed; people hurried to place containers there. Bosko filled the first jug and immediately closed it.

"Why are you here?" shouted a woman in the crowd. "Why is a Serb allowed to collect water?"

"Shut up," a man responded.

"Why should she shut up?" responded another man. "Why do we allow them to come to bread lines and water lines? Do we know who his friends are? And what they may be doing?"

"This is not right," said another man. "They do not belong here."

"That's right, they don't belong here," yelled another woman, and she grabbed the filled water jug out of Rita's hand. "Get out of here, both of you."

A crowd of people had started to encircle him and his mother. Another woman pushed Rita out of the crowd. Bosko grabbed his mother and, holding onto her, stared at the woman and said in a lethal tone, "Do not touch her."

The anger felt by the crowd of men and women was palpable. He had to get his mother out of here. Slinging the tethered jugs over his shoulder Bosko grabbed his mother's hand. He'd turned his head just in time to grab the hand of a woman who was about to strike Rita. He was about to fling her out of the crowd that had encircled them.

"Stop. Enough," said a voice. It was the man who had told the woman to shut up. He walked up to Bosko and his mother. "Leave now. You have what you came for."

"Don't come back to this water station, next time you won't be so lucky," said a woman, and then she spat at Bosko's feet.

"Go," said the man. Bosko held onto this mother, and they

pushed their way past everyone.

Bosko knew that in another second, tempers would flare out of control. Mothers, fathers, sisters, and brothers in Sarajevo were being killed by Serbs in the hills and snipers in the city. The sight of him and his mother at the water station—two Serbs taking precious water with them—inspired a sudden rage amongst the others waiting in line. The jugs of water could have been ripped away from him and Rita, and that would be only the beginning of the end for them. They hurried away from the water station.

"It's okay, Mum, we'll be home soon." Rita tried to smile and look reassured by Bosko's words. He held onto her hand as they hurried along. How was she going to protect Bosko?

When they were ten minutes from home, two militia cars flew past them, heading in the direction of their apartment building. The moment they reached the hill and stood on the rise, Rita let out a mournful cry. Their apartment building had been hit by tank shells, and it appeared that the entire building had shifted off its foundation.

Bosko grabbed his mother, the jugs of water still strapped across his shoulders. Their neighbors, the few who remained in the building, were leaving and taking out whatever they could. Rita sped toward her home. She spotted one of the few friends she had left and ran to her.

"Gordana, are you okay?"

"Yes, my dear, only my wits are shattered. Curse those bastards for what they've done. Rita, I can't talk. There's so little time. We must go before this building falls on top of our heads. Or those bastards decide to make Swiss cheese out of us."

"Where will you go?" Rita asked.

"My son came over and we're taking whatever we can with us. Get out of here, Rita. This place can't be inhabited anymore. Fatmir is also taking his family away. You must go too. What a life. What a shitty life," Gordana said. "What did any of us ever do to deserve this?" Rita hugged her friend. "Hurry, Rita. Bosko, make sure you take care of your mother."

"I will."

"Go on, Rita. Hurry, they're watching." Gordana pointed toward the mountains. The militiamen were assisting as much as possible with loading up household items into a car. All the other tenants, none of whom had cars, were carrying or strapping on as much as they could carry, or loading things into metal shopping carts and strollers or on bicycles. An entire lifetime of memories was being left behind in their apartments. Militia lookouts were scouting the area with binoculars for any sign of snipers.

"Mom, let's go in and see what's left. We need to determine the actual damage inside." Bosko and his mother moved toward the entrance. Entire apartments had been blown away, exposing their space and the personal effects of the inhabitants to the outside world. "Keep going, Mom. Don't look."

When they reached their third-floor apartment, all Bosko could think about was how lucky they were that it had happened while they were gone.

Bosko pushed open the door and waited a few moments. Parts of the ceiling collapsed in small and large chunks. He turned to his mother. "Wait here."

"I'm not staying outside."

"Yes, you are. Now wait here in the hallway." He kissed her on her forehead and stepped inside.

"Bosko."

"Shh," he admonished her without turning around. Pieces of wallboard and plaster ground beneath his feet. A very large piece of sheetrock fell inches from where he stood, creating a mushroom dust cloud that rose up to the ceiling.

Rita let out a gasp and stepped over the threshold.

"Stay where you are," he yelled, covering his face with his arm. Large cracks appeared all over the ceiling and walls. When he turned toward his parents' bedroom, he could feel a draft. He retraced his steps. The windows and the glass doors to the balcony were still there, boarded up behind the wood and the thick, drawn curtains.

Finally, he motioned for his mom to enter. "Take only what you need," he said, pointing to one of the closets in the hallway, "and what you can run with. We're leaving."

"Leaving to go where?"

"Admira's."

"I—can't."

"We have no choice." He saw her move in the direction of her bedroom and stepped in her path. "Stay away from your bedroom." He pushed her gently back into the hallway.

"All my things are in there. Your father's things are in there."

"We're leaving them."

"I can't leave those things; they are my life. I will not!"

"You will do precisely that, Mother. Because none of those things matter. Your life is not about things. We have to leave them. Everything. We don't have much time." He remembered what Matko's mother had said in her letter. They had gone to Konavoski Dvori to get their *things*, and it had cost five lives.

"Bosko, I can't simply leave our home. I can't," she said in anger.

"Mother, listen to me," he said, holding her back. "Things can be replaced. We fight back by living. That's the only way. It's what Father would want you to do."

They could hear the neighbors in the hallway. Gordana was the only neighbor to enter their apartment. The other neighbors who had remained in the building were too scared to stay any longer than was needed. They didn't bother coming into the apartment to say their good-byes to Bosko and his mom.

"Rita, my son has finished loading the car. My God—what do I say?" They embraced each other.

262

"We'll come back when this is over. Won't we?"

"Yes," Rita said.

"Where will you and Bosko be?"

Bosko spoke up. "We're going to stay with friends; we'll be okay. You've been a good friend to us, Gordana. Be safe." Bosko hugged her tightly.

"You as well, my boy. Make sure to take care of yourself." Gordana was Muslim. She knew the predicament that Bosko and his mom were facing as Serbs. She tried to hide the fear she was feeling for the both of them.

"Mother!" Gordana's son called as he appeared in the doorway. "We must go." Rita hugged her friend again and the next moment they were gone.

"Mom, we have to pack," Bosko said, urgency in his voice. "Mother—"

"Yes, I know."

"Bosko, Rita." An elderly woman's voice broke the silence. Rita turned to the doorway.

"Radmilla, my God, are you okay?" Rita ushered the old woman into the apartment.

"I'm fine—it's a nuisance, this is."

"Where are you going, where will you be staying?"

"I'm staying here. Where will I go?"

"You can't stay here.'

"Why not?"

"This building is about to collapse."

"Let it. I'm old. I've lived long enough."

"Radmilla, your boys—where are they? Bosko and I can take you to them."

"Listen, dear, I came down to check on you and Bosko. Where is he?"

"Bosko," his mother called out to him. He came running out of his bedroom.

"What is it?"

"We need to take Radmilla to—"

"No you don't!" the old woman replied sternly. "I'm staying. I'm too old to be running about out on the streets. Where are you and Bosko going?"

"To my girlfriend's," replied Bosko. "Radmilla please let us take you to—"

"No, I'm not going anywhere except upstairs. I will see you later, maybe. Come give your babysitter a kiss. You haven't gotten too big for that, have you?" Bosko leaned forward and kissed her on both cheeks.

"Rita, be well and God bless. Bosko, take care of your mother." Radmilla kissed Rita and then turned and shuffled out the door and up the stairs to her apartment.

"Mom. Mom!" Bosko snapped his mother back to the reality of the moment and away from staring at the hallway into which Radmilla had disappeared.

"We can't just leave her," said Rita.

"I'll check on her the first moment I can. But we have to go now. Mother—please, we have to go."

Rita was trying to understand what had suddenly happened to all of their lives. It had been turned upside down and into utter turmoil.

"Mom, come on, let's pack," said Bosko, pressing his mother's arm gently.

"Yes, okay." Her voice was calm as she walked to the hall closet and took out a traveling bag. She began to fill it with some of her clothes. Bosko took out his army duffel bag from a second closet and did the same. Both their bedrooms had sustained major damage. Bosko noticed that some parts of the walls of both their bedrooms had actually been blown away. The explosion had exposed the interior of each room to the hills.

"Bosko... I need my personal things. You know, personal

264

things?"

"Go to the bathroom and take everything you need," he said. He crawled into his mother's bedroom on hands and knees. The wind blew into the apartment through the large opening in a wall, and some lightweight items like papers and Rita's unraveled yarn that was lying on her bed were lifted up into the air, and swirled around. Other items had simply been sucked out of the room with the sudden change of air pressure caused by a hole being blasted into the bedroom wall. Realizing that he was too exposed to possible snipers, he sat as low to the floor as possible and used his legs to scoot backwards while pulling the chest of drawers with him toward the bedroom door. If he could get it to the doorway, he could tear out the back of the dresser so his mother could access her things. Inch by inch, Bosko pulled it toward the door. Once it blocked the doorway, Bosko ripped out the thin backing.

"Mom, come on, get your stuff now. Stay hidden behind the dresser, and make sure your head is below the top of the bureau. I've pried away the wood, so you should be able to get what you need. I need to go to the closet. Hurry." Rita began packing her underwear and brassieres. Bosko searched for his own underwear and found them covered in dust and ash. He laughed at the absurdity of scooting around on the floor in their bombed-out apartment, searching for their personal undergarments, while explosions continued all around them. The laughing stopped when the building shook violently again.

After half an hour, Bosko tried to hurry his weeping mother. "Are you ready?"

Rita shook her head and began to sink to her knees. "This is my home. This was my home."

Bosko gently pulled his mother to her feet and held onto one of her hands while he slung the duffel bag over one shoulder.

Rita couldn't bring herself to walk away. "I can't, I just can't."

She kept weeping and trying to break free from Bosko's grip.

"You must and you will." He guided her out of their apartment. She tried to cling to the walls and the side of the door, but Bosko forcefully pulled his mother along the hallway toward the stairs. Two pieces of luggage were all they had. All he knew was that he had to find a way to get her out of Sarajevo. First, they had to get to Admira's home—and that was four miles away.

Bosko pushed open the entrance door to the building, and with his khaki duffel bag slung over his left shoulder, and his mother's hand held tightly, he began to walk, picking up his pace and dragging her along. There was a militia unit that remained on the street on the lookout for sniper fire while others in the group were helping a husband and wife lift the few belongings they had scrambled out of their apartment into a wagon that the man was going to pull; as he headed off with his wife and two daughters to some "safer" place. Rita pulled Bosko's hand; she wanted to say her good-byes. But Bosko just held onto her hand and dragged her along. He knew there was no time for any good-byes—time only to run.

In just a few short seconds, she was keeping up with Bosko, realizing that this was not the time for her to be a burden and slow them down. Mother and son, holding each other's hand, hurried along. Rita didn't bother to look back at their apartment building in which she and her husband had lived for over twenty years. "Stay with your son," a voice said to her. "It's how you can protect him."

A broken city was strewn all around them. Debris, bloodstained sidewalks, and blown-up cars, trucks, and trams littered each side of every street. They were running now, over the rubble of destroyed buildings. The sound of glass being shattered in office buildings could be heard constantly. Bosko still held onto his mother's hand firmly while with her other hand she held onto the one bag of clothes and toiletries she was bringing with her.

Bosko kept checking to see that his mother was not out of breath and could still run.

She nodded, she was okay. So they kept running till they came to an intersection where a handful of people were standing behind three sections of a fifteen-foot high wall of steel. They were screens erected at many intersections to protect pedestrians from snipers.

They all stood listening to the crackling sound of automatic weapons being fired and which at times seemed to be getting closer to where they were all huddled together. Bosko was now even more determined and frantic to get Rita to Admira's home. He looked at everyone standing at the barrier, who were all at different stages of making a decision of whether to wait or dart out from behind the screen and hope today would remain a lucky day for each one of them. Rita raised their entwined fingers and kissed Bosko's hand.

An elderly man, who seemed in a daze and completely lost to the world and to what was happening to them in Sarajevo, stepped aside. Bosko kept looking at him and then turned to all of them and said, "None of us will die today. Understand?" They all nodded. Rita felt the tears gathering in her eyes, but she wiped them away before they could roll down her cheeks. "We're going to run," he said, turning to his mom before giving her a hug. "We'll be there soon." Rita nodded. "Are you ready?" She nodded once more. They held onto each other's hand tightly.

"God be with you," said someone. In that same moment, mother and son were running.

A ferocious wind had picked up and was blowing against Bosko and his mom as they desperately tried to run against it, but it kept forcing their footsteps backward. They began to slide backward on the sidewalk, unable to take a single step forward. He kept pulling his mother along.

"Bosko—wait son, can you slow down?" Rita was exhausted.

It had all been in Bosko's imagination. The ferocious wind was all in his mind. That feeling of making no headway was his sense of desperation that it was taking too long to get to Admira's.

"No, Mum, we can't stop." He took the suitcase out of his mother's hand and, holding onto it with his left hand, he made them pick up their pace once again. He heard the sound of his breathing; it was dull and low sounding and it felt as if his whole face were encased in a mask, and that what he heard was the sound of his breath reverberating within that mask.

Others were running just like they were, and sometimes in the same direction. Everyone who had ventured outside was a target. Some did not make it to their destination: a young woman, an elderly man, a teenage boy. They had all been shot and their bodies strewn across the street or sidewalk. Their loved ones would in time begin a desperate search for them. Bosko pulled Rita into a doorway. She couldn't stop herself from lowering her head, and she began to weep, shaking her head in utter despair. The sight of the dead, of the young and old being wantonly killed, was a sight that she could not bear to look at anymore.

His mother's words of the things she'd remembered that had happened to her as a young girl in that time of madness kept repeating in Bosko's thoughts. He knew he would not rest till he found a way to get his mother out of this hell. He would do whatever to keep her safe. To not let the past catch up with her. Grabbing her hand once more, he glanced at Rita and together, mother and son flew out of the doorway.

Chapter Twenty-Three

July 1992

Bosko sat on the back porch steps, fidgeting with his hands. It had been almost three weeks since he and his mother had left their severely damaged apartment and Admira's family had taken in his mother and him. It had been sheer bliss for Bosko to be with Admira day and night.

"Need company?" Zao asked as he opened the kitchen door and stepped outside to join Bosko.

"Of course," Bosko replied. He was about to stand up when Zao placed his hand on his shoulder and sat next to him.

"What's on your mind?" They both stared in the direction of Sarajevo as they listened to the distant sound of the explosions and watched the unending smoke rising from the city's destruction. Their location seemed to be safe for the moment, but they knew it could all change in a heartbeat with a major assault by the Serb forces. It hadn't happened yet. Bosko knew that word would soon get out to the militia that two Serbs were living here, and then they would come for them and drag them back to the city. He had to get his mother out of Sarajevo before that happened.

"Is there anything I can do to help, Bosh?"

"No. It's for me to do," Bosko whispered. The two men remained silent. "When we were leaving the city, running through alleyways and intersections, huddling with others behind walls, I started to get a sense of it, Zao. Sarajevo has succumbed to a strange and unhealthy mood. It felt as if the city's spirit was just a day away from being completely broken. The expression on everyone's face told me they believed this was the end."

Zao patted Bosko's hand as he listened.

"My mother must get out. Her greatest sin now is that she's a Serb. She has to leave the city and me. She knows I won't leave

Admira, but she has no future here. I can't bear to see what little life and joy she still has left finally destroyed. She has to go to our relatives, a brother and sister in Serbia; they will take care of her. Do you know how much I hate the sound of that word? But that is the only place she'll be safe."

Zao kept silent. "This is a reoccurring nightmare for every Slav, isn't it, Zao?"

Once again, Admira's father remained silent.

"Our continuous, barbaric freak show." Bosko understood there was only one choice left to him. He had to return to the city and find a way to earn a living among the dead and the dying, amid the rubble and garbage, the wild dogs and flies, the stench, and the bloated dead bodies. He would have to face being a Serb in Sarajevo. But first, he had to find a way to get his mother to safety, to convince her to leave him.

"Zao, you and Zena have done enough. I need to do the rest. Mom can't stay here forever. Your neighbors don't like it one bit. They know two Serbs are living here. The militia will come and force us to go back, and then you'll be in danger too for having harbored two Serbs."

"Forget what my neighbors think. I'll deal with that. As for the militia coming here, what can they say? Your home was destroyed. They can't force you to live on the streets."

"They *can* force us to do anything. That's why my mother and I must go, now. I can't let anything happen to you or your family because of us. She can't stay in Sarajevo, and I can't stay here much longer. We have an old friend. He was my brother's best friend. It seems from all of the stories I kept hearing from neighbors, and the rumors on the streets, that he's been involved in the exchanges of families separated by the siege in Sarajevo. I don't know all the details, but if there's anyone in Sarajevo who could make this happen, it will be Mladjo. He's my only chance to get my mom out."

"She won't leave you."

"She will. She has to."

Bosko stood and walked down the stairs. He turned to Admira's father and said vehemently, "If she doesn't, then I may see her die in front of my eyes. And I won't let that happen. Do you understand me? I will *not* let that happen."

Zao stood and reached out to grasp Bosko's shoulders. "What can I do to help?"

"You've already done it." He squeezed Zao's shoulder. "Now is the time for me to do what I must. And I'm counting on her seeing how impossible it is for me to protect her. I'm counting on her seeing how dangerous it is for both of us, and that I have a better chance of surviving this, knowing she's safe. I'm counting on her being able to accept it."

Zao looked straight at Bosko. "I will do what I can. You have my word. But Rita knows if she leaves here, she'll never come back."

"Come back? What will be here to come back to?"

*

Three days later, under the cover of dawn, when it appeared that there was a lull in the bombardment, Zao drove Bosko and his mother back to the outskirts of the city and to one of the heavily guarded roadblocks into town. Little was said, but in their silence the paramilitary forces signaled their disapproval.

Bosko was searched, but no one touched his mother. He wouldn't allow it, and neither would Zao. A Muslim man had allowed two Serbs to live with his family. Zao hugged Bosko close and then Rita too, for everyone to see, and waited at the checkpoint until they disappeared from sight. Bosko had shown his ID card to the militiamen. Every male over eighteen years of age carried an ID card. The militiamen manning the checkpoint

271

closest to Admira's home knew full well who Bosko was; he had passed through this checkpoint every day to get to Admira's. He was a Serb. Admira, who would also pass through the checkpoint to see Bosko in Sarajevo, was Muslim. The militiamen had started to hear rumors that began circulating in the city of a couple that travelled eight miles every day to visit each other. No one knew who this couple was or how this rumor got started and who had started it. But as time wore on, the men at the checkpoint realized it was Bosko and Admira who were the couple. They decided to take bets to see who would be the first to be killed. So far neither Bosko nor Admira had allowed anyone to collect on their bet. Bosko and Rita made their way through other heavily guarded checkpoints and barricades in the city toward the one man who could make Rita's escape possible, a man who had become famous in Sarajevo for his recent exploits.

In the city, nothing had changed. The destruction and killing continued around the clock. The streets were littered with the dead. A place of palaces was now simply a morgue.

Certain sections of Sarajevo were under shelling from dusk to dawn, but as morning approached, the bombardment waned. That was the time when people emerged from their hidden warrens in the ground, from cellars, and ditches. Without sleep and in shock, despairing for their lives and their loved ones, they ventured out into the world, easy targets for snipers.

Rita looked at the faces of these people. The more she saw the sense of determination and defiance in their faces, the more she questioned what she was about to do. Rita spotted a woman her age who walked with unwavering steps despite the sound of small-arms fire all around them. She seemed completely unconcerned for her safety, focusing only on where she had to go.

"Come on, Mom. Don't slow down."

"I need to rest."

"Not now."

"I must."

Bosko scanned the area for a safe place. He led his mother into a two-story brick building that had once housed a flower shop on the ground floor. The store appeared like every other building in the city—shards of glass all over the floor, gaping holes in walls and ceiling. The second floor had been partially blown away. Bosko gently pushed his mother back as far as possible into the vestibule, while he used his boot to brush away the broken glass that surrounded her on the floor.

Rita's eyes darted back and forth, but she wouldn't look directly at Bosko. The image of the woman they'd seen made her feel like a coward. *How can I leave Bosko? Have I gone mad?*

Bosko divided his attention between what was happening outside and what was occurring with his mother. She sat on the floor in silence, filled with a sense of shame.

Finally, she spoke. "I can't."

"You can't what, Mom?" He stared out of the round opening in the door.

"I can't just leave you like this. I can't simply run away like this. Others aren't going. I won't either."

"We can't have a conversation here. It's too late."

"It's never too late. And why can't we have this conversation now? Would you prefer to have it in a cafe? I'm not going. I won't do this. I won't leave you."

Bosko's thoughts turned razor-sharp. He had but one chance, only one moment to convince his mother that this was the only way. He wasn't going to see her die. Bosko stared into his mother's eyes as he sat down beside her.

"I can't. I won't," she sobbed.

"Mom, listen to me," he said in a soothing voice. She wouldn't let go of him. "You must leave me. If you love me, you must. Do you love me?"

Rita nodded. "I've always loved you more than anything in

273

my life."

Bosko moved back a few inches, out of his mother's grip, so that she could look straight into his eyes. "Father would say I'm right. You would listen to him. Now listen to me. You must do this. If you want to protect me, then you must leave. I worry about you and Admira all of the time. If I only need to worry about her, it will make all the difference in the world. That is how you can protect me, by not forcing me worry about you, too."

"My place is here. We will find a way to live in Sarajevo."

Bosko rose to his knees and felt pieces of glass digging into his skin. "Look at me," he said, placing his hands on his mother's cheeks so she could see his resolve.

Rita kept shaking her head. Her resolve was equally strong. "We live moment by moment, and there are no second chances for any of us. Dad would know it. Do as he would ask you to do, as I am asking you."

"If I leave, I'll never see you again." Rita burst into uncontrollable sobbing. The sound came from the pit of her soul, from a mother now faced with the thought of losing her child.

"Mother, look at me—you *will* see me again. You will see *us* again. I promise." He grabbed Rita and hugged her. "Look out there; look at our world. Did you think it could happen again? Would you ever think you would be hiding with your son in a bombed-out building in Sarajevo? Living out the same moments you did when you were a little girl? Did you?"

Rita turned her face away.

"Dad would have protected you no matter what. If you truly love me and believe in me, search your heart. Wouldn't Dad be telling you to keep your son safe? You know he would."

She stared into his amber eyes. No one in all of Sarajevo had eyes as beautiful as Bosko's. His mother believed him, but she didn't want to. She wanted him to be safe but didn't know how she could make it happen. By leaving him? It's a mother's duty to be there for her children.

"I promise we will come to see you, Admira and I. You'll see us soon. Do this for me. Please, Mom. Do as Dad would want you to. For me."

Rita wiped away her tears and caressed Bosko's cheek. "I love you so much," she said, her voice trembling.

He held on to her hand and said, "I love you more."

Bosko helped his mother get up from the floor. He peered through a small opening in the wooden door, watching and listening to the explosions and gunfire all around them. The timing had to be perfect. She pulled him close into a tight embrace.

"Ready, Mom?"

"Yes."

"Let's go. Now."

*

Mladjo rocked his wooden chair back and forth. Djoka, his partner, sat across from him in a soft leather chair, sipping his Refrosk.

A young Croatian man who was a gangster and part of Mladjo's criminal group stepped into the room. Mladjo's militia group, comprised of criminals, had joined a vast and fractured internal security force of many civilian militias in the city.

"Two people are here to see you, Mladjo. They didn't give names."

"I don't speak to people without names or appointments or money."

The door behind the young man opened wider. "We have names," a voice said.

"Bosko?" Mladjo jumped up from his seat and went to embrace him. "What are you doing here?"

Bosko glanced at Djoka.

"Don't worry about him. He's as corrupt as I am. Come in, come in. What brings you to this illustrious place of murderers and psychopaths?"

"We—I need your help." Bosko's voice was unsteady.

"Who is we?"

Bosko turned and stepped through the door, returning a moment later with Rita tucked close by his side.

"Rita?" Mladjo's voice softened the moment he saw Bosko's mother. He hugged her tight.

Djoka stood and Mladjo introduced them all. "Rita is the only real mother I've ever known," Mladjo said.

"She raised me, along with Bosko's older brother, who was my best friend. Sit, please. Let's have some tea."

The young militiaman left, shutting the door behind him. Bosko didn't know where to start. The words didn't come easily, and with every passing second of silence, he could sense his mother losing her resolve.

The fearful look in Rita's eyes didn't go unnoticed by the gangster. Mladjo leaned against his desk and said, "I wanted to drop by or just speak with you when this all started to happen, say hello, but what could I have said?" Mladjo shrugged. "I did have some of my colorful associates check discreetly every so often to see that you and your mom were well—as well as can be, under the circumstances. But I thought it best to stay out of your lives. Mixing with a known and convicted criminal is never healthy, especially in these times, since Muslim and Serb have become enemies. You're my enemy now too, Rita. Imagine that." Bosko kept silent. Rita stared at her hands clasped in her lap.

Mladjo laughed out loud, not because he felt a sense of irony about the situation, but out of a profound sense of anger at the idea of Rita as his enemy. "Anyway, I'm glad to see you are both safe."

276

Rita nodded but remained silent.

"The two of you must remain out of harm's way as best you can. I can try to make things easier for you and your mom."

"No, it's not that, Mladjo."

"Then what? It's no easy feat keeping alive these days."

"Yes, no easy feat." Bosko's tone was soft. He didn't know how to blurt out the reason he had come to see him. Seeing Bosko's and Rita's discomfort along with their continued silence, Mladjo began to say in a humorous tone.

"The current situation calls for a psychopath, many psychopaths to exact a price on those who are trying to kill us. My criminally minded friends and I are exactly that kind of people. Our gangs have killed many of those bastards in the mountains and ones who hide in their rat holes gunning people down. We've hunted them down at every opportunity. I find it interesting how psychopathic tendencies are now needed and have been called upon to help our city and its law-abiding citizens to survive this madness."

"Mladjo, we came here—."

Rita's resolve crumbled. "I can't do this. It was a mistake. I want to go back to my apartment, to my home."

"Mother—"

"Mladjo, I'm sorry we intruded. I need to go back to my home."

"What home, Mother?"

"Rita." Mladjo could see how upset and confused she appeared. "Don't you remember this police station? I spent more than a few nights of my youth in this station. Dragan came here to bail me out more than once."

Bosko's mom nodded, acknowledging Mladjo's words. After a brief moment, she said, "I can't leave. We must go back to my home."

"Rita, you've come to visit, just as you and Dragan did those

277

many years ago. We couldn't have tea then, but I would like to now and catch up on things. Do this for me. Please stay."

She nodded. Mladjo bent down and kissed her on the cheek.

Mladjo sat next to Rita on a plush leather sofa. He took her soft hands, which had once upon a time fed him, and held them between his massive palms.

"There is only person I never wanted to disappoint and that was Dragan. Do you know why?"

Rita shook her head.

"He never judged me. You and he never did." Then, just as suddenly, Mladjo's tone turned from being reflective to one of serious business as he squeezed her hand. "You came here for a reason?"

Bosko jumped into the conversation before his mother had another chance to speak. "Yes, I need your help to get my mother out of the city as soon as possible. I heard that you do these things." His tone was desperate.

"Yes. I can help."

"I'm not going," Rita whispered.

"You are." Bosko's voice was adamant.

Mladjo raised his hand to Bosko. "I think what Bosko meant to say, Rita, is that if you leave, his chances of survival vastly improve. Isn't that what you want—for Bosko to be safe?"

She nodded.

"Rita, we're all faced with making decisions that none of us ever thought we would. To be forced to do things that should never be asked of any human being. Mothers must leave their sons, who now have a mark on them, simply because they are Serbian. And me? One of Sarajevo's most notorious criminals is now one of its strongest defenders. How do you explain such things? Little makes sense these days. What matters now is that I can arrange a direct passage to safety for you. So you've heard about this foreign exchange program we've got going?" It was a lame attempt at humor. No one in the room smiled or laughed.

"Our neighbors used to talk about it all the time," Bosko answered, determined to come away from this meeting with his mother agreeing to leave.

"It's simple. We exchange a Muslim for a Serb, or a Croatian. That type of thing. Families are reunited from both sides of the barricades and in many cases have a chance to leave Sarajevo itself. Rita, will you go to Serbia to be with relatives?"

Rita nodded. Bosko couldn't tell if his mom was nodding to acknowledge that she had relatives in Serbia, or agreeing to go.

The door opened and the young militiaman entered with a tray in his hands. It held three ornate cups and three unopened tea bags, milk, and sugar. These items were impossible for most people to find.

Djoka took the tray from him and placed it on the table.

"What are you doing with yourself these days, Bosko?" Mladjo poured hot water into a cup, added milk and sugar, and handed Rita her tea. "I remember how you take it," he said as he smiled at her.

"I'm currently unemployed," Bosko replied.

"Well, there are still ways to survive. Where are you living?" he asked.

"We live with friends on the outskirts of the city. Not far from the roadblocks and checkpoints."

"These friends of yours, are they Serbian?"

"No, they aren't," Bosko said. "We are staying with my girlfriend's family. Her name is Admira. She's Muslim." Bosko's face lit up at the sound of her name.

"Rita, when you're safe with your relatives, Bosko will have room to breathe, not worrying every day about keeping you safe. He's already thinking of Admira and how to keep her safe. I can see it in his eyes."

Rita lowered her head.

Mladjo turned to Bosko. "I have a very good memory for names. You said your girlfriend's name was Admira. We met. You introduced us. Some years back I met you with some of your friends at a bicycle shop. You had an accident coming down the hill, if I remember correctly."

"I did." Bosko smiled.

"The owner of the bike shop and I came to terms with regard to how much he should be paid for the bikes you had destroyed."

"I remember."

"She struck me as being very strong willed."

"She is. Isn't she, Mom?" Bosko answered, still holding Rita's hand.

Rita smiled and squeezed her son's hand. "Yes, she is."

Quite abruptly, and with a sense of urgency in his voice, Mladjo said, looking at Rita,

"I'll send word to you Rita, soon. There are no papers to fill out. No officials to stamp documents." Bosko nodded; his mother remained silent. Without taking his eyes off Rita, Mladjo remained seated beside her. His voice was tempered.

"He will have Admira. It is what all Sarajevan men need in these times: their women and their strong will. Without the strength of our women, it is doubtful we will make it." Rita finally lifted her head. Her gray eyes met Mladjo's. "Mladjo, please protect Bosko. He will be alone. He'll have no one except Admira and her family."

"I'll watch over him."

Bosko stiffened. He wasn't a coward; he could take care of himself.

"You've done the right thing to bring your mother here."

"I know," Bosko said in an unwavering voice.

Mladjo nodded slightly as he and Bosko observed each other. In a quiet tone, he said,

"You've remained in our city. A Serb. Someone very special

280

has obviously caused you to stay. You could have left and gone to the mountains like so many other Serbs when you had the chance —you didn't. Or you could leave with Rita, yet you choose not to. You don't want to leave, do you? She must be very special to make you care more for her than for your own well-being. Because you know that by killing women and children from their rat holes, these Serb vermin have put a mark on you, one that won't go away for a long time."

"These are not my friends or my family, these Serb vermin whom you speak of. They have no meaning to me. It's as if they never existed. They don't deserve the acknowledgment of ever having lived, these Serbs you speak of."

"Fair enough," Mladjo answered. "I'll send word very soon."

"You don't know where we're living."

"Where you are staying is no secret from those who want to know." Mladjo kissed Rita on her cheek. "Don't worry, it will be okay. These things happen. What can you do?"

Mladjo had always possessed a wry sense of humor. Bosko put his arm around his mother as Mladjo opened the door for them.

"Get home safe."

"You can count on it." Bosko and his mother walked toward the entrance door. Rita felt an indescribable sense that she was betraying her son, yet also a reluctant belief that she was doing everything she could to keep him alive.

Djoka said to Mladjo as he closed the door, "Be careful this war doesn't turn you into a philosopher. It's a weakness in these times and might be the death of us both."

*

"Let's go," Bosko said as he pulled his mother forcefully, running across the street. Everyone around them dispersed in

281

different directions, running for their lives. Bosko and his mother began the dangerous journey back to the safety of Admira's house. Bosko's intention to keep Rita safe while they waited for word from Mladjo only deepened like a root into this soul. The shelling grew worse. He'd become deaf to the sound of the explosions and the people's screams. A voice inside his head kept telling him to get her to safety. It was the sound of his father's voice.

Chapter Twenty-Four

August 1992

Admira tasted a certain sweetness in the early morning air that hung above their home, and she breathed it deeply into her lungs as she sat on the concrete stairs in her backyard sipping her coffee. She blew on the steam rising up from the cup. She had left Bosko alone as much as she could so he could spend as much time with his mom as she needed and wanted. Admira thought about her quiet moment with Rita and how she had promised her that she would take care of Bosko. She would protect him, knowing in her heart that they would never, ever be separated.

Sarajevo in the distance appeared like a burning heap of ash and rubble. She could see the unending white and black smoke rising upward into the sky. Yet it remained, its existence continued, a reminder to its besiegers that it was not going to vanish as easily as they had once believed. Admira shuddered at the thought of how the lives of young and the old, of men and women, were being taken every hour of every day, yet the blood that flowed down the streets and into gutters of their city had become the indestructible mortar that kept the city's *walls* still standing.

The more Sarajevans that were murdered, the harder and stronger their will became to survive and defend their city. Her coffee cup rested at her side, the steam still rising out of it. Her shoulders sank and Admira leaned forward and rested her face in the palm of her hands. The same sweet-tasting air she kept breathing in had in it the presence of a great sadness.

The screen door swung open and seconds later Admira felt Bosko's hand on her neck. She raised her shoulders and pressed her cheek against his fingers.

"Sit." He did. She handed him her cup of coffee.

"How is Rita?"

"Sad. Upset. But I won't let her change her mind."

Turning to Admira, who felt Bosko's breath against her neck, he said, "I'll never be able to thank your parents enough for taking in Mom."

"You're family, Bosh."

"Good to know." His comment brought a smile to Admira. "There's been something on your mind. What is it?" he asked.

She placed her hand on Bosko's thigh, exactly the way she'd done on that first day of the New Year when they sat and sipped their coffee and talked of poplars swaying in the wind and Sarajevo having a dual inclination.

"We don't fight." Admira's voice was soft.

"What do you mean?"

"We've never fought, do you realize that? A real knock-down, drag-out fight. Why? Couples always fight, but we never have."

Bosko laughed at Admira's comment. It was true that in all the years the two of them had been together, they hadn't had a fight, a real fight.

"Okay, when do you want to have one? I'm up for it."

"There's a reason I'm saying this, Bosh."

"I know." His tone was soft as he squeezed her hand. He got why she was saying it. The normal everyday experiences of being a couple no longer touched them. Being able to fight with one another was normal about life, about being a man and a woman. But now there was nothing normal about their lives.

"I hope for that day. I long for it to come when you and I can have a fight; fight every day and every day make love."

"What else do you wish for?"

"I want you to get angry at me for something I've done. And I want to get angry at you for something, for the many things you do. I want it to happen every day. I want a family. I want you to never stop loving me. I want to cook great meals for all of us. I want to shop for food with you. I want to be able to nag you."

"And what else, my Gypsy Girl?" He asked playfully.

"I want you to come home drunk and we fight about it. And then I want you to throw me on the bed and ravish me, and I'll fight you even as I enjoy every moment of being taken by you. And I want to spend money. I want to be able to waste it on frivolous things and not feel guilty about it. And I want us to never, ever stop doing every day, normal, boring things that couples say and do."

"Then we'll do all of these things."

"They don't know how lucky they are." Said Admira. "Those couples that are together who take it all for granted. Every single thing that you and I can't do anymore. They don't know how lucky they are that they can be boring with each other.

"It makes me so angry that we were stopped from being able to do it—to live life as a couple, that whether they like it or not are forced to feel every good, bad, and simple thing that happens to a man and woman. Those bastards shooting at us took that away from us."

In the distance, they could see the black and white smoke continuing to billow up into the sky while they sat on the concrete stairs. Bosko lifted her hand and kissed it.

Admira's tone was soft, but it was deliberate and intense. "What we do instead is to live our lives by repeating the same actions over and over again, every hour of every day. Actions that do only one thing keep us alive. It's become a story not worth telling anymore." Turning to Bosko Admira continued, "I want so desperately to be living in the kind of world, in which we should be. I want to—"

Bosko grabbed her. Admira was on the verge of tears.

"I want those same things," he whispered. Bosko, like Admira and like every other Sarajevan, had come to fully understand and experience the banality of survival and the banality of death. It was what all of their lives were now reduced to being. That the

285

death of every Sarajevan was significant to those who loved them was so true, yet it also remained true that no greater philosophical question was answered by their dying.

"How boring a story we Slavs continue to write about ourselves," she said, "and for the rest of the world to want to read about. Why should anyone care about us—we wretched Slavs." Admira leaned against Bosko. His arm was wrapped around her waist. Their breathing seemed to become one and the same and their chests rose and fell in unison.

"What I do know," he began to say, "is that it takes great strength and perseverance for us to repeat the same actions every moment of every day as we do our best to survive and live another day, defying those who are bent on killing us all. It's a boring exercise for all of us. To keep trying to survive one day to the next. The same action repeated day in and day out. And for many it will have been an act of futility because in the end their lives will have ended."

"Shh," she said. He could have been talking about their future and what lay in store for them. Admira slid onto his lap and buried her face against his neck. Holding her tight and pressing her chest against his he continued, "If every action, from the smallest to the most daring and most caring that we do, is boring, repeated over and over again without any end in sight, then let's keep doing it. Let's never stop doing it for each other, not now, not after this ends, not ever. Let us never forget what it took to survive, and what it took to beat them. What we've been forced to become in this city is to be better than we would otherwise have been."

She grabbed Bosko's arms, saying, "And I promise to never stop telling you the same thing over and over again, that we will always be together and that we will never be separated. And I promise you that I will repeat the same movements of my face when it's pressed against your neck."

"And I promise, Gypsy Girl, the same gesture of holding your hand and of kissing you the way I always do as many times as I can. Because I can't stop myself. And I'm not sorry that we haven't spent time fighting about something that was so unimportant to our lives. Do you know why?"

"No, why?"

"Because there are so many men and women now at this moment in our city who wish they could take it all back."

"Take what back, Bosh?"

"Those moments they'd spent doing and saying things that were hurtful to the person they love. A person who has now been taken from them. I would change nothing from that first moment when we met. And I would take this life over any other offered to me because it is with you."

Admira was sitting on Bosko's lap, her breasts pressed against his chest, her face pressed against the side of his neck. They held onto each other. In the distance lay their city. Black and white smoke kept ascending upward. The explosions had gotten more intense.

*

"Admira, come and join us. I've already gammoned Dad twice. It's no fun anymore."

"In a while, Tonya," her sister said. Admira sat with Rita in the living room. The cat kept crossing between the two of them, seeking affection. Getting all their *sugar*, Admira often said.

Rita clutched the yarn in her lap. She'd been knitting the same sweater for months. Not much yarn was left and definitely not enough for two sweaters, as she'd planned.

"All I want is to go back to my home, even if it's about to collapse. To be in my living room and bedroom and be with my husband, but I know it will never happen," she said, her voice

287

cracking as she held back tears.

Admira hugged Rita. "If it were me, I would be going mad too. All I can say is that he'll be with us. My Dad will do everything to keep Bosko safe, and I'll never leave him." Rita stared into Admira's eyes. "I will never leave his side. I promise."

"Someday you will make quite the daughter-in-law."

"You and I both know it. Bosko had no idea what he was signing up for the day he met me. I'm spooky, you know."

"Spooky?"

"And very strange."

Rita began to laugh.

"It's all true." Admira slid closer toward Rita. "Think only of the day when you'll see your son standing next to you, as he did when he hopped off that train the first day back from the army and landed on the station platform just a few feet away from you."

"I love you so much, Admira—so much!"

"Finish the two sweaters while you're with your sister and brother so Bosko and I can come and get them."

"Admira..."

"Yes?" Admira leaned forward and held Rita's hands. "What is it?"

"Do you think this war could ever separate you and Bosko?"

"Only a bullet could ever do that."

*

Bosko's mother was seated at the kitchen table with Tonya. Zao was standing next to his wife. Bosko and Admira were standing next to Rita. Djoka had arrived with news. His militia confederates were waiting outside in their car.

"We are ready. Tomorrow, be at the police station by 11am."

"Where is my mother going?" asked Bosko.

"You and a number of other Serbs have safe passage to enter a Serb-controlled area in the city. Once you are safe and on the other side, you will take a bus with the others headed for Belgrade. Muslim and Croatian men and women in Serb- controlled areas are waiting to be reunited with their families in the city. They have been separated from them since this madness began. Bring only one small suitcase with you."

"Thank you," said Rita softly. Saying nothing further, Djoka turned to leave. Opening the door, he stopped and turned to Rita. "It'll be fine. We've done this many times before. You're lucky— very lucky." He stepped outside on the concrete stairs and shut the door.

"Mom." Bosko knelt beside his mother, who was seated at the table. "This is great news, you'll be safe." Staring at her son and without saying a word, she lunged at Bosko, grabbed him tightly, and wept uncontrollably. She had only twenty-fours more with her son.

*

Rita closed her eyes, but sleep didn't come, just a shiver deep in her veins. It was early morning. Hours of her life had passed in quiet solitude, every moment of which she thought about Bosko. She was leaving him. Djoka had personally delivered the news.

The guilt in her heart for leaving her son haunted her every moment she'd remained awake. Her only comfort was that Bosko would be with Admira and her family. And now Mladjo would also help watch over him.

Bosko knocked on the door and waited for his mother to answer.

Zena appeared next to him. "Give her a moment, Bosh. Come, Admira has made everyone coffee." Zena took his arm and they went to the kitchen. After a few minutes, Rita joined them at the kitchen table. The girls remained in the living room.

Zao walked into the room and pulled out a chair.

"I have nothing to give either of you for all you have done," Rita said.

"Ah, but you have. You've given us Bosko," Zao said as he placed his hand over hers. "We'll take good care of him. You must take care of yourself. This will not last forever. What has been destroyed will have to be rebuilt. Families will reclaim each other. You will see. Bosko is my son, too."

Rita did something she'd never done before except to her husband. She lifted Zao's hand and kissed it.

"Mom, it's time." Rita said nothing but gave a slight nod. Bosko stood next to his mother, and she wrapped her arms around him. Zao was going to drive Bosko and his mother to the closest checkpoint, as he had done once before. Driving would give Bosko and his mom some quiet moments together. The road was far enough away from the heart of the city, on the outskirts, rarely traveled and generally ignored by the gunners in the hills. It was also heavily guarded by militias, who knew Zao and his family. Rita stood and embraced Zena. The Serbian and Muslim mothers held onto each other like family. They each had a child who shared a fierce and uncompromising love for the other.

Admira and Tonya finally joined everyone in the kitchen. No one knew what to say next. Bosko imagined moments like these have happened to other people. There was an ordinariness to it, good-byes can seem that way, but this was no ordinary goodbye. There was a banality to this moment as well. Rita was leaving—and that was it. For a split second Bosko felt that at any moment he'd wake up. Against the backdrop of what was happening to all of them, the killing, the murder, the death of the innocent. There was a simple goodbye that was taking place in a simple kitchen in a simple Muslim home. How unreal this moment seemed to be.

Without saying a word, Bosko held his mother's hand. Rita gripped his fingers and, pressing against him, she followed Bosko as they walked out of the kitchen.

Tonya and her mother stood pressed together on the porch.

"Wait, Bosko." Rita turned around. Walking back up the concrete stairs to Admira's sister and mother, Rita took hold of Tonya's hand and said, "Be safe, Tonya. Watch over your mom and dad. And take care of Admira. She's a wild thing."

"We know," Tonya answered.

Rita smiled, kissed Admira's sister on both cheeks, then returned to the car. Admira waited for her by the gate to the fence. Rita reached out and held Admira. "I will miss you so very much."

"Don't forget to knit us the sweaters. We're coming to get them."

"I promise." Rita kissed Admira and whispered, "Take care of each other, no matter what."

"We will, Rita." Admira hugged Bosko's mother tightly. "We will always be together."

Zao put Rita's bag into the trunk.

"Mom, we don't have much time." Bosko opened the rear car door. Rita took a last look at Admira and her family, then climbed in. Bosko got in beside her.

Zao started the car and in seconds they were gone.

*

Their second time into the city involved hiding and running from explosions and hidden snipers. Bosko was on high alert, his senses razor-sharp. He had to get his mother to Mladjo. Their fate today was not guaranteed; even the slightest thought of providence being on their side would be a split-second distraction that could prove fatal to one or both.

Rita was beside her son. She was determined to survive on these streets as they ran and sought constant cover from the eyes of their assassins. Bosko and his mother were across the street from the police station and were concealed behind a burned-out truck, waiting to make their mad dash. It was ironic that he was taking his mother to this station in Sarajevo. It was the same police station that Gravilo Princip had been dragged into the afternoon of June 28, 1914, minutes after he had shot the archduke and his pregnant wife. On that day, a twenty-year-old Serb did not know the repercussions of what his act of murdering two people would unleash.

Bosko, holding his mother, was about to run across the intersection with her. He too was a Serb about to enter the same station. The repercussion of his act of getting his mother out of Sarajevo was simple. She was going to live.

Holding onto Rita's hand, he realized that Mladjo had purposely chosen this police station to be his headquarters. It was a reminder to him and all those in the city who knew him. This station remained a symbol of the atrocities that would be committed because of the act of one man. Its brick and stone remained strong, intact, no part of its structure seemingly ready to be consigned to rubble and the past, much like their ethnic hatred. Its windows had been sealed up so tightly that no outside light seeped in. Large concrete and metal barriers had been strategically placed around the front of the building to avoid it being car-or truck-bombed. And because Mladjo and his men were the back-door conduit for exchanges between Serbs, Muslims, and Croatians, the building wasn't a target for shelling.

Bosko knew that Mladjo's criminal network extended into many parts of the city. For the moment, criminals and defenders stood side by side against a common enemy. His contacts with each side ran deep, and everyone kept their word, so none of the exchanges had ended in disaster. Without Mladjo and his ruthless gang, which was feared by both Muslim and Serb, more blood would have been shed by both sides if such trades went awry. None had, so far.

"Ready, Mom."

"I'm ready, son." She kissed his hand, and, on the count of three, they emerged from behind the burnt-out truck and ran as fast as they could.

*

When they arrived inside of Mladjo's militia headquarters, Bosko and his mother sat on the leather sofa in his office. Mladjo's men were expecting them this time and had ushered them there to wait. The interior office was furnished with comfortable chairs and sofas and kilim carpets from Sarajevo. Lace covered the tables, made by Muslim Yugoslavs. Rita's palms sweated. Bosko held his mother's hand tightly.

"I will see you again," Rita said to Bosko, holding back her tears.

"Yes. You will," he replied. Rita and Bosko seared the image of each other into every pore of their being. "Are you sure you have enough money to pay for the bus trip to Belgrade?"

"Yes, plenty," she said softly.

Djoka entered and said in a cold, flat voice, "It's time."

Rita immediately wrapped her arms around Bosko. But she had resolved to believe that she would see her precious son again. She gave him a mother's look of fierce tenderness. Tears gathered in the corner of her eyes, but not a single one rolled down her cheek. She reached up and kissed him on his lips.

They followed Djoka to a small group of men and women who were also leaving, all thanks to Mladjo.

"Rita," Mladjo said as he approached. "You will be on the other side soon." Mladjo meant the side controlled by the Serbs.

"And they will put you on the road, and then it's a bus ride to your family in Serbia." He embraced her and whispered, "I will watch out for Bosko."

She nodded. It was all she wanted.

"Thank you, Mladjo." Bosko could not have sounded more relieved. His mother was finally going to be safe.

Mladjo shook Bosko's hand firmly, but kept his emotions in check. He was inscrutable. An invaluable quality in a leader, Bosko thought.

"I have matters to attend to," Mladjo said, and turned and walked away. He saw no need to prolong the goodbye. He'd said enough.

Some of those also leaving looked despairing, others ashamed. A door opened next to the brick wall of the jail. It was a "keep" that had incarcerated some of Sarajevo's most notorious criminals. No longer being used for that purpose, it opened to give these strangers their freedom when the city itself had become a prison. Rita couldn't take the first step toward the door.

Bosko placed his hand on his mother's shoulder. "Finish the sweaters so Admira and I can come get them."

A man motioned to them to start walking.

"I love you, Mom."

PART SIX

Chapter Twenty-Five

September 1992

A month passed. A few days after her departure, Rita had gotten word to Mladjo by a messenger used by the militia who traveled delivering news to both sides when loved ones were resettled. He was Mladjo's personal "emissary," and would not be harmed by either side. She was safe and living with her brother and sister in Belgrade. She'd also been able to contact Serge in Italy.

For the first time since the siege had started, Bosko and Admira felt a sense of hope. They partied at Admira's home. Seeing how happy it had made Bosko to know his mother was safe made Admira even more certain about keeping their lives intact and unchanged. They were going to make it; they were all going to make it.

"I don't want you to go," Admira pleaded with Bosko once more. She hadn't stopped pleading with him since he'd made his decision to go back into Sarajevo. They stood together near the fence of the backyard, with Bosko holding onto his khaki duffel bag.

"I have to, Admira. You know I have to."

"Papa says you can stay, he doesn't care what the neighbors say or feel. This is his home."

"Yes, it is—and it's yours and your family's. And nothing must happen to them because of me."

"Let me come with you."

"Not yet. I have to fix up the apartment. I don't even know if the building is still standing. And if it is, whether the apartment is empty and habitable."

"What if you can't stay there? Will you come back?"

"I'll find Miro, and he and I will find a place together. Admira —I don't know about a lot of things but I need to find out. I will come to you."

"When?"

"When I am done. Promise you will wait for me to come to you. Promise me, Gypsy Girl. Do I have your word? You will wait for me to come to you. And you will not run headlong into the city looking for me. Promise me."

"Bosko..."

"Promise me on your love for me that you will wait for me to come to you no matter how long it might take. No matter how long it takes."

She shook her head no. A few moments later, she shook her head yes. Admira knew this is what she had to do—wait. She hated having to do it. It would drive her mad doing it. But she had to do it. Bosko had to focus on surviving in the city and face whatever would come his way. She had to honor it; she had to believe he was going to be okay. They had made it so far, they had dodged and outrun the bullets and the explosions. But they were going to be separated when she had promised it would never happen. Never again, she uttered into her soul, would she let herself be separated from Bosko—not ever again. She leapt into his arms, and he held onto to her.

"I love you, I love you." Whispering into his ear, it sounded to Admira as if she were screaming it because she wanted the whole world to hear it. Her family was standing at the kitchen window watching Admira and Bosko saying their goodbyes.

"Dad," said Tonya, turning to Zao as if to plead with him to stop Bosko from leaving.

"Tonya, Bosko can stay but he won't. I cannot stop him."

Bosko knew he couldn't stay with Admira's family. He was a Serb. Their neighbors were harboring a growing animosity toward him. And now no Serb could simply leave Sarajevo if he wanted to or even if he could. Every Serb could become a potential sniper if he were allowed to leave the city, or become another man behind the guns in the hills firing down on Sarajevo. Every day he remained, he made her family the focus of the enmity of their neighbors. His mother was safe—that's what mattered. Now he would be able to take care of himself.

Bosko slung his duffel bag over his shoulder. Looking at the kitchen window, he saw Admira's family and waved to them. They did the same.

He kissed Admira the same kiss he always gave her. It was a kiss that said, I will see you again. Then Bosko opened the gate and started down the gravel road toward Sarajevo toward his future.

With both her clenched fists, Admira started banging the top of the fence, feeling powerless and so very fearful for Bosko as she watched him finally disappearing into the distance.

*

Djoka stood at the door to the apartment.

"You knew I was here?" asked Bosko.

"We make it our business to be aware of many things."

"Come in."

Djoka followed Bosko into the apartment. The three other militiamen decided to remain in the hallway.

"This building is a tomb. It'll collapse at any time, no wonder no one lives here."

"There is one other person. My babysitter."

"What?"

"Radmilla. She used to babysit me when I was a child. She refuses to leave. I am in good company; she'll take good care of me."

Djoka smiled, just barely, at Bosko's comment.

"It's the only place that I can call home," said Bosko. "As you can see, there is much work to be done to make it habitable."

"You will be doing more than housekeeping and house cleaning in the coming days. Be at the station tomorrow at 8 a.m. sharp. Miro will be there as well. Has he visited you?"

"Yes. He's staying at—"

"We know where he's staying." Djoka's response was curt. "It's good you have at least one friend in Sarajevo."

"Why is it good?"

"Why do you ask questions? Don't be late," Djoka snapped, and, giving a quick look around the apartment, turned and headed for the door.

Bosko went back to the task of cleaning up the apartment, which had sustained continuous damage since that day he had left with his mother for Admira's. As he was about to enter the kitchen, a massive explosion occurred outside, not far from his building. It was followed by another and then several more after that. He stood still as the building shook. The concussions reverberated throughout his body. He felt his bones rattle. He remained still and slowly lifted his eyes up to the ceiling. Was it about to collapse? Was he, as Djoka said, going to be entombed?

Throughout the evening and into the late hours of the night, his neighborhood was bombarded by massive explosions and his building kept shaking and trembling as if at any moment it would collapse. He brought Radmilla, to be with him, and together they sat and sipped many cups of weak tea throughout the night in the dim light of flickering candles as their home, along with the neighborhood, seemed to be on the verge of crumbling into rubble.

"It's like when you were a baby," Radmilla said. "Here I am, taking care of you again."

"You are," he said, squeezing her cheek gently.

"It was good to hear that your mother is safe."

"Admira and I will see her soon," Bosko said confidently. In the dim candlelight, as he stared at what continued to remain the strength of Sarajevo—its women—Radmilla heard Bosko say, "Tell me some stories of those times when you would babysit me, Radmilla. Was I a good boy?"

"No—trouble, always trouble, always wanting to go outside and play. You were like every young boy, always wanting to play games. You couldn't stand to be home."

And as he listened to Radmilla speak, he closed his eyes. If it was going to end this way, then his last thoughts would be of Admira.

*

"Do you know what this is about?" Bosko asked Miro. They had arrived separately to meet at the police station, and sat on the same bench as Rita had just before she'd had to say good-bye to her son.

Miro shook his head. He as well as Bosko were in the dark about what Mladjo wanted from them. Miro noticed that Bosko had what looked like a smirk or a smile on his face.

"What are you smiling about? Whatever is going on, it's not funny."

"No, it's not."

Miro lowered his head and said under his breath, "How are we going to survive this—how? I barely have any more food, there's been no water or electricity in my building for over a month and no one knows when it will come back." He sounded desperate, like every other Sarajevan who was possessed by the same thought.

"We will," Bosko said emphatically. His smile remained. It was because he and Radmilla had survived last night when it seemed that at any moment they might be buried under tons of rubble. For a brief few moments, as he sat on this familiar bench, Bosko allowed himself to start to believe that maybe he was protected by some strange unseen force. That he and Admira would survive this siege. They had so far, against all odds, travelling the four miles each way to each other's homes under a hail of gunfire and countless explosions—every day. He opened his eyes. They were going to make it. He could feel within his chest, where the beating of his heart grew stronger, that they would live and survive this time. Miro kept staring at Bosko and at that strange smile on his face.

Djoka stepped out of the office and, looking at both men, said, "Inside."

They followed him into Mladjo's office. Mladjo said nothing to them except to point to two empty wooden chairs. Bosko and Miro sat down. Bosko more than Miro maintained eye contact with the gangster, who rested back against his oak desk.

"It's time to talk about your future," Mladjo said. Miro and Bosko were sitting beside each other. Bosko seemed more relaxed. Mladjo noticed Miro avoided making eye contact with anyone. It seemed to the gangster that Miro's thoughts ran deep and were unsettled.

"I will try to assist as much as I can in these next days and months." Bosko nodded. Miro remained still. Bosko understood exactly what Mladjo meant. News had traveled fast throughout the city and to his neighborhood. Bosko had been "noticed" as being a friend of a vicious criminal. Mladjo's star was rising politically and in the criminal world. It gave him great cachet among many Sarajevans. He and his criminal friends had been among the city's first defenders when the siege began. Bosko and Miro's relationship with Mladjo would act as a buffer and protect them from being singled out by many Sarajevans who had suffered the brutal loss of a loved one at the hands of a Serb and who might want to exact revenge.

"It will never be understood or fully appreciated what it feels like, what emotions run through a person's head and heart, when they know that the moment they leave their home, it could be the last thing they do in this life."

Neither Bosko nor Miro responded.

"And only in a time of savagery like the one we are facing now will a person fully appreciate the gift of life and being alive. Don't you think?"

"Yes," Bosko replied, staring at his hands. Miro simply nodded.

"Even as I speak, we can hear the explosions outside. Someone will die very shortly; many will die today."

Bosko looked up at the gangster. His words were a clear reference to the fact that the people who were about to be killed were being killed by Serbs. He and the gangster stared at one another.

"They will be killed by a single bullet, or simply evaporate because a shell landed and exploded a few feet from them."

Was he just a coward? Was it just that simple? Bosko kept thinking. He had not participated when the demonstrations for peace to prevail had first begun in Sarajevo and in other parts of Bosnia. He had stayed out of it. When he finally did add his voice to the throngs demonstrating for peace, it was already too late.

"It has become an art form in Sarajevo, being killed. That is how they see it, those bastards in the hills. Every person killed by their hand is their own personal work of art."

"Your point?" Miro asked.

"There is no point, Miro, to what is happening to all of us. Only that we are living a reality that no one could have imagined." Looking at Bosko, the gangster said, "Your father always used to tell me that this city was a place of palaces. Saraj Ovasi. I will always remember his words."

"Not anymore. Now it's the city of the dead and the dying,"

Bosko said ruefully.

"But we will prevail. We must," Mladjo was unequivocal.

At hearing the word "prevail," Bosko asked himself if it were really too late. Could he still make a difference? A suppressed anger began to resurface in Bosko. It was telling him to do the one thing he swore to himself he would not and should not do.

"What makes you so sure we will prevail?" Miro's tone sounded disdainful. "That's not a city outside beyond this cozy jail. It's a gray, cold, lifeless cemetery. We should give them the city in exchange for all of our lives. Let them have what's left of it. Let it be plowed into the ground and forgotten for all time."

The gangster curled his fingers into a fist as his face lost all color. His eyes narrowed as he glared at Miro.

"And by doing that, Miro, what would it say to the dead?"

"They're dead, Mladjo. But we're alive. This is just a city—"

"No! It is not just a city. It's our city! Worth its price in blood to the last person left alive. Understood?"

"Not mine," Miro retorted, raising his head to glare back at Mladjo for the first time. "Not my blood," he repeated.

"We shall see," was Mladjo's retort.

Bosko had been listening to Miro and Mladjo speak but what he was really hearing was his own inner thoughts. A very familiar anger and rage had resurfaced, that he had always believed he could suppress, an anger that kept telling him to join Mladjo's militia as one of those men who hunt down the Serbs in the hills or the snipers hiding in their rat holes, who were killing men, women, and children.

He was a Sarajevan, not a Serb! He would not be killing his ilk or his kind. These were monsters that should not be granted mercy when found. Bosko felt himself losing control of himself, of every rational thought. Was he capable of killing? Yes, he silently screamed at himself.

"As I was saying," Mladjo continued, "we must discuss your

future. You'll both be working with my militia."

"What do you mean, working?" Miro asked.

"I have given each of you certain duties to perform. You can't simply sit around waiting for this siege to be over and do nothing while others are doing everything to keep Sarajevo from being wiped off the map."

Bosko and Miro nodded. Bosko knew that it had to be this way. He had to show his loyalty to his city, to its citizens, to Mladjo who was now their quasi protector.

"These duties are required of both of you, and you are to do them without question. Am I making myself clear?"

"Yes," Bosko answered. It took Miro a few seconds before he responded affirmatively. He and Bosko still didn't know the specifics of their duties. But Miro realized that it was Bosko's connection to Mladjo that might shield them from the worst retribution that many others believed should be their punishment.

"You will both be with other members of the militia. This group includes some of my more colorful associates. Who they are is not your concern. Leave it at that. Understood?"

Miro nodded, Bosko remained silent. Then standing up, he said, staring at Mladjo, "No. There is something else I can do. Put me into your unit that hunts down these bastards."

"Bosko—wait," Miro cautioned Bosko.

"I must do this." Djoka kept observing both men, in silence. "My dad once told me to be proud that I am a Serb. I am." Mladjo remained silent. "But I have no love or loyalty toward any Serb who is responsible for what is happening to Sarajevo. Their deaths are good news to all of us. I will find them, and I will kill them."

Mladjo walked over to his bar cart and poured for himself and Djoka two shots of Refosk. Handing a glass to Djoka he turned to Bosko.

"What would Admira say to this choice you've made?"

"It's my choice. She has nothing to do with it."

"Hmm..." Mladjo sipped his Refosk, then gulped down the remainder and, slamming the shot glass onto the table, he turned to Bosko and said, "No, it's not only your choice. I don't think Admira wants to see you turn into a monster."

"I will live with what I become."

"Indeed."

"Do we have a deal?"

"No," replied the gangster.

"Why not?"

The gangster observed Bosko and Miro intently. "Neither you nor Miro are killers," he said. "The kind that is needed at this time. It requires a certain clear, detached thinking and lack of empathy for those you will kill; and a lack of conscience over the fact that you know you are—a psychopath. And neither of you are capable of being one—that is, at least for the moment. Yes, for the moment. Pray that there never comes a day when you, Bosh, have found a reason to want to kill and not stop killing.

"Only one thing could make that happen, and that is if the most precious thing in your life is taken from you. Pray that the day never comes. Because when it happens, it turns peaceful people into monsters."

Bosko's heart beat faster. The thought of something happening to Admira took his breath away. What if he held a lifeless Admira in his arms? Wouldn't he then become that monster? Wouldn't he seek out vengeance against every Serb he could find? Their eyes met. It was clear they knew what the other was thinking.

"There are enough killers and monsters amongst us in Sarajevo and in her beautiful hills. I won't be responsible for creating one more. No, it will not be by my hand, Bosko, but by your own— should you become a monster."

Bosko sat down and stared at the floor. He knew he could

become this monster. After all, he was a Serb, it was already in his DNA, just waiting to be released.

Leaning against his desk and picking up his shot glass, staring at its beveled edges for a brief moment, Mladjo said, "I keep thinking of something Bosko. There must be an answer to what happens when all of this is over. How do lives begin again? How do we marry each other again? How do we build again? You and Admira and, yes, Miro, you and your wife, all of us will have to find a way. That is how we'll win as survivors when this ends."

Mladjo's words never rang truer than at this moment. "So for now you will need to be patient and smart," he added.

Bosko nodded. Miro remained focused on the floor.

"Be here tomorrow morning at seven o'clock to receive the details regarding your new duties. That is all. I think we understand each other."

"I believe we do," Bosko answered.

*

Bosko had done everything possible to make a livable life for him and Admira here in their city of death. Their two lives spent together, was the only thing that mattered.

He stood back and took in all of the work he'd done in these last several weeks. He went through a mental checklist to see if he'd forgotten anything. At the same time, he went over everything he'd already done in preparation for Admira's arrival. Items he'd found and didn't need had been bartered away at the makeshift markets that had sprung up in the city. Any kind of linen he found that was not soiled Bosko used to barter with the ambulance drivers, who used the linen for bandages. He'd been on the lookout to stock up on toiletries, like toothpaste and toilet paper, especially shampoo and conditioner for Admira. Soap for his fifty-cent Serbian head was just fine. Any canned goods, crackers, pickles anything that was edible he bartered for or had scavenged for in his bombed out city.

Electricity and water were still being delivered to the building intermittently, and he'd found a wood-burning pot-belly stove and brought it back from one of the many outdoor markets, pulling it home on a sled he'd devised while dodging bullets and explosions. It would allow him to heat the apartment during the winter months and also boil the water that for all Sarajevans was no longer uncontaminated. He examined the crude form of plaster that he mixed together and used to patch up the gaping holes in the ceiling and walls.

Radmilla was the only other resident in the building. She had told Bosko and Rita that she was going down with the ship.

Bosko sat on his field bed in the living room and took a break from stacking scraps of wood against the wall. He was back in his apartment on Kosovo Hill. Miro was by his side every day, working alongside him. While Admira remained with her parents, Bosko had spent every moment away from his militia duties fixing up the place for her so she could join him.

He and Miro were part of a militia unit whose duties, among many things, was to hunt down the snipers once their location was discovered. Bosko detested himself for not getting involved sooner in making his voice heard, like so many other Sarajevans had already done.

Now his and Miro's contribution to their city's survival was to work closely with spotters in their unit who, after discovering a hidden sniper's location, would relay it to Bosko, who would immediately transfer the sniper's location into a code that was radioed to militia units who remained concealed close by, waiting to receive this code so that they could race off to root out the sniper before he had the chance to kill again. Bosko looked forward to that moment when, after having relayed in code the whereabouts of a sniper, news would arrive that he had been found and executed.

Every day Bosko searched the other abandoned buildings in his neighborhood and well beyond, rummaging and scavenging for material he could use to repair the walls and parts of the ceiling.

Any usable items, utensils, or tools, he brought back to the apartment. He knew he could trade them for supplies he and Admira would need in order to survive. Whenever he found food of any kind that had been left and not discovered by squatters, it was like finding a buried treasure. He'd become delirious after discovering a few dry biscuits or unused tea bags, and especially canned goods, like peas or corn.

If he happened upon candles of any kind, or light bulbs, or a working lamp, it brought him to tears. Nothing worthwhile was left in any of the apartments once Bosko had completed his methodical ransacking. After weeks of scavenging and working to make his home as habitable as possible, he was ready. The usable portion of the apartment consisted of a kitchen, bathroom, and living room. The electricity did still miraculously show itself for brief intermittent moments, but never lasted very long.

The only way to navigate through the apartment, especially during the night when the sunlight wasn't streaming through the two-inch-holes cut into the wood that covered the windows and sliding glass doors, was to burn candles if you had them; if not, then homemade kandilos was the other alternative. They had to be made continually. Bosko had made a dozen with the help of Miro. After collecting a dozen glass jars, they filled each one half with water and half with oil. After cutting five to seven millimeters of cork, Miro would then hand it to Bosko who would then drag through the cork fringes pulled from the carpet in his mother's bedroom and from a section of carpet he ripped up off the living room floor.

Then Bosko would take a very short metal or tin strip and

would place it above the opening of the glass jar. This was so that the wick would stay above the oil. Through that metal strip ran the carpet fringe soaked in the oil. The light from the kandilos was how countless Sarajevans navigated their apartments each and every night.

It was a world, their world, lit only by fire.

*

A gaping hole in his parents' bedroom had been sealed with a thick, blue U.N. plastic tarp he'd found that was used to cover the food trucks when they were allowed into the city.

Once the tarp was in place, he placed the mattress and box spring against it. Finally, Bosko shut his parents' bedroom door for the last time and sealed the opening with another blue tarp. He had blocked off the passageway leading to that bedroom with a few wooden bureaus he'd dragged out from the other abandoned apartments. He'd stacked them one on top of the other in the hallway. Eventually, he'd take them apart and saw them into pieces for firewood.

On this day, he'd spent a long time sitting in the hallway, feeling terribly lonely. He was without his mother and father, and he missed them a lot. But he and Admira would be together soon, and that fact kept his mind clear and allowed him to focus.

He realized how lucky he'd been that no one had scavenged their apartment after he and Rita had left it in such a hurry. It gave Bosko for just a fleeting moment a sense that it must have a meaning that he could come back to his home. It had to be a good sign, a possible hint that, as he struggled to survive, fate would grant him a few breaks. There was not a Sarajevan, not a man woman, or child who did not need fate to keep granting them some small kindness.

Bosko was ever so glad that the fear of being entombed kept

those who were homeless away. The building leaned dramatically to one side, so squatters who came and stayed in other apartments didn't venture past the first floor. Bosko's apartment was on the third floor. The building rattled and shook with each nearby explosion. It was abandoned, except for him and Radmilla and so none of the new rules for keeping a building secured for its inhabitants applied.

In countless other buildings of the city the entrance door remained locked at night and residents and neighbors took turns guarding the building. No longer did the names of the residents remain on their doors. Names were even removed from letter boxes. Whether you were Muslim, Croatian, or Serbian was no longer important for being able to survive in Sarajevo. Remaining anonymous and unified was vital. They were fighting for their lives and their homes against a common enemy who wanted to divide and obliterate them from history.

*

Tonya walked into the kitchen after having turned off the radio in the living room. The same news of what had been happening these last weeks and months was being repeated. No one wanted to hear it. She picked up a handful of her mother's garden zucchinis on the counter and washed them in the sink, then joined Admira, who was dicing some of them, getting them ready for her mother to make her zucchini soup. There was nothing new to talk about, and only one thing to consider. Was Bosko okay? Admira was certain that if something had happened to him, Mladjo would have sent word. She had to believe that Bosko was okay and that he would keep his promise to her to come to her, when he could.

She slammed the knife on the cutting board. She was beside herself. Every bit of news they had heard was that the

309

bombardment had gotten much worse. Bodies were piling up on the streets and sidewalks and were just left there to rot. She had to be next to him—yet she wasn't, and it produced an uncontrollable anger in her for being here in her home, away from Bosko, and for what was being done to all of them. She wanted to kill, to inflict the same horrors being inflicted on them on those who were responsible.

Zena placed her hand on Admira's shoulder and, turning her daughter around, said,

"It's enough, Tonya and I will finish the zucchinis. Go join your father; he's chopping wood. It might do you some good as well. Go on."

Admira pushed open the screen door and jumped off the concrete stairs onto the grass. Zao looked up at his daughter just moments before he brought down the maul and split a log in half. Without waiting for her dad to say a thing, she began to collect the split logs strewn about the yard and started to stack them on top of a cord of wood pressed against the side of the house that was already four feet high. She had done this since she was a child, and always the way her dad had taught both his girls. Zao continued to split the logs. Admira bent down, picked up the metal pitcher, and walked over to the outdoor well. She began to pump the handle of the well and, holding the opening of the pitcher under the mouth of the pump, she watched as the water gushed into it.

She reached down to pick up a glass lying on the grass, she blew away the dust that had collected on it and filled it with water. "Dad, you need to drink water." She handed him the glass, and then, without a second thought, she poured the rest of the cold well water over her father's head.

"Ah, my God, that's cold. I remember when your mother would do this. Ah—it feels good."

Wiping the water off his face and handing the glass to his

daughter, he dried his hands against his pants, grabbed his ax, and split another log.

"So, what's new?" he asked.

Admira let out an enormous laugh and then wrapped her arms around him. "Sometimes, Dad, you really can make me laugh."

"Glad to hear it," he said, holding onto her. "He's fine. Bosko made you a promise to see you again, and he'll keep it."

*

Bosko left his apartment with a sense of urgency. There were many things that he couldn't stop himself from thinking. The most pressing being that in the last month, he had noticed how a sudden shift in the line between those who were defending their city and those who were bent on its destruction could suddenly and irrevocably change and cut him and Admira off from one another. What would they do if that happened? He had no answer.

Getting to Admira today was a must; she had to know. Her parents had to know. He wasn't just coming to visit them. They had to know he wanted their daughter with him in the city. He was bringing the worst news to all of her family. But if they were cut off from each other that would become unbearable for both of them.

He forced himself to turn his face away from the corpses lying on the street. Stay focused, he kept repeating to himself. You can be seen. You have to get to her and show her how selfish you are because you want her to be with you. Now run, a familiar voice inside of him commanded Bosko. They were all running in every direction. The screaming of victims hadn't ended. The gurgling sounds made by those who were shot in the neck or stomach and had not yet died, their sound filtered up into the stale

311

air that clung above their city.

Run, Bosko, run.

*

Zao had drunk his third glass of water while sitting comfortably in his chair in the backyard, watching Admira wield the maul. She, much more than Tonya, enjoyed having to do this chore, and in her youth had spent many hours chopping wood in the backyard. Every few seconds a crackling, splitting sound permeated the air. It was the sound of a fresh ash log split in two by one stroke of the maul. She was wearing her overalls. Every day it was the same for Admira: she would help her dad in the garage, or she would help her mom bottle her preserves or help with the cooking, and when she wasn't doing that, she was chopping wood.

Admira knew she had to keep her hands and mind occupied. Having time to think was not the best way to spend her days while waiting for Bosko. Zao was relieved to have a break from chopping wood. He observed his daughter.

"I made a promise," Admira said moments after splitting another log. "I promised—" She turned to her father, the wooden handle resting on her shoulder. "I promised I would never again complain of long, uneventful days—when they happen to us again. I want, I crave, boredom."

She placed another log on the chopping block. She knew as did most Sarajevans of how lucky they had been to enjoy a lyrical if uneventful life living in one of the most beautiful hamlet cities to be found anywhere in the world, until all of a sudden their lives had been turned upside down. But even then, she said to herself as she held the wooden handle of the maul in both hands, ready to strike another log. Even as the war came to them, every Sarajevan had somehow found a way to navigate through its

312

horrors.

The sound of splitting the log broke the silence. Admira looked down at it and thought of how they had weathered the siege by visiting each other every day. Prior to that eventful day when it all began, she and Bosko had had no conflict in their lives. They let no one get in their way, and no one separated them or threatened them. They always got along and hardly argued. How very boring of the two of them, thought Admira. And how she longed with every fiber in her being to have that boring life back once again.

"You know something papa?"

"What?"

"If I could reach out to tell every man and woman out there in this world, I would say, looking into their eyes while holding onto them and shaking them, be happy with the boredom of your life. Be happy you can repeat as many times as possible the day- to-day things you do in life. Live every moment for the moment's sake. Do not spend a second thinking of tomorrow; it's promised to no one. And without love you have nothing at all. It is the only thing that matters in life. That's what I would tell them, Papa, that's what I would want them to understand. How lucky they are to have such a life and to never take it for granted because in an instant, it can all be taken away."

With one thunderous swing of the maul, she split the log in two.

*

Bosko could make out in the distance the outline of Admira's home and the homes of her neighbors. He hadn't as yet passed through the last checkpoint before beginning the long walk down the familiar gravel road that led to Admira's home. 'Be vigilant' that voice reminded him. He had let his guard down for just a

313

moment not thinking to look around the immediate area and see how others were reacting. Everyone who ventured outside was a pair of eyes for someone else.

He couldn't help it: Bosko was so happy. A month had passed since he'd been in Sarajevo, and in that time he'd fixed up the apartment as best as he could. He'd be seeing Admira and her family soon. Did he really think that taking her away from her family was an honorable thing to do? Once again he heard those words that had never left him.

Have you ever been in love... the kind of love that cares for nothing and no one, only for what is selfishly loved?

Bosko's palms began to sweat. How would he begin to tell her parents that he wanted to have Admira with him? "Just go, you fool you're almost there. She's been waiting to see you. Think of nothing else."

Should he call out her name as he got closer? No, that would alert their neighbors. Should he just walk up to the door and knock on it, as if today were just another ordinary day and he had come like he had in days past to pick up Admira? How should he enter their home, bringing the news that he wanted her to be with him?

The explosions and screeching of cars barreling down the road snapped him back to reality.

Admira was at the well, pumping water into the metal pitcher. Her father was watching her. She was so despondent. Placing the pitcher on the grass, she sat down on the brick outcrop that also acted as a pedestal for the pump. Her father split a log. Admira became lost in her thoughts. Then, forcing herself to do it, she stood up. "Do not think of things. Do not think of anything," she reminded herself, and went back to filling the pitcher with water.

"Dad!" Admira's tone was loud as she pumped the gushing water. "Don't—please." She didn't like hearing that familiar sound. A few moments later, she heard it again. She spun around, staring at her dad. "What are you doing? Please don't."

"I haven't done anything."

"Stop whistling."

"I'm not—I didn't hear a thing. I'm splitting the logs."

A few moments later, they both heard it, a whistling in the distance. They both turned their heads toward the road. Admira ran to the fence, holding onto the pitcher with both hands, the water sloshing all about and soaking her.

"Bosko!" she screamed. The moment he saw her standing at the fence and heard his name, he picked up his pace and then he started to run. She flung open the gate and bolted toward him; in just seconds, he was standing a few feet from her. He'd been whistling that Bosnian folk song, about a Serbian boy in love with a Muslim girl. It was the only way he could think of to announce himself as he approached her home.

Admira felt as if she'd kissed Bosko a thousand times. All he wanted was to hold onto her and not let go. The opening of the metal pitcher was turned toward the ground, the water streaming out; the pitcher slipped out of her fingers.

And lo, in the garden, in the shade of a jasmine,
There with a pitcher in her hand stood... Admira.

*

Everyone was seated at the kitchen table. Zena had served Bosko a plate of cevapi, with somun bread. It was a smaller portion than what she had served Bosko in the past, yet he was so grateful for having it. He ate his food diligently, at times looking up from his plate and staring at Admira's family. He felt so unworthy of their kindness; it made it all the more difficult for him to tell them the news.

Admira and her family kept quiet. She filled his water glass.

Bosko stopped eating. Placing the last piece of bread back onto his plate, he looked up at Zao and said, "Miro and I are with the militia. Mladjo has given us a job. We are part of a unit that hunts down the snipers."

"Bosko," Admira said, turning him toward her. "No you mustn't do—"

"I'm not. I wanted to. I volunteered to. I can do it. Kill every Serb who is doing this. But Mladjo said no. He said I'm not a killer... not yet."

"He's right, you never could be."

"Yes, I could!" His tone was adamant. Grabbing both her arms and staring into her charcoal-black eyes, Bosko repeated, "Oh yes, I can."

"Son, Bosh," Zao said. "Mladjo is right. That is not who you are, or would ever wish to be."

Bosko lowered his head. "I don't know who I am anymore, Zao. But I could kill them. I would hunt them down and kill them all."

"Stop. Do you hear me? You are not that person." Admira squeezed his hand, resting on the table. "Don't ever say that Bosh. You are the best of what a man should be."

Bosko remained silent. Knowing that he had to tell her family that he wanted Admira to be with him in Sarajevo. He rested back against his chair and looking at her mom and then her Dad. They heard him say.

"There's one more thing. The fighting in the city has gotten much worse. The shelling has intensified both day and night. There is talk that there will be door-to-door fighting in the streets soon. By the Serbs in the city who will be joined by those everyone believes will be coming down from the mountains— against the rest of us. The barricades that separate neighborhoods constantly change. I don't now know when I will be able to visit next.

"Zao, I want Admira to be with me in the city. I know what I am saying is selfish, and I have no right to ask it. But if we are cut off from each other. I don't know when we'll see each other again."

Admira's father kept staring at him. Tonya was silent. Admira was staring at her dad, with an all too familiar look. Zao began to shake his head no.

"You must go." Everyone looked at Zena. "You must go with Bosko." She was staring at her eldest. Zena realized that her daughter had to be with Bosko. It had become far too dangerous for them to keep travelling back and forth to see each other. And how would she and Zao ever be able to stop Admira if she decided to hurl herself into the city looking for Bosko because she hadn't heard from him in months? Nor could Admira accept just waiting for the news to arrive, telling her the worst had happened to Bosko. There were no good options left for her and Bosko, and Zena knew it. She looked at her husband, who hadn't taken his eyes off his wife. "They have to go, Zao. It's the only way they can be safe. Mladjo is there, he will protect them. They can't do this anymore."

"Mom—thank you." Admira was on the verge of tears. Tonya got up from her chair and went over to Admira and hugged her, and wouldn't let go of her sister.

"You'll have each other to watch over." Zena reached across the table and held both Admira's and Bosko's hands.

Their city had become a cauldron of death. But they would watch out for each other. Zena knew that together her daughter and Bosko always seemed stronger, because together their lives became aligned and purposeful. Perhaps that would also become their shield and protector.

"Quickly, now. You must pack. I have money. Bosko, you and Admira will take as many preserves and food as you can carry back. Admira, hurry. You and Bosko must leave before it gets

317

dark."

Admira jumped up from the kitchen table, and Tonya did the same. "Go with your sister and help her to pack. Zao and I will get the preserves. Bosh, finish your food. Come on, we don'thave time to waste."

Bosko turned to Zao, who hadn't taken his eyes off him.

*

Two hours had passed since Bosko first arrived at Admira's home. Now they were standing on the concrete stairs in the backyard, with her holding onto her bulging suitcase and Bosko holding two bags filled with food.

"Mom, I'll call as much as I can, as long as the phone keeps working. And we'll visit whenever we can. Tonya, take care of them—promise me."

"I promise. And you," she said, looking up at Bosko, "take care of my sister."

"With my life, Tonya."

"Dad—"

Zao didn't give his daughter a chance to say anything more. He grabbed her and said, "Do every boring thing you've ever wanted to do and keep doing it."

"I promise, Papa."

"Think of only each other. Live only for each other. You will be fine. Now go. Hurry."

Bosko and Admira trekked across the yard, through the gate in the fence, and stood onto the gravel road. Her family stood by the fence.

"Every boring thing—remember that."

"I promise, Papa."

"Thank you, sir."

"You have what matters most to the both of us—never

318

forget it."

"I never will."

Their breathing became aligned, and with each breath was felt a quiet joy.

"Till the end of days, my crusader... till the end of days," she whispered, just as they took their first steps toward their city.

Chapter Twenty-Six

Late September 1992

Bosko had cut a channel two inches wide and almost the entire length of the sheet of wood that covered the balcony doors. He placed a thick black cloth over the space. He had drilled many holes into the wood that covered the windows. The holes provided only a peephole view, but the two-inch wide channel provided a "letterbox" view of the world outside. They saw a beautifully composed shot of Sarajevo, a city which seemed to be convulsing. It was being wrenched and contorted into submission like a wrestler trying to free himself from a death grip.

The first evening he and Admira spent together in the apartment, they'd stood for hours on a chair and looked out into the night and into their city, with only the light from a handful of lit kandilos surrounding them. Looking through the channel cut into the wood, they were like two voyeurs watching the destruction of their city, mesmerized by the horror of what had become of their lives. Holding onto each other, they watched the bullet trails of light streak across the night sky, breaking up the blackness with bright colors of red, green, and blue light. It had a terrifying brilliance.

They watched their city being systematically destroyed, but the spirit of Sarajevo hadn't been broken—not yet. She continued to live, tormenting her besiegers by whispering into their hearts and minds: I am not Carthage. I am not Troy.

*

"Come in, Miro. It's open," Bosko said. He was expecting his friend; anyone else wouldn't have bothered to knock. The look on Miroslav's face when he entered the living room conveyed what was in the hearts of almost everyone in Sarajevo—their spirit

321

hadn't been broken, but it had taken a terrible beating. Lately, Bosko sensed a distance in his friend. He was alone and he hated it. Bosko knew Miro envied him for having Admira at his side.

His family and his new bride were gone; he felt like he was a third wheel whenever he joined Admira and Bosko, but still he spent a lot of time with them. Loneliness and jealousy were eating away at him.

"Grab a seat." Bosko patted Miro on his shoulder before he walked into the kitchen.

Miro looked around the living room. "You've changed things a bit since I was here."

Near one end of the living room were three chairs and a table constructed out of bricks they'd scrounged from the rubble in the hallway.

"I like it," Miro said. "It's very modern. Minimalist. Like artwork you'd find in a museum."

"Glad you approve," Bosko spoke from the kitchen. "Thanks for always coming to visit us, Miro. I know you think this building is going to collapse at any moment."

"Who cares anymore. Which is better? Being crushed to death in a building or shot dead in the streets? What does any of it matter now?" Miro leaned back on a familiar cushioned chair that had been in Rita's family for years.

"I like your new fireplace. It's more of a potbelly stove. It should keep you and Admira warm in the winter."

Bosko had built an exhaust pipe for it, the end of which stuck out of a small hole in the wall for the smoke and fumes to escape.

"Keep all three of us warm, you mean. I dragged it all the way home from the market and dragged it up the stairs. I even fixed the hot plate finally. Admira cooks quite well on it." Bosko entered the living room from the kitchen holding two mugs of black tea.

"Where is she, by the way?"

322

"Upstairs visiting Radmilla. Here, take the mug. She refuses to leave, too. Admira and she have become good friends. They need each other to gossip, and it's nice for them to have another woman to talk to. She'll be back soon."

"I guess this is how you're going to stay warm this winter." Miro was staring at the stacks of wood piled up against the wall.

"Looks like it," Bosko said, thinking of all the trees in Sarajevo that had been cut down at alarming rates. Birch and poplars, ash, plum, apple, cherry, and pear trees were being felled daily. Door frames and the doors of destroyed buildings, handrails and shelves from abandoned stores, wooden stools, even entire bars from restaurants were ripped out and taken away. Wooden crosses and Muslim wood markings from the cemeteries would be next.

"I walked past a garage the other day that had been hit by mortar. I could still feel the heat from the burned wood. But I was able to salvage quite a bit, as you can see."

"I'll try to bring some wood for you and Admira to burn in that contraption, and I'll sleep in your hallway. I hate being alone, Bosh. I hate it!"

"Stay with us, you fool. As often as you want, and in here, not the hallway. How could you even think that? And you don't have to bring wood. We're in this together."

"I miss Biljes so much. I'm going out of my mind." Miro's tone suddenly changed from one of despair to a kind of controlled excitement. He began to pace the room. Bosko put his hand on Miro's shoulder, but he shrugged it away. "Maybe you and I can get there—to Paris."

"What are you talking about?"

"Don't pretend you haven't thought of getting out of this dead city."

"No, I haven't. I won't be separated from Admira."

"Take her with you."

323

"Take her where?"

"To Paris. To wherever we'd end up going."

"No one can just leave Sarajevo. Haven't you noticed?"

"Oh, I've noticed."

"So, then, what are you talking about?" Bosko was getting more irritated by Miro's comments.

Miro knew he had to be careful about what he said to his friend. "What did her mom and dad say when you told them the news that she was moving in with you?"

"They said very little."

"Must have been your charm." There was an edge to Miroslav's words.

"Hey, listen to me." Bosko grabbed his friend and held him tight. "Until that day comes when you're with Biljes, you're going to have to spend all your time with us."

"Thanks, Charmer Boy." Miro pushed him away gently and began to pace again. "I love her as much as you love Admira. I despise having to spend another day without her. If I could, I'd be on a bus or plane, whatever way I could, to get out of this graveyard. Good intentions won't protect you or me. This isn't my war or yours, and I have no intention of offering up my life as some sacrifice. I'm not Mats."

"No, you're not. I never confused the two of you," Bosko said.

"Go ahead and despise everything I'm saying, but I don't intend to be heroic in someone else's war. Listen to me. We could ask Mladjo to get us out of here. I'm sure he could. You know he could. He's your ace in the hole."

"What about Admira?"

"Take her with you."

"You want me to run away like some coward. Do you think I could ever look into her eyes if I did? How could she still love me if I asked her to leave with me? I'd become a coward in her eyes

—in my eyes."

"She would love you no matter what."

"I would take her home to her parents and make them promise me to keep her there, while I lived out my life here to whatever end, before I would ever leave Sarajevo. This is my city and I'm not going to abandon it. Or Admira." Bosko threw down the bundle of wood he'd tied up and gave his friend a puzzled look. Miro had never been so desperate, and Bosko sensed it. He reached out to him, but Miro backed away again.

"It's easy for you to say these things. You have Admira."

"You'll be with Biljes one day. Listen to me, it's going to happen."

"Ever the optimist. When, when is it going to happen? You don't know if it will; it may never happen."

"You have to believe it will."

"I'm not the optimist you think you can turn me into. Why can't you understand that?"

"Well, I am; we all have to be." Bosko's tone softened. "Miro, for as long as people will remember, it will be said that Serbs started this war in Sarajevo. And it's true. It won't matter to anyone that Serb families, mothers, and daughters have also been killed. It won't matter that not every Serb wanted this to happen and many even fought to prevent it from happening. The world will remember this siege, and will always think of us as being the monsters who brought an end to Sarajevo, if that is what happens. I will stay here till that day comes and goes. This is my home. I am a Sarajevan."

"And if it should end in a bad way? What will you and Admira do?"

"We will be together; that's all that matters."

"I have to find a way to escape. I can't keep running and hiding like an animal. I run by the bodies in the street as if they don't exist. As if they never existed. They rot away with no one knowing who they were. Where's the grace and pity that should have come with their deaths? I haven't showered in days. I never know when I'll get something to eat, if this morning is the last morning I'll wake up to.

"We're dying like dogs. Worse than dogs." He grabbed Bosko and shoved him against the wall. "We're going to die—you, me, Admira—all of us. We're all going to die!"

"Don't you ever say that word to me again, Miro."

Miro's comment triggered a very palpable anger within Bosko. "Take it back. She's not going to die."

"Alright, she's not going to die. Mats thought so too, but now he's dead. You're always the fucking romantic. That's what will get you killed. You have a chance. Take it. It's pitiful that you know someone who can help you escape from this hell, and you won't take the chance."

Bosko stood there looking at his friend. "I really don't know you, do I?"

"Your pride will be your end."

"Not pride." Bosko slammed Miro against the wall. "I. Gave. My. Word. I swore that I would stay with her and neither heaven nor hell on this earth will see me break it. And she swore to me that it would be the two of us till the end of days."

"And what will happen to you, when that day comes? A Serb in love with a Muslim girl? What do you think they'll do to you? If the city does fall? Don't make the same mistake Mats did. Learn from it. The only loyalty you should have is to yourself and to no one else. We can leave this accursed graveyard."

"Are you not listening to me?"

"You're a Serb in love with a Muslim girl. Can't you understand that! You're both despised by each side. Everyone knows. Everyone. They see you with her, when you are out there in that hell. How do you think it makes them feel? A Bosnian Serb with a Bosnian Muslim. It's like you're throwing it in their faces. Think, Bosko, it only angers them even more. You're fuc

326

—"

"Don't even think of saying it. Not everyone feels as you say, Miro. This is Sarajevo, this is what we've always done. The way we've always been."

"Bosh, listen to reason. When that day comes and this city falls, you'll be made into an example, and so will Admira. There's only one way to protect her. She has a better chance without you. Do what I'm saying. For God's sake, it's the only choice we have as Serbs."

"Miro, this conversation is over. Enough. You don't know what you're saying. First you tell me I should take Admira with me, then you say I should leave her." Bosko's face was red with anger and his hands shook. "You're desperate and not thinking straight. We have each other, and we will make it."

"No, we won't Bosh, we won't."

"Then so be it."

Miro looked at his boyhood friend with utter disdain. "I have no intention of offering up my life for what has always been a godforsaken city."

"You don't believe that, Miro."

"I do, more than anything in this world. I believe this city should be forgotten forever."

"We can't give up, Miro. We can't." Bosko was fighting his own sense of futility. Would they in Sarajevo ultimately prevail, and if they did, how would it happen?

"Listen to me," Miroslav asked in a quieter voice. "If I find a way to leave, to escape, will you go with me?"

"No." The tone of Bosko's voice was meant to end the conversation. He peeled his friend's fingers from his shoulders.

"I'm going to ask you this one last time. If I find a way to get out of Sarajevo, will you come with me?"

"No. Understand? No."

"Is that your final word?"

"Yes."

Admira heard Bosko and Miro arguing earlier in the day and had stopped in the hallway and listened as she'd walked down from Radmilla's apartment. She'd waited for them to finish their argument before coming into the apartment. Miro had come over, and they ate their entire meal in silence, after which Miro left abruptly.

"Bosh, don't be angry at Miro," she said as they settled in their field bed laid out on the living room floor. "I heard you both arguing earlier today. I stayed outside and listened and came in after it was over."

"I don't want to talk about it."

"Don't be angry at him."

"I'm not." He raised his voice at her. "I'm not." He said in a softer tone. "Don't you think I know how desperate Miro is? How much he misses Biljes? My God, I took you away from your family because I couldn't bear to be separated from you. And I brought you into this hell. It's the only thing that makes being in this hell bearable—having you beside me. Miro is alone. And I don't know how to help him."

They lay together side by side, till Admira turned over onto her side and raising her thigh and then her body, she practically climbed on top of Bosko. He held her in an embrace. It was quiet, their little world. Outside the explosions continued. Their world was getting smaller and darker. They were together, but their dearest friend, he was alone.

*

Admira tried to put it out of her head, Miro's sense of desperation and their inability to help him. She remained focused on what she had to do to help them all. She packed everything she intended to sell into a bag and headed off to one of the markets. Today, she went to an open-air warehouse market. Yesterday, she'd been at the Ciglane marketplace trying to sell or barter her meager things for items like homemade candles, soap, lighters, matches, toilet paper, or any kind of canned food.

Most of the folks who participated in the market were women, but some men sold miscellaneous items like axes and irons or handmade stoves that could be used for heating during the winter, if they didn't blow up.

Long ago people had begun to scavenge among abandoned cars for batteries and headlights. If still intact they could provide light for a living space. Sarajevans had learned not to use a regular light bulb—they drained a battery quickly. Instead, like Bosko, they had chosen the small light bulbs from abandoned cars, gathering as many as they could find. Bosko only needed a battery for them. He could also plug in a radio, if he had one. Intact batteries were incredible treasures and impossible to find. Admira and Bosko had looked for them in vain.

She stood next to an elderly woman who was selling items of her own. The line of women stretched shoulder to shoulder in front of slabs of concrete tables propped up on thick concrete pylons. All of her items were lined up perfectly in front of her. She smiled at anyone who stopped by to check out what she had, trying to appear cheery and as obliging to any possible customer. After an hour, she hadn't sold a thing.

Admira became despondent; it seemed like nothing she had was of any value to anyone today. She told herself to stay a bit longer and not go home without selling something. Closing her eyes for an instant, she opened them and looked up at the sky, asking for help.

A man appeared out of nowhere, his hand outstretched to her. "What is it?" she asked.

"A book."

"I don't need a book, I need—"

"Yes, you do."

"No, I don't."

"Listen to me. I don't feel like carrying it home and I noticed that you haven't bought or sold anything, and I have. I'm going home. Here, take this." He handed the book to her. "Take it. See what it says." Admira looked at the spine of the book.

"Lenin's—"

"Yes, Lenin's bullshit. It's big and heavy and I have more copies. Trust me. You do want it. It burns well and long, good for when winter comes. Go on, take it." He practically pushed it into her chest.

Admira held the book. "Thank you."

"Don't thank me. Thank Lenin and all that bullshit he wrote." The elderly man walked away, and Admira watched him with a smile.

Another twenty minutes passed and she still made no sale. A voice inside her said, Go, Bosko is waiting. She wrapped up her items and tossed them into a bag, zipped it shut, and slung the strap across her chest. She waved to the other women and started to walk away. She quickened her pace, eyes darting back and forth, always ready to run or jump into a crater in the street—if one existed—at the first sign of gunfire or worse. Admira had almost reached the entrance at the far end of the market when the silence was shattered by an enormous blast behind her. She was thrown to the ground and her ears began to ring. It became hard for her to breathe. The oxygen was sucked out of the space.

Admira rolled over onto her back. Dozens of people were on the floor with her, some were conscious while other had their eyes closed. She tried to get up but couldn't; her ears began to throb with the ringing she kept hearing. Get up, she commanded herself. She reached out and tried to grab onto anything to help her raise herself off the ground, but there was nothing she could

330

hold onto. The ringing sound began to fade, and in its place she began to hear the screams and groans coming from every corner of the market.

Admira rolled herself onto her belly and then, with all of her strength, was able to drag herself up onto her hands and knees while she choked on the dust and pulverized debris that saturated the air. Finally, she stood up and pulled her bag full of items toward her. She knew she should run. Instead, she turned around. Within a moment of the explosion, everything went silent, followed by screams of agony from the injured and the dying.

Admira saw a man who had been severed in half at the waist. His torso and legs were separated by a distance of five feet and the blue and white checkered shirt he wore was covered with blood and entrails. She saw his mouth open as if he were about to speak, to disclaim the event, then his eyes closed.

Body parts were scattered all over the market. A white-haired woman in her sixties kept pushing her way through the crowd, calling for her daughter, "Nevena." She kept frantically calling out her daughter's name. Her face was contorted with the ultimate fear and anguish of a mother whose worst fears are realized about her child. Admira started to walk toward her, dragging her bag alongside her.

"Nevena," her mother called out frantically once again. Admira also started to call out her name—why, she didn't know. She only knew her mother would be doing the same, calling out her name in desperation. The sound made by this mother searching for her child turned from one of anguish to anger to despair as the realization sunk into the marrow of her bones that the worst had happened to her daughter.

Admira heard her let out a wail from the pit of her soul. She had found her daughter—what remained of her. People tried to stop her from approaching the remains of what had been her daughter, but she violently kept swinging away at them. And then she knelt down on the blood-spattered ground and, with her bare hands, began to scrape off the floor what remained of her child into her arms. The sounds she made, this mother who collected the remains of her child should have made God finally intercede. But God did not.

"Where is God," Admira kept screaming. "Where is God?" Admira didn't know what to do. She wanted to help but didn't know how.

"What should I do?" She kept yelling to anyone who might know, but many had started to run, fearing another explosion was imminent. Others bravely remained and assisted the wounded and dying as best as they could. People's clothes became drenched in blood as they knelt beside the dying, whose blood poured out of their bodies like an open faucet. A man knelt next to another man who was still alive and severely wounded, trying to push the man's guts back inside his open torso.

Everywhere Admira looked were bits and pieces of what had been human beings just moments ago. While the most sorrowful sounds came from the survivors, they were mixed with screams and moans from the injured. The worst were the soft, gurgling sounds of those about to die.

A man with salt-and-pepper hair covered with blood beckoned to Admira.

She ran to him, searching her bag for something she could tie around his leg to stop the bleeding.

But he wasn't calling to Admira to help him, he was motioning her frantically to go, to run. He'd lost one leg that had been ripped away from the knee and only a few strands of muscle from his thigh held the other to his body.

"Go!" he pleaded as she knelt next to him. "Run." She nodded. Then turning and unable to see clearly what was in front of her, she started to run with the crowd. Where should I go? She didn't know.

332

Screams from the marketplace victims haunted her every step. She couldn't go on, and she wasn't sure where she was going or how far she'd run. Admira put her hands up to her ears, still hearing their screams. Dropping to her knees next to what had been a ten-story building, she tried to catch her breath. She should have stayed; she should have helped. A voice in her head said, No, Admira, there was only death awaiting you if you'd stayed. Didn't you make a promise to yourself that you would not die without Bosko at your side?

Where was God? Where? She damned God for being invisible. How could there be a God? Her heart raced and her inner voice kept telling her to run. Run. Run, Admira. But she was frozen and couldn't move. She rested on both knees, pressed against the inner wall of a bombed-out building. She knew she needed to get up, but she didn't have the will to do it. Then she said his name—Bosko. She said it again and again. Each time she spoke it out loud, she felt her resolve grow stronger. Admira inched up from behind a pile of rubble and looked around. At least she knew where she was. Guessing she was a half hour from Kosovo Hill, she continued on her journey home. To Bosko.

Setting her sights on a building about two short blocks away, she wasn't sure of her best course of action. Should she run from the start or emerge cautiously? Deciding that quick was better, she lunged to her feet.

*

Bosko had been pacing the living room all afternoon, waiting for Admira to return. The days either of them went out alone, to the market or the bread line or to get water, were the hardest. They knew it wasn't practical to be together twenty-four hours a day and survive as a couple. As with every other couple, they had to find a way to live and overcome and stay in love and not lose

333

hope as the hand of death held firm and tore at the fabric of their desperate lives.

Each time Admira ventured out of the apartment, he cursed his very existence and that he had subjected her to this life. Bosko often questioned whether he was doing the right thing for them, staying together in Sarajevo. It was an extremely selfish thing for him to want, and yet he couldn't help himself. Without her, what was the point of being alive?

He'd been standing by the door for at least a half hour, waiting and listening for a familiar sound. Then he heard it, the echo of her footsteps coming from the stairwell, her shoes crunching down on the rubble and grit on the stairs.

"Admira?" he called as he flung open the door. She flew into his arms. Her bag with its contents fell at her feet.

*

No silence is greater than that which comes from fear. They remained in the bathroom, with only the light from a few kandilos. She hadn't stopped shaking or crying. He'd had to clean her. She needed to be cleansed of all of the sounds and sights from the marketplace. Although she objected to the use of the precious water they had saved in every container they had; he poured the water over her, Bosko insisted. It peeled away the layer of hate that had glued itself to her skin the moment the explosion took place. When he finished drying her, he wrapped her in a thick towel, lifted her into his arms, and walked into the living room.

Admira lay on her side on the sofa, pressed against Bosko. Not a sound, not even the sound of their breathing, could be heard as they lay with arms and legs wrapped around each other. Bosko ran his fingers through Admira's curls.

Shafts of sunlight blasted through the holes in the window

coverings. He pressed Admira closer, and she sank against his chest. She wished in the silence that she could disappear inside of Bosko.

Powerful and uncontrollable emotions ran through him. Finally, he said, "You could have been—"

"No, not without you," she said, reaching up to press her fingers to his lips. She closed her eyes. Today she had cheated death. Its grasp had come so very close. She remembered the faces of the dead and the dying, and the sound of weeping family members who were themselves badly injured, suffering the torment of watching a loved one die.

Bosko was beginning to question their life together. Mats had always said that the siege would come to no good end. Miro had pleaded with him to ask Mladjo to get them out of the city. Was Miro right? Admira would be safer with her parents, at least for now, and maybe the city would never fall and she would remain safe. How long would she be able to survive in the city with him?

"It was you." Admira's eyes were still closed and she was reading Bosko's thoughts. "You called to me; I heard your voice telling me to come home. You saved me."

335

PART SEVEN

Chapter Twenty-Seven

December 1992

Admira went into the kitchen, feeling incredibly tired, filled with the same fatigue as every other Sarajevan. In their hearts and minds they felt the bending, and heard the snapping, of their resolve, which stood in defiance of their besiegers. How much longer could they stand up against this onslaught before their surrender and defeat? When would their city succumb to complete oblivion?

Come on, snap out of it. Make them lunch and yourself some tea. Think of that day when you will see Rita. Admira focused on making her boys some lunch. Miro had brought with him two books of matches the other day. A wonderful find. They were so thankful for them. She lit the hot plate and placed the kettle on top. Through Mladjo's influence, Bosko had been able to get two small but full propane tanks that he could connect to the handmade contraption that was part grill and part hot plate with an area that emitted a small but steady flame. Being frugal with the gas, they could make those two small tanks last for months. Using a tea bag that had been used three times before, she set it into a cup and waited for the water to boil.

Today's lunch would consist of bean pâte on two slices of bread. Admira had been able to buy a small bag of pepper, a jar of mustard, and some mysterious seasonings. She'd made the pâte last night and covered it tightly in a jar. Bosko and Miro would take it with them this morning when they left with the militia.

A month had passed since the bombing at the market. The image of a mother searching for her child amongst the dead was seared into Admira's thoughts. It was a moment she knew would remain with her for the rest of her life. Word finally had gotten around that more than forty people had been killed and twenty others had been seriously wounded. Bosko and Admira had avoided talking about that day. She especially didn't want to talk about it because she was certain Bosko would forbid her to be alone in the city. Admira also knew that the argument that would follow would be beyond anything they'd ever experienced.

Just let him try. He doesn't know the meaning of spooky if he thinks I'm abandoning him in Sarajevo.

The image of a mother on her hands and knees, scraping the remains of her child into her arms, made Admira shut her eyes and grab onto the counter. How could all of this have happened?

"Breathe," she said out loud. "This will end, and you and Bosko will have prevailed."

Placing her mug on the counter, she reached for a precious loaf of bread and cut four slices. She'd decided to wait until the very last minute before waking Bosko. Miro wouldn't arrive for a couple of hours and then the two men would head off to their duties. She couldn't sleep and had to find something to do to keep her busy. Making their lunch now would free her up to do and say all the boring things with Bosh she promised herself she would continue to keep doing. To simply exist next to him, side by side.

Sometimes she would catch Bosko staring into space for a brief moment, alone in his thoughts, and she was certain he was thinking of his friend. So much was unknown. How was Vails doing? And where in the world was she? Was Biljes beside herself not being able to be with Miro?

After spreading the homemade bean pâte onto the four slices of dry bread and wrapping them in wax paper, she poured heated potato soup into thermoses, one for each of them. In these times of scarcity, every item was precious. Every evening Bosko returned the waxed paper to be used another day. Neatly stacking everything to the side on the kitchen counter, it looked as if she'd prepared two school lunches for her kids.

Rain lashed against the windows. Hopefully, it would continue after Bosko left. If so, she would go outside to collect as much rain water as possible and bring it back to be stored for the toilet, doing laundry, and washing their hair. Admira knew of a location where the rain would be channeled through a broken pipe jutting out of the side of a bombed out office building not far from their apartment. She desperately needed to shampoo her hair but felt guilty about using the precious little water they had for something so trivial. Collecting the rain water to use to wash her hair alleviated any sense of guilt.

She and other neighborhood women gathered there with buckets on rainy days, always happy to see a familiar face when they did. Some faces never returned, but the ones who did respected Admira. They knew she had chosen to stay with Bosko in the city where two steps in any direction might be your last. She could have stayed with her family where she would be safe. In their eyes, she was one of them.

*

Bosko and Miro were positioned with the militia in two separate buildings a few blocks from the Holiday Inn, an infamous perch for snipers close to the main Sarajevo boulevard, Ulica Zmaja od Bosne, also known as Sniper's Alley because it was lined with hidden sniper posts. Snipers, the militia, and Sarajevo's citizens were now caught in a dance of death with each other.

Mladjo's men and two other militia groups were attempting to ferret out as many snipers as possible. No one knew how successful the outcome would be, but the ongoing rampage of death had to be stopped at all costs. The boulevard was lined with many tall buildings, providing snipers a wide-open view of

Sarajevo's citizens. People had to leave their homes and move around the city, but in doing so they also offered up their lives to the person with a finger pressed on a trigger.

Three militiamen remained hidden in a room on the fifteenth floor of an abandoned office building closely monitored by their brethren nearby. Only members of the militia were allowed in the building. Each member sat carefully concealed behind a window, peering through their high-powered binoculars, scanning individual buildings for any sign of possible sniper movement.

The militias in the city and Mladjo's associates were all that stood in the way of preventing the killers from completing their grizzly task. Most snipers changed their positions immediately after they had shot and killed someone. Others were so well concealed, they remained undetected a mere two hundred yards away from their potential victims.

Bosko watched as the three militiamen scanned the large office buildings that lined the boulevard for any possible location that might be an ideal spot for a sniper. If a sniper was seen, they immediately relayed the coordinates of the area or specific building where the sniper was located to Bosko, who then translated it into code that only the militia units on the ground could decipher before heading out to raid the suspected sniper's nest. While he waited, Bosko sipped a spoonful of hot potato soup from his thermos cup. The rain kept pouring.

*

Admira had tried to let herself feel that certain joy that always overwhelmed her when walking in the rain. She was a farm girl, and carrying these buckets of water back and forth to the apartment and up three flights of stairs to fill up the tub, and then back down again was not burdensome for her. She had met the other women who were doing the same thing filling their buckets with the water gushing out of the exterior broken pipe of an office building. They'd all agreed that just before their last run back home if time permitted, to do what most women love to do, gossip. They were all together now and so they hugged each other tightly, this was their last run with their buckets of water so they made sure to make the most of it and chat. She had traded her bean pâte recipe for yet another recipe for macaroni and rice. Sticking out her tongue and tasting the rain brought a smile to Admira's face.

"I'm not sure I'll make it back home. I've stopped caring if I do or I don't. I just don't know for how much longer I can keep doing this?" Said a very disheartened housewife who was standing next to Admira.

"Off course you will make it." Admira admonished her, grabbing her hand, and then hugged her tightly. "Never think that way. We can't let them win. We women are much stronger than those bastards hiding in the hills."

The other three women who were holding onto their buckets of water nodded and were all on the verge of tears.

"My clothes are soaked and I smell so bad. I cannot take a bath because my family needs water to drink, to cook with, even to flush the toilet. I'm so ashamed to lie next to my husband smelling the way I do." Said another woman.

"Don't sell your man short," said Admira, breaking into a smile. "A woman's scent, no matter how pungent, is always alluring."

They started to laugh, but not too loudly.

"I must go, me and my pungent smell." They all nodded. They also had to get back home. It was raining hard. "I wish I could run through the street naked and let the rain clean me."

Admira turned to her saying. "You know what I think? I *will*." To their amazement she began to disrobe. She took off her bra, and rolled up her pants, while leaving her thin blouse completely unbuttoned. The rain poured across her chest and breasts. Seeing Admira's wanton disregard for any modesty, the other women followed suit. They giggled even though they were so afraid.

"Tonight we'll be fresh and clean for our men and we'll tell all of them how it happened." The women laughed at Admira's comment. "Alright ladies, now let's run." They all nodded and hugged each other tightly once more, not knowing when or if they would see each other again. In seconds they'd scattered, running in the downpour, having disrobed as much as they had dared.

And as they ran with their breasts exposed to the rain and the wind, their hair and bodies completely soaked, their plastic buckets filled with precious water that kept sloshing about, they were overcome with a sense of freedom and invincibility. Their killers, if they were watching them running half naked through the pouring rain, holding onto their precious buckets of water, would have realized that they were in fact staring at the strength that kept the walls of Sarajevo from crumbling. Its women.

Admira hurried herself along, the tub was almost completely full. It was a complete downpour and she was being showered by it and it felt so glorious.

And then something very odd caught her attention, and Admira almost fell head over heels on the slippery sidewalk. Stopping and standing completely still, rain pouring down on her, she saw a white swan gliding peacefully down the side of the street buoyed on top of the rushing water that was flowing toward a drain.

She realized she was out in the open where anyone could see her, and she immediately began to hurry home, but after just a few steps she stopped again. A peacock emerged from a building and started to walk down the sidewalk next to the gliding swan. Escaped or set free from the zoo, they were together, roaming in a melancholy partnership. Their sadness made less so by the fact that they had each other.

342

Every new day was a holiday. Simply living another day was reason enough to celebrate. Christmas was just a week away. Admira was ecstatic, as were so many other Sarajevans, even as their loved ones, friends, and neighbors died around them.

On this day, she held a very special book in her hand. They would have to burn it soon, but she couldn't bear to see the first page destroyed in a fire. Oh what happy days those were, when she and Bosko and all their friends thought of nothing more than enjoying life, making love, and their future. When her man had made love to her with such passion and gentleness. Well, she thought to herself, that last part hadn't changed. Admira pressed the book against her chest, thinking that if that moment came and their city fell and all that she and Bosko had left was each other, that was all that mattered. Their unbounded love for one another. Life, existence, and survival—what did any of it matter if you weren't loved?

Admira placed the book next to the one by Lenin, near one of the scrap-wood piles Bosko and Miro had tied and stacked. Someday, those happy times would return.

Before they burned the book, she'd ask Bosko to read it to her one last time. Perhaps its poetry would make the flames burn brighter and hotter. They needed all the fuel they could get their hands on for their makeshift potbelly stove contraption. She and Bosko were always scavenging for wood or anything that would burn. Everyone in the city did. It was a never-ending process that continued throughout the year in preparation for the coming winter.

This Christmas, Muslim and Christian alike would rejoice together because they'd all managed to live for one more year. They would celebrate along with the people in New York, Rome, London, and Paris.

On days when she was home alone, Admira bundled up and

343

left the wood-burning stove alone. They needed all the precious wood they had piled up inside the apartment, so their potbelly stove fireplace remained unlit. She was a farm girl and could handle their small hovel becoming cold, sometimes very cold. She bundled herself up under layers of clothes and blankets. She walked around the apartment with her arms wrapped around herself, rubbing them to keep warm, or read her university book by the light of the kandilos. When the sunlight shone through the holes in the wood panels covering the windows, she would position herself on the floor so that the beams of sunlight covered her body, providing her with a little warmth. Just before Bosko arrived home each evening, she lit the stove to heat up the apartment.

Admira unwrapped decorations she'd been collecting for months. She'd managed to keep them hidden from Bosko, having carefully placed some wreaths behind the wood stacked against wall. Her hands trembled from being cold as she arranged her mother's vegetable baskets near Bosko's makeshift fireplace. Sadly, the baskets contained only half a bag of flour and one precious piece of coal to be used on New Year's Eve, to continue her father's ritual. Admira held a red and a gold ribbon, each of which was tied to one white and one green Christmas ball. She shook her head, thinking as she smiled, of how her Muslim family always celebrated Christmas.

She attributed it to her dad having sung in a Christian choir where he must have also sung Christmas carols. Ever since then, he'd caught the bug for celebrating a Christian holiday. Admira laid out the two ornaments on the floor. She had fashioned three wreaths out of strips of cloth, pieces of wood, dry branches, and twigs that she had accumulated over the summer. She'd already tied over a dozen acorns and small red ceramic apples together with red ribbons that were fashioned into bows and hung them in every crack and hole on every wall of the living room. Admira had saved one red bow for Bosko. It was his to place wherever he wanted.

Admira heard Bosko's footsteps coming up the stairwell; he was taking two or three steps at a time.

"Admira," Bosko called out. "I have it—the loaf of bread." He practically leapt into the room, raising his hand, showing her his much-sought-after prize of the day. A loaf of bread.

Bosko stopped talking and froze in his tracks because of what he saw. The sun was setting, its bright shafts of light no longer penetrating the apartment through the holes drilled into the wooden planks covering the windows. It was a room lit only by fire, by the flickering orange and red flames of the burning kandilos that Admira had hung on the walls and that emitted an ethereal kind of light. Their space took on a surreal look, a dreamlike quality.

Bosko walked up to one of the three wreaths she had made and hung on the wall. He ran his fingers over the twigs and branches, feeling their rough and rustic surface against his fingertips.

"When did you do all of this?" he asked as he took in the ribbons hanging along the exposed brick wall, and the acorns and red ceramic apples attached to them.

"When you left."

"And all of these decorations, where did you get them?"

"I've been collecting them each time I go out. I'm always on the lookout for things. Do you like it?" She wanted Bosko to love their very simple Christmas decorations.

"It's beautiful," he said. She walked up to him; they said nothing more but kissed each other. He would follow her scent trail from this moment on into the night, and it would be a silent, passionate love pairing that would last for hours, or even days.

"What would I do without you?"

"You'll never need to know," she said, looking at him,

wearing nothing under her favorite red plaid shirt of Bosko's. She had fastened only one button, and the fabric swayed back and forth with her every movement, revealing another kind of present for Bosko.

She brought her hand forward from behind her back and, lifting up her arm, she showed Bosko the red bow she had saved for him. He could place it wherever he wanted. He took it out of her hand and very carefully hung its small metal hook onto a button hole.

"Gift giving is going to start a little earlier for the both of us, this year."

A massive explosion outside caused the building to shake, more explosions followed and would continue into the night and early morning. The gunners in the hills were going to do their best, day and night, to break the will of the city's inhabitants to make them celebrate this holiday season by mourning the passing of their loved ones. The building shook again. Their future hung in the balance.

Chapter Twenty-Eight

Spring 1993

Bosko had been summoned to Mladjo's office but didn't know why. He'd been waiting outside on a wooden bench, going over and over anything he or Miro might have done to cause a problem. Nothing came to mind. Bosko glanced around with trepidation at the other men. They managed many of the gangs and militias that prowled the streets of Sarajevo, keeping her citizens safe while trying to ferret out the snipers.

On occasion, he'd catch them staring at him. It wasn't difficult to figure out what they were thinking. Why was Mladjo protecting him and Miro? If it had been up to most of them, Miro and Bosko would have been severely beaten and their bodies discarded on some lonely street. Bosko tried not to show fear in his eyes as he stared back.

"Bosko, come on in." Djoka stepped out of the room and motioned Bosko to come inside.

One of the men in the outer office followed Bosko with his eyes. *Has someone he loved been killed by a Serb? Probably.*

"Sit down. Have some sweets," Mladjo said, his tone giving no hint of the reason Bosko had been summoned to the police station.

Bosko helped himself to a handful of sweets on Mladjo's desk. He carefully wrapped them in his handkerchief and put them in his pocket to be shared with Admira and Miro later. Djoka closed the door.

"Is there something wrong?" Bosko asked.

"Some people might think so." Mladjo's reply sounded somber.

"What do you mean?" Bosko didn't know what to think. Mladjo was inscrutable.

"Relations, Bosko... relations."

"I don't understand."

"My fiancée's family doesn't think too highly of me."

"Fiancée?" Bosko was surprised. Mladjo never hinted about having a fiancée. Mladjo remained silent but focused on Bosko.

"I'm a disreputable type, but I still intend to marry her and she has accepted my proposal. Congratulate me!" Mladjo stood, arms open wide.

"You're getting married?" Bosko hugged Miro tightly.

"Indeed I am. Bosh, I asked you to come because I would like you and Admira to attend the ceremonies."

It took Bosko a few seconds to reply; he was still taken aback by the gangster's admission. "Mladjo, we'd be honored."

"I wish Serge and your parents could be there."

"I do, too."

"Anyhow, let's think of only the future."

"Yes, let's. When's the wedding?"

"We were waiting for the right moment. It's what we're all doing in Sarajevo, waiting for the right moment to do what we must. This is March, so a March wedding sounds good to me."

"Admira and I would be honored to be at your wedding, Mladjo. Thank you."

"Good to hear. There will be many political types there. One especially insisted on coming. He's a mover and shaker these days inside the president's inner circle. When I met him, he was a political prisoner. Years ago, when I was in prison, I saved his life, and now it's come to mean something in my life. He'll be at the reception with his wife. Perhaps if he has time, I'll introduce you and Admira."

"I could use some political connections these days," Bosko replied. Mladjo said nothing in response to his wry comment. He studied Bosko's face for a moment before asking, "What about you and Admira? When will you get married?"

"Just like you, we're waiting for the right moment."

A slow smile spread across Mladjo's face. "A toast, then, to waiting for that right moment," Mladjo said, handing Djoka and Bosko each a glass of *Omis*, a sweet Muscatel.

With a great sense of relief, Bosko drank his wine. He understood why he and Admira had been invited. Important guests would be at the wedding—political allies, people who made things happen. The word would spread that he and Admira weren't just friends of Mladjo's, but much more. He knew Mladjo wanted anyone who might want to harm them to think long and hard about what it would mean to do so. Mladjo was a defender of their city, a vicious gangster, and a drug dealer. He ran a protection racket and came to the aid of Sarajevans in their hour of need. His criminal power had been solidified, and now he had political aspirations and was courting strong connections. In these tough times, being ruthless and getting ahead required a profiteer who knew everything about making deals.

Being invited to his wedding provided an extra layer of security for them. Mladjo was doing all of this for Bosko and Admira because of what Rita and Dragan had once done for him, in his greatest hour of need.

*

"He'll be alright," Miroslav said, trying to comfort Admira, who heated up some water for tea in the kitchen. "He hasn't done anything wrong. It's a failing of his. I keep pointing it out. This is probably about the profits from the petrol and cigarettes. Maybe we're going to get a bigger cut. I know, I know, you don't approve of us being involved in the black market, but selling pots and pans won't cut it. We all need another source of income.

"What Mladjo gives us is minuscule compared to what he and his cronies get for selling petrol on the black market. Defenders and gangsters have to also buy everyday necessities. It's our salary

349

for being good soldiers. Those few extra Deutsche marks Bosh and I get make a big difference. Mladjo can't be seen showing us any special kindness or favoritism when it comes to money. People will get a lot more jealous about that then they already are of his willingness to protect us from so many folks who would like to see the worst done to Bosko and me.

"So he pays us only a fraction of what the other militiamen get from the deals his gang makes with corrupt UNPROFOR soldiers for petrol and other things. It seems to have so far done the trick. Kept everyone calm and happy, that we get hardly any money for the work we do in the militia. At least Bosh has been able to buy shampoo and conditioner and even get some sausage. He told me he paid Deutsche marks for it."

Admira remained silent. In order to survive, it was impossible to remain corruption-free in Sarajevo.

"We've all sold out in one way or another, some less than others, but everyone has sacrificed some or all of their morals. How else are we going to survive? We can't be Boy Scouts, like the Americans say."

Admira nodded but remained silent.

"Hey, don't worry about him. He knows how to take care of himself. You'll see. As soon as Charmer Boy walks through that door, he'll have good news for us."

"We could certainly use some," she said as she dropped two tea bags into separate mugs. When the kettle boiled, she lifted it off the hot plate and poured the hot water.

Miroslav tried to imagine that it was him standing next to Biljana and she was making him a mug of tea, and that they were together in Paris with their glorious future ahead of them. He had become so jealous of Bosko for having Admira.

They walked out of the kitchen and sat next to each other.

"Miro, what happens to the people you and Bosko help the militia find?" She turned and looked at him.

"Best not to think about it. I don't. Each side has become remorseless in their actions. When these bastards are found and dealt with, it means one more Sarajevan has been allowed to live." She lifted her mug and blew away the rising steam. Miro couldn't take his eyes off her, thinking of his wife once more.

Admira sipped her tea, keeping her thoughts to herself as she waited for Bosko to return.

Miro turned his head toward the door. Someone was climbing the stairs.

"I think that's Bosko now."

Admira began to breathe easier. She silently gave thanks as he walked in. "Well, Charmer Boy?" She jumped out of her chair and ran to hug him.

"So, what did Mladjo want?" Miro tried not to sound concerned.

"Nothing." Bosko took off his shoes and placed them against the wall.

"Nothing?"

"Have some tea." Admira offered him her mug.

"Thanks. Oh, there was one thing."

"What?" Miro asked, still trying to appear calm.

Bosko ambled over to the chair and plopped down, trying to remain casual as he took a sip of his tea.

"He insisted that Admira and I come to his wedding."

"What?" Miro jumped out of his chair. "Mladjo is getting married? I didn't even know he had a fiancée."

"I don't think many people do know, that he's engaged let alone had a fiancée."

"Well, how do you like that? A gangster and thug who's profiting from the siege is also getting married in the midst of this madness."

"He said it was a good time to do it," replied Bosko.

"Yes, timing is everything, and he's shown a remarkable

351

ability to remain at the top of the food chain."

Admira was looking at Miro and was certain this news only made Miro yearn to be with Biljes even more. Miro became silent and seemed to fidget. He hated himself for not being able to do what Mladjo and Bosko were able to do. They'd held onto their women.

"We've been invited to the reception," Bosko said in a matter-of-fact way.

"Who is he marrying?" Miro asked.

"She's quite attractive. I saw her photograph; her name is Lejla. It's the happiest I've ever seen him. But I told him we couldn't go," Bosko said.

Admira was sitting on his lap and slid off immediately. "Why, Bosko? Why did you tell him that?" Admira was so disappointed. "Never mind. It's okay, I'm sure you had your reasons." She hadn't danced with Bosko in such a long time. She longed for a party— to be with people where they could talk and laugh and feel human again, even if it was for just a brief moment in their lives.

"I told him you didn't want to marry me, that the relationship was over, and, therefore, we couldn't go together."

"You did not." Admira grabbed Bosko and shook him. "What really happened? Did you really say we couldn't go?"

"I said I couldn't go unless—"

"Unless what?"

"Unless a very pretty, headstrong, impossible-to-win-an-argument-with girl would agree to go with me."

"Really? We're really going? Oh my God. I would love to be with people, laughing and drinking." She grabbed Bosko and kissed him all over his face. "We're really going? Is it true?"

"Alright—my God. Yes we are going—happy?"

"Oh, so much."

Bosko was happy to see Admira so joyful. "Miro," Bosko said, turning to his friend.

"I understand, Bosh, only you and Admira were invited. It should be quite a wedding,"

"Miro, I'm sorry, he didn't—"

"Don't be sorry. Every good thing that happens to you happens to me. He's your family's friend. It makes sense he'd invite only you and Admira."

"Thanks for understanding."

Bosko's friend smiled as he raised the mug to sip his tea.

"Miro, we'll bring back tons of food and drink," Admira said, hugging him. "We'll have a party of our own after, and invite as many friends as we can to come over. Wouldn't that be great?"

"I think it's a great idea," Miro replied as he continued sipping his tea.

"Mladjo asked me when we were getting married," Bosko said.

"What did you tell him?"

"We're waiting for the right moment."

"What did Mladjo say to that?"

"Only that it was what every Sarajevan is doing these days. We're all waiting for the right moment to do something."

Miro stopped staring into this cup while he sipped his tea. "Tell you what," Miro said. "I'll give you both a ride."

"Really, Miro?"

"Yeah. We'll manage not to get shot up. Besides, you're going to be all dressed up. Can't have Admira and you covered in dust and rubble, running to a wedding party. I'll get one of the militia cars. Are they going to say no?"

"That's exactly what Mladjo said he would do—send a militia car to pick us up. But you giving us a ride is even better. Thanks, Miro. Djoka is coming tomorrow to give me the transit papers to get us through the checkpoints. We should have no problems. The car will be marked with Mladjo's gang sign so everyone will know who it belongs to. It's not a guarantee to make us bulletproof, but it won't hurt either. This is perfect." Bosko hugged his friend.

If Miro was hurt for not being invited to the party, he didn't show it. "I'll get the car from the police station and drive here to pick you both up."

"Thanks, Miro."

"It's what friends are for."

"Miro, please light the *kandilos*; only one match to light all three. Okay?" Admira said.

"We even ration matches," he said, taking the match box out of her hand.

"Well, at least we still have the sunlight." Shafts of sunlight poured into the living room. Holding onto the unlit match, Miro began to weave in and out of the sunlight, almost as if he were doing a strange dance. He wasn't sure why he was overcome by this need to dance, but he couldn't stop himself.

"I hope you can eat macaroni and rice again."

Miro nodded. Admira headed for the kitchen, and Bosko followed.

"Did you see him dancing?" she said, handing him a plate.

"Yes," Bosko replied, trying not to laugh.

"What's gotten into him?"

"Probably thinking of all that food and drink we'll be bringing back. Let's eat. I'm hungry."

Admira served out four portions. "This is for Radmilla," she said, putting aside a small bowl for their friend. "How many ways do you think I've cooked macaroni and rice?"

"One day we'll make a list." Bosko kissed her.

Bosko left the kitchen and joined Miroslav, who was standing on a chair and peering through the long, thin channel Bosko had cut in the closet doors covering the sliding glass doors.

"The city will still be there after we eat. Come on. Admira has served our food."

Miro continued staring out toward the city and beyond.

"The food is going to get cold." He tapped his friend's leg and Miro stepped off the chair without saying a word.

"Here we go," Admira said as she brought out the plates. "Come on everyone, sit." They took their usual places on the floor, sitting on a mat. Bosko had poured for each of them exactly four ounces of water; everything had to be rationed. He glanced over at Admira. She knew Bosko was feeling bad that Miro hadn't been invited to the reception. But Miro showed no signs of being hurt over not being invited. His only outward reaction to the news had been to dance in and out of the shafts of sunlight. And now a repose seemed to relax his entire body, as if it were being supported by something, perhaps a pleasant thought.

Admira did notice that while he ate his food, he never looked up from his plate at either her or Bosko.

Chapter Twenty-Nine

The reception would be close to one of the heavily guarded city checkpoints that separated Serb-from Muslim-controlled areas; Miro knew no one would question his presence. He had the transit papers to cross the various checkpoints in the city in order to transport Admira and Bosko to the reception.

Miroslav looked at his watch. He'd wound it exactly at ten this morning and checked every hour on the hour to make sure it was working. It was five o'clock in the evening. The reception and celebrating would begin at eight. At seven, he would pick up Admira and Bosko, and it should take them no more than twenty minutes to get there, taking into account any problems like bombs and snipers. Today, nothing would touch any of them. He was certain of it. He would remain alive. His escape was preordained.

Dressed casually, he appeared normal and had even managed to hoard two full packs of cigarettes. If necessary, he would share a smoke with any of the militiamen and gangsters who would be on guard outside the reception hall. Miro carried all of his Deutsche marks—the few he had—in his pocket. It was the only currency that mattered at the moment.

Miro looked around the apartment. He wasn't leaving a home, or a city he still loved. He was leaving a graveyard, a killing field, a death camp. *Who wouldn't do what I'm about to? Anyone in my shoes, given such an opportunity, wouldn't think twice.* There comes a time when a person has to make a choice. He'd chosen life and had been waiting, like every other Sarajevan, for the right time to make a decision.

Mladjo had even said so.

Finally, it was time to go. He opened the door to Biljana's apartment and stood there at the threshold for a moment. He'd left her apartment in immaculate condition—even the bed was made. The scavengers were welcome to it. Someone would stumble upon it and decide to hide there or make it home. Gripping the doorknob, he shut the door with a thud. It was a symbolic sound, as if sealing his past and awakening his waiting future with his wife.

*

Admira had tried to keep her emotions in check during the two weeks leading up to Mladjo's wedding. Now that the day had arrived, was it wrong to feel so ecstatic when so many others could not? It had been a year since the siege began and the murder of countless Sarajevans, since their desolation had just about obliterated all sense of hope. It wasn't wrong to feel this happy; it couldn't be. She'd kept repeating the last three words to herself.

She tried to breathe normally. Bosko saw her excitement and it made him happy; it had worn off on him. They were about to celebrate life and being alive. Admira had been extravagant this evening and had lit as many as fifteen *kandilos* and placed them all in the bathroom, and then told Bosko to stay out until she was ready.

"What's taking so long? Why can't I come in?" Bosko stood at the far end of the hallway.

"In a minute," Admira replied. The *kandilos* provided enough light for Admira to see that her hair was perfect. Sweeping a hand over her forehead, she checked that every strand of hair was in place. She'd swept her hair up and back away from her luminous face in a style from a film. She remembered Bosko telling her about the movie *Now, Voyager* with Bette Davis, and how much he'd loved it and how she'd worn her hair at the end of the movie. It was exactly the way Admira had done hers for him tonight. It was one of her favorite movies too. They would prevail just like Bette Davis's character had done in the movie.

"Now?"

"Not yet."

"Oh my God—Admira."

"Patience. Will we dance?" She called out enthusiastically from the bathroom.

"Till our feet ache," Bosko replied impatiently.

"And will we laugh and sing?"

"Till we lose our voices."

"And will we toast with champagne?"

"To everyone. Now, come out."

"Close your eyes. Wait. Blow out all the kandilos in the living room."

"But it will be pitch black."

"Just do it, Bosh."

After a few seconds, he said, "Alright, I blew them out. Now what? I can't see a damn thing."

"Stay where you are." Admira opened the bathroom door, paused at one end of the hallway and then walked slowly toward Bosko. Her image grew clearer with each step she took. She emerged from the darkness, surrounded by the glow from two *kandilos*, one in each hand. She stopped, and stood just a few feet in front of him. Bosko's jaw dropped. His heart beat faster, as they stood staring at one another, just like it had that morning they'd met in front of The National Arts Theatre. She'd taken his breath away then, just as she was doing it now.

"I hope you approve. It's the way you like it."

He just stared.

"Say something, Bosh."

"You look so beautiful—oh my God. And you remembered."

"I did. Now, will you do something for me?"

"Anything."

"Do you remember what they said to each other at the very end?"

Bosko nodded. Admira offered him one of the *kandilos*. Reaching up, she placed her palm against his cheek.

"Tonight, let's not ask for the moon or wish for anything we do not have."

"Okay, Gypsy Girl. Tonight we will not ask or wish for anything we do not have, because we will most certainly have the stars. And they will burn for us, like the flickering of firelight."

Bosko placed his fingers under Admira's chin and lifting her face, kissed her on her lips.

"Tell me those words once more."

Without hesitating he said. "Agar firdaus bar roo-e zameen ast, Hameen ast-o hameen ast-o hameen ast."

The flames of the kandilo's flickered against every word he uttered.

"You should not do this to me; seduce me like this. I have no way to fight back."

"Good. I mean to take away any chance that you ever could, Gypsy Girl."

They both turned their heads toward the door when they heard Miroslav climbing up the stairs, "Miro's feelings are still hurt because he wasn't invited. Don't act too excited."

They walked to the door together and opened it.

"Ready for the big night?" Miro asked with a beaming smile.

"You bet," Bosko replied.

Miro took Admira's hand. "You look stunning."

"Thank you."

"I guess we're all set. Let's get going, you two."

The three of them emerged from the building and sprinted toward the car. Admira and Bosko took turns looking at the reflection of Miro's face in the rearview mirror. He kept his eyes on the road driving like a demon to avoid the rubble and didn't glance back at them once.

"Miro, after you drop us off, don't hang around. We'll get the militia or some of Mladjo's gangster buddies to drive us home, like we agreed. We'll be fine, so don't worry about us."

"Okay. Whatever you say." The car swerved back and forth on the street as he avoided gaping potholes and obstacles in their way. Speed was essential to get where they were going. Admira bumped or leaned into Bosko every time the car took a wide turn or steep incline. She laughed. She and Bosko were so happy. The way Miro drove made it seem they would outrun anything fired at them. Bosko tugged on her hand and she squeezed it gently, giving him a reassuring look. "It's okay. Everything today is going to be okay."

Approaching the reception hall, which was located in a heavily guarded block of buildings, they watched cars pulling close to the entrance and invited guests getting out.

Miro pulled into line behind a procession of cars.

"Doesn't this seem a little conspicuous?" Admira asked, thinking that everyone present made a lovely and extremely well-dressed target.

"Mladjo has an insurance policy," Bosko answered.

"What do you mean?"

Holding Admira's hand, he said, "The reception is in the basement in a big hall. The first and second floors are packed with civilians—men, women, and children. All of them Serbs. They were rounded up today, and brought to this place. All of them have family members outside the city or in Serb-controlled neighborhoods, and many of them are waiting for a Serb-Muslim exchange. How could they not agree to be rounded up and made hostages? You can be sure there will be no shelling of the reception hall and no snipers' firing here. Not tonight."

The men at the door motioned for them to pull up. Once stopped, Bosko and Admira got out. They waited for Miro to step out of the car and join them.

Bosko said, "Be safe getting home. I'll see you in a couple of days. We've both got some time off to recuperate from this shindig. Mladjo's orders."

"I'll do that."

"Thanks for bringing us." Bosko hugged his friend, and Admira kissed him on the cheek.

"Hey, have a good time. Enough for me too." Miro grabbed Bosko again. "Enjoy yourselves. I'll see you again, count on it."

"Of course you will," Bosko replied, puzzled.

"Take care, Admira." She turned around and waved to Miro. A sad look crossed her face for a moment and Miro saw it. She wanted him with her and Bosko. It wasn't right for him to be left out.

Bosko grabbed Admira's hand. Militiamen and many of Mladjo's gangster associates were all dressed in suits. Some had even managed to wear tuxedos, doing double duty as guards and ushers. Bosko took out the invitation from his breast pocket and handed it to one of them. The guard recognized Bosko and waved him and Admira ahead with the other invited guests. They turned back toward Miro, who raised his hand, and they waved good-bye once more.

Miro pulled slowly away from the crowd of people arriving in other cars. All the guests had been driven and given a safe-arrival guarantee. Miro could see himself travelling at the speed of light, racing toward the gates of freedom as he drove away, waving and nodding at each militia guard. No one bothered to inspect his vehicle, where he had hidden the codes, the same codes used to relay the location of a sniper to militia units who would race off to root out the sniper before he had the chance to kill again. Miro had written everything down on a small notepad, which he had stuffed under the driver's seat. As he drove away, he rolled up every window; to him, it felt as if he were only moments away from bursting free into a new life, a life with his woman. The woman he loved and who was waiting for him a world away.

The ironies kept piling up for Miro. He wanted to let out a belly laugh and not stop. He had the opportunity to escape the city of the dead and the dying because he was not invited to a wedding reception, and was making his escape in a car belonging to one of the groom's criminal friends, a car emblazoned with the gang sign to further protect him. He told himself that this meant life had no meaning, no sense, no purpose, or justice. It never did and never would. He was going to live while others were most definitely going to die. Existence in this world meant that if you were not one of the strong, you were one of the weak.

He continued to drive along the road past Sarajevo's main railroad station. This was the same station that he, Bosko, and Mats had departed from and returned to after twelve months of army duty. It was a derelict place now—battered and destroyed, like all of the hopes and dreams that he and his friends once had. The night was cool, and a soft breeze blew down from the hills. Miro didn't hear any explosions. He grabbed the handheld radio next to the driver's seat, turned off onto a side road, slowed down, and then turned off the headlights. He parked the car in the shadow cast by a bombed-out building. Slowly turning a knob on the military radio to a frequency he knew the Serbs listened to, Miro whispered into his radio. His voice had a gravelly tone.

"I am a Serb. I wish to talk to someone who can approve a trade." He said nothing more and then waited. The seconds passed and then a whole minute. Once more Miro raised the radio to his mouth and said, "I am a Serb. I wish to speak with someone. I have something you want." He waited, but still there was no reply. He lifted the radio a third time and repeated the message.

For another moment, there was silence, then a crackling sound, coming from the radio and then a voice said, "What is it you want?"

Miro held his breath and waited a few seconds, not wanting

to sound as desperate as he felt.

"What is it you want?" asked the voice once more.

"To leave," he replied.

There was a brief silence and then a lot of laughter.

"Would you be laughing if I told you I have the codes the militia use to track and kill your men? If you had them, you could save the lives of fellow Serbs. I am a Serb."

Silence.

"I don't hear you laughing now."

After a few moments a voice said, "How is it you know we are Serbs and not Muslims?"

"Would I be talking to you if I wasn't sure?"

"Come to these coordinates I will give you. Are you in a car?"

"Not just any car. You will recognize it when you see it. Do not ask any more questions. Everything will be answered when I get there."

The voice on the other end of the radio rattled off some numbers, then said, "Once you arrive, stop and do not get out of the car. We will come to you. Understood?"

"Understood," Miro replied. "And you should know that if you kill me, you might have the codes that are in my possession, but more importantly, you need me to show you how to decipher them so that you understand what they mean. Keep your trigger-happy snipers from doing anything stupid. I'm on my way."

Miro dropped the radio onto the passenger seat. He drove away slowly, heading for the coordinates, watching as he got closer to where he needed to be for his fellow Serbs to emerge from the darkness. He hadn't bothered looking in the rearview mirror from the moment he'd driven away from the reception. Nothing was behind him except death. What lay ahead was all that mattered. He pressed down on the gas pedal.

"I'm coming to you, Biljes," he whispered. "I'm coming."

The next day Bosko and Admira slept until early evening, not getting out of their field bed for anything. They remained immobile lying together. Their heads hurt. Their bellies were full. They were exhausted. They were also very happy. Once, they would have woken up much earlier, feeling ravenous, but the times had disciplined appetites in Sarajevo. They'd learned to ignore the hunger, but last night they had also gorged themselves on food and drink while they'd had the chance.

As promised to Miro, they'd brought home as much food as possible. "Screw how it looks. We're all starving," Admira had told Bosko, as they loaded up bags of food and fruit and bottles of wine and carried them out to the militia car that brought them home. It would make Miro very happy, and they would have a party of their own and share it with friends. Even Radmilla had promised to join them. They slept the day and night away.

Admira awoke first on the second day after the wedding reception and did what she loved to do—watch Bosko sleep.

Bosko opened and then closed his eyes. "We danced, didn't we?" he mumbled. The insides of his mouth felt like the coarsest sandpaper.

"Till our feet hurt," she said, not feeling nearly as bad. He had a massive hangover.

"Whatever I drank, I don't want it again. I remember being given something called Sarajevo cognac."

"You drank quite a bit of it. I brought a little home."

"Oh dear God, you didn't." Bosko opened his eyes again.

She reached across his chest, picked up a bottle, brought it to her lips, filled her mouth, leaned over, and kissed Bosko, sending a steady stream of cognac down his throat.

He gulped it down. "I can't move. Where's my head? Help me find it. It's a big Serbian head. You can't miss it. I can hear it screaming, 'What did you do to me last night?'"

"Let's stay in bed." It was a lazy second day after the party. The shafts of sunlight were still quite bright, shining in on them, the bed, and the living room. Admira figured it was early afternoon. Sleep was still the best thing for the two of them. Their entire beings were drained of all energy and purpose.

"Outstanding plan," Bosko mumbled as he slid his arms around her. She lay on top of him. They didn't hear the intermittent sound of gunfire and the constant explosions; they'd forgotten where they were. Nothing else mattered except to dream of dreams.

PART EIGHT

Chapter Thirty

Admira and Bosko slept through the entire first and second day after the wedding. The Sarajevo cognac had an anesthetic effect; it literally knocked them out for two solid days. The third day was spent detoxing their bodies and trying to walk in a straight line. Bosko and Miro had been given a brief reprieve of a few days by Mladjo from their duties on Kosovo Hill. Admira and Bosko kept expecting to hear Miro's knock on the door. Fun time had ended, tomorrow it would be back to surviving. They'd put some things aside for him to take back to his place. It was late afternoon of the fourth day and Admira was making tea for herself when Bosko heard footsteps in the stairwell.

Bosko turned to Admira. "Well, he's finally here. Do we have enough hot water for another cup?"

"Not only hot water, but unused tea bags!"

They expected Miro, but as the sound of the footsteps grew closer, they realized more than one person was approaching their apartment. Bosko got up. "Maybe it's Miro and a friend, but who? They're going to fall over when they see what we shanghaied from the party."

He opened the door as Djoka was about to knock. "Another party?"

"Not quite, Bosko."

The other two men at Djoka's side remained silent.

"What is it?"

"May I come in?"

"Of course."

The others remained outside. Bosko glanced briefly at their expressionless faces before he shut the door. He stood behind Djoka and made a funny face at Admira.

367

Admira tried not to smile, but she did.

"So what's up?" Bosko asked cheerfully. "Want some tea?"

"No thanks. I need you to come with me," Djoka said in a subdued voice. "Mladjo will explain."

"Explain what?"

"It's best if he tells you in person."

"What is it?" Admira asked as she moved to Bosko's side. Instinct told her something was wrong, but she had no idea what it could be.

Djoka asked, "Shall we go?"

Sensing something was awry, Bosko quickly jumped in. "Djoka." He walked up to him and wagging his finger playfully continued. "It's a surprise. If you say anything more, you'll give it away."

"What is?" Admira asked again, putting her arm around Bosko's waist, holding him back.

"You'll spoil the surprise, Admira, if we say anything more."

"What surprise?" Admira asked, looking at Bosko.

"It's a surprise and you'll have to wait. I'll be back and tell you all about it."

Touching the tip of her nose, he winked at her before he turned to Djoka and said, "Come on, before you give too much away."

"Bosko—wait, what's going on?"

Realizing that Bosko was trying to calm Admira's growing distress, Djoka said, "Bosko is right. He'll tell you all about it later." Djoka even managed a quick smile.

Bosko slipped on socks and boots, grabbed his jacket, and kissed her. "Stay out of trouble, and stay home," he said as he followed Djoka out and closed the door behind them.

*

On the drive to Mladjo's police station office, Bosko remained silent. The emblazoned gang sign on the car would keep

368

them safe from bullets, at least that was the hope. Bosko sensed quite rightly that none of the three men, Djoka especially, was in any mood to talk. For the life of him, Bosko could not figure out why Mladjo would want to see him so soon after his wedding. Why wasn't he still on his honeymoon? Had they taken too much food and drink with them?

When they arrived, Bosko walked briskly and confidently into Mladjo's headquarters. But he noticed that when he made eye contact with any of the men, they looked away. Every other time he'd been there, they stared at him. But now they avoided looking at him. Djoka didn't bother to knock. Mladjo was sitting behind his desk.

"So what's the surprise? Outstanding party by the way," Bosko said, strolling in, feeling confident and queasy at the same time.

"Sit down." Mladjo motioned for Djoka to shut the door but remain in the room.

This didn't go unnoticed by Bosko, nor did the fact that there were no sweets or coffee on the table. Mladjo had been a practical joker all his life, at other people's expense. He'd done it to Bosko when he'd summoned him to his office to tell him about his wedding. The manner in which he'd done it made Bosko's imagination run wild with every possibility. *Is he doing it again and having a laugh again at my expense?*

Bosko was expecting his friend to break out with some strange thought or laugh.

"When did you see Miro last?"

"What has he done this time?"

"When, Bosko?"

"When he drove us to the reception."

A long silence followed. Mladjo stood behind his desk and looked directly into Bosko's eyes. "Your friend is not with us anymore."

Bosko felt like his heart was about to burst. He dropped into a chair. "Is Miro—I shouldn't have let him drive back alone."

"That's funny you should say that."

"Is he okay? Has something happened to him? I don't understand."

"Let's see what you do understand." Mladjo's comment caught Bosko off guard. "After Miro left the reception, it was assumed he would go home." Mladjo's mouth contorted into a snarl. "When he didn't return the militia car the next day or the day after, I thought he had decided to do a little celebrating by himself and had gotten drunk. He was free from his duties on Kosovo Hill. He just had to return the car. But after the second day, I sent my men to search for him. There was no sign of him in his apartment. My men did finally find the car, but not him. The car was completely torched, destroyed."

"Where is Miro? Is he alive?" Bosko got out of his chair thinking the worst had happened to his best friend.

"That's a question we asked ourselves when the car was found abandoned. Where was your friend? A massive search turned up nothing."

"I don't understand. Is Miro alive?"

"He's alive." Mladjo's response was curt.

"So he is here, and he's alive." Bosko was so relieved. "Maybe he's just—"

"Just what?"

Bosko didn't have an answer for Mladjo. But as he remained standing with a million thoughts running wildly through his mind, a recent memory came back to haunt him, of that moment when he had a fight with his friend, who had begged him to leave Sarajevo.

"Since we were unable to find Miro, it left us with only one possibility to consider. What if he were to somehow find a way to escape the city?"

The very thought he'd just had, had now being spoken by

Mladjo. Bosko fell into the chair behind him. He began to squirm in his seat.

"For Miro to be able to succeed, he'd have to have something of great value to bargain with for his escape. And he would have to be certain it would work, because there would be no second chance to contact the Serbs and offer what he had so that he could gain his freedom. The night he drove you and Admira to my reception was the one night Miro had complete freedom of movement in the city to travel anywhere without being stopped and questioned and the car being searched."

Each second of Mladjo's speculation increased Bosko's feeling of dread. He couldn't imagine what his friend had done or what the gangster was alluding to.

"Miro is very much alive." Mladjo repeated once more slamming his fist on the desk. "There." Mladjo pointed in the direction of the Serbs and the mountains.

Bosko gripped the arms of the chair. "How do you know this?"

"One of our units on Kosovo Hill was contacted. Actually, it was the unit he served in. I don't know if he meant it to be as a joke. Having the Serbs contact his unit to indicate that one of theirs had made it over, and they implied that if it were so easy to get past the checkpoints, they would be coming down from the hills very soon."

"But how could he just leave, just disappear without anyone knowing?"

Mladjo's eyes were ice cold. Bosko instantly realized that Mladjo had been made a fool of on his wedding day. He couldn't bear to look at the gangster.

"My wedding celebration and the papers that authorized him to travel in a militia car, unescorted with very little restriction, provided Miro with the cover to desert us and his city."

"But how did Miro do it? How could he?" Bosko's voice

371

grew loud in anger.

Mladjo remained silent.

"I would have known. I would have sensed it. This is not possible, he wouldn't leave us. "I knew him like—"

"A brother? No one ever knows a person totally."

Bosko was hunched over, his face resting in the palms of his hands. His heart raced as if he were being chased by some horrific monster from a childhood fairy tale. It had to be a bad dream from a horrible hangover. "Wake up," he heard himself yell. "Wake up. This is not real." He swayed and almost fell out of the chair onto the floor. He couldn't look at Mladjo. *What had Miro done? Why had he shamed them all?* Again he protested. "I would have known. This is not possible."

Mladjo remained silent.

"Miro could not do this. He would not." Bosko's voice cracked. Nothing he'd heard in the last few minutes made sense. "He must have been kidnapped, forced to do what he did. It has to be."

"But it is not what happened, Bosko. It seems that Miro was waiting for the right moment. And it seems to me that I once reminded you of that." Bosko kept refusing to believe what he now knew was true. "We all live our lives in this city waiting for the right moment to do what we must. You want me to believe that you knew nothing, suspected nothing?"

Bosko looked up at Mladjo for only an instant before staring down at the floor once more. He remained silent.

In that brief moment when their eyes met, Bosko saw it. A visible layer that could only be described as a frenzied violence glazed over Mladjo's eyes, the very same kind that shows itself in monsters, men who are psychopaths and possessed by boundless bloodlust. Mladjo had been made out to be a fool. He had been taken for a ride; the irony of Miro escaping the city in one of their militia cars made it all the more offensive.

372

"This is a complete surprise to you? Is that what you want me to believe?"

"Yes, it is."

"This friend of yours—no—this *coward* shared every moment with you and Admira. He ate at your table. Shared the little food you and Admira have, worked beside you in the militia, and you're telling me that not one time, not even for a moment, did you suspect a thing? This you want me to believe?"

"I—"

"What, Bosko?"

"He—"

"What?" Mladjo slammed his fist on the desk.

Bosko remained silent. This angered Mladjo even more. Bosko rested his elbows on his thighs and kept staring down at the wooden floor. Finally, in a weak voice he said, "He—"

"He, what? The truth, Bosko. What are you not telling me?"

Even Bosko began to doubt that he hadn't suspected that Miro had a plan. It was more that he didn't want to believe it. Bosko knew he had to answer Mladjo.

"He said he wasn't like Mats, a friend of ours who was killed in Konavoski Dvori. Miro once told me, this is not my war. I have no intention of offering up my life as some sacrifice. I'm not Mats. Miro was desperate to be with his new bride. It was all he talked about, and it became his obsession. That had to be what drove him to do this.

"He begged and pleaded with me to ask you to get us out of Sarajevo. He was certain you would do it for us. But I said no. I will never leave Admira. He said if the city falls and it's found out that I am Serb who refused to join his brothers in the mountains, because of loving a Muslim girl, they would make an example of me. I told him I didn't care." Bosko raised his head and looked at Mladjo once more. "I can't leave her. I'll never leave Admira."

"So you knew how desperate he was and at no time did he

373

hint or did you suspect that he would find a way to escape?" Mladjo moved closer to Bosko, his hand near his gun.

Djoka took a step toward them, certain Mladjo was about to draw his weapon and shoot Bosko if he confessed that he suspected something.

"Miro was obsessed with the idea of being with Biljes. He begged me to speak to you for help and I refused. So maybe I am responsible for his actions. I should have realized he would do this. But how could I?" The gangster and Bosko stared at each other. "We never spoke of it again. I told him to never bring it up."

Mladjo moved his hand away from his sidearm.

"I don't understand." Bosko stared at his old family friend, bewildered. "How do you just *leave* Sarajevo?"

Mladjo leaned against his desk, studying Bosko's face, taking in his look of utter disbelief. In a soft tone he replied, "He had his two-way radio and the codes."

The moment Bosko heard the word "codes," he almost slid out of the chair. The enormity of what Miro had done to gain his freedom, instantly became clear.

"Miro, your friend, used the codes to bargain for his freedom once he was close enough to contact the Serbs on his radio. For two days before we discovered that he had shared the codes with his fellow Serbs, they were able to listen in on our frequency. Knowing what the codes meant, they were able to warn their snipers before they were located. Two days may not seem like a long time, but in forty-eight hours, a lot of mothers, fathers, brothers, and sisters have been killed. Their killers, whom we might have found, escaped. The codes have been changed, and we continue to improve on scrambling the frequency so they cannot listen in."

Bosko slipped out of his chair onto floor. His best friend, with whom both of their lives had been inexorably entwined, had betrayed his city, a city that still refused to surrender or die.

"Get off the floor," said the gangster.

"Do you understand what this means?" Mladjo knew Bosko was now a condemned man.

"I understand perfectly. My friend chose to escape and live at any cost, and that makes me just like him to everyone else. I will have to live with it." Bosko's body shook as he sat on the chair.

"This is a war, Bosko. What each of us does matters; it affects us all."

"Miro is not in the mountains with a gun in his hand. This much I am certain of." Bosko could barely breathe.

"Are you?" Mladjo asked. "And what makes you think that next week or next month he won't change his mind?"

"Miro wants only one thing. He's only ever wanted one thing —to be with Biljes. It's the only thing that matters to him. Nothing else."

"Let us hope so, Bosko. For your sake and Admira's."

Bosko's blood curdled at hearing the words.

"You say he hasn't got a gun in his hand, looking down on Sarajevo's citizens, about to kill them. Let's hope that you are right about this, since it appears that you were not so observant about many other things."

"I'm sorry for what Miro has done."

"Sorry, Bosko? Sorry! This is how your boyhood friend pays you back? He ate at your home, broke bread with you. Admira fed him, taking food out of her own mouth so he wouldn't starve. And this is what he does to repay you?"

Bosko had no answers for Mladjo. His eyes never left the floor.

"His friendship with you meant he was also my friend, which meant he lived a lot longer than he might have."

"Mladjo, I don't know how to—"

"Save it. I'm surrounded by men who betray me all the time. I understand it—they do it for money, for power, the things I have that they want. But Miro betrayed *you* because he's always been a coward. You just refused to see it."

Bosko grabbed his head, feeling that it was about to explode. He gritted his teeth and shut his eyes.

"You must be very careful from now on. Both you and Admira." Bosko heard Djoka's words but didn't look up. "You— for all the reasons we both know—and Admira because she is sharing your bed. I do not have to tell you the possible dangers that might arise from this fact."

Bosko's stare remained on the floor; he was unable to look at either man. In a calm and deadly voice the gangster said, "The difference between you wanting to stay with Admira and Miro wanting to escape to be with his woman is that you and Admira are willing to accept death as the price for being together. Miro and Biljes were not. It is in these barbaric moments, which no person could ever fathom happening, that a man and a woman will be called upon to show a most profound human trait: courage."

Bosko lifted his face, meeting Mladjo's eyes. Those had been the same words spoken by Mats when they'd all stood together on the walkway for the last time. *When there's no choice given, then an act of courage is called for. This is mine because there's no other choice for me.* Courage had kept them defiant against their besiegers and tormentors. It kept them alive. Now, more than ever, Bosko missed having Mats next to him.

"Go home."

"What do you want me to do? Just tell me. I'll do it," Bosko said, feeling desperate.

"There is nothing for you to do except to protect Admira. She's the only thing of real value you have ever had in your life. Go home to her."

Bosko rose to his feet and stood still, looking for some words

376

to convey how sorry he was. With every passing second, it kept sinking in deeper and deeper that he would be seen as another traitorous Serb. A Serb who, like Miro, would also one day betray his city, as so many of them already had.

"Mladjo, you've done more for my family than I deserve. I am truly sorry." No apology could mean enough or compensate Mladjo enough for Miro's betrayal.

Bosko headed for the door. He was disgraced and bewildered and was now a marked man. Before he opened it, he turned and stared at Mladjo and Djoka once more.

He opened the door. Everyone in the outer room turned and looked at him. Miro's words echoed in his head from that day when they had watched Mats leave under a cascade of falling snowflakes.

"He's doing what he has to. In the end, we all will—whatever that might be."

*

Djoka shut the door and turned to Mladjo. At first the two men were silent.

"His militia days are over. None of the men will be able to stomach being anywhere near him," Djoka said, breaking the silence.

"If you were Bosko, what would you do?"

"Do?"

Mladjo turned to Djoka.

"There's only one thing to do. Leave the girl, come to you so you could get him out, then find Miro and kill him. Betrayal such as this breaks all the bonds of friendship forever."

"You would leave her to face what might happen if the city falls?"

"Yes," Djoka replied. "Without hesitation."

377

"Bosko will never do that." Mladjo's voice almost sounded wistful.

"She's a fool if she stays with him, and he's a romantic if he lets her. Romantics and fools always lose in life and in war."

"Perhaps."

"They don't have a chance. You know that."

*

Her hand wouldn't stop trembling as she poured them each a cup of tea. Admira didn't know what to think or how to act after Bosko had told her what had happened. She began to funnel through her mind every thought Bosko might be having about them. It made her feel very uneasy. Already she felt a tension growing between them. It began the moment he'd told her everything and then became very silent as he sat by himself on their field bed. Admira turned to leave the kitchen, and the two mugs she was holding almost slipped out of her hands. She quickly placed them back on the counter and pressed a hand over her mouth. She didn't want Bosko to hear her crying. *How could Miro just run away? How could he have left them in such a way—as if they'd never mattered to him?*

Miro's running away felt to her as if some part of her body had been torn away and she was only half of her former self. Admira didn't know what to do. She felt like curling up into a ball on the floor. Now they were truly all alone, with only each other to live for—and die for.

The silence in their apartment grew deep and cavernous. Life at this moment made less sense than at any other time in the past year. Admira held onto the counter and prayed to God with all her strength for guidance. God hadn't listened to any of them. This much was true. God knew that all Slavs were pitiless, never knowing how to live amongst themselves. "Perhaps this one time, will you relent?" she begged and fell to her knees. "And show me what I must do? Please help me."

Her heart broke for him. What was she to do? What could she do? "Be still and think," she heard herself say. Admira shut her eyes and curled each hand into a fist. Not even this would separate them. She swore it under her breath. The sound of her beating heart grew louder. The answer came to her. *Listen to your heart. Listen.* Here in the pit of hell was their paradise. This place, this home, where they'd first made love to each other was where they would stay together. Nothing was going to separate them.

Admira stood up slowly. She was compelled not to give up or believe the end was near. Even as a child, she'd always been unwilling to accept things as they were, only willing to make them as they should be. Taking hold of the two mugs, she walked into the living room. Bosko still sat on their field bed. For a moment, all she could do was stare at him. He was so terribly wounded by Miro's betrayal.

Nothing she could say would make a difference. Perhaps it did not matter, she thought to herself, because the day would come when this daily hell in which they were living would end and she and Bosko would still be together. The only thing that mattered, all that ever would, was to be together. Admira took a deep breath, filling her lungs, her entire being, with the familiar smells of their apartment. The smell of burning wood and ash, and of her cooked macaroni and cheese. The scent of Bosko and of her. Even the smell of the exposed pieces of plaster that clung to the walls. It was all symbolic of their will to live, to persevere. It was the scent of their life together. It permeated the air around them, soaking into the sheets on which they made love. It was the same scent that filled the lungs of everyone in their city with that same determination, a refusal to surrender to their besiegers.

Joining Bosko on their field bed and offering him his tea, she watched the flickering light from the *kandilos* that illuminated their

379

hovel.

"Tell me," she asked. "Share with me Bosko, tell me what you're thinking."

He just lowered his head and remained silent. Bosko didn't want to tell Admira what he was thinking, not yet.

"It's not important now. I just want to stop thinking. I'm so tired of everything."

"Me too."

After taking a few sips, Admira placed the mug on the floor next to the bed and lay down. She was wearing one of Bosko's thin flannel shirts, the one with the red checkered squares. It was her favorite—worn, soft, and snuggly. He leaned against the wall, his long legs stretched across the bed. Placing her head on his lap, she looked up at him, so many questions swirling about in her mind. He began to play with her hair. It was something she loved. The minutes passed and she began to feel her eyes close.

"Don't stop," she whispered. "Not till after I fall asleep." They were both exhausted, and there were no words left to say. Their only friend was gone. They had been abandoned. Neither one said a word. He continued running his fingers through her black curls. Finally, she closed her eyes and fell into a gentle sleep. Bosko stayed awake; his eyes were wide open, burning with a realization as bright as the single flame from the *kandilo*. The shattering sound of explosions continued as their city crumbled around them. Its citizens hid in basements and concealed warrens that were hastily dug or simply discovered. Bosko kept passing his finger back and forth through the flickering flame. Each time he did, a ring of fire formed around his finger. He and Admira had been plunged into a different kind of fire.

Bosko kept hearing Miro's words: *This is not my war. I have no intention of offering up my life as some sacrifice. I'm not Mats.*

Because his Serb friend had betrayed his city and was now safe among the very people who were besieging her, there wasn't a soul in Sarajevo who would not look at him with hatred and suspicion. Where one traitor was hatched, another could be found in the same nest.

He slid his fingers deeper into Admira's curls as he watched her chest rise and fall with every breath. They had believed that nothing could ever separate them. Every bad thing that could happen had already happened to them and their city during the past year. Their city had survived, barely, and so had they— because every Sarajevan wanted to live. But something far more lethal had happened to Admira and Bosko that seemed worse than all the explosions and sniper fire they had endured. While Bosko was deep in thought, the light flickered and his black shadow seemed to jump off the wall—an apparition that gave him silent counsel.

"We would have made it, Miro. You know we would have," Bosko whispered. His voice cracked as he repeated the words, which in time lost all of their meaning. He lowered his face until his lips touched Admira's, and, as softly as he could, he kissed her, not waking her. Admira was lost in the land of dreams. He closed his eyes. *Had the bombing stopped? Were any explosions taking place?* If there were, why could he hear only his thoughts and nothing else?

*

Admira woke, stretching out an arm to touch Bosko. His place on the bed beside her was empty and cold. She turned her head and raised it slightly, not having fully opened her eyes.

"Bosko?"

"Yes." He reached forward to hold her outstretched hand. He had spent all night resting against the wall.

"You didn't sleep?" She tried to get up, but Bosko gently pressed her back onto the sheets."

"Rest, it's not like we have a lot of things to do. Did you sleep

381

well?"

"Yes; strangely, I did. Were you awake all night?" she asked again, touching his cheek.

"I dozed off now and then. I feel fine—really."

"You should have slept. You can't go outside without rest."

"I know."

"Then you'll stay indoors with me today. We'll hang out and play *caroms*. I beat you the last time." Bosko kept silent. "We still have plenty of food and drink from what we brought back from the reception," she said, trying not to feel guilty.

"I know."

"I'll make us breakfast," she said as she pushed away to get up.

"I already have."

"You have?"

"Yes, one scrambled egg with bread, a little butter, and jam. I'm keeping it warm in the kitchen. I'll be right back."

She sat up and pulled the sheet to her waist. Bosko went to the kitchen and returned holding a breakfast tray.

"Here we go." Bosko set the tray in her lap. "The tea water is heating up."

"What would I do without you?"

He smiled—not his usual smile—just a smile. He was locking every image of her into his memory.

The slice of bread slipped out of her hand when she noticed her small suitcase, its straps buckled tightly between the loops, resting against the door. "No," she cried, and pushed the tray away. Bosko tried to hold her but she shoved him away with all her strength. He grabbed her, but she kicked him with both feet. In an instant, she was standing. "No. I will not." Her voice was like stone. "No. No. I will not."

"Stop with this temper tantrum and act like a grown woman."

"How dare you say that to me! It's me, me you're talking to."

It was only then that she realized he was fully dressed and had been waiting for her to wake up. "Don't do this, please, don't do this."

"Listen to me."

"No. I won't. I won't. I won't." She put her hands up to her ears and tried to run away. But he grabbed her and lifted her off her feet.

"Let go of me." Her voice was hard. A rage built within her toward him like nothing she'd ever felt before. She pummeled him with her fists and slapped him across his face. With every blow, her tears flowed. Finally, her fists came to rest on his chest; she was completely exhausted and spent.

Bosko slid his arms around her and held her.

"You must listen to me. I don't know what's going to happen, but whatever it is I must face it alone."

"Let go of me."

He released her.

Admira stepped back. So many emotions roiled about in her heart.

"You're going back. Do you understand me? I don't care if I have to carry you all the way. But you are going back."

"How dare you think you can make a decision, any decision, about *us*, and not talk to me about it!"

"This does not concern you. It's about me and Miro."

"You and Miro? Miro has nothing to do with it. Who's in this room, except for you and me?"

"Admira—I'm afraid of what will happen to you if you stay with me." Without giving her a chance to say another word, Bosko said in a low voice, "We've done more than anyone ever thought possible. Walked those miles every day to see one another even if it was for just a few hours. We've run and hidden... and starved... and laughed and cried. I've made such glorious love to you on our field bed. And you've done the same to me. But if you stay here, I'm just like Miro, wanting something so desperately and getting it the wrong way."

"Getting what the wrong way? What are you talking about?"

"He left to be with Biljes. I understand that. It's the way he did it that was wrong. I want you to be with me, but to keep you here is wrong. It's the wrong way to do it, knowing what can happen if you stay. I won't do it. Don't you understand what Miro has done? For two days, men, women, and children have died at the hands of those killers. They could have been a neighbor's friend or a mother or father. He stole those codes to bargain for his freedom—the codes we used to find those bastards. When people find out what he's done, everyone will believe that someone they loved was killed because of Miro's actions. They will take their vengeance out on me because in some way I was to blame."

She pulled him away from the wall and wrapped his arms around her.

"Bosko, my love, you must never retreat or surrender to those who have no soul, to those who have forgotten what it is to be human."

"Admira—"

"No, you listen to me. To be apart now makes everything that has happened to us and to everyone else meaningless. If we're not strong enough to stand up to these murderers, if we let them separate us, it's not Miro who will have caused it. It will be us."

Bosko shook his head and turned away from her.

"Look at me."

Bosko looked up at the holes into the wood covering the windows. His eyes followed the shafts of light as they beamed across their living room and onto the floor.

"Bosko of Kosovo Hill, you look at me."

He turned to Admira and lowered his eyes away from the beams of sunlight.

384

"Yes. It is a deep, deep sorrow if it's true that anyone has died because of what Miro did. I will get on my knees and beg for their forgiveness in the streets of our city if I should meet anyone who has lost a loved one because of what he did."

"Then... you know, you must go back."

"Do you hear it?"

"What?" he replied, looking away as he leaned back against the wall and slid down to the floor. Admira fell to her knees next to him.

She looked straight into his eyes. "The laughter. Can't you hear it? It's coming from the mountains. They're laughing at us. They can see that in the end you and I are not strong enough to realize the only thing that matters while they do everything to destroy our will to live, to survive, is to *be* together. Or is the real truth that you and I were never really strong enough? Because we were never tested until now?

"And now that we have been, you want us to fail the test. Is that what you want? All those days and months of running and hiding and yearning to be together—do you want all of that to mean nothing? Should it be swept away in an instant because we're so scared of what might happen?"

"Our neighbors or just strangers could drag you out of my arms, and that would turn me into a monster. You can't be near me, anywhere near me, not now. It's too dangerous. What Miro has done—"

"I don't care about Miro. No one is ever going to take me away from you. They'll never possess the strength to do it. Don't you dare give up!"

"Admira, this will end one day. One day, it will. We'll be together on that first day of peace. I promise you. I will come to get you."

"No, you won't." Admira's fear was knowing that if she left Bosko, it would seem to everyone that she believed he was guilty

385

in some way for what had happened—and that would be fatal for Bosko. If she left him now, he would be by himself and not even Mladjo would be able to protect him. As much as he wanted her to leave, she knew she had to stay. Seeing that she had remained with him, a Muslim girl with her Serbian lover, might make enough people think that she would only dare to stay because she knew he was innocent—because the risk was so great in doing so.

"I can't protect myself and I certainly can't protect you. But I'm not afraid to die."

The very words opened up a pit in her heart and she screamed inside at the thought of Bosko—she immediately put the image out of her mind. Closing her eyes for a brief moment and searching in her heart for the right words, she took Bosko's face between her hands. "Don't ever say those words to me. You will not die without me at your side. This I know crusader. This I know. If you send me away, I'll keep coming back. I won't stop. I'll keep walking past the bullets and the shelling and the corpses in the street."

"Your father won't let you. I will die in my city but not on my knees and not with your blood on my hands. I'm not without the rage of my ancestors. You are going home."

"I am not! Just you try," she yelled at him.

"When you're safe with your parents, I'll deal with my fate as a Serbian, always knowing in my heart that I'm a Sarajevan."

In that instant, Admira knew Bosko's heart would turn black and he'd fight his tormentors if she was not with him; he'd fight them with the rage of his ancestors, on every corner, on every street, at every moment, until the fight was over. She knew she had to do something, otherwise he'd die a horrible death.

"This isn't about me being safe. It's about being together. You stayed when you could've left. Mladjo would've gotten you out a thousand times over. Instead, you came to me every day. You stayed because you love me. Don't ask me to do anything

386

less. I will come back. Father will not be able to stop me. I'll bang on your door and keep banging till you let me in, and if you don't answer me, I'll stand outside on the sidewalk for everyone to see me. I won't move. I won't. You know I will do this. I will find a way to run away from home in the night, in the day, it doesn't matter, but I will find a way, and when I get here, I will stay outside on that sidewalk for all to see until you let me be with you again."

Bosko remained silent. He knew Admira meant it.

"Look at me and answer me with your heart. With your heart, Bosko. It's the lie that kills lovers, not the truth. If you lie to me now, you will kill us as surely as a bullet will. I am your Gypsy Girl. I speak the truth. You will not die without me by your side. I know this in my heart. Do you truly want me to leave?"

Tears had formed in Bosko's eyes as he listened, knowing she was right. He couldn't look at her. He felt so ashamed. He wanted Admira to be with him but couldn't say it.

"Look at me."

He couldn't.

"Tell me you want me to go away, that this is the truth in your heart."

They sat together the two of them in a silo of silence, with only the brilliant shafts of sunlight waiting to bear witness. To the truth that was in Bosko's heart.

"Lie to your Gypsy Girl."

"No," he barely uttered the word. And at that moment it was Bosko's heart that became illuminated with the truth, for Admira and him to bear witness. The shafts of sunlight blazed down on each one of them.

She held him tight and kissed him. "Oh, yes. Yes, be selfish. Love me selfishly, always," she cried as she kissed him. "This is the time for us to be selfish. Promise me you'll always be selfish, that you'll never let me go. Promise me." She held his face in her

387

hands and looked at him with tear-stained cheeks. "Always together. Promise me."

"I promise."

"We will always have the stars to look up to, and they will always look down at us."

*

Two weeks had passed since Miro had fled the city. Bosko knew that he had to tell Admira's parents what had happened. Admira knew how much her family would be happy to see her and Bosko. They had remained safe. Taking time off to visit them had been extremely difficult with Bosko having his militia duties to perform—but that fact was no longer the case. Being pragmatic at the same time, Admira realized that visiting her family would allow them to bring back a few of her mother's preserves, not a bad idea.

All of their neighbors living in nearby buildings and all along Kosovo Hill had by now known what Miro had done and that Bosko was his friend. Neither Bosko nor Admira knew what would greet them each day when they travelled out onto the streets. Today would be no different as they tried to reach her parents' home, but they had to do it, they were not going to lock themselves away and hide. They had to remain a part of it delve deep into the midst of the chaos of the siege; of people running for their lives. The whizzing of bullets above their heads. It was a scene that described all of their lives in an unfolding, unending hell.

They observed their world, each other, and everyone one else who was out on the streets attempting to survive for one more day. Admira was the first to look up at a building they ran past, it too caught Bosko's eye. The innumerable metal pipes sticking through holes dug into the outside walls of the building were attached to the makeshift stoves in each of the apartments which provided heat during the cold winter months. He'd vented their own apartment the same way. The ventilation was to avoid carbon monoxide poisoning and smoke suffocation, which had already killed so many. For some, it had been no accident.

They ran holding onto each other's hand.

*

"What else?" asked Zao.

"That's it, Zao, that's how Miro was able to get out of Sarajevo."

Her whole family was seated around the kitchen table listening to Bosko recount what had happened. Everything, from the joy and fun they had at the wedding reception to finding out later what Miro had done. The mortar explosions and gunfire that they dodged and ran away from to get to her parents' home didn't seem nearly as dreadful as having to tell her parents the news. And who, after hearing it, Bosko believed might insist that Admira stay with them for fear of what might happen to her if she remained with him.

But Admira's parents did not insist that Admira rethink staying with Bosko. They both knew better than to suggest it. They already knew that Bosko and Admira had fought about it. They could both see it in Bosko's eyes. They knew their daughter. She would have never accepted being separated from him.

"Okay, so it's done. Miro made his choice. But the both of you still have to survive. How do you plan to do it?" asked Zao, knowing he had to inject a voice of reason and purpose into a discussion about a very bad situation.

"I don't know, Zao, and I'm not going to lie to you or Zena. I don't know."

No one mentioned it, but Bosh and Admira had lost quite a

bit of weight. Both their faces were gaunt, and Admira's clothes hung on her as if they were two sizes too big. They were struggling to survive day by day.

"I go to the U.N. station on Kosovo Hill for their food packages. Sometimes I'm able to get one, and then there are times that there aren't enough to go around. We've been surviving on them, so far. It has oil, sugar, soap, even some cheese and six cans of beef. We stretch a package out for as long as we can. And there's the bread line. I'm in it every day. Two hundred and thirty- three grams for each loaf—it's ingrained in my brain. There's also the scavenging I do. I've been able to find things in the garbage dumps that I am then able to barter for other things we need or have run out of."

Zena cursed Miro under her breath in a way only a mother can. Her daughter's life and that of Bosko were dangling on a precipice.

"Have you had problems?" asked her father. He was asking about how Bosko was being treated when he ventured out onto the streets.

"I get a lot of stares. People purposely bump into me, but I just keep walking." Bosko didn't mention that he had been spat on. He had never mentioned it to Admira. "I don't blame them." He looked at his open palms resting on the kitchen table.

"I've got some things I want you both to take back." Zena broke the silence and got up from the table. Turning to her youngest, she said, in a marshaling tone, "Tonya, help me to get some things for your sister and Bosko." Tonya immediately got up out of her chair.

"Sis, come here, give me a hug," said Admira. Bosko kept staring into his palms. Her father remained silent. "I'll help you guys." Admira stood up. Then turning, she tousled Bosko's hair playfully before leaving the kitchen with her sister and mom.

Zao sat across from Bosko at the kitchen table. The women

390

were outside in the shed picking out bottles of Zena's preserves. The shadows that had crept into the kitchen were made by the late afternoon sun. Almost all of Bosko was blanketed by a black shadow. A single ray of sunshine, which had pierced through the space of the drawn window curtain, illuminated just one side of Zao's face.

"She won't leave me, Zao."

"I know."

Bosko looked up at her dad.

"I don't want her to leave," said Bosko, sounding so guilty for having said it.

"I know," replied Admira's father.

*

Bosko cleaned the kitchen and swept the floors, retied the stacked wood, and made more *kandilos* for them. Admira had cooked a very weak lentil soup, which they would eat in small portions for a whole week. They had visited her parents a few days ago to give them the news of what had happened. It had gone better than expected, so they both were feeling very upbeat. Their plan was to make the foodstuffs they'd brought back from the wedding last for as long as possible. Admira worked hard at reining in her fear. Bosko's anxiety over Admira's well-being made him extremely sensitive to any sound outside the apartment. *Are there people gathering outside on the stairwell, waiting to drag me out and attack her?*

By chance, the electricity had come on at two o'clock in the morning and then they had running water, but for how long they couldn't know. Whenever that happened, it was a race against time to wash and clean things, take a bath, bake a loaf of bread. Water was more precious than food. Somehow just enough pipes in their building delivering water to the apartments remained intact. Long hair was washed in exactly one and a half liters, the whole body was washed in two or three liters, and utensils of any kind were cleaned in cold or lukewarm water.

As the days passed, they realized there were no groups of people ready to rush up the stairs and drag them from their apartment. No knocks on the door late at night by neighbors who had left nooses made from wire and had attached them to their apartment door. So they both began to relax. Admira's only recent sadness was having to scrape a precious fried egg off the floor, the one she'd hurled at Bosko in a fit of uncontrollable rage. Once more they'd willed themselves to stay together; their only thought was that to live without each other was far worse than the alternative. They now had to live with an even greater hardship. Miro's betrayal had cut off all avenues for Bosko to eke out a living. The paltry sum he and Miro would receive for their militia duties no longer existed. The food donations from the U.N. now, more than ever, meant whether they would have food to get by or would have to starve. And he had to scavenge the city every day for anything he could barter for items they would need.

Admira and Bosko knew that he had to go into the city and face whatever awaited him. Bosko dressed in the bathroom while Admira watched, leaning against the wall.

"I'll be okay," he said, turning to her.

"I know you will," she replied as she joined him in the bathroom and turned down his collar. He'd tied a collection of metal pots and pans together with a piece of string through the loops of the handles so he could carry them slung across his shoulder. They had belonged to his mother. He was limited to selling pots and pans—if anyone would buy from him at all. And he'd continued to scrounge around in bombed-out buildings and abandoned cars for anything he could barter with at the marketplace. Bosko tried to remain optimistic. Treasures were occasionally found; they never knew when it would happen.

Radmilla had bought some items from him, but he'd been too ashamed to take any money from her.

They had half a loaf of bread and a handful of potatoes left, but no meat or vegetables. Perishable food from the reception had had to be eaten right away. Everything else had been stored away in tin cans. Nothing was ever wasted.

"I'll try to get us a U.N. food package if I can, and I'll try to sell more of my mother's pots and pans. They're in good shape; surely someone's going to want them. I'll be back soon," he said as he slung the pots and pans over his shoulder.

She straightened his collar once more. "And I'll be waiting."

*

The stench in the air came from a combination of sources. Living in the city meant dealing with exploding shells, piles of garbage rotting everywhere, and unclaimed bodies that had been left to the dogs and the weather. Claimed by both, the corpses lost all their human features and eventually became only scraps of clothing. At times, it was impossible to tell if a corpse had been a man or a woman. Fires raged from buildings, big and small. A haze of smoke was everywhere, mixed with smoldering ash and wood. The only fresh scent in Sarajevo came from overturned earth being dug for a grave. Almost every inch of soil in the city had been dug up to bury the dead.

Bosko needed to find food because he and Admira were desperate. Travelling to her parents' home to get fresh vegetables from her mother's garden or her bottled fruit preserves was always a dangerous thing to do, but now they would have to do it more often.

As he walked, the sound of gunfire wasn't close enough for him to duck even slightly. Before him, countless buildings lay in ruins. The Ali Pasha Mosque's roof had blown off a long time ago, its minaret completely destroyed and reduced to rubble. The Church of St. Joseph had also been peeled open like a sardine can, its once-believed hallowed interior now a prostrate witness to an ambivalent God. Rain, snow, and ash were the only tribute that fell from heaven, from a God that seemed neither Christian nor Muslim.

He watched as mothers and wives walked down the street. They'd become like their mothers before them—expert laundresses. They washed clothes in whatever water they could find running from broken culverts, gutters, broken water main pipes, or rainwater collected in every conceivable container. The river worked, too, if you were able to avoid the snipers. Washing machines were a thing of the past.

Ahead of him, a sign was posted on a wall: *We have lost four thousand tons of weight, give or take a kilo here and there since this siege began. Look for further updates.*

He glanced at his watch. Curfew started at ten o'clock at night and ended at five in the morning. He knew he had plenty of time as he headed to one of the humanitarian aid centers. *Have I done the right thing, allowing Admira to stay with me?* Bosko shook his head as he walked. Doubt remained.

As he drew closer to the aid station, he hoped to be lucky enough to get some purification pills for the water they'd collected. They boiled the water, then treated it with a single pill. A white pill for two liters, and a green pill for five liters. The pills were under the strict control of the military, the police, and UNPROFOR.

Bosko also hoped he'd be given a USA packet, as they were called. One aid packet could be stretched to feed up to five people for a while, if used with imagination. If there were any left at the aid station, he would beg for one, and if he had to get on his knees, he would.

"Bosko, is that you?"

At first Bosko didn't hear them call out his name. His back was turned to a half dozen young men about the same age as him who had been following him ever since they'd seen him. Bosko's thoughts were on getting an aid packet. They were foaming at the teeth. Six young Muslim men who shared a Slavic heritage with Bosko, but it had no meaning to them. To all of them, Bosko was a traitorous Serb just like his friend Miro. Why was he being allowed to live while countless others were being killed by his kind? They were disheveled-looking, and they hadn't taken a bath or shower in a couple of weeks; running water for even just a few minutes was almost non-existent in every part of the city.

Each was holding onto a club or large wooden stick.

"Hey you, are you Bosko?" the leader of this wolf pack called out once more.

Bosko turned around, a smile on his face.

"What are you smiling about, traitorous pig?"

The word stung Bosko like a sharpened barb. His face burned.

"That's right. You."

Bosko didn't recognize the young man who was about his age.

"I'm Bosko, and I'm no pig."

"No, there's no mistake," the young Muslim said as he and his four cohorts surrounded Bosko. "Do you see his head? Look how big and misshapen it is. It's filled with the monstrosities that we know are in the head of every killer Serbian pig."

Bosko fought the impulse to make a fist.

It was swift and occurred without any hint or warning. An onslaught of fists, wooden clubs, and sticks struck every part of his body while steel-toed boots crashed into the side of chest. He was pummeled down onto one knee. He fought through the pain and refused to let himself fall down onto both his knees. At first he tried to push them away, as the hardened tips of boots crashed against his ribs. The clubs and wooden sticks kept crashing against every part of his body.

Bosko fought back, grabbing the clubs while trying to yank them out of the attacker's grip. He curled his large fingers into a fist, and while he was being struck over and over, he was able to hit one of the young men in the throat, but it had no effect. He kept fighting back through the rage and pain, feeling different... like he was a Serb.

It ended as suddenly as it had begun. Barely a minute had passed since Bosko had been kicked with heavy boots and beaten with clubs and wooden sticks on the streets of Sarajevo, as if he were a rabid animal that needed to be exterminated. The young Muslim and his friends stepped back, smiling. "That was just to tenderize you," the leader said. "You're going to feel pain like you've never felt before. When we're done with you, that Muslim whore will be next. We have very special plans for her. But everything happens in its own good time."

The six men took turns spitting on Bosko—once, twice, three times, in his hair, on his face, in his eyes. "This is just the beginning. Tell that to that whore of yours, if you see her before we do." They laughed and walked and then started to run in the direction of his apartment.

Bosko rose to his knees, holding his side. Each time he tried to draw a breath, the pain in his ribs sliced through him. He stood and wiped away their spit with his hands and the sleeves of his shirt.

A few people had stopped to watch, but no one had interceded. They knew who he was, who his friend had been. He held his side. As he looked at the expressions on the faces in the crowd, their faces revealed nothing and everything. *You're a Serb*, their eyes said. He'd held back his blows because he knew he must, and because the words of Milošević on the Field of Blackbirds repeated in his head. *Allow us to forget that at one time we were brave and one of the few that entered the battle undefeated.*

He was calling to Bosko once more to make right the injustice being done to him, to fight, to destroy, to annihilate. *Should I have picked up a brick and bashed their brains out? It would have stopped them. I could have taken care of them. Word would have gotten out that I'm not to be messed with.* Instead, he'd held back. Now they thought him a coward; he'd made it worse. No, he said to himself, you did the right thing. To fight now would rob Admira and him of any chance they might still have to survive this together.

He looked down at a brick on the street and shook with rage. Only his own fear of using it calmed him down. A dirty page from an old newspaper blew across his feet. He picked it up and began to wipe away the spit from his hair, and then he remembered what they'd said about Admira. His journey to the aid station was forgotten. He discarded the newspaper and began to walk as fast as his aching side would allow him. He kept up his pace, ignoring everything around him—including the snipers. His mother's pots and pans clanged and banged against his shoulders as he tried to ignore the pain in his ribs and back.

A few of his neighbors, who had remained his friends, said hello to him as he rushed past them. He ignored their greetings. His focus was on reaching her. She had to be safe. If anything had happened to her—if they had harmed her—he would find them and kill them all.

It is a luxury to think as you do. To think, you could never become a killer. Only one thing could make that happen for you, Bosko: if the most precious thing in your life is taken from you. Mladjo's words haunted Bosko with every grueling step.

He reached their building out of breath. His nose was bleeding profusely. Bosko discarded the pots and pans onto the sidewalk outside of his building. Bosko grabbed his side; his ribs felt as if they'd snapped and the jagged ends had pierced his lungs. Collapsing onto one knee outside the entrance door to his building, and gasping for air, he tried with all of his strength to rise to his feet and breathe. He held on to anything he could use to pull himself up from his knees. When he pushed the entrance door open, he fell against the wall, wanting to call out her name, but he didn't. He struggled up the stairs, grabbing the railing as he tried to whip his body upward, until finally reaching their door on the third floor. "Hey, Sweetie, it's me. Open up." He heard Admira's footsteps. "I'm back. I told you I wouldn't be long."

Admira opened the door and let out a wail as she looked at his face, at the blood dripping from his nose and from the sides of his mouth. Bosko held his side, as he practically fell into the apartment. Admira grabbed him and placed his arm over her shoulder. Together they hobbled inside.

Chapter Thirty-One

Admira felt his rage bubbling below the surface of his wounds. More importantly, she saw the hurt in Bosko's eyes. She wondered what he would have to do to prove to everyone that he wasn't the enemy.

"Let me," she said as she gently helped Bosko take off his clothes. His torso was black and blue. A bulge had formed above his sternum, and both shoulders were a deep purple.

Bosko rested against the bathroom wall as Admira slid her hand across the front and sides of his chest to check for broken ribs, not finding any. She thanked God. The same invisible God that everyone prayed to in Sarajevo.

Bosko watched her, and while he did, he couldn't shake Mladjo's words from his head. It was true. He would turn into a monster if anything happened to her.

"This is going to sting," she said, dabbing the cuts on his face and lips with rubbing alcohol. She stood, picked up a dry washcloth, and wet it with water from a plastic jug. Bosko reached out and held her hand. She smiled and kissed him. "Let me finish, and then we can eat." He didn't take his eyes off her. "What is it?"

"I'll kill them all. I will. They will see a monster rip out their-"

"Stop it! Why are you talking like that?"

"They said they would find you and—"

"Just stop. Do you hear me?" She caressed his cheek and he pushed her hand away.

"If anything should happen to—"

"Nothing is going to happen to me. Understand?"

"They said..." Bosko lowered his head as his voice tapered off.

"Shh. I don't care what anyone said. We're together. Nothing is going to separate us."

What have I done by letting her stay with me? Bosko worried.

Admira kept Bosko at home after his encounter on the streets with the Muslim gang. She wasn't going to let him out unless they were together. They had to be seen. Bosko was spoiling for a fight, something she knew could not happen under any circumstances.

"I'd really like to go out by myself. I can handle it, Admira," Bosko said, raising his voice.

"What you would *like* to do is not my concern," she replied raising hers. "Today is water day. We'll do it together, and whatever else we plan on the spur of the moment. We will dodge what those psychopaths have planned for you and me, and everybody else in Sarajevo. Now, pick up the plastic jugs and let's go. What are you waiting for?"

She walked out and he followed, shutting the door to the apartment. Not waiting for Bosko, she skirted down the stairs with him right behind her. The empty plastic water jugs bounced against his back and shoulders. His entire chest and back were black and blue, and he had bruised ribs on each side of his chest. Admira had nursed him from the moment he'd stepped into the apartment. It was the first time that Bosko had ever been assaulted in this way, and both she and Bosko realized it was just the beginning. He'd stopped spitting up blood and could just barely stand up straight, but not without wincing in pain. The empty plastic jugs tied on a rope and bouncing against his back made him grimace.

Her voice echoed up the stairwell as she raced ahead of him. "Let's go, you Serb, I don't have all day." Without trepidation, she planned to meet whatever was awaiting the two of them beyond the entrance door. Fifty liters of water was what Bosko and Admira intended to get. It was their ration. The moment they stepped outside of their building and their own little world, they were once more faced with the stark reality of how everything in their city had changed. Running side by side, they watched the city transforming itself in slow motion, even as it moved like a roll of film on fast-forward, showing scenes of Sarajevo's destruction.

More than once Bosko saw the enmity in the eyes of the people he and Admira passed by on the street. People who recognized him, who knew what Miro had done. People who wanted justice, who required revenge. People filled with rage and who needed to show it, vent it, wherever and whenever the opportunity arose. Someone had to pay. To the men across the street, many of whom recognized Bosko, he was most deserving of their hatred. He was a Serb with a traitorous friend. They all knew it. His kind was responsible for the atrocities in the city. Wounded children were being carried from hospitals in Sarajevo onto transport planes flying to Britain and Europe, never having a chance to say good-bye to their parents, who had no idea where their children had been taken.

A few kilometers from Sarajevo, it was Bosko's kind who had forced fifty men, women, and children into a bus and then blew it up. Maybe it was his Serb friends and family members who were causing countless numbers to be maimed or killed by mortar shells, tank shells, and dum-dum bullets every day. Stoning a Serb man on the streets of Sarajevo was nothing compared to that.

It was his kind, the Chetniks, who had dug in around the airport with their guns and prevented much-needed food and medical aid from being distributed to a desperate, starving population. They prevented antibiotics and drugs, which sat unused in warehouses, from getting to the gravely ill and the wounded, who were dying for want of them. Tons of food lay untouched and rotted on the tarmac and areas surrounding the airport.

His kind also possessed some of the few phones that still worked, and were using them to inform other Serbs, directing them to targets, telling them where to aim and whom to shoot. There were not enough stones in all of Sarajevo to hurl at his kind, because their atrocities were infinite.

"Stay close to me," Bosko said as they hurried along. "And watch out for the rubble."

The stares he and Admira kept getting from people seemed to be coming from all sides and from all around them. They held hands, knowing it wasn't a smart thing to do, but needing to stay connected. They ran and rested and ran some more, desperate to try and get to the water station as soon as possible. They arrived at Kulouviceva Street. A huge banner marked the Hotel Belgrade, or Hotel Sarajevo. People in Sarajevo debated about which hotel it was, it all depended on whether you were one faction or the other. Ever since the banner had been unfurled, it concealed innocent people on the thoroughfare from the psychopaths. It was one small victory for the besieged. As they kept walking, and kept listening for any sound that meant they should dive for cover, they saw the banner flutter in the wind. Ironic that such a shield was made of fabric, not armor.

"Pig!" someone shouted at Bosko from across the street. "Look, another Serbian traitor." continued a man who was standing across the street with two large stones clenched in each hand. Wherever Bosko went in the city, someone always recognized him. "He thinks he should be allowed to get water." And with that, the man threw the rock he was holding in his right hand at Bosko. It grazed Bosko's cheek; he'd moved his head just in time. He stepped in front of Admira to shield her. No one stopped to intercede or to say anything.

Then a second man, who had been walking very quickly and who had heard what had been said, yelled out to Bosko. "Go home and take that whore with you. We know who you both are."

Bosko and Admira kept walking away quickly but avoided

running. If they did, they might have incited both men and then others might start to chase after them. More people who had been walking briskly slowed down when they heard both men start to yell at Admira and Bosko.

"There he is, the friend of that traitor," said one of the men, who slowed down his pace and was building himself into a frenzy of anger.

"Yes, why are you out here?" shouted the second man. More people were looking in Admira and Bosko's direction.

"We should drown them in the river, then they'll have all the water they need."

"Drown them, that's what we need to do. Drown them!"

Bosko fought the urge to run. Admira, too, knew not to incite anyone; it would only make the situation worse.

"Your day will come, Serb—your day will come."

They kept their pace steady and kept walking. Admira held Bosko's hand firmly, and that metallic taste of fear filled their mouths once again.

They hadn't stopped their quick pace and avoided eye contact with anyone. They had to fill their plastic jugs of water; it was their only thought. The water station was getting closer. They would need to be greeted by good "neighbors" who would not force them away. If they did, Admira and Bosko would have to walk to another water station, and then another, till they were finally able to fill their plastic jugs.

As they got closer to the river, they watched people, young and old, desperate to fill their buckets. The river had also turned into a sewer for the almost completely destroyed water system. Each time, they would carry the water home, along the way they would look to collect anything that would burn in their potbelly stove so they could boil the water while also using the pills they were given by UNPROFOR. But microorganisms, bacteria, and viruses still plagued the water supply even after boiling and treating it with the pills.

Sarajevans couldn't understand how the reservoirs and water pumps were not defended by the U.N. protection force. It would have allowed Sarajevans to have the most precious gift of life— water. But U.N. forces had decided it wasn't their job.

Explosions, coupled with the shrieks and cries that followed, had long ago become monotonous. It was Sarajevo's requiem. They held onto each other's hands even tighter as they waded deeper into their city of the dead and the dying.

The streets of Sarajevo had become desolate and abandoned. Admira looked at Bosko without saying a word. She didn't have to; he understood her thoughts completely. How *easy it is for a city to be plundered and destroyed. For a civilization to fall. How easy it is to be overwhelmed by those who seek to kill you, when you yourself have no such thoughts regarding those who seek to destroy you.*

How could our experience be explained to anyone—and possibly understood? Bosko thought to himself. *Have we been so blind for so long to our impending destruction?* She asked herself. *Have we brought this catastrophe upon ourselves?* Now each one of their lives had been made suddenly worthless. It had happened overnight, the moment the guns encircling their city began their bombardment —the moment the murdering of her citizens commenced. Yet the signs of their impending annihilation had been foretold by their leaders.

"We can't stop, Admira." Bosko pulled her along. Their every action was to survive even as they both looked at what seemed to be the end of their world. The ending of the sound of chirping birds, children's laughter, the rustling of leaves in the wind. In their place, Sarajevo's concrete streets and sidewalks were littered with countless burned-out and destroyed cars, trucks, and trams. Littered throughout the city, they appeared as rusted metal coffins. And the bodies of once-living, breathing human beings now littered the streets abandoned to the rain, snow, and sleet.

Everywhere they looked and every step they took in any direction, Admira and Bosko faced buildings burned to the ground or standing only as charred husks, left as reminders of their former history. Admira and Bosko knew their lives had been reduced to a medieval existence. Starving people roamed the streets along with stray dogs released by their masters who could no longer feed them. Together, dogs and men scavenged mounds of uncollected garbage, competing with each other to find something to eat. Dead bodies remained plentiful for the dogs.

Admira and Bosko, crouching low and holding each other's hands, approached one of many large buildings reduced to rubble. They needed to rest. He pressed her against a wall, into the shadows, and shielded her body with his. A van, a makeshift ambulance, careened past them and pulled up to a building that served as a hospital. Bosko and Admira watched as the back door of the van flew open and a man, bleeding from his wounds, was carried on a stretcher through the front doors. A few moments later, one of the men who had carried the wounded man came running out, jumped into the back of the van, and emerged seconds later carrying a leg intact up to the thigh.

Bosko stepped from the shadows and peered in the direction they were headed. Suddenly, a sniper shot through the windshield of a car speeding along the debris-strewn road. The car came rushing toward them, out of control, the driver dying from a single shot to his head, his body in convulsions. Bosko grabbed Admira's hand and they ran. His bruised ribs ached and throbbed. He was hobbling as they sprinted as fast as they could to make their escape. Seconds later, they felt the force of a tremendous blast behind them as the car slammed into a building and exploded into flames.

They had cheated death's grasp once more. Yet a life was taken. It was remembered and forgotten at the same moment it had happened. There was no time to think of the piteous waste of such an act. It happened every hour of every day in their city. And it did not alter Admira and Bosko's reason to be outside. Water, they desperately needed water. Life was only about surviving.

*

Bosko adjusted the knob on the small radio that was attached to a battery he and Admira had found in the wreckage of a car. The small car had been hidden behind a burned-out tram and was barely noticeable, otherwise someone would have stripped it of all its valuables long before. When they'd spotted it, Bosko had crawled on his hands and knees through the wreckage while Admira remained hidden and on the lookout. With the few tools he always carried, he was able to pry the battery loose and they ran home carrying their newfound treasure.

Bosko spent the next day cleaning the exterior of the battery of dirt, rust, and grease. And then with their fingers crossed, he connected the wires from the battery to his radio and waited. Admira leapt into his arms when a station came on. Bosko had no way to recharge the battery, so if it had been dead when they'd brought it back to the apartment, his only choice would have been to sell it to someone with the ability to recharge it. Even then, it would be worth a small fortune, maybe even a few thousand Deutsche marks on the black market.

At Sarajevo's Center for Security, an announcer known for his wry, gallows sense of humor was speaking. "Last night I joined others who were staring out at the city from the doorway of a building where we hid. We were all waiting for the shelling to stop or slow down so we could make a run for it. Everyone exchanged small talk, even joked a little, and between the explosions the silence was filled with nervous laughter."

The announcer explained that a woman who was huddled next to him said, "I was at my brother-in-law's apartment

406

yesterday. He still has his father's radio and batteries that work. And yesterday those crazy men from the underground radio station started to play that song by Queen, 'We are the Champions.' My brother-in-law told us that those guys at the radio station put out the word they were looking for some loudspeakers because they wanted to blast the song out to those shitheads in the mountains."

The announcer continued to say that apparently the group all began to laugh because they knew those crazy guys really wanted to be in show business, but had to settle for a war to showcase their talent. "Then someone in the crowd repeated, 'We *are* still the champions. We're still here, and you know we'll continue fighting till the end.'

"The woman added, 'Isn't that the craziest thing? They wanted us to find them some loudspeakers with everything that's going on. Where would we find such a thing?'

"We could place an ad in the papers,' one man replied. And we all started to laugh and couldn't stop. And then you know what happened next? Another man, and a proud Sarajevan who was huddled with us, began to sing the whole song. Then we all started to sing the song with explosions happening all around us and people running for their lives. Some people who ran past our hiding place almost tripped when they heard us singing; we could have been the ghosts of the dead singing that song by Queen.

"How do you like that, boys and girls? Only in Sarajevo is such a thing possible. After we finished singing our song, I have to tell you we felt so invigorated; it's difficult to explain. It felt as if we should march down the street kicking our heels up in the air like those American dancing girls, the Rockettes, while shouting out 'we are the champions.' We didn't. It would not have been a good idea. Finally, when we agreed it was a good time to run, we all shook hands as if we'd been introduced at a cocktail party and wished each other God speed.

"As we ran for our lives in different directions, I know we all noticed a narrow ribbon of light stretching across the horizon. It was the last golden sliver of the setting sun falling behind the mountains like an eye full of sleep that finally disappears behind an eyelid. Our mountains will always remain the eyelids of our fair city; the sun that falls asleep behind them will always allow us in Sarajevo to dream a dream... never a nightmare. Well, we all know that's not true anymore.

"But we will always dream here in Sarajevo. We will dream of dreams and we will never stop. Those in the outside world who watch this grotesque show from the safety of their living rooms need to know that we remain generous and kind to our fellow Sarajevans. It's not out of a shared misery, but because we will never forget what remains beautiful about our city and about ourselves."

Admira walked out of the kitchen into the living room and sat on Bosko's lap and they both enjoyed the treat of listening to the announcer. "Yes, once in our fair city we only dreamed, we dreamed of dreams... once, long ago. Who shall be pardoned and who shall be punished? Do we know? Will it matter? Oh, well. Now on to more pressing issues. The Pagans and Huns have fired from Lukavica barracks onto our venerable newspaper. Mad dogs that they are, yet nothing will stop the presses at *Oslobodenje*. It is not advised to visit that area to pick up your morning coffee and newspaper. We'll make an announcement when it's safe.

"The Mongol hordes have been suffering a terrible sense of defeat and depression. We just refuse to submit. What can I say? Sarajevans remain masochists. For that reason Milošević's sycophants have expressly targeted long lines of any kind in Sarajevo. Stay away from any bakeries that are still open, or the district offices chucking out ration cards. Churches and mosques are definitely a no-go. God will have to be found some other place if you have any prayers to offer up. Water and electricity, so coveted by all, still remain very reluctant and recalcitrant brides. We will let you know of the imminent wedding night we are all waiting for, when the brides appear and do what brides are expected to do. Go out if you must, but stay home like you should."

The radio went dead for a few moments.

"Have a wonderful morning." The announcer's voice came back on. "And in this arena of death, you who are about to die, we salute you."

Admira remained on Bosko's lap, and they held onto each other. It was all that they could do.

*

Muslim gangs regularly targeted Serbian men, who were beaten severely simply because they were Serbs. Bosko was a Serb. His Serbian friend had deserted the city by bartering away codes to the enemies. The rage felt by many who knew Bosko's identity was palpable. Whether Admira's presence beside Bosko was any kind of deterrent, she didn't know. She only knew that being with him meant they were stronger than apart.

"I'll be back with the bread before you know it."

"How many times do I have to tell you? We'll get the bread together, all two hundred and thirty-three grams. One person can't possibly carry all of that. Besides, I'm not going to wait here each time you go out. I can't bear it. So if it's water, or bread, kerosene, wood, daffodils, or snails for our salad that we need— I'm going to be at your side. We'll face everything like everyone else. I want everyone to see us together." She wrapped her arms around his neck and kissed him softly on his temple and whispered, "We are each other's protector. You are my lover. I have had no other. I am your oath, and you are mine forever. I do not fear anything. Neither should you. So, stop arguing with me!"

409

Bosko remained silent as he held on to Admira. She knew by the way he held her how much he was afraid for her safety. The Muslim thugs had said they had something planned for her. That thought kept Bosko awake every night. Yet for her to be with him day and night wasn't practical either. Should she stay at home with Radmilla? He was certain that to leave her alone with Radmilla was not the best choice, but it was probably better than to have her exposed on the streets with him each time he had to go out.

"Don't worry so much. We will outlast them."

Whenever they made trips out of the apartment, insults about his family were shouted at them. Most of the time he and Admira ignored them. Complete strangers, people with pent-up fear and anger, almost anyone who knew who he was and what Miro had done, vented emotions toward them.

He bore it in silence, held her hand more tightly, and kept walking. Men deliberately bumped into him, sometimes knocking him to the pavement, giving the Serb snipers seconds more to find their human target. They saw no difference in Bosko or his tormentors. They were both fair game.

Admira suffered the indignity in silence with him. When men knocked him down, she'd grab Bosko's hand and help him back onto his feet, staying by his side and ignoring the snipers. Admira would turn and glower at those men. Occasionally, she'd see it— the shame in their eyes—if only for a moment. His tormentors would tire of it. Admira was certain. They just had to outlast them by simply doing nothing.

He and Admira counted each day that passed as if it were a minor victory. They'd survived together. On this day, they were on a bread run to get their meager ration and return home together.

Without warning, a jagged rock hit his back. Bosko stumbled forward. But he had enough presence of mind to raise his arms, shielding Admira. A second rock smashed against his temple close to his eyes. Bosko turned around and pressed Admira against his chest as an onslaught of rocks smashed against his back and head.

"Let me go, Bosko," she screamed. But Bosko wouldn't let her move as he pressed her against his chest.

"Let me go!" She screamed once more. Admira wanted to pick up the same rocks, run across the street, and bash out the brains of every single one of the men, the animals, who threw them. Instead, Bosko held onto her, protecting her. People on the sidewalk hurried past, doing nothing to intervene. They assumed the man being stoned was a Serb; it's what they all deserved. No one came to their aid.

"Bosko, let me go!" He stood his ground and held her even tighter. To run would have been fatal for both of them. Admira looked into his eyes, and then realized what he was doing, and stopped struggling. He felt her body relax, then her arms slid around him, pressing both hands against the back of his head and neck. She was trying to protect as much of him as possible as the rocks kept smashing against his back and head. Admira felt every stone and its dreadful impact against her lover. It seemed to her that all of Sarajevo was watching and by not helping, were also participating.

Blood coursed down Admira's fingers as she pressed them against Bosko's head. The rocks had done their job. The back of his scalp had been sliced open and blood streamed down his head and neck. He remained silent and held onto Admira. The rocks stopped. The men who had been throwing them had gone into such a frenzy they'd forgotten where they were. Realizing that they were as much of a sniper's target as Bosko, they took one last look at Admira and Bosko, spat on the sidewalk, and ran.

Bosko began to cough violently as he bent over and fell to one knee. While others rushed past, running from the sound of gunfire and explosions, Admira remained at Bosko's side. Wiping the blood from his temple and scalp with the hem of her dress, she helped Bosko to his feet. They stumbled on, hopefully in time to get their bread ration.

PART NINE

Chapter Thirty-Two

"Would you let me—" Bosko shook his head and looked away from Admira.

"Bosh, please," She said.

He remained silent. They'd gotten the last loaf of bread and come home. A victory that was neither minor nor major, just a victory. Now darkness had covered the city except for the bullets breaking up the blackness with their trails of red, yellow, and blue light. Admira went into the kitchen and rested for a moment against the counter. She knew she had to clean his wounds, but he wouldn't let her.

"Think, girl. What do you need to do?" she whispered out loud.

Bosko refused to clean the wounds or the blood that had hardened into scabs all over his scalp, neck, and face. When they'd arrived home, he'd changed his clothes, putting on a clean shirt, and then sat on the floor next to the bed in complete silence. While he sat, she left the room and once in the kitchen, she removed her bloodied dress.

"Hey, you. You big, stupid Serb." She walked out of the kitchen and stood in front of him, her legs spread apart, hands firmly on her hips.

"Want to feel like a Serbian warrior ravishing a Muslim princess gypsy girl? Think you got it in you, or have a few rocks made you soft?"

It took Bosko more than a few seconds to pry his thoughts away from the reality of a few hours ago and the anger and rage that had built up inside him. Rolling his eyes up to meet hers and trying to smile, he stared at her lapis blue bra and panties.

"I'm spoiling for a good fight."

"Me too. But first you will have to seduce this Gypsy Girl into fulfilling every desire that your dark Serbian heart might have. Can you handle it?"

"I believe I've still got something left in me."

"Good. Because it won't be easy. You'll have to fight to take what you want. Want to try and win against a Muslim today?"

"Will the victory be hard won?" Bosko asked, his smile growing.

"Like you can't imagine."

"You know I would enjoy a good brawl."

"Don't move. I'll be back." He watched her run into their bathroom. He tried not to think of any of the events that had taken place on the street. Admira sensed what Bosko might be thinking about what he should do. Now was not the time for them to fight about anything. She wasn't going back to her parents, no matter what. Grabbing a plastic jug of water, a couple of clean washcloths, and some rubbing alcohol, she marched out of the bathroom. Bosko sat still, eyes shut.

"Don't move, but keep your eyes closed," Admira said as she knelt beside him. First, she wet the facecloth and began to gently wipe away the dried blood of his wounds, starting at the back of his head.

Admira caressed his swollen lips and the numerous abrasions and lacerations on his face. She kissed him gently everywhere on his face, except the wounds. Dipping the cloth into water again, she wiped away the hardened scabs. Then she poured some of the alcohol onto the second cloth and gently pressed it against the opening of each wound. Bosko's eyes remained closed. The alcohol burned, but he made no sound. The only reality at this moment was his difficulty in keeping the worst of his thoughts from entering into his head.

She tried not to imagine what he might be thinking—about them, about her.

414

He leaned forward as she knelt on the mattress. She pressed her chest against his back and began to clean his scalp where one jagged rock had sliced open the skin. He needed stitches, but where could Bosko go to get a few stitches? People in Sarajevo with life-threatening injuries weren't able to get any medical care. Admira gently and meticulously worked to clean his deep cuts and lacerations. Finally, she got up and took the supplies and bloody rags back into the bathroom. She smiled at her reflection in the mirror. Admira removed her bra and panties and slipped on her favorite red cotton plaid shirt. It was one of Bosko's that hung on a hook on the bathroom door. She left the shirt unbuttoned. Opening a small plastic container, she removed her diaphragm, filled it sparingly with gel and placed it inside her. She longed for the day when she wouldn't need to use it and they would have a brood of kids. She ran her fingers through her hair, and then reentered the living room with a grin on her face and sat next to him on the field bed.

"So how hard must I fight?" He kissed her shoulders.

"As hard as I resist," she said in a sultry voice.

"Guerrilla warfare?"

"Nothing but," she answered, pulling Bosko down onto the bed and sliding on top of him.

There comes a moment, a sliver of time, when two lovers unveil all of who they are to each other, when the only thing that matters is love—theirs for each other. They feel as if they have all the time in the world because they are so overwhelmed with the spirit of the other, that there is no sense of a moment, its beginning or its end. They were made of each other and for each other, and somehow, in some way, every step taken in life was meant to be taken together.

Admira pressed her bare breasts against Bosko's chest. In a city of the dead, two lovers, no more special than anyone else, were as marrow and bone are to each other. She wanted to take away his pain and make it hers. He had protected her, no matter what, and always would. She wanted him to see how much she loved him and to realize that they were here in their own secret place where only tenderness existed. It was a place only they knew and would never forget—a private world, where all he could want and need from her was his to take. Admira pressed her soft hands against his cheeks and they rolled over with him on top of her. He moved in such a way that she hardly felt his weight pressed against her.

He kissed her, and it was a kiss of joy and sadness. He was silently telling her that all was well at this moment, and even though it might not be that way tomorrow, it didn't matter. Admira kissed him tenderly, without care for the future. They were living in the moment. The moment was all that mattered. The moment would become the future. She didn't stop kissing him because when she hesitated, Admira saw his doubt, his anger, his sadness, his abject fear of losing her. They had become something unexplainable— whatever becomes of two sentient beings in love—pure energy, in its human form. She kissed his broken temple. Tomorrow it would be healed. Then his lacerated forehead. The next day it too would be healed. Admira kept kissing his wounds as he caressed her breasts, and their passion, their fear and sadness, were coupled with only one thought as Bosko entered Admira. Tonight, they were alive, real, and embedded in each other.

*

The shimmering flame beside her on the floor wavered and flickered. Admira was wide awake. It was not so long ago that they had made love. "Dream of dreams," she'd whispered to him as she watched him fall asleep. Pulling her pillow to one side, she slid her hand underneath and carefully removed a letter he'd written to her many years ago while he was in the army. She never left their home without it. It was always tucked away somewhere on her body, usually close to her heart. Resting back against her pillow, Admira unfolded the page carefully and read in near darkness. It took her breath away and made her feel jubilant. That was the only word she could think of each time she read his words.

Dear Admira,
Every night when I go to bed, I cannot sleep because I'm thinking of you.

She stopped to let a wave of emotion pass. Once centered, she began again.

Dear Admira,
Every night when I go to bed, I cannot sleep because I'm thinking of you. The days and nights have never felt so ordinary and without purpose as they seem to me now and will always be, when we are apart. I keep thinking of that first night we met.
If such real and fantastical moments can happen to two people like us, then I have to believe there was a purpose to why it happened. I think of none of the trials and tribulations of life when I'm with you. It's as if we've created our own world to keep us real and worthy of each other, and perhaps that is exactly what two people in love must always do. What is outside of that world can often be so cruel.
I think the purpose of life is to be happy. To enjoy the gift that is to be alive, to feel that butterfly on your shoulder, to walk in a valley that is a paradise. I think the best part of me would die if I should lose you. No, not die, I meant perish. For this is what happens to a heart, never allowed to love that which it was always meant to... and I know it is no one else but you whom I shall always love.
B.

The flames flickered and then were extinguished.

Many loud footsteps echoed on the stairs outside their apartment.

"Stay there," Bosko said, turning toward Admira who dropped the only university textbook she had left onto the chair. She stood. He opened the door as wide as he could. No fear.

"You are Bosko Brkić?"

"I am."

A man about the same age as Bosko, who was clearly part of some local militia, stood at the door to their apartment. He possessed an air of confidence that could also be seen in the four other Muslim men standing with him. They were all well-armed and were all Slavs. But it did not matter, they were all now divided into camps of Serbian, Muslim and Croatian. Bosko didn't recognize them from the unit on Kosovo Hill. After Miro defected, Bosko was no longer needed, or trusted, in that group. The men standing at the door were all clean-shaven and looked as if they had showered recently.

"You are required to report to the police station at this address on May 17, two days from now," the man said, handing Bosko a slip of paper with the address on it. Bosko looked at it. It was in one of the most bombed-out areas of the city.

"If you don't show up at that time, when you're found you'll be arrested on the spot."

"Why must he do this?" Admira asked as she stepped into plain sight, defiant.

"Loose ends to tie up," the man said.

"What do you mean by loose ends?" Admira's tone was combative.

"The militia needs further information from you." The young man looked at Bosko with disdain. "Regarding how your friend Miro was able to slip through all of our checkpoints and escape.

418

We certainly wouldn't want anyone else to be able to do so again. In two days, present yourself at the police station." He looked at Bosko, turned around, and walked down the stairs with the others.

Bosko closed the door and pressed his finger against Admira's lips. "Not yet. My tea is still warm and you haven't finished the chapter you were reading. Let's do those two things first. Come, sit down."

"No. I don't want to sit." In that instant Admira's skeleton of beliefs crumbled. Until now, every fear she'd had about Bosko had been kept in check by her singular belief that he'd always be okay because they were together. No matter how many times he was assaulted and beaten with no one to intercede, they'd survived. Regardless of having to dodge sniper bullets, Admira would not lose her resolve. They would outlast this war. She was certain they would prevail. To believe in anything else was to let doubt creep in, which threatened their survival, and perhaps most important, it would be giving in to their enemies. She looked around their hovel of an apartment and began to weep.

Bosko lifted Admira into his arms and sat on the only wooden kitchen chair left in their apartment. She wrapped her arms around his neck and leaned her head against his shoulder. They sat for a long time, not saying a word. The shafts of sunlight pierced through the covered windows. Bosko watched small dust particles dance around in the beams of light. He and Admira were not much different, whirling about like those particles, trapped within a given space.

"Say something," she whispered finally. Bosko remained silent. She held onto him even tighter. "Please say something."

"I thought—"

"Yes?" Her tone was filled with resignation.

"I believed that if we just hung in there. If I waited, I... we would outlast this war. It's going to end. We know it is. All we have to do is hold on for one more day, one more week. And then that day will come, and all of this will be over. Someday."

She tried to respond, to say something to Bosko, anything but there were no words or thoughts that entered her heart or head. They had two days left to be together. To go to the police station would be unthinkable, to not go would be fatal. She ran the tip of her finger over the cuts and bruises on his face and neck. It couldn't end this way. "There has to be a way," she said, "to remain together."

"We have... I have... no choice."

Admira lifted her head and felt that familiar, slow-burning wave rise ever higher. It was a wave of determination to never accept the way things are, only what they could be. She slid off his lap and stood, planting her feet on the wooden floor like a statue from antiquity. Her eyes were full of worry, but her tone was unwavering. She had found a way.

"We must—go. We must leave."

"No," he replied and stood. "No more being chased. And I won't hide with you. This time I'll take you home and you'll go because there will be nothing here to return to."

"This is not our home anymore." Her tone was cold.

"Admira," Bosko reached out his hand and she took it. He pulled her closer to him. "It's possible they only want to talk to me, to tie up loose ends, like he said."

"Bosko, don't you dare think of going." She pulled her hand away from his as tears welled up in her eyes. She backed away from him. She knew they meant to kill Bosko. She wiped away her tears, and with all the resolve she could muster, she said, "Bosko, my love, don't give up now."

"I haven't given up. There's nothing else I can do but go. This is my home; the only home I've ever known. This is where it must end. I won't be hunted down on the streets like a dog because I'm hiding."

"If you do this, you'll have to kill me first. I promise you, I'll do it, I'll do it now. I'll walk out onto that balcony because it means you've given up. I may as well do the same."

"Pack your things. I'm taking you home," Bosko said, his voice getting louder and angrier.

"I'll rip those doors down and walk onto that balcony. So just try taking me back. Try it," she screamed at him with equal anger.

"I have no other choice. It's all been taken away from me. And even if I could, I would not—will not—run. I'm not Miro."

"Bosko, what would your father and mother want you to do?"

"It's my decision."

"No, it's not. You have a mother and she lives, praying and waiting for the day she'll see you again. It's not your decision alone. How dare you say that! Rita told me to take care of you and I intend to do just that, you stupid ignorant Serb." She was so angry at him and loved him so much at the same time.

"Do you think your mother or father would let you go to a police station? There's only one real shame that comes from all of this, and that is to allow killers to do as they please. That's something we can't allow to happen. Listen to me." She walked up close to him and pushed him gently against the wall. "You must convince Mladjo. He must get us out of this place, out of our city."

"Where would we go?" Bosko appeared almost amused by Admira's plan.

"There is only one place. To your uncle's, where your mother is."

"How could I take you to Serbia? A Muslim girl?"

"So now I have become a Muslim?"

"No." He grabbed her and shook her. "You are mine. If we go to Serbia, they will try to take you from me. And if they try, I'll kill them all."

421

"There's never been anyone you have had to kill—not Serb or Muslim—and there never will be. Understood? We'll be together with Rita."

"No. I can't. I won't."

"Look at me. We're not going to lose each other. Not after all you and I have been through. We must leave the city, and one day we will return."

"Your parents will hate me. They'll never agree to it." He collapsed into the chair.

"Who is making this decision—them or us? Who?" Admira would never accept the situation for what it was, only for what it could be.

"Admira, I can't take you to Serbia, to a land of psychopaths. My God."

"Bosh." She knelt in front of him. Her tone became soft, like steel that bends when it's molten. "We can't let them win. It'll be okay. You must believe it. We just have to get to Rita. She's not a psychopath. So there must be others who aren't. Think of how happy she will be to see you, to know that you are finally safe and I kept my word."

Bosko was trying to make sense of all the feelings and emotions he had about right and wrong. He rested his head in his hands.

"You're not a human sacrifice. Not for Serbs or Muslims, not for anybody. Isn't that what your father would say?" She placed her hand under his chin and raised his face to look at her. "Now tell me, because I know how much you loved your father. Isn't that what Dragan would say?"

Not as things are but as they should be; it would always remain that way with Admira.

*

Bosko's hands trembled as he buttoned his shirt. His hands had seemed so immature nine years ago when they first met. Now

422

they appeared as the hands of a man, one who could take care of himself and Admira, no matter where they were—and yet they were trembling.

Admira stood in the bathroom doorway, watching.

"I seem to be having a problem buttoning my shirt."

"Let me." Admira's nimble fingers buttoned his shirt. "I won't be with you, and I always swore I would be at your side, but there isn't much time. I have to get our things together. I know you'll come back to me—I know it." Bosko felt the blood drain from his face. She pulled him toward her and kissed him. "Think only of us and that we are meant to be together." Bosko nodded. "I will see you soon." Bosko stepped back. "Go and then come back to me. Bosh..." She pulled him back toward her. Staring into those familiar, amber eyes, Admira said.

"Just as the butterfly was once a caterpillar, you and I were something different before we met. We were always meant to become something grander." And she hugged him. The same boring, wonderful hug she'd been giving him for the longest time. He headed toward the door, holding her hand. The door opened. "I'll be waiting." She kissed him with total abandon. A chill crept through his body as he left the apartment and disappeared down the stairs. She listened to the sound of his footsteps become softer, and finally there was nothing but silence.

Admira closed the door and sank to her knees.

Bosko hurried along the abandoned roads, paying no attention to how he was going to get to Mladjo's. Other thoughts consumed him. *What is the truth? Have I given in too easily to Admira? Is it utter madness to even think of taking her to Serbia?* And yet to stay in Sarajevo was suicide. *How can I do that?* Bosko started running. Explosions went off all around him. He dove into the doorway of a former bakery shop that had seen better days. He cut his pants on the shattered glass covering the floor. Staying out of sight, he peered through a crack in the wall. He watched the carnage around him as he rested against a wall. He closed his eyes and imagined a time when he would have waited at the counter in line with other people to buy loaves of freshly baked bread and every kind of pastry to enjoy with Admira. Their aroma had once filled the shop and the street outside.

That was the past. Could it ever be the future? Their future, standing here together? They would order *sljivopita* and *jabukovača*, *ruske kape*, *oblande*, and *krempita*, he told himself. He had to believe it was possible. If Admira were standing here next to him, she would have told him in a heartbeat it was true, and they would be back. *If she can believe it, why can't I? Have I forgotten that she's my Gypsy Girl, believing in the impossible?* He desperately wanted that life for them together. A growing sense of optimism welled up inside of him.

The time had come to choose to live and be with the only person who counted in this life. Together they would step into the unknown. Adrenaline coursed through his veins. He peered out through the door to the bakery, knowing he'd come back with her. Nothing could keep them away. He'd bring Admira and their children back here and they would stand in this very spot and he would tell all of them of this moment. *Go now*, he heard a voice urge in his head.

He flew out of the bakery and didn't stop running while flashes of light from spectacular explosions seemed to chase him. He jumped almost effortlessly over and around the debris and rubble and burnt-out cars and corpses. The scent of limes filled his nostrils—not death, only the fragrance of limes.

Bosko knew there were very few exit points from the city, and all were being watched, even the one that Mladjo used for exchanges. There was nowhere that he could go to try and escape the city. Bosko realized what these men really wanted was for him to run and hide so that when they found him, they would drag him through the streets of Sarajevo, naked and in chains, like a conquered slave and enemy for everyone to see. He was a Serbian dog, a traitor like his friend.

His shirt buttons had burst open from the strain caused by his running so fast and hard. His head was filled with only one thought: to be with her always. He was out of breath from repeating those words by the time he approached the concrete stairs. The adrenaline seemed to have taken over his veins. Here it was, the rusted metal door to Mladjo's headquarters. When he pushed it open, it groaned like a trumpeter announcing the arrival of a warlord. There was no reason to think Mladjo would be available. If he wasn't, Bosko would just wait. If they let him. Would Djoka be there? He was arriving unannounced, with no idea of what he was walking into.

The hallway was well lit, unlike the bombed-out ruins where normal people lived. These men were adept at keeping a regular flow of electricity into the building.

"Bosko?"

Bosko turned his head. Djoka approached. Though he thought Bosko a romantic for staying in Sarajevo and Admira a fool for not leaving his side, the idea that they would welcome the worst should the worst happen made Djoka reluctantly admit that the two of them were very brave indeed.

"Here to see the married man?"

"Yes," Bosko replied hesitantly.

"You're in luck. He's still here."

Djoka knocked on Mladjo's office door and, not waiting for an answer, just opened it.

"Bosko." His gangster friend's tone was reserved. "Come in. Sit."

Bosko sat but said nothing.

"Our friends in UNPROFOR want to renegotiate our petrol deal. It's becoming difficult to make a profit these days, with some of these corrupt blue helmets from the U.N." Mladjo said.

When Bosko didn't reply, Mladjo looked at him more closely. "What is it?" Bosko had stayed away from Mladjo, and from this

425

building, from anything that would connect him to his friend. He knew that Admira and he had to survive by themselves without his help. But now here he was once more, and once more was about to ask his friend for his help one last time.

Bosko's eyes shone with sadness. He stared at his own hands, then looked at Mladjo. What he had to ask of him required he do it as a man. Mladjo had to see his face, his resolve. "I need your help one last time. I need to leave Sarajevo. *We* need to leave."

Mladjo leaned back against his chair. To Bosko it seemed as if he'd done it in slow motion.

"What has happened?" Mladjo knew with absolute certainty that Bosko would not be here with him if it weren't something very dire. Admira was in danger. It was the only reason Bosko would come to his headquarters to ask for his help.

"Earlier today some men came to visit. They said that I'm required to come to this other police station within forty-eight hours. If I don't, they'll arrest me. It seems that's what they have in mind, regardless. Here's the paper they handed me." Bosko reached across the desk, holding out the slip of paper.

Mladjo pulled the paper from Bosko's hand. He read the address. "Did you recognize any of them?"

"No."

"Are you sure?"

"Yes."

"Whoever handed this to you must report to someone who heads a police militia unit in that zone they've asked you to come to. It's a unit I'm not familiar with, but that's not surprising. There are so many in the city claiming to act in its defense. You said we —"

"Yes, that's the way it is," replied Bosko without any doubt in his tone. "There is only one place left for me to go." He hesitated saying the word. "Serbia, to be with my mother and her family. It's where we have to go, to live amongst Serbs, but nothing will

426

happen to her, I swear this to you. Nothing."

A long silence filled the room. Mladjo kept staring at Bosko. He was taking a Muslim girl to live amongst the Serbs. Did he truly understand? Did they truly understand what such an act meant for Admira to do?

"Alright Bosh—" Their eyes met. "If this is your choice, yours and Admira's we must move quickly." The two men stared at each other. "She is very brave, Bosko."

"Yes, I know."

"You and Admira must leave by the Vrbanja Bridge. You cannot leave by the route your mother and others took. That transfer of people won't happen for a week. They must know this —that's why they have given you forty-eight hours to show yourself. There's only one other choice and it's not a good one, Bosko, but it's our only choice. Because no one will suspect that we would do it."

"Then it will have to do," replied Bosko.

"It's at the end of our world, it's become a no-man's-land," said Djoka.

"But it's the only way out of Sarajevo for you and her," continued Mladjo. "It's surrounded by every armed group. They all keep a keen eye on one another. There's no cover and no place to hide. Nobody dares to go there. But it's the only escape route available for you and Admira. Do Admira's parents know?"

"Not yet. We didn't know if you'd be able to help me." Bosko tried to smile. "I mean, us. If you couldn't get us out, my only other choice was to take her back to Zao and her family. And I know she'd fight me with every breath to prevent it from happening. She would hate me and never stop hating me for it." Bosko stared at his sweaty palms. Admira's words echoed in his thoughts. "She said she'd walk out onto our balcony if I left her. She is mad and willful and—but I would find a way to take her back, if you couldn't help us."

"Bosko, Admira may be all of those things, but most of all she is in love. Be here, both of you, at three o'clock this afternoon."

Mladjo wanted to say a lot more about this choice they had made but held his tongue.

And Bosko could easily imagine the gangster's thoughts. *A Bosnian Muslim girl daring to live among Serbs. It's madness.*

Hearing the words "three o'clock" made Bosko think they would be free. He looked at his friend and asked, "How can it be so easy?"

Mladjo said nothing.

"To just leave this—hell? We all should be able to leave. It's grotesque that I can but others can't."

"You want to make sense of war? It's war; there is no sense to it. No sense can be made of who lives and who dies."

"Why do you stay, Mladjo? You could have left long ago."

"I am a profiteer. I've become rich from all this misery. It's not always easy to make a living in this world. War and brutality— they are opportunities for a man like me. I've always been an opportunist." The gangster's last words sounded eerily malevolent.

"I think you hide behind this persona, the man whom everyone fears, because a gangster should have no conscience or care for anything or anyone but himself. You have enough money, more than enough to start a grand life somewhere else if you chose. I think you stay because this is your home being destroyed and you can't abide seeing it, so you stay to defend it by any and all means possible. But more than that, I think in the deepest pit of your soul you despise a sense of helplessness. So many people in this moment can't help themselves."

Bosko saw the gangster's changing emotions subtly reflected on his face.

"It's something you have known only too well. My father

once told me that you were a man who required many things in life and that one day you would know if all of it had brought you any happiness. I think he was right—it hasn't. Perhaps you've found another way."

Mladjo stared at Bosko.

"I'm running away. I swore I never would. But I am. I'm no better than Miro. I'm just like him."

Mladjo frowned and shook his head. "Do you think I would help a man like Miro? You're nothing like him. That's the war and madness talking. Not you. If you were anything like him, you would've gone with him the night he left. You've stayed out of love and respect, for your girl and your city. You are a Serb who is willing to die because you won't be separated from the woman you love. What Miro did by stealing codes and running away was done out of cowardice and self-preservation, not love. Don't ever forget it."

Mladjo's words did little to comfort Bosko, who tried to force a smile in acknowledgment.

"After the guns are silent, when we look at what we've done, we'll realize that a Sarajevan is a Sarajevan. This is where we belong. Many things will be said about this time when it's over. Much will be written about why it all began. Those who have watched it will have much more to say and write about, than we who lived through it, but only we will truly understand the meaning of this experience."

"Will we?" Bosko asked, doubt showing on his face.

"Yes, Bosh, we will. Sometime in the future, in some location you and I have never heard of, the bastards who started this will get together to end it. They'll sit down in a room and, after having eaten and drunk their fill, they'll sign a paper ending this war and dividing everything like a pie. The pain and suffering these times have caused will be forgotten, as if none of this ever happened. We, all Sarajevans, we will always remember. Always." Mladjo stood and walked around his wooden desk. Bosko rose to his feet. "Come back today after you've been to her parents. I'll have all the details by then. You'll leave at nightfall."

"Today?" Bosko shook his head in disbelief.

"Tonight."

"Thank you." It was such an inadequate response.

Before opening the door, Mladjo put his hand on Bosko's shoulder and said, "There's a Muslim proverb, that says: 'To love only one woman is to have a little bit of eternity dropped into your hands.'"

Bosko remained silent, but his eyes were shining with gratitude.

*

Sitting on the floor of the living room in the shafts of sunlight, her legs folded beneath her, Admira pressed flat a piece of white paper against the tray used for serving tea and tried to gather her thoughts. They were leaving. What could she say to her parents in just a few words?

> *My dear Mom, it seems we are leaving and what happens is God's will. Papa, I know you and Mom will not agree that we should be doing this. And I understand. Please understand that I cannot be without Bosko. I am selfish and willful and I have always been this way—please forgive me. Please...*
>
> *I will let you know as soon as we are safely on the other side. Bosko and I will be coming back to Sarajevo—nothing under heaven or on earth could keep us away. This will all end one day and it will become better. I believe this with all of my heart. Everything will be fine, like the war never happened. Don't worry about me. Think about yourself and Tonya. It will be much easier for me because there is a part of me that will always feel like I have*

abandoned you. Forgive me for being the person I am.
  I love you so much.
  Your Admira

She folded the letter and stuffed it into the pocket of her jacket. She turned her head, thinking she heard a sound coming from behind the entrance door. She remained completely still and listened. Admira practically jumped out of her skin. There it was again. Someone was knocking on the door.

She'd packed their things the moment Bosko left. She knew not to take all their clothes out of the closet in case those same men came back unexpectedly. Hiding the two small suitcases in the bathroom behind the shower curtain, she went into the kitchen and grabbed a knife. Her hands were shaking. As the knocking continued, she raised the hand that held the knife.

"Who is it?" she asked. She put her hand on the doorknob, counting in her head, *one, two, three,* then swung the door open.

"Ah, Admira. It's me," Radmilla cried out.

Admira lowered her arm.

"Why didn't you answer me?" Admira held herself back from yelling at Radmilla while her chest kept heaving and her breathing was erratic.

"Dearest I have only one good ear, I didn't hear you say anything."

Admira lowered the knife and embraced Bosko's babysitter.

"My God." Radmilla stood, mouth open in shock holding onto Admira. "I don't know which is worse, being afraid of armed men in the building or having you open the door ready to slice me up like a loaf of bread."

"I'm sorry, it's just... it's just. I didn't know who it was."

"Would you like some tea, my dear?" Radmilla dug her hand deep into her frock pocket. "Here, I brought you and Bosko four more unused tea bags I found in my cupboard. I've always

431

preferred mine loose in a teapot. It's stronger that way, but those days are long gone." She held Admira's hand and opened her fingers to press the teabags into her hand. She followed Admira into the apartment, waddled over to the wooden chair and plopped herself into it.

"We'll each share a bag," Admira said, "I'll heat up the water. Radmilla, where did you get the tea?"

"I've been cleaning out my cupboards. I've collected a lot of junk over the years. I saw them pressed up in the corner of one of the drawers. Lucky for us."

Before Radmilla could say anything more, Admira disappeared into the kitchen. She needed a few moments to catch her breath.

The water boiled quickly. The electricity had been on for the last half hour—a good sign of things to come. Bosko's teabag from earlier was scrunched up in a corner of the sink. It had been used at least three times. *When this all comes to an end, I will drink coffee and only coffee three times a day for an entire year.*

"Here we go," she said as she approached Radmilla with two cups of steaming black tea.

"You know, I've never been very good at small talk." Radmilla put her teacup on the floor and took Admira's hand. "You can't hide that something serious is troubling you."

Admira clenched Radmilla's hand as the elderly woman leaned forward.

"What is it, my child?" Radmilla turned her good ear toward Admira.

"We have to go."

"Go? Where are you going?"

"I'm going with Bosko."

"Yes, but where?"

"To Serbia."

Radmilla heard it with perfect clarity and the look on her face defied description. "My child, why would you do that?"

"We have to. Those men who came earlier today want Bosko to go to the police station in two days. If he does—" Admira's voice began to quiver. "If he does, I'll never see him again. Our only chance is to go to Serbia to his mother where we'll be safe."

"What friend could do this?" Radmilla asked. The tone of her voice implied that she didn't believe for a single moment their leaving could be possible. Nobody could just leave Sarajevo.

Admira began to tell Radmilla about Mladjo.

"But, darling, don't you understand what you're doing?" Radmilla asked.

"It'll be no more dangerous than dodging bullets."

"A Muslim girl in Serbia. Think about it, my child, think."

Admira reached down and kissed Radmilla's hand. "I love him. It hurts so much that it's unbearable when I'm not with him. Even now, all I can think about is when he'll be home. I'll die if I'm separated from Bosko."

"On my God! Every young person thinks that when they're in love. Don't tell me about love and being young. I was no different at your age. That's what being in love is all about, but you will see that lovers can survive being apart. It doesn't seem that way to you now, but itwill. You'll see."

"I love him and he loves me. His heart kept him here, not his head. He could have gone, he could have left me, but he stayed because of me. Should he have listened to his head or his heart? Should I now leave him?" Admira hugged Radmilla, who had become her adopted mother. "Don't worry. You'll see; it will all work out. We've made it so far, someone is watching over us."

"But child—"

"Radmilla, we will make it. We know the butterfly is on our shoulder."

"What do you mean by that?"

"Oh, nothing. We'll get a message to you so you know we're

433

safe. I promise."

Radmilla saw the determined expression in Admira's eyes.

"Sit and enjoy your tea. I still have a few things to do."

Admira hurried back to the bathroom to open up the suitcases. Had she taken everything they would need? She'd packed a few other items besides clothes. There was a bottle of water, less than half a loaf of bread, a container of her bean pâte, a bottle of her mother's preserves, two *kandilos*, and an apple with a red ribbon attached to it.

Returning to the kitchen, she took her time wrapping some very dry crackers in a cloth and ran back and stuffed them into her suitcase. If they were to do this, they would have only one chance at it. It meant that she and Bosko would have to remain very calm. Neither of them could seem nervous if they were stopped. They must avoid any situation that might arouse suspicion. Trust no one, suspect everyone. If Bosko returned with good news, it meant her silent prayers had been answered; there was a God after all, and perhaps *they* were worth his intervention.

Radmilla sat quietly as she watched Admira run to a secret little place behind some tied-up piles of wood stacked against the wall, behind which was a wooden box. Grabbing the box, she opened it and removed all of Bosko's letters and that one page she'd torn out of the book. Then she put everything back the way she'd found it, darted back into the bathroom, opened her travelling bag, and carefully placed all of his letters, except one, between her clothes.

When Admira returned to the kitchen, she hugged and kissed Radmilla, and said, "I'm almost done."

They had to go to her parents' house the moment Bosko came back, to tell her dad and mom. She had to look into their eyes, and Tonya's, and make them believe that she was going to be okay. Someone was watching over her and Bosko. Admira didn't know what news Bosko would come home with, but she

434

had to believe that Mladjo would help them one last time. For a moment, she was lost in her thoughts. *You're wrong, Papa, there is a God and God hasn't forgotten us.*

"Our tea is still hot, let's finish it." Admira sat back down with Radmilla, blowing into her mug as she watched the steam rise. They remained silent. Soon her ears picked up the faint sound of footsteps in the stairwell heading toward their door. Admira jumped up, spilling her tea on the floor. Radmilla reached out and took the mug from her. Admira ran to the door and flung it open. For a brief instant there was no expression on Bosko's face, and Admira's heart began to sink. Then he smiled and nodded. They fell into each other's arms.

"He will do it; it's done," Bosko whispered into Admira's ear after he closed the door. "We don't have much time." They walked into the living room. "Radmilla, what are you doing here?" Bosko bent down and gave her a kiss on the cheek. One look at Radmilla and he knew Admira had told her everything. Bosko knelt down next to Radmilla. He'd known her since he was a toddler.

Radmilla shook her head and began to cry. She didn't want to listen to what Bosko had to say.

"Shh," Bosko said, remembering the hours he'd spent in her lap as a boy.

"Children, this is foolhardy. It is."

"Radmilla, look at me," Bosko said.

Radmilla turned her head.

"We will—"

"Come back," Admira said, quickly finishing his thought.

Radmilla knew of nothing she could say that would make a difference. Bosko noticed that Admira was wearing her running clothes. Her hair was swept back to make her more aerodynamic, as she often joked.

"Children, wait..." Radmilla begged them.

435

"We can't," Admira replied, getting to her feet. "This is our only chance." She went to the bathroom and brought out their two small suitcases.

"There's one thing more I've got to do," Bosko said. "Remember that night when we stood on Ruza's balcony and you showed me Sarajevo as I'd never seen it?"

"I remember."

"I want to see my city that way once more."

"Do it." Admira's voice was defiant.

Admira took Radmilla by her hand and they walked into the hallway with her two suitcases. There was a loud cracking sound, like dry wood being snapped in half.

In a matter of seconds, Bosko had pulled the boards off the sliding glass doors. Their city. There it was. The mountains, the *kafana*, everything that Bosko knew stared back at him in glorious panorama. He breathed in the sight of Sarajevo. A sight they hadn't seen for almost two years. Bosko stood motionless.

Admira ran to him and pulled him aside. "That's enough." He'd lingered a little too long in the same spot. "If you can see the hills, the hills can see you."

They huddled by the doorway with Radmilla. Bosko's heart was racing. "Thank you, Radmilla, for everything you've done for Admira and me. I will tell our friend to look in on you," Bosko said as he embraced her.

Admira was ecstatic. Someone was truly watching over them. Mladjo had seen to it that they could leave. Her prayers were answered. Her heart soared.

"We'll get word to you as soon as we can, I promise," Admira said, hugging Radmilla. "Here, take this," Admira reached into her pocket and removed the ripped page from the book. She placed it into Radmilla's hand. "Bosko used to read this to me whenever I'd ask him, and then we'd make up stories about our future when we huddled under the blanket to stay warm. Keep it safe for us until you see us again."

"I will be waiting," Radmilla said, wiping away her tears.

Admira took Radmilla's hand and kissed it. She and Bosko watched as she walked down the hallway and then climbed up the stairs toward her apartment. They waited to hear her door open and then shut.

"It's done," Bosko said. "One suitcase each is all we're taking. Are you sure?"

"No matter what my mother and father say to you, you must not give in to them. You must listen, not with your head, but with your heart. Promise me, my love," Admira said, her charcoal eyes ablaze.

"I promise."

"Promise me again."

"I promise."

"Forever."

"Forever."

Bosko turned his head to take one last look at their apartment. He closed the door gently. Then they were gone.

PART TEN

Chapter Thirty-Three

Zena stopped folding the dry clothes she'd brought in from the clothesline in the back yard. Zao called out to her, and then she heard voices. It was Bosko and Admira. Zena moved so quickly that as she turned, she bumped her hip against the bedroom dresser. She rubbed it and rushed toward the kitchen door, too ecstatic to feel any pain. Admira was home.

"Well, I didn't expect you two for at least another week or so," Zao said, wrapping his daughter in a tight hug. "It's so good to see you both."

Admira usually liked to tease her dad, but this time she remained silent.

Bosko extended his hand to Zao, barely managing a smile.

Tonya noticed a difference in Admira and Bosko. Something was wrong. It was obvious in the way her sister hugged her; their embrace lasted longer than usual.

"Give your mother a hug," Zena said, still rubbing her hip as she stepped off the back porch stairs into the yard.

Admira's face lit up when she saw her mother, as it always did. Her mother was the center of her world.

"What a surprise."

Admira said nothing. She just kept holding onto her mother.

"Let's go inside," Zena said.

"It's good to see you, Sis," Tonya said, hugging her a second time. She was now absolutely certain something had happened. She knew her sister well enough.

Admira sandwiched herself between her mother and sister, slid her arms around their waists, and the three of them walked toward the house. She glanced back to make sure no one saw the two small suitcases hidden behind the garage.

They entered the kitchen. Zena wanted to show Admira some of the new jam she'd made from the wild berries that grew along the property. She would give them as many jars as they could carry.

"Wait, Zena, please," Bosko said. Admira held her mother's hand and gently nudged her to sit down at the kitchen table.

"Yes, Bosko, what is it?" Zena asked, frowning at Zao, already seated at the table.

Bosko sat and turned to Zao. They were two men who loved the same woman. "We are leaving, Zao. I'm taking Admira with me."

"Leaving? Where are you going?" her father asked, confused. A worried look crossed his face.

"Serbia."

The moment he uttered the word, Admira and Bosko knew that the world lost all meaning and sense to everyone except them.

Before Zao or Zena could speak, Bosko told her parents everything that had happened. As he spoke, he could sense Admira's calm resolve.

"You must not do this. I forbid it." Zao slammed his fist on the kitchen table.

"I must," Admira said,

Zao ignored his daughter. "Bosko, why are you doing this? Why would you take Admira to Serbia?"

"Papa, you already know the answer to your question. I'm going because we're never going to be separated," said Admira forcefully. She kept staring at her dad. "And if Bosko stays, they —"

"Bosko, if Mladjo can get you out, then you must go," Zao said. "But Admira can stay here and wait and—"

"No, that is not what I will do," Admira said firmly. She'd never spoken this way to her parents before. "We stay together,

440

no matter what!"

Zao stared at his daughter, but his thoughts were for Bosko. "Think about what you're doing, of what you're asking Admira to do. How can you think of taking her to Serbia?"

"She'll be safe with me and Rita."

"Safe? You can't truly believe that."

"I do, Zao. Safer than where we've been living in Sarajevo."

Zena felt the tug of her daughter's hand under the table and heard her silent plea. *Help us, Mother.*

Zena sent Admira her own silent message with her eyes. *How can I help you? How can I accept my daughter going to the Serbs?* This time her mother refused to be on Admira's side.

"Answer me. What makes you think you can protect Admira in Serbia?"

"I can't answer you, Zao. I can say only that with these hands, I will protect her."

"We are all Slavs." Zao jumped up from his chair and walked to the sink. Lowering his head, he tried to find the right words to stop them from this madness they had planned. "We are all Slavs," he said once more, "but to the Serbs, she's only a Muslim. Protect a Muslim girl in Serbia? Think, Bosko. You do have strong hands. But it's not enough. It's what you will not be able to do that matters. There are people on both sides, on every side who have lost everything. They will despise you when they see you with Admira. What do you think they will do when they find out? Offer you good luck? I'm not even talking about the soldiers and what they will do. Have you considered them?"

"We'll get to my mother. Once we're there, we'll be okay."

"No one is safe. You should know that by now. We Slavs would eat our own kind to prove a point. They will drag Admira out of your mother's home and drag her through the streets of the city."

Bosko thought he'd prepared himself for all that could be

441

said, but as the moments passed, he began to rethink what they were about to do.

Admira saw it in his face. She tugged her mother's hand once more under the table as she watched Bosko's resolve start to crumble. His goal in life had been to keep her with him and keep her safe. Would he be able to do it in Serbia? Admira remained silent. To say anything at this time might only further convince Bosko of the truth of her father's words. And if he changed his mind, she was trapped. He would leave her here and go back into Sarajevo and then to the police station. Her father would do everything in his power to keep her here. *No, Bosko, don't listen with your head. Listen with your heart.* She sent him this message with her eyes, which had never left him.

Tonya reached out and held Admira's other hand. Zena could see her husband choke back his despair.

Zao spoke in calm, slow words. "It's not the bombs and bullets you must fear but what's in the hearts of those you'll meet. Try to understand that. You can't hide from it the way you and Admira have hidden from bullets. It will be all around you like a disease because it's already infected the air you breathe."

Zao's words cut Bosko deeply he knew Admira's father was right. Bosko said nothing. He looked down at his hands folded on the kitchen table.

No, Bosko. Don't think about what my father has said. Think only of us and that we must always be together. Admira hoped Bosko would hear her silent plea.

"What more did Mladjo say?" Zena asked softly, trying to be a calming force, though her heart was divided. She would always remain a loyal wife, and yet deep down in the pit of her soul she knew what Admira felt—her willful, unyielding daughter who'd always followed her heart and loved Bosko, who had once said so eloquently, "You are the life that breathes in me." At this moment, Admira looked so vulnerable and so resolute.

"It's as I said. He told me we must go to Vrbanja Bridge."

"And then we cross it," Admira replied confidently. "And we'll find our way to Rita. It will be okay, Papa."

Zao's body shook as he tried to control his emotions. He hadn't heard a word spoken by his daughter.

"We want your blessing, Zao. Yours and Zena's," Bosko said quietly.

"How can I give you my blessing? In marriage, you would certainly have it, but not in this. What you're asking is wrong. This is something you must not do." There was no going back for Zao, no inch of compromise. He could not and would not accept their plan. He felt an overwhelming sense of helplessness and despised the existence of love. Admira's love for Bosko made both of them blind to the extreme danger and utter thoughtlessness of their plan. "It is madness, Bosko. Use your head."

A dreadful silence followed Zao's words. He was right, and Bosko knew it. It was madness to take Admira with him—and yet. The silence went unbroken. Bosko kept staring at his hands resting on the kitchen table. *Leave her*, he heard himself say, in his mind. *She has always been with me.* He answered himself back. *What is more important, her life or her love for you?* Bosko clenched his fingers into a fist. He was moments away from answering the question. *There is no life filled with any meaning if what means the most to you is no longer in your life*, he kept repeating to himself. He lowered his head. His fists remained clenched. *Take her. Take her with you.*

Bosko lifted his head, but not to look at anyone except Admira. Their eyes met. It was as if they were staring at each other like they had done on that first New Year's Day. When they had met, the two of them, on a quiet, snow-laden morning. It seemed to Bosko that at this moment, he was seeing Admira for the first time in the daylight and she appeared even more alluring than she had the night before, just as it had been on that first New Year's morning when she took his breath away and with it

443

all of their earlier fears, fears that were crushed into oblivion.

And as it had been those many years ago, it remained the same at this moment; the seconds passed and the rhythm of their breathing became one, with a quiet joy. His fears were crushed into oblivion.

No matter what my mother and father say to you, you must not give in to them. *Listen with your heart, not your head.*

Her words echoed inside his bones. She smiled at him, a desperate smile, holding back the tears with every ounce of strength.

"We're going," Bosko said, looking right at Zao.

Those were the two most romantic words Admira had ever heard. He'd kept his promise and listened with his heart.

Zao was silent. In his mind, he could see Admira at every age that had led her to this moment. Now he had lost her, his little girl. Nothing he'd said had made any difference. Without saying another word, Zao left the kitchen and went outside. The screen door snapped back. Bosko got up, his heart pounding. Admira, Tonya, and her mother stood too, and the four of them stood huddled together.

"When do you have to leave?" Zena asked.

"Tonight," Bosko replied.

Zena silently cursed Miroslav's name as she walked to the kitchen window. If he had remained a true friend, her Admira wouldn't be in this impossible situation.

She looked out at Zao, who stood by the fence, shoulders hunched forward.

"When I get there, Mom, I'll call you as soon as I can. Maybe it's a good sign that your phone still works. If it's not, Mladjo will let you know. It's going to be okay."

Zena tried to smile at the enthusiasm in her daughter's voice as she gazed out at her husband through the kitchen window. Yes, maybe having the phone still working meant everything

444

would be okay and Admira would call and tell them she was safe.

"Yellow," Admira said as she reached down and picked up her cat. "Did you come to say good-bye?" She stroked him under the chin, his favorite spot. In seconds, he'd settled onto her lap, purring. "Take good care of them while I'm gone."

Watching her daughter, Zena was reminded of Admira doing the exact same thing as she'd waited for her ride to a New Year's Eve party.

"When do you think you'll get there?" *There* being a safe place on the Serbian side.

"Real soon, Mom."

"Does anyone else know?"

"Only those who need to," Bosko answered.

"We have to go, Mom."

Her mother nodded.

Admira kissed Yellow, then gently put him down on the floor. She had one last thing to do. "I'll be right back."

Admira entered her parents' bedroom, reached into her jacket pocket, and took out the letter she'd written them. She put it on their dresser. Admira looked around at the bedroom. "I love you both," she whispered.

Her mother stepped into the room. Admira had known her mother would follow her; it's what a mother would do. Zena wrapped her arms around her daughter.

Admira stared at the two of them in the oval mirror of Zena's vanity. "Mom, if you were me and this was happening to you and Dad, would you leave him when you knew in your heart and soul that the two of you had everything in the world to look forward to? Would you listen to your parents? Or would you do as I know we must?" Admira looked at her mother's reflection in the mirror and then turned around to hear Zena's answer. "Would you leave your own Bosko?"

Zena stared at her daughter with tears in her eyes. She shook

445

her head. "No." She was barely able to say as she stared at her firstborn child and hated herself for telling Admira the truth. She would never have left Zao—no matter what. She couldn't lie to Admira.

"Nothing will separate us, Mom. I promise. I will always be by his side."

Admira and Zena returned to the kitchen, arm in arm. Seeing them, Bosko tried hard to push away any more doubts about their decision. Admira saw it in his eyes. She shook her head just a little, but he saw it. *Don't give into your fears.*

Zena wrapped her arms around Bosko. She pressed her cheek to his and kissed him. "Take care of my Admira."

Then she stretched out her arms to Admira, who rushed to embrace her mother. It would be a while before they would see each other again.

"Thank you," she whispered into her mother's ear.

All that Zena could do was to hold onto her daughter tightly.

Bosko felt Tonya's hand grip his. "I will miss you. Don't let anything happen to her."

"We'll be together, I promise."

Tonya moved closer to her sister and they held each other.

Bosko looked down at his hands, weighed down by the fears Zao had shared with him. Staring at his hands, he whispered to himself. *With these hands, I will protect her.*

Suddenly, Zena turned to Admira. "Money. What will you do for money?" she asked.

"Mom, we have enough."

"What do you mean? How much?"

"Shh... enough. The only money that matters anymore is Deutsche marks. We have a few. We must go," Admira said, knowing it was up to her to say it.

Zena nodded as tears welled up in her eyes. Bosko stood by the window and said nothing as he watched Zao enter the garage.

Tonya sat at the kitchen table weeping. Bosko picked her up and set her on her feet. She kissed him on his lips and wrapped her arms around him.

"With my life, I will protect her," he said.

Admira pushed open the screen door and waited for Bosko to join her. They stepped out onto the porch and walked down the steps holding hands.

"Wait," she said, and she walked toward the garage. Stepping inside, she saw her dad arranging her mother's bottled preserves. The familiar smell of axle grease and motor oil greeted her.

She walked closer to her dad, whose back was turned to her while he fiddled with the jars. Her father remained silent.

"Papa."

"I do not agree with what you are doing. It is not right."

"Papa, it's what I must do." Admira turned her father around and, looking at him, she said, "And I promise when I come back, you and me, we'll fix that truck of yours. It'll be like old times. There are so many things that need fixing." Zao stood still. "We shouldn't fight, Papa."

"We aren't," he replied. She took a bottle of preserves from his hand, and placed it on a rickety table. Zao said nothing, trying to hold back his tears.

"I know you don't agree with what we're doing. And I can't ask you to understand. But Papa, how can I leave him now, when he could have left me so many times? He stayed because of me. Because he loves me, Papa, more than anything in this world he loves me. Bosko has remained a man, and it was you who taught me how to look for that, how to recognize it. You taught me. He's not like Miro. He didn't run away. Bosko is a man. And now when he has no choice and has to go, I must be with him. He needs me. I need him."

Admira faced Zao and hugged him "Just know that I will always love you, the first man I ever loved in my life. Take care of Mom and Tonya, and try not to be a disappointment to them." Admira kissed her father on his cheek. He remained silent. He couldn't wish her good-bye or good luck. A superstition of his made him believe that to do so might bring about the worst possible end. So he remained silent, as his heart broke in these last moments of looking at his firstborn. Admira turned and very slowly walked out of the garage. Her father said nothing; she had hoped he would.

Admira grabbed Bosko's arm. While she'd spent those precious minutes with Zao, he had picked up their two small suitcases. They walked toward the fence, lifted the latch to the gate, passed though, and shut the gate behind them. Bosko and Admira waved to her mom and sister. Her mother blew her a kiss and waved again. They were going to be okay, Zena told herself in every possible way a mother could. Tonya couldn't stop her tears, but raised her hand and waved to her sister. Admira blew her one last kiss before she and Bosko turned toward their city, the gravel road beneath their feet.

With all of her heart, Admira wanted to turn around. She'd always timed it right. Her father was always there, standing by the fence waiting for her to turn around and smile at him, as they would wave to one another. But Admira knew her father. This time there was no need to look back.

Chapter Thirty-Four

They said very little to each other on the walk. It was a strange feeling to be journeying back to Sarajevo with the intention of leaving again almost immediately. Exhausted, they passed several checkpoints guarded by armed militia. Soon, they would avoid them completely in order to escape.

Exploding shells jolted them out of their melancholy. Bosko grabbed Admira and they made a mad dash for the side of a building. While he pressed her against the wall, the shelling continued but the explosions grew farther away.

"We're near the zoo," she said.

"You'll see, Admira, one day all of this, even our zoo, will be rebuilt. And we will visit with our sons and daughters."

She nodded and hugged him as they stood huddled against a building, hidden in its shadow, knowing that the last creature in Sarajevo's zoo had perished some time ago. It had been a female bear whose death was seen on TV all over the world. It was a solitary death. Some of the creatures had been used as target practice by snipers, and others perished because the last remaining zoo officials were too afraid to go out in the open in order to feed them. Monkeys, lions, wolves, llamas, tigers, and camels all died agonizing deaths among the putrid stench of rotting carcasses and skeletal remains.

"I curse them all for what they did." Admira was now more determined than ever to leave their city, and to be with Bosko, even if it meant living with the accursed. They waited until the shelling was far enough away, then grabbed each other's hand and ran.

Admira and Bosko were like so many couples they saw. Running frantically through the streets holding onto each other and their meager possessions. It was such a normal a scene to witness. As were the images of corpses rotting in the streets. Two more blocks and they'd be at Mladjo's. Bosko worried that they were too out in the open. *Are we being watched? Have we been followed from the moment we left the apartment?* He didn't know. Wouldn't it seem obvious that he would try to escape Sarajevo, even contact Mladjo for help? Why wouldn't they follow him but remain out of sight, and then just grab him and Admira?

Even though Bosko had been attacked and beaten up many times, he also knew that appearances were very important in Sarajevo. So that it wouldn't appear to the outside world and the journalists that Muslims were persecuting Serbs, he sensed they might stay away. Bosko knew without doubt that his would-be captors were aware of Mladjo and that he was a friend and also a very dangerous ruthless criminal. So, he was hoping they wouldn't follow him and would keep their distance. Bosko was also hoping that they would be paranoid enough to think so, though it was not true, that Mladjo had some of his men secretly keeping an eye out for him and Admira. And if they saw anything suspicious, the gangster's men would move against the perpetrators. The outcome would be ghastly for those who were captured. Bosko was hoping that there would be just enough paranoia on the part of his enemies to keep them at bay, and that they would wait the forty-eight hours before they came looking for him. Just long enough for him and Admira to disappear.

*

Admira squeezed Bosko's hand. "We are leaving, and we are doing this for your father and mine, for all the grandparents, for Mats, and everyone who has suffered. This is for all of them, but most of all it's for me. I won't lose you. Now come on."

The hinges groaned and creaked just before they entered Mladjo's headquarters, Bosko turned around to see if anyone was watching them. Admira pulled him inside. Was it three o'clock yet?

The militiamen and Mladjo's gangster cohorts greeted the couple with stares. Bosko didn't know what they were thinking. Some might be envious of them getting out of the city, others probably hated him for being associated with Miro and having a Muslim girlfriend. Bosko couldn't help but keep thinking to himself, as they sat together, *How could this plan for me and Admira to escape Sarajevo have been kept a secret?*

He sat with Admira on a wooden bench, clutching her hand. She remained quiet and calm. This was simply a short trip they were taking, and they would be back. After those first moments of being glared at, no one seemed to give them another thought. Heavily armed, and concerned with staying alive for another day, men entered and left the building, focused only on matters relevant to their lives.

"You're on time; it's almost three. Good." Djoka approached. "Follow me."

*

Mladjo was pouring himself a glass of brandy. He turned toward the door as Admira and Bosko entered. He said nothing except to observe them. She looked back at Mladjo. They'd met for a second time at his wedding reception; the first time had been years ago, when Bosko and Miro had destroyed the bicycles they had ridden while racing down the hill.

The encounter at his wedding reception had been brief, and only socially acceptable pleasantries had been exchanged. It seemed strangely intimate, though it was not the perfect word to describe the moment. There was something about Admira that felt very familiar or kindred to Mladjo. Perhaps it was that he knew she was brave and resolute in a manner he understood.

Whatever it was that he'd sensed about her many years ago, it

451

was also true today. Her life force remained strong. Admira tried to find any disapproval in his eyes, but Mladjo was inscrutable. Finally, he walked over to her and extended his hand. "Glad you could make it."

"As am I," she replied, keeping one arm wrapped around Bosko's waist as she shook Mladjo's hand firmly with the other. He raised his glass, sipped the brandy, and set it down on the desk.

"Sit, please."

Djoka shut the door. Mladjo gave them a larger-than-life smile, which lowered Bosko's anxiety, if only for a moment.

"Would you care for anything? Tea? Coffee?"

"None for me," Bosko said.

"Me either," Admira replied.

Bosko was obviously nervous. It was harder to tell with Admira.

"There has been a slight change. You will leave in the morning, not tonight. The people who will be waiting for you on the other side of the bridge were not able to be at the rendezvous point by tonight. They will get there early in the morning and will be waiting for you." Admira's chest heaved upward and then sank with a great sense of relief. She and Bosko were one step closer to leaving Sarajevo, if only to return soon, which they intended. They would leave in the daylight and not be skulking away like thieves in the night. Miro had abandoned them and their city under the cover of night.

"It will be a sunny day with white clouds, I think, a beautiful day for Bosh and I to take a very important walk," Admira said.

Mladjo continued. "Your contacts will give you safe passage after you cross the bridge, and make sure you get out of the city and beyond."

"Who are they, these people who are willing to help?" Admira asked.

"One is an old friend. He's a Serb on the Serbian side. I am the Muslim on the Bosnian side. We've had dealings before. Our families knew each other before all of this, but it's not our past friendship that makes him do this. He still has family in Sarajevo and wants to get them out. You and Admira are set to go first. When you are safe and on the other side, his family will follow. Your problem was urgent. That is why you're going first.

"And as I said, the bridge is surrounded on every side. It's forbidden to go there, not that anyone would dare to. Those men who came to your apartment will never suspect that you and Admira will be there. That's exactly why you will use it. I have dealt with all the parties involved. My contacts will be waiting for you. When you have crossed the halfway point on the bridge, whistle. They will want to remain hidden till the very last moment before emerging to get you. You won't be able to see anyone, but they'll be close enough to see you. Wait for the return whistle, then follow the sound to its location where they are hidden. Once you are just a few feet from their hiding place, they will emerge quickly and will guide you off the bridge. It will take only seconds for all of you to disappear from sight.

"It's time." Mladjo stood up. It took Admira and Bosko a few moments to understand that it really was happening. In a very short time they would be out of Sarajevo. Bosko was the first to stand. He was still holding onto Admira's hand when she got up. Neither of them knew what to say. Looking at Bosko, Mladjo said, "You and Admira will have to find a place to stay until morning. Luckily for you there are many destroyed and abandoned buildings to choose from near the bridge."

"What time should we be at the bridge?" asked Admira.

"They will get there just before sunrise. When you choose to—"

"We'll be there to meet them early in the morning, when it's sunny and there are puffy white clouds dancing in the sky."

453

"How do you know it will be this way tomorrow?" asked Mladjo.

"Because I wish it," Admira replied.

"Then it will be so," said the gangster, allowing himself to break into a smile. He walked up to the both of them and said, "Be careful, and stay out of sight till it's time."

"We will," Bosko said. "No one will see us. We'll be careful."

"Make sure that you are," Mladjo said, as if it were an order. "Say hello to Rita when you see her. Give her a hug for me."

"I will," Bosko replied.

Bosko embraced his family friend. Once more he'd come to his rescue. Mladjo released him and shifted to stand in front of Admira.

"I wish we'd known each other for longer, Admira. When this silliness is over, I'd like it if you and my wife could be friends."

"I would like that." Instead of shaking his hand, Admira stood up on her toes and kissed Mladjo on his cheek. She whispered into his ear, "Thank you for all you have done. I'll never forget it." He acknowledged her words with a simple nod. Mladjo walked over to the door and turned to them just before he opened it. "This is as far as I go."

"I understand," Bosko replied. Admira held onto Bosko's arm as he took hold of their suitcases. He looked at Djoka, who also smiled at Bosko and gave him a nod, which Bosko returned.

Djoka stood by Mladjo and watched the couple walk toward the metal door and listened to it groan as they pushed it open. He turned to Mladjo before stepping out of the room. "You've done everything you can. Whatever happens now is out of your hands."

Mladjo said nothing, but stepped back into his office and shut the door.

*

They moved through the streets, hiding, pressing against walls that remained standing, crouching on their hands and knees

454

beside destroyed cars and buses, crawling along the streets and sidewalks from one safe spot to another.

At times they both thought they were being followed. During those brief moments of overwhelming fear, it paralyzed them and they were unable to take another step, but they had to they knew they had to continue and not give into their fears. Stopping, huddled together by the side of a building, hiding in the shadows, they glanced in every direction at a desolate, concrete road surrounded on both sides by dozens of bombed-out buildings. No-man's-land.

They walked and ran and hid. Every step of the way was calculated, as they carefully inched their way along, their city that was disappearing all around them. When they finally entered into this no-man's land, they were surrounded by what was truly an apocalyptic place, void of any life. The only things that remained were shelled and burned-out buildings, exploded cars, the twisted wreckage of trams, and hundreds of electric poles leaning to one side and resembling broken arms, wires dangling and powerless. Holding hands, they entered the building he'd chosen for them to hide until morning. It was a burned-out husk of what had once been a three-story office building. The smell of damp concrete occuring from exploded water pipes permeated the air.

"We should stay in the lobby away from the windows." Admira nodded in agreement. Loose plaster, bricks, lighting fixtures, and other parts of the building were strewn across the lobby, much of it burnt and twisted.

"It's perfect," she said as they lowered themselves onto their hands and knees, making their way toward what might have been a reception area. No wooden furniture of any kind remained; the cold floor was covered in dust and debris.

"Let me find something to throw on the floor."

"Okay." She touched his cheek. Bosko searched the lobby for something to cover the bare concrete floor. Every few moments, no matter where he was in the lobby, he turned back to look at Admira.

"I'm okay," she finally said. "No one's going to come and steal me. Bosh, really, it's okay. It's going to be okay." He nodded and tried to smile, but couldn't. The lobby windows had all been blown out and they could clearly see the outside world that surrounded them. *Have we been followed?* The thought kept hammering away at Bosko. "Bosh," she called out to him in a soft voice. "It's okay. Come on back. We won't be here for long. Come here." He hunched over, then dropped to his hands and knees and crawled over to her. They huddled together in a corner. Admira opened her small suitcase and removed two *kandilos*. She took out the matches and lit each one. It was still daylight outside but inside the building it was dark. The flames flickered as the lovers held each other tightly.

"I wonder if Rita has finished our sweaters. Won't she be surprised to see us?" Admira asked, trying to break the tension. They were almost there, and she needed Bosko to know her faith in his decision. She snuggled up against him.

"Will you make a garland of lime leaves like you used to and put it in my hair the first day we come back?"

"The first day and for as many days as you want me to, because we will have all the time in the world."

She kissed his eyelids and pulled Bosko to her until they were so tightly pressed together they could feel the other's heartbeat.

They shivered as the wind blew into the open space. The building shook and the *kandilo* flames wavered.

"It will be okay," she said softly. "They haven't managed to separate us, and they never will."

The minutes passed and then an hour and another. Soon evening became night, and they held each other while they sat awake, silent and lost in their thoughts, or dozing off. As the hours passed, they slept in shifts. When Admira squeezed his hand, Bosko would respond in kind even in his sleep.

Each in their own way had willed for morning to hurry and meet them. They were ready.

White, puffy clouds filled the sky. Admira could see them through what had once been large windows looking out on Sarajevo. She guessed it was almost eight o'clock in the morning. They'd huddled together all through the night, dreaming of dreams when they could. Now everything seemed as it should be and she was ready to burst out of the building with a strange giddiness. Bosko felt it too. It was the same feeling they'd had that New Year's Eve night years ago. The future was theirs then; it was theirs now.

"I'm sure your mother has finished the sweaters she promised."

"I know she has. Are you ready?"

Admira nodded and said, "Everyone is waiting. The man with the whistle, and your mom with our sweaters."

"Give me your hand." Admira held hers out to him. "Ready, Charmer Boy?"

"Ready, Gypsy Girl."

"I like that. Charmer Boy, Gypsy Girl."

Each carried a suitcase in one hand. They entwined their fingers and left their ghosts behind them.

Admira said nothing as they walked side by side. She held Bosko's hand tightly. It had been only a few minutes, but the silence between them was beginning to feel like a dull ache. She began swinging their clasped hands back and forth as they walked the desolate road, which was void of any signs of life. An eerie silence permeated the air. Not one tree existed. No birds sang. Nothing but an unearthly calm surrounded them and the ruins of a city.

This place, this no-man's land, had been forgotten and was an aching reminder of a siege where the victims would accept death

457

before the dishonor of surrender. A blue sky was awash above them. The sun shone its glorious face. Admira's grip on Bosko's hand tightened.

On every side, and in front as well as behind them, lay a ghostly gray and blackened wasteland. A misty blueish hue was painted into the air that began to blow in short gusts around them. It was quiet except when the top half of a telephone pole, which had broken off but still remained attached, would now and again swing back and forth. The twisted sinews of metal made a grinding and groaning noise as the broken half swung back and forth in the wind.

Buildings remained but were uninhabited. Their white and pastel-colored exteriors had been blackened by constant explosions, their insides rotting away from fire and decay. Everywhere were wires and electricity cables strewn about on the streets. Burned-out and rusting buses, trams, and cars littered the roadway, and in no place was there not a stench of decay. The only sign of life were weeds that had sprung out from cracks in the road.

Bosko lifted her hand and kissed it. She had the scent of jasmine.

"Are you scared?" he asked softly.

"Yes, no—"

"They're watching, whoever they are."

"So let them."

A sudden gust of wind blew between them and almost immediately, hundreds of the white, puffy crowns from the tops of dandelions went floating upward toward the sky.

"Look, there it is. We're almost there." The bridge beckoned them. He tightened his grip on her hand, their fingers interlaced.

"Yes, almost," she whispered.

As they approached the halfway point on the bridge, someone whistled. Bosko whistled back. They were going to

458

make it. She could hardly believe it. Her eyes widened. Bosko took a few steps ahead of her. Almost free, she said to herself. She began to skip toward him.

The first shot rang out. It landed just in front of him. Instinctively he jumped in front of Admira to protect her. A second bullet tore open Bosko's chest above his heart that still continued to beat. Bosko was in a dream; he felt his eyes get heavy. He heard Admira call out to him as he felt himself falling forward. He tried to turn his head to look at Admira, but he couldn't. His barely opened eyes saw a misty moonlit night when he'd met a girl and they had stood on a balcony looking out on Sarajevo, whose lights burned like the flickering of a firelight.

"Bosko," Admira screamed as a bullet pierced her flesh.

Bosko's head smashed against the ground and his arms lay stretched out behind him, his palms facing upward as if he was reaching behind him to grab hold of her hand once more.

"Bosko!" Admira cried out again as she fell to the ground. "Bosko..." She called out but barely heard herself. Reaching out with both her hands, Admira began to crawl forward, pulling herself closer till she was next to Bosko. When she reached his side, he was so still. He was dead.

"No..." Her voice trembled as she nestled her face against him. A tiny stream of tears sparkled on her cheeks in the bright sunlight. She pressed her lips against his soft hair. And with every ounce of strength she had left, Admira lifted her arm across Bosko's back and held him. Her eyes felt heavy and began to close, and with her last breath she whispered, "Wait for me, my love, we'll get there together."

The white, puffy crowns from the dandelions, which had risen up toward a clear blue sky, began to descend and fall upon them like a thousand white clouds.

Zena lifted her head from her sewing when the phone rang. The first ring seemed to go on forever. It rang again. She jumped up. How many days had passed since her daughter had left, she didn't know and had stopped counting. On the third ring she finally grabbed it and cried, "Admira. Admira. Hello, baby, is that you?"

"Hello, hello," the stranger repeated. "Am I speaking to the mother of Admira Ismić?"

"Yes, you are. Is she there? Please put her on."

"Hello, yes—"

"Admira," she said again.

"I'm calling from a militia outpost near Vrbanja Bridge. I need you to confirm a report regarding the death of your daughter —"

Zena dropped the phone. She shook her head, hearing the words from this stranger, but not understanding them. Gripped by indescribable pain, she staggered across the living room, knocking over chairs, feeling her life being crushed into oblivion. She pushed the kitchen door open to the backyard with no idea where she was going. She stumbled down the back stairs and walked in a daze across the yard. Falling to her knees, she wanted to call out to Zao but couldn't. Zena grabbed a hold of the bell and shoved it with all her might while barely able to utter the words she cried out.

"Come back, Admira, come back... your Mama wants you to come back. You've gone too far... I can't see you... come back." The deep, dulcimer-like ring of the bell echoed beyond their home, but not far enough to bring her eldest daughter home.

Epilogue

Admira and Bosko lay together on the bridge for many days. All sides argued over who had been responsible, but ultimately no one took responsibility for their deaths.

They were buried in a Serbian cemetery at the same time that ceremonies took place for slain Serbian soldiers.

Admira's parents declined safe passage to attend the ceremony.

Rita attended.

A Serbian priest at the graveside said prayers for Bosko, since he was a Serb. He declined to pray for Admira because she was a Muslim.

Rita wept as she placed the sweaters she'd promised them on each of their coffins.

After the siege of Sarajevo ended, Bosko and Admira were re-interred together in Sarajevo's Lion Cemetery, where they lie today, in a well-maintained grave surrounded by marigolds in their City of Palaces.

No one knew about Bosko's letter to Admira which was buried with her, with them. Almost all of it was destroyed except for the last few words on a crumpled, burnt page. They were Bosko's words, from his heart to his Gypsy Girl.

I think the purpose of life is to be happy. To enjoy the gift that is to be alive, to feel that butterfly on your shoulder, to walk in a valley that is a paradise. I think the best part of me would die if I should lose you. No, not die, I meant perish.

For this is what happens to a heart never allowed to love whom it was always meant to... and I know it is no one else but you whom I shall always love.

-The End-

ABOUT THE AUTHOR

 Author Victor Harrington might easily be said to have the quintessential family history of a writer.

The family adventure began in 1850 with Edward, an Englishman in the British army stationed in India. Edward survived the carnage that was to follow the Great Indian Mutiny, and went on to wed a Muslim princess whose family lived near the city of Agra.

Enter Evangeline Grace Wilson, the only daughter of an American Presbyterian Missionary, who would marry the author's great, great, grandfather, John Patrick on December 24, 1896.

The author and his family make their home in New York City, a city from which Evangeline Grace Wilson had left with her father, a little over one-hundred years ago. Victor's journey to New York from his childhood home in Canada makes the circle complete.

Living in New York allows him to witness the continuing drama of individual lives unfolding, and reinforces the fact that human joy, suffering, and redemption are quite literally felt the same way in everyone. The author loves to eavesdrop. The thoughts shared by one person to another can provide the material for what can become a compelling story. He has placed into his memory countless stories that were worth hearing, and were whispered from both the living as well as from the ghosts that haunt his city.

Victor has worked in the financial services industry for the last sixteen years.

He has completed his second novel.

Copyright © 2016 by Victor Harrington.

All rights reserved. No part of this publication may be reproduced, distributed or transmitted in any form or by any means, including photocopying, recording, or other electronic or mechanical methods, without the prior written permission of the publisher, except in the case of brief quotations embodied in critical reviews and certain other noncommercial uses permitted by copyright law.

http://www.victorharrington.com/

Publisher's Note: This is a work of fiction. Names, characters, places, and incidents are a product of the author's imagination. Locales and public names are sometimes used for atmospheric purposes. Any resemblance to actual people, living or dead, or to businesses, companies, events, institutions, or locales is completely coincidental.

Paperback interior and cover layout by
Matthew Wayne Selznick / MWS Media
https://www.mwsmedia.com

Cover art by
Miladinka Milic
http://www.milagraphicartist.com

Charmer Boy, Gypsy Girl/ Shannon Harrington. -- 1st paperback ed.

ISBN 978-0-9962316-2-6

www.ingramcontent.com/pod-product-compliance
Lightning Source LLC
Chambersburg PA
CBHW071243250626
47163CB00002B/310